TWELVE TALES
OF HORROR F SUSPENSE

Lee J. Minter

Lee J. Minter
Top Circle Publishing

Printed in the United States of America
First Printing 2020
First Edition 2020

ISBN 978-1-7340930-2-5

Library of Congress Control Number: 2019915091

10987654321

Dead End, Twelve Tales of Horror & Suspense is a compilation of horror anthologies written by the author of the best-selling hit "**In Sheep's Clothing**" Twelve stories that will take you down the darkest corridors of your imagination and into the abyss where nightmares come true and monsters are real. Now please pay attention to the road signs as you take a midnight cruise down a lonely dark and isolated stretch of twisted roadway. That takes you to a rusted old yellow bullet holed, cobwebbed sign, that lets you know you have come to the end of your journey; you have reached the end of your road, you have come to a *well you know, enjoy.*

Dead End "Twelve Tales of Horror & Suspense

" The First And Last Name In Horror"

"Beware of demons that come as friends, and masquerade as angels"

~ Mintboogie

Dedicated to family, friends, and fans here and abroad. Thanks for all your love and support, but most of all, believing.

CONTENTS

FOREWORD BY THE AUTHOR

Have you ever had a dream that you are driving down a dark and lonely stretch of road and you have no idea where you are going, but you can feel that there is some dark and compelling force taking you on that unknown journey to only God knows where? And you do not know what to expect when you get there may be something good or maybe something bad or maybe some of both.

Have you ever had that dream where the landscape and your location seems familiar, but you keep getting lost, and you cannot find your way home or back to your location no matter how hard you try – a dream where you become lost in a maze or a labyrinth of purgatory hell.

Worst, have you ever dreamed that not only were you lost, but you were lost and naked. All of you in your birthday suit exposed to the world to see, but yet no one pays you any attention it as if people are oblivious to your nudity.

I have heard that you can control your dreams by the way you perceive life consciously thus your conscious thoughts will transfer over to your unconscious thoughts and give you better abilities to control your dream-world for better or worse.

If that is so? Might that theory be possible, especially when it comes to lucid dreaming, whereas you are in a state between unconsciousness and consciousness not quite awake but not quite asleep? Caught somewhere in the middle.

But getting back to my original question, I like many no doubt, as I am sure you have before. Have gotten lost while driving on unknown roads in unfamiliar locations and felt a sense of pending anxiety that if my car broke down and I ran out of gas, I hope that I would be capable of handling whatever came my way, good or bad.

What if this was just you? And your car was broken down on the side of an isolated and unfamiliar road. And the trusty car navigation or cellphone application that you use erroneously led you to a strange destination that was off the grid.

Could you trust an unfamiliar stranger that came along to help you? Or should you safely wait inside of your car on the roadside service that you called earlier to arrive to get you out of this jam?

Should you? Would You? Could you?

After tinkering with your car's engine that fails to start back up again, you begin to regret that you slept through Automotive101 in High School. Now safely back in your car, you look around at your desolate surroundings, with no other soul in sight. What is that noise you just heard, rustling in the bushes not too far from your car? Nothing you tell yourself, just your imagination running wild.

Your eyes catch sight of a beat-up yellow sign glowing eerily in the dark at the end of the road, its words almost hidden by the overgrown foliage covering its message. But make no mistake you make out what its faded two words tell you, wait what is that rustling again in the bushes, is that footsteps you hear now approaching your car from behind? Your eyes go back to the old yellow sign pulling you in as the stench of death hits your nostrils full force! Beads of perspiration begin to form oddly on your forehead in seventy-five-degree weather. You turn the key again in your ignition in one last desperate attempt to start your car, as a weak grumble finally erupts from your engine.

"Fuck you Automotive 101," you curse underneath your breath with a grin on your face. Who? Needs you.

As you put the car in drive and begin to back up off this isolated patch of a road you barely get three feet before your car shuts down on you again.

What was that rustling again? You catch a glimpse of a shadow of something large moving quickly in the brush ahead by the sign.

You hear something approaching again, but this time it is a familiar sound, yes, the sound of an engine, you look in your rearview mirror as the bright lights from the tow truck illuminates your car up, almost blinding you. A smile comes back on your face as you chastise yourself for being so foolish.

Nothing to worry about you say, you will be back on the road before you know it, as you get out of your car to greet the tow truck driver, why is he carrying an ax in his hand?

Fear now hits you again as you turn back and look at that reflective diamond-shaped yellow sign again. A sign that earlier foretold your past and now your imminent future.

That you have reached the end of this road and come to the beginning of a chilling destination, whereas it all starts and begins at a … Dead End.

¾ Enjoy

EDDY

My Eddy has always been an unusual and special child ever since he was an infant and into an adolescent. He never cried much as an infant, and I do not recall him putting up that much of a fuss as he got older, unlike his older brother Robert Jr. and sister Cary who was quite a handful at the age of thirteen years old, where most children find themselves transitioning into adolescence.

The only serious issue we had with Eddy was a medical anomaly, as a child he was born and diagnosed with a very rare stomach condition that prohibited him from eating any normal food, so our doctors put him on a diet of special high protein shakes that had all the nutrients according to the doctors of normal food sources.

I often felt sorry, for our Eddy that he was not able to enjoy the comforts of regular food like most children his age, a cheeseburger, and fries or a slice of pepperoni pizza due to his medical condition. So thus, I think in a lot of ways rather it was intentionally or unintentionally I overcompensated in my affection and attention shown towards Eddy that left his older siblings sometimes feeling jealous.

They all love their little brother, of course, and I do not think they held it personally against him having a rare condition that was no fault of his own. But still, because our world seemed to revolve around "Eddy," I hope that they knew that my love for him was equally and no less than my love for all of them.

Other than Eddy's rare condition, you can say me, and Robert had the typical West Virginia family in our community of Augusta VA. Our lives were built around work, our children's education, sports, and plenty of family vacations and of course not to leave out the sixth member of the family our golden retriever named Manny.

That is until they came the night of the thunderstorms like a lightning bolt right out of the sky and change life as we knew it forever.

* * *

After the children had been born Robert and me due to our good jobs and steady income had been afforded the blessing of being able to purchase our gorgeous dream home in a rural part of Augusta on twelve acres of scenic land, surrounded by lush green trees and nearby wildlife.

We had moved down to Augusta five years ago from Washington D.C. with our family of six, yes, that's including our dog, to start a new chapter in our lives from the hustle and bustle of city life in the East Coast. We thought it would be a good change for the kids as well as a good opportunity for us.

Robert immediately embraced the solitude of our semi-rural life in Augusta and our children after some resistance due to no doubt loss of friends and changes in their school and social life appeared to adapt to this new chapter and beginning in our lives gradually and just as well.

That is until the night the storm came, and what the storm brought with it that would inevitably change all our lives forever.

THE STORM

"Honey did you hear we got some bad weather moving in tonight from the east coast," Robert said, as he removes a small bottle of Minute Maid orange juice from one of the grocery bags, open it and took a sip out of it.

"Yeah I heard, that's all they been talking about all day long on the news," his wife June responded as she helps unpack the groceries they had just brought.

"Mom, did you get the iced oatmeal cookies I ask for?" Robert Jr. said as he enters the kitchen.

June reached in one of the numerous bags on the counter and pulled out a pack of cookies and tossed it to her son.

"Yes dear and try not to eat all those things before dinner."

"Mom, I am not a baby," he replied.

'Nope, just a big ass cookie monster," his sister Cary teased.

Robert Jr. gave her the finger as he bit into his cookie.

"Man these things are like crack," he said, licking the crumbs off his lips.

Cary rolled her eyes up in her head at her brother.

"Have you ever tried crack stupid?"

"Nope," he answered.

"Then how would you know?" she said annoyed.

"Because I think this white icing is actually melted crack spread out on an oatmeal cookie," he said, taking another bite.

"Robbie, you are so dumb!" she said, laughing.

"Enough talk about crack, help me put these groceries up you two," their mom June said.

"Hey hon, I am going to the shed and make sure things inside there are secure for tonight," Robert Sr. yelled back to his wife June in the kitchen.

"Okay, dear," she said.

"Rob go give your dad a hand."

"But I thought you wanted me to…"

June cut her son off with a look on her face that meant business.

"Coming dad!" he yelled out.

"Where's Eddy?" she said.

"Where is the little NASA future astronaut normally?" Cary said, rolling her eyes again.

"Up in his room on the computer," her mom answered.

"Bingo!" said Cary.

Chirp, chirp!

June looked at her watch, which was synchronized to Eddy's meal times to alert her when it was his meal times, because of his special diet.

"Go get your brother it's time for him to have his dinner."

"I don't know how he survives off those milkshakes?" Cary said.

"The same way you survive off of hamburgers and french fries smart ass," her mom said.

"Definitely not the same," Cary said with the eye roll again.

Cary was right June thought as she watches her leave to fetch her brother. Protein shakes, and solid food was in two different food categories. But when all was said and done the only one thing that truly matters to her, and that was that these special protein shakes provided the necessary sustenance to keep her and Robert's son Eddy alive, for a very, very, long time she hopes.

The see-through bagged protein shakes were all line-up and organized on one-side of the double refrigerator, all different flavors from chocolate, strawberry, too vanilla and some exotic flavors, like cheesecake flavor, mint chocolate chip, and a meat by-product shake, that Eddy seemed to enjoy, but his big brother Robbie found absolutely gross.

Eddy coming from his bedroom upstairs greeted his Mom as he entered the kitchen. He was a slightly built young man with dark features and eyes that seemed to belong to someone much older than his age. He always appeared to his mom to be staring past you or through you when he was looking right at you when you were conversing with him.

"Hi Mom, what's for dinner?" he said, as he sat down in the kitchen at the table.

"Meatloaf, mashed potatoes, and green beans," she answers back, as she took one of the chilled protein shakes out of the refrigerator and puncture the premade hole on the side of the pouch with attached straw like a Capri Sun drink.

"Smells good," Eddy said, as he took the protein shake from his mom and began slowly drinking it thru the straw.

June tried to hide the shame of guilt; she felt as she watches her young son consume the drink. Guilt knowing that he would probably never be able to share a real family meal with his brother and sister at the table. A family meal with all of them.

"How's your stomach?" she asked.

"Fine, mom," he said, his mind seemed to be elsewhere.

June stirred up the mashed potatoes in the pot some more and then turned off the burner to them when she decided that they were cooked. Oh, how she wished that Eddy could taste some of her cooking, but of course, not at the risk that it would… she did not want to think such thoughts, so her mind went to another place, a safe place.

"Hey, mom do you ever feel that you don't belong in this world?" Eddy said.

Eddy's question not only immediately snapped her mind out of the mundane task of preparing dinner but caught her off guard as well.

What a strange question she thought before she struggles to answer. "No, I can't say I do, why would you ask that…"

"Man that storm is coming in quick," her husband said, as him and Robbie Jr. entered the house.

"Hey, Eddy, how's it going bud?" his dad asked as he tousled Eddy's head full of thick curly hair with his fingers.

"Fine dad," Eddie said.

"I haven't seen you all day where have you been bud?"

"In his room on his computer in nerd zone," his big brother answered for him.

"Fuck you, Robbie!" Eddy shot back.

"No fuck you geek!" Robbie Jr. said.

"That's enough! I don't want to hear anymore F-bombs out of you two. If I do, I am going to wash both of your mouths out with the same damn soap!" said their father.

"Uggghhh," said Eddy.

"Now apologize to your mother."

"Sorry, mom," both of the boys said in unison, but not very convincing.

"But I am not sorry, about the geek comment Eddy."

"That's okay; you're just jealous because I am smarter than you," Eddy said, looking his brother straight in his eyes.

"Yeah a smart little asshole," Robbie Jr. countered.

"Enough!" said their mother firmly.

"Now go get ready for dinner, Robbie."

Eddy cracked a smile he loved getting the best of his big brother when he could.

She looked back over at Eddy. "Not nice," she said.

His father had a smile on his face too. "Well, he is right," he said.

"Not nice," June said as she hit her husband with the dishtowel trying not to laugh.

"Well, he is the only one I know that master calculus at twelve in our family," Robert Sr. said.

"I know honey, but we don't want to make our other children feel inferior," June said softly.

"We don't have to they do it every time they open their mouths," Robert replied.

"You're bad," June said, kissing her husband on the lips.

Eddy watched the interactions between his parents intently almost as if he was studying them.

"Hey, bud how is the astronomy coming along?"

"Fine dad, I saw a new telescope on eBay I want you to take a look at," Eddy said with excitement in his voice.

"What's wrong with the one you got?"

"Nothing but this one is awesome! Pleaseeee, dad."

Why did I open my big mouth, his farther thought? "Sure son, after dinner," his father conceded.

"Awesome!" Eddy said again.

"I wonder how much awesome is going to cost me?" His father said quietly underneath his breath.

"You want another shake?" His mom asks.

"No I am full, mom thanks."

Manny ran in the kitchen wagging his tail as Eddy reached in a dog biscuit jar on the counter and handed him a treat, patting him on the forehead.

"Hey, you want to go for a walk boy?" He said to Manny.

Manny let out a excited bark with his tail wagging in response to Eddy's question.

"Don't be too long a storm is coming in," his mom reminded him, as he got out Manny's leash and hooked it to his collar.

"No worries, Mom, I am just going for a short walk," he said.

The sound of crackling thunder erupted from outside.

"You better hurry, son, just a short walk," reiterated his dad.

"Okay, dad I got this," Eddy said reassuringly, somewhat annoyed by all the fuss over a simple walk.

"Oh by the way, did you hear about old Mrs. Watersons cat?" His dad asks.

"No, what happen to her cat?" June said.

"Her cat's been missing for five days now, and she is stressed out of her wits about it," Robert said.

"Wow that's a shame," June replied.

"Yeah dad, that's too bad," Eddy responded with as much empathy he could falsely muster up in his voice.

"Yeah, it is, her husband just passing away recently and all, that cat is all she pretty much got," he said.

"Well hopefully it will turn up soon, you know how cats are," June said.

"Hopefully, but you want to hear something strange that's like the fifth missing cat in this neighborhood in two-weeks," Robert pointed out.

"That's weird," June said.

"I wonder if its coyotes."

Eddy cleared his throat to get their attention "Ahem, I'll keep an eye out for her cat."

"Thanks, son, be careful," said his mom.

"Hey, where are you going squirt?" Cary said as she entered the room.

"To take Manny for a walk."

"Can I come?"

"Sure."

"Cary dinner is ready," said her mom.

"I know, I'll be right back, I am sure that meatloaf is not going to get up out the meatloaf pan and walk away, *unfortunately*," she said sarcastically.

"What was that young lady?" June asks sternly.

"Nothing mom," Cary said.

Eddy cracked a smile again on his face, amused by his older sister's rebellious personality that he envy in many ways.

"I told you, every time they open their mouths," Robert said with a grin to his wife.

"You might have something there," his wife June said, shaking her head sideways.

Robert laughed.

"Wind gusts of up to 45-50 mph (ca.-80 kilometers per hour) are predicted for tonight's storm a wind advisory is in effect starting at 8:00 pm to 12:00 am, midnight. We advise all residents to be safe and stay indoors in a safe place and limit your travel until further notice," said the weather reporter on a nearby television in their living room.

"Sounds like it's going to be a rough one tonight, honey," Robert said.

"I hope so," June said teasingly, as she set the rest of the plates on the table for dinner and another protein shake on the table for Eddy.

"Do you think our boy is getting enough protein from those things?" Robert asked, concerned.

"I hope so," June answered back.

Robert picked up the shake reading maybe for the one-thousandth time its outer package *"Nutrition 228 calories. 7.5g fat. 1.5 saturated fat. 30 carbs. Protein source: Lab milk and bio-enhanced protein powder, made and packaged at Apex Food Processing and Distribution Facility in Hidden Valley California."*

"What in the hell is lab milk?" he said, staring curiously at the package.

June heard the sound of their kids returning with the dog and took the protein shake out of her husband hand and sat it back down on the table.

"Something that keeps our son alive Robert, now get ready for dinner," she said.

"That's not what I meant June," he said.

"I know dear, but can we have this discussion at another time," she asked.

"Hey mom we're back," said Eddy as him and his sister entered the house.

Robert looked in the direction of his kids, maybe June was right this wasn't the time to be discussing (again) the mysterious ingredients in his son's protein shakes but you better believe he thought to himself this topic just wasn't going to go casually away, and never be brought up again.

"You are right dear," he said, kissing his wife June on her forehead.

"Another time," he conceded.

The kiss on the forehead June knew was Robert's usual way of telling her I am going to get back with you regarding this matter later, but for now, just savor your momentary victory.

He did not give up that easy, but nor did she, that is she thought why their son Eddy was still alive and thriving.

He was, after all, like the boy in the bubble, but without the bubble, of course.

But it was more to Eddy then just that he was their miracle baby and despite his digestive issues, he had defied all the doctor's odds and had matured into the healthy young man that unlike most people only needed these special protein shakes to keep him alive. Special protein shakes with *lab milk and bio-enhanced protein powder.*

* * *

"You have a very special boy here," Dr. Dick Dickerson told her, (**See Zombie Pimp a Night Turner Tribune Novella 1ˢᵗ edition**) the man who was not only behind the breakthrough research of the special protein shakes but instrumental to making sure Eddy got prescribed and supplied these pouches of liquid food to sustain his life as well.

When she and Robert had heard that Dr. Dickerson had perished in a fire from a gas explosion at the facility that he worked at, they were devastated. She felt after all, they had owed him everything for saving their son.

But even in death, he did not disappoint them, because unknown to them he had made special arrangements to make sure that Eddy would continuously receive a lifetime supply of his miracle shakes until a cure could be found for his condition. What a thoughtful and caring man June thought who had even reached out beyond his grave to help them.

The crackling sound of thunder erupting broke June's thoughts, as the first fall of rain start beating the outside concrete pavement around her house. As she looks through her kitchen window where condensation begins to form, she could see the branches of the tree and leaves flapping back and forth violently as the wind begins to pick up. It wouldn't be long she thought before the storm arrives tonight, and hopefully, it will pass without incident just as quickly as it arrives she reasons.

But no need to worry any further she thought, by then her and all of her family members, would probably be tucked in the bed safely, sleeping off their meatloaf dinner. Better yet her and Robert found thunderstorms the perfect time to make love because it drowns out the sounds of them making love to each other while the kids were asleep, or, so she thought.

The steady sound of rain could now be heard beating against the roof of their house against the sound of gushing wind as June, and her husband put away the last of the dishes from dinner in their dishwasher to be clean.

Robert walked over to June and gave her a gentle kiss on her forehead.

"That meatloaf was delicious babe, what's for dessert?" He said grinning, rubbing his stomach.

"The kid's ice cream and pound cake, but you seem more like a cool whip and Maraschino cherries kind of guy to me," June whispered in Robert's ear.

"I see a fourth kid on the way," Robert said.

"Don't push your luck," June said slapping Robert on the ass.

"Can you guy's go get a hotel room?" Cary said, rolling her eyes, as she texts something on her cell phone to a friend.

Robert looked over at his daughter and back to his wife.

"Just joking about that," Robert said, throwing his hands up in the air, as he and June burst out laughing.

"What's so funny?" Carey said.

"We were thinking about extending the family dear," June said, as she sat the cake and ice cream down in front of her daughter.

"Please think again," Carey said, as she cut a small piece of pound cake off with her fork.

"Well that's rude we can use another sister," Robert Jr. said, grinning.

Carey gave him the finger.

"Or a little brother," Eddy shouted out, as he slurps on his shake.

"Hey, hey, guys we were just kidding," Robert Sr. said.

"That's what you said, and Eddy came along," Carey said still on her phone.

"Watch that attitude young lady and please put that damn phone away until after dessert," June said.

"Mom, really?" Carey said definitely.

"Yes, really," her mom answers back non-conceding.

Carey put her cell phone away reluctantly at her mother's request.

"Now let's have some civility at this table please," June said.

"Amen," Robert Sr. said.

" This pound cake is delicious mom," Robbie said, grinning.

"Suck ass," Carey murmured.

Her mom cut her a sharp, discerning glance.

"Sorry," Carey said softly.

"No fourth kid, rubber time," Robert Sr. said quietly to himself.

"I heard that," June said grinning as she kicks his foot underneath the table.

"Heard what?" He said, playing dumb and laughing.

Carey excused herself from the table.

" Dad, Mom, why we keep putting off her exorcism?" Robbie joked when she had left and was no longer within earshot.

"Actually we are in the process of getting it sanctioned," his mom responded, jokingly.

"Carey is just going through puberty she will be alright," Eddy said.

"You know something, champ; I think you are right." Robert agreed, taking another bite of his pound cake.

"I still think a priest is a good idea," Robbie said.

"Hey, guys how about a good movie tonight?" June said changing the subject.

"With popcorn, mom!"

"With popcorn Eddy," she answered.

Although he could not eat it, he liked the smell and would take the popped kernels and inhale the aroma of them in his nostrils.

June knew her family was different, but it is their differences she knew that made this her family for better or worse. One rebellious kid, one kid that was a smart ass athlete and one kid that possessed a genius IQ but could only stomach special protein shakes.

As the sound of thunder erupted again, it awoke Manny from his slumber, and he started barking.

Oh!' and their faithful and beloved golden retriever.

June noticed right away that her daughter Carey must have left her attitude upstairs in her bedroom because when she came down to enjoy the movie with her family a "lighthearted comedy" her attitude had completely changed, and she was pleasant one could even say sweet. She helped make the popcorn and get the beverages together for family movie night or maybe unknown to her mom, and dad the reality was an ex-boyfriend named Jason that neither approved us was secretly now back in Carey's life, and now life was good again.

At least for now.

* * *

Robert felt good inside of her, June thought, as she rhythmically moves her hips in cohesion to his deep strokes inside of her against the background noise of outside thunder. It had been a while since the two of them had been intimate and made love to each other because of the busy schedules they both had. And if all it took was a thunderstorm to bring the both of them together she thought for some marital playtime then maybe she would deliciously appreciate the next storm even better that comes there way. "Fuck me," she softly moaned in Robert's ear as his penetration felt even deeper now as the sweat rolled off his body onto hers and inside of her mouth as she savored the salty taste of his perspiration on her tongue.

Robert pulled out of her just before she was about to come and took her inside of his mouth, June moaned again and arched her hips, instantly exploding in his mouth as his tongue masterfully hit her g-spot as he savored his extra dessert for tonight.

Robert flip her over and entered her again from behind as June met him stroke for stroke bringing him to a groaning climax as she tightens herself around his throbbing piston causing Robert to tremble orgasmically inside of her, as he releases his hot load inside of her treasure box.

A loud explosion suddenly erupted from outside of the house startling them both as Robert pulled himself outside of his wife and almost fell out of the bed before she grabbed him by the arm preventing his fall.

"What the fuck was that?" He said startled.

"I don't know?" June replied, as she wiped herself off with a nearby towel and began putting her panties back on.

They both knew that it would be just a matter of time before their kids come knocking on their door and the last thing they wanted to do was greet them in their birthday suits, as they both now hurriedly got dressed in their sleepwear.

"Maybe a nearby power line," June said, right before the loud knocking on their bedroom door proceeded by Manny's even louder barking begins.

"Come in," June said, as her and Robert now comfortably dressed met their children halfway at the door's entrance.

"Wow, did you guy's hear that?" Robbie said excitedly with Eddy standing right beside him yawning.

"Yeah, we couldn't help but hear it, where is Cary?" His dad asked.

"I don't know, in bed I guess, you know she sleeps like a rock," Robbie said.

"Yeah, I know, but go check on her anyway," his farther proposed.

"Awww, Dad," Robert protested.

"Now!" His father shouted out, slightly annoyed.

"Okay, you ain't gotta shout!" Robbie grumbled, as he proceeded towards his sisters room.

"Moron," Eddy said underneath his breath, giggling at his brother's expense.

"What did you say?" His Mom said, cutting him a serious glance, he did not think she had heard him or anybody else for that matter.

"Nothing mom," he said his eyes downcast, but still snickering.

"Cary's still sleep!" Robbie yelled back at his dad from across the upper hall.

"Let her sleep," his dad answer back as they begin to descend the stairs to investigate the source of the explosion.

* * *

"This is some good shit you got," Cary said as she took a drag on the blunt Jason had rolled.

"No this is some superb shit," Jason said, correcting her, as he took the blunt out of Cary's hand and took a longer toke on it and began coughing.

Cary started laughing "Slow down baby we still have a lot of it left," she said shaking a large Ziploc bag of marijuana that Jason had handed over to earlier after she had sneaked out the house and hooked up with him against her parent's wishes and without their knowledge.

"So how did you get out the house again," he asked, as he took another toke of the joint and passed it back to Carey.

"I stuffed my bed covers with clothes and my shower cap with socks to make the head to appear as if I am still sleeping in my bed, then I climb out my window and down the awning," she said proudly.

"Man that sounds like some Alcatraz shit," Jason said, laughing, as his eyes wander over Cary's body.

He missed that tight little body of hers and how she smelled when they were together, and he regretted cheating on Cary recently with an ex-girlfriend, and hope Cary would forgive him and give him a second chance to make things right.

Good weed was a start, he thought.

"You know baby I missed you," he said.

"With or without your dick in her?" Cary replied.

"Both," Jason said sarcastically.

"Asshole," Cary said, punching him in the side of his arm.

"Ouch," Jason squealed out as he grabbed his arm in pain, laughing.

Cary started laughing, no longer able to hold a straight face and play the scorned girlfriend. Jason may have been an asshole, but he was also a funny asshole to her that she just so happen to be madly in love with as well.

" You know that bitch doesn't mean anything to me, I love you," Jason said as he softly held her face and kissed her on the lips, slipping a feel on her breast as she brushed his hand off her boob.

"Slow your road down dude I am still mad at you," Cary said, as their lips touched again this time their tongues flickering in and out of each other's mouth.

Jason looked over the inside of the shed that they were sitting in it had plenty of room for him to get some booty in he thought if Cary decided that she was no longer going to hold his transgressions over his head.

Cary's eyes followed Jason's she always knew what he was thinking maybe because she was thinking the same thing too, after all, it had been a while since she had given him some booty.

Then the explosion happens, powerful enough to rock the shed that they were sitting inside as illumination from the explosion lit up the shed from the inside, a strange glow now pulsated from the outside giving the shed an eerie ambiance.

"What the fuck was that?" Cary shouted out!

"I don't know," said Jason looking just as startled as Cary.

The both of them cautiously exited the shed, instantly catching sight of the large luminously glowing object about fifty meters from them on the ground.

"What the fuck is that a plane?" Jason said as they walked towards the unidentified glowing object.

"Dude does that look like a fucking plane?" Cary said, unable to believe what they were looking at in her backyard.

They both now watched as a hatch opens on the mysterious oblong-shaped aircraft emitting a bright glow then something large emerged from the aircraft, something not of this world, a monstrous size Arachnid that look nothing like the ones on earth and it was headed in their direction at lightning speed.

"What in the fuck..." Jason said, unable to get all of his words out.

"Run!" Cary shouted as she grabbed her ex-boyfriend by the arm and took off for her house, she could see the silhouettes of her family in the darkness coming out of the house.

"Go back in!" Cary shouted at them as they sprinted for the house for safety.

Jason slipped and lost his footing on the wet grass, and that mistake was all it took before the Arachnid was on top of him tearing him apart like a giant shredder as it pulverized and disintegrated his guts with its giant blade-like legs, as it emitted a shrilling noise that penetrated the night air. Jason screams soon faded as his body was ripped apart like it had been through a tree shredder.

Cary picked up her pace and was now screaming at the top of her lungs her face all bloody from the cast-off of her ex-boyfriend's blood.

"Cary?" Her Mom screamed out.

Cary hit the porch, all bloody and distraught met by her father and mom.

"That thing just killed Jason!"

"What-what- in the hell are you doing out here young lady?" Robert shouted at his daughter as she ran right past all of them directly into the house.

"June did you see that," he said.

"Dad," Robbie said his voice trembling.

"What the hell was she babbling about," Robert said.

"Dad!" Robbie said louder grabbing his dad's arm, pointing towards the monstrous creature that's headed their way.

His dad could not believe what he was looking at running across his lawn.

"What in the hell is that? ..."

"Everyone "get" in now!" June screamed out and not a second too late because as soon as her husband shut the door behind them, the monstrous Arachnid came crashing into the locked door behind them with all its weight almost breaching it.

"Guys move everything you can against this door," Robert ordered his children.

Before he could say anything to his wife, she was way ahead of him and coming back downstairs with two rifles and handguns in her possession that she had taken from their gun safe.

Emergency Operator: *"911, what's the emergency?"*

"My boyfriend has just been killed by a giant spider monster or something? That came out of a UFO, and we are under attack, we need the police over here now!" Cary screamed into the phone.

Emergency Operator: *"Miss, did you just say someone just been killed?"*

"Yes by a giant spider that came out of a UFO!"

Emergency Operator: *"Ma'am have you taking any drugs because you're not making any sense, giant spider, UFO's."*

June snatches the phone out of her daughter's hand after overhearing her conversation with the 911 operator.

"Bitch yes UFO get someone over here fucking now! This is not a joke we are under attack."

Emergency Operator: *"Who am I speaking to now?"*

"Her fucking mother, you fucking moron!"

Emergency Operator: *"Excuse me?"*

Gunshots erupt as the Arachnid attempts to breach the door again.

Emergency Operator: *'Ma'am is that gunshots?"*

"Yes, send the fucking police, the National Guard, whoever now!" June said as she hung up the phone and ran over to one of the front windows.

A shrilling noise like they had never heard before erupted from the outside again, a noise that they had all only heard fictitious creatures like *Godzilla* in cheap monster movies from Japan make.

"I can't believe that thing killed Jason," Cary said, shaking with the gun in her hand.

"Cary you need to get a hold of yourself, what did you mean by UFO and that thing came out of it?" Her dad asked, holding her by the side of her arms.

"Me and Ja -Ja- Jason heard the explosion and when we came out the shed we seen what look like a long metallic object on the lawn and then its hatch open, and that thing came aft-aft-after us," Cary said, stumbling on her words.

June watched out the front window as the massive creature retreated and seemed to be plotting its next move while it was assessing its injuries, her son Robbie manned the other window with a .44 magnum.

The sound of a window breaking from upstairs and glass shattering, jarred everyone's attention to the second level of the house.

Robert looked around at the frightened faces of his family, June, Cary, Robert Jr. but one other face was missing, Eddy!

This was the first time in the melee that any of them had noticed in all the confusion that Eddy was missing and no longer in their presence.

"Where in the hell is Eddy?" June said before her husband could get the question out of his mouth.

But both of them already knew.

"You two hold it down here!" Robert instructed his older children as him, and June proceeded upstairs.

Halfway up the stairs, a scream erupted that immediately sent both of them into a race up the stairs into the room where the scream had come from in the house.

What they both came to face with instantly froze the both of them in their tracks, as they watch the Arachnid creature attempt to pull their son Eddy out the window it entered through. Its blade-like legs with pincers on each end wrapped around his small body as he held onto the bedroom furniture for an anchor, screaming in fear.

They both snapped out of it awaken by their son screams and instantly went into action as Robert begins fiercely stabbing at the creature's legs with a long knife that he had tucked in his waistband.

June got close enough to the creatures massive head and begin firing into its face blowing out some of its multiple red orb eyes that seemed to move in synchronicity with each other as the creature locked in on its prey – them.

A plasma-like dark liquid exploded out of its face as the bullets from her 30.06 tore into its ugly mug.

The creature finally released their son from its grip and quickly crawled back down the side of the house followed by rapid-fire from June's rifle, that lit into its hull as it shrieked in pain as it scurried away. .

June watched out the broken out window as it made its way down to the surface, took a few steps, and collapsed on her front lawn.

June turned around and quickly embraced her son Eddy in her arms, sobbing.

"What in the hell are you doing up here?" she asked.

"I don't don't know," he said, almost in a trance-like state.

"I-I-I just felt a strange compulsion to come up here, almost like a voice told me to mom."

"What voice?" His mom asked confused.

"It's okay champ, you stay with us now and don't leave for nothing, understand?" His father said.

Eddy nodded his head nervously yes.

The sound of sirens in the distance could be heard now approaching their home.

"Now let's get our asses downstairs and give your brother and sister a hand."

"I think we killed it," June said.

"What?" Robert replied.

"After I shot it a few more times, it appeared to collapse and die."

"Take Eddy downstairs babe, I am going back to check," said Robert.

"No, let's wait the police will be here soon."

"It's okay babe after I check I'll be right back down," Robert assured his wife.

"Don't be too long," June said, worriedly.

"I want." Robert assured her.

* * *

June watched as Robert went back up the stairs and disappeared back off into the bedroom, as she and Eddy came down the stairs and entered back into the living room where her children were keeping guard she could see the red and blue strobes from the police cars approaching their property.

"Robert come down the police is here!" she yelled upstairs to her husband as a weight seem to instantly lift off her chest seeing that they had reinforcements now only minutes away, maybe only seconds away... from death!

June and her children watched in horror as more of the Arachnid creatures appeared out of the darkness and ambushed the four officers as they exited their patrol cars, they never had a chance as the Arachnids quickly ripped them apart between futile gunshots and even futile screams.

June and her children let loose with the artillery they had, but to no avail, the Arachnids kept coming, as one made its way to the porch, Cary hurled a homemade Molotov cocktail at one hitting it! As the cocktail exploded the creature burst into flames as it retreated on its spindly legs squealing while engulfed in flames.

Distraught, June yelled for Robert again, but he did not answer back, so she made her way back up quickly to the bedroom only to see Robert now hanging out the bedroom window, but his legs were still inside.

"Robert!" She called out to him as she cautiously approaches him. "Robert?"

June pulled at his pants leg, and that is when what's left of him from the waist down slid back in as she screamed out in shock at the chilling site of her husband's now torsoless and headless body.

June sat there shaking and stunned as tears rolled down her face staring at what was left of Robert's body, until she finally got enough nerve up to approach the window again.

She raised the 30.06 towards the outside of the window as she cautiously looked out below for the remains of that thing that she thought she had killed earlier.

The ground below was empty and it was eerily silent as well she noted.

* * *

A bead of perspiration rolled down June's face as she walked back slowly from the window and that is when the creature lunged up at her from the outside of the window, and she instinctively let loose with the 30.06 blowing its brains out through the back of its skull.

As it hit the surface below this time, it did not move.

June grabbed more ammo out of the gun safe and ran downstairs to the sound of more screaming and gunfire to engage in the battle that her children was now immersed in, only to be hit by a intense glowing light from the outside that blinds all of them and stops her in her tracks as everything now goes dead silent again.

They all now watch helplessly and in horror as an eerie reddish orb now enveloped Eddy as he faced the house surrounding by the Arachnid creatures, who stood guard, an orb that was almost in the shape of an egg.

Eddy said one thing before his body begin splitting in half, from the top of his head and a creature emerges from it covered in a gelatinous ooze, a creature that looked like the ones that surrounded him, but with more human-like appendages attached to its slimy arachnid body.

"Mom, I have to go home," the creature said.

One of the few neighborhood cats left had the misfortune of wandering near the creatures as they made their way back to there mothership. As soon as one of the Arachnid creature sense, its presence a reptilian tongue shot out of its mouth and caught the cat as if it was a fly on a toad's tongue. The cat let out a hiss, but it was too late as the reptilian tongue retracted the small furry beast back into its acidic mouth and its sulfuric juices begins digesting its feline meal.

The earth rumble again and just as quick as it had arrived in a flash of blinding light, Cary and her other children watched helplessly as the Creatures mothership disappears into the nighttime sky into oblivion.

* * *

June needed to understand what the hell had just happened and something told her that the answer might be somewhere in Eddy's bedroom as she searched through his room feverishly looking for answers. It had been hours now that she had been searching and nothing seemed out of the ordinary in his room. That is until she noticed what appeared to be a loose floorboard underneath his bed. She then had her son Robert Jr. help her disassemble the bed so that she could better access the floorboard.

June slowly lift the floorboard up and then another, as she stared at what the floorboards had hidden, Eddy had hidden. There must have been hundreds of them, all different sizes and colors. She picked one up and inspected it with the dangling metal tag on it that said *my name is Kitty; I belong to Ann Waterson,* Manny shuffles over tail wagging and sniffs the cat leash and whined as June dropped it back inside the floorboard.

She was wrong, she thought, her son or it? Had an acquired taste for more than protein shakes.

THE SPELL

M ike Castellini a Las Vegas crime boss, and his crew had just one little thing to take care of before he made his weekly visit to what he considered was a hole in the wall strip club but with one saving grace or two, pick your choice. It had some of the best goddamn pastrami and corned beef sandwiches that you could bite into and some of the best eye candy that money could buy making love all night to a strip pole. He also had another interest invested in this strip club classily name Puss n Booties – money.

He wanted to know what the hell was going at that joint? Mike had heard, through his street sources that most of his loan sharking clientele was now dropping all their borrowed money at this place instead of the local Casinos around town. Thus, giving him zero probability of possibly ever seeing a return with interest on his money again.

Sure, he knew, these joints work hand in hand, that is to a certain point. It was just as easy to get an addiction to fantasy women on stage sliding down steel poles as it was to one arm bandits, gaming tables, and the glitz & glamour of the Las Vegas, Casinos and its make-believe scenery of striking it rich for the average Joe or Joan.

But in the infinitesimal chance that one did hit it big, the make-believe was any random joker could have them both. That is until his or her luck ran out. Like the poor bastard in the back of Mike Castellini's spacious Lincoln Continental trunk, all tied up and ready for a skinny dip in the cold dark waters of Lake Mead.

Mike could hear the man moaning, gagged in the back of his spacious trunk. This bum owed Mike thousands, plus interest and Mike had got tired of waiting to be paid back.

Because one thing Mike Castellini knew for sure, empty promises did not pay debts, cold hard cash did.

Mike lit up a big cigar and order his driver/goon to turn up the classical music on the radio to drown out the man's pathetic wailing.

Another car filled with some of his other goons trails cautiously behind him.

Mike took a sip of his cognac and placed the glass of liquid gold back in a pull-out tray.

The black waters of Lake Mead glisten in the night as both cars pulled up next to the boat dock. All the men exited the two vehicles, four strong.

One of his goons pop the trunk of Mike's car, reached in, and help the reluctant tied-up passenger out of the car's spacious trunk.

"Come on, chump, it's time to get your feet wet," he said chuckling.

The fear of the inevitable could not have been more evident in the man's eyes as he struggled to speak through his gag.

Mike motion with his cigar to one of his goons to pull the gag down from off the man's mouth. Everyone, he thought when facing their execution was at least entitled to their last words, no matter how self-deprecating they may be.

"Please Mr. C, please, I will pay you back I swear, I have a – a – a- family, don't do this!" the man begged for his life, as he cupped his hands together in prayer.

"I have a family too, you know," Mike coldly said as he relit his cigar.

His debtor nervously nodded his head in acknowledgment.

Mike pointed his finger at him. "And when slimeballs like you don't pay me back what they owe guess what?" he said.

The man was too scared to answer the question and rightfully so; he knew what was coming.

"They and you are taking fucking food right off my family's fucking table!"

"That's what!" Mike shouted out to his captive, who appear to had been already worked over by Mike's men by the swollen slits for eyes he was now looking through at Mr. Castellini and his surrounding goons.

"I know, I know – I fuck up, Mr. C, but I can make this right, I swear on my grandmother's grave."

Mike walked over to the man and patted him on the side of his face. "I know you can make this right, "Mickey boy." Trust me you already have."

"What-what- I don't understand? Mr. Castellini."

"What's to understand? It's simple, consider your debt paid in full," Mike said cheerfully.

"Close the books on his debt Vinnie," he orders.

Mike walked away from the now kneeling man that was still pleading desperately for his life.

"No-no-no-Mr. C!"

"By the way, don't forget to say hello to your Grandma for me," Castellini said.

One of his goons quickly steps in his place raised his gun with a silencer attached to its muzzle to Mickey's head. He pulls the trigger on his boss

Mike's command. A flash erupts from the muzzle of the silencer; As the goon closes the books on the man's debt for good.

Mike disrespectfully flicks his cigar or at least what is left of it onto the dead man's body.

"Now you are paid in full Mickey boy," he says unabashedly.

One of his three goons, looking on had an ear to ear grin, on his ruddy face.

"I think our boy Mickey is ready for that swim now boys," Mike said, as he lit up a fresh cigar.

"You have any idea's boss?" Vinnie his number one goon asks.

Mike took a puff of his cigar. "Yeah, make it look like a bullet to his head, and his ass was toss in Lake Mead."

His crew laughs.

"Gotcha Boss," said Vinnie.

After what took his crew only ten nasty minutes to prep Mickey's body for his late-night swim in Lake Mead cold waters.

A faint splash could be heard in the cold dark distance of the night as two of his men took the body out on a rowboat and toss it over the boat's side into the murky depths of the lake.

His henchmen got back to the dock, their pants legs, and arms wet.

"Ditch the fucking boat and dry-off, gents, we are headed back to Vegas, for some fun and entertainment, orders of the boss," Vinnie said, to the other goons with a grin on his face.

"Sounds like a plan to me," said one of the goons.

"What's the name of that joint again?" the big goon holding the saw-off shotgun asks.

"Puss n Booties," Vinnie answers.

"Sounds like a classy joint to me," he said with a grin on his face.

They all laughed, almost oblivious to the body they dispose of with concrete weights attached to it sinking further down to the bottom of Lake Mead, further down to its cold watery grave.

The sound of the engines starting back up broke the silence of the night as Mike Castellini, and his crew drove their vehicles out of the dock area and hit the hardball back towards the city lights of Las Vegas Nevada.

Mr. Castellini lit up another cigar in the back of his Lincoln, a "Gurkha Black Dragon" inhaling its rich earthy spicy aroma. It was a cigar he normally saved for special occasions; well, this was definitely one of them he felt.

He was closing the books on all his debtors and was now about to find out where in the hell all of his goddamn money was going? And if this strip club was the source, then he had no other choice but to strong-arm in and take over the joint and kick the owner out on his ass with a few dollars still left in his pocket, and that was being generous, he thought.

Yeah Mickey, was sipping on bubbles Mr. Castellini thought, and they weren't champagne bubbles either. Some people had to learn the hard way he guessed.

"Hey Vinnie, turn that up!" he said to his driver as he listens to the classical aria "Nessun Dorma" sung by Luciano Pavarotti.

"Puss n booties? What kinda mook names his club that?" he said.

Vinnie chuckled. "I don't know; you got me, boss."

"Well, I guess we are about to find out?" he said solemnly, as he admired the label on his Gurkha Black Dragon Cigar.

In New Orleans, two weeks before Mike Castellini and his crew decided to throw one of their clients into the cold waters of Lake Mead, the proprietor of the strip club that they are visiting, a gentleman or not. Depends upon whom you ask? Who went by the distinct name of "Marius Chandelier" is on the hunt for a stripper that goes by the name of Eldorado, that he had concluded might just be the key to bringing his strip club out of the red and putting it back on the map. Thus keeping his club out of the hands of the mob, and guy's like Castellini and his crew.

He had an offer to make her like the Godfather he thought, an offer that she couldn't refuse. All expenses paid, plus room and board and a ten-thousand-dollar upfront bonus if she agreed to follow him back to Vegas, and work in his club.

It was a generous offer he knew. But if this broad was as good as the word out on the street was about her? He figured he could make his investment back up in a month, or maybe less.

His search for her and his sources had led him to a strip club name Sirens in the French Quarter of New Orleans.

As he entered the strip club, he sat down at one of the tables close to the stage.

He would not be disappointed, as he listens to the emcee and deejay of the club introduce, the next dancer on stage.

"All right folks here is someone special you been waiting for all night, the sensational and tantalizing *"Eldorado."*

Eldorado had a stage walk with bounce and attitude to it, that was nothing less than captivating, to say the least. And now, as Marius Chandelier laid eyes on what he thought was a living and breathing goddess right before his eyes, he was not disappointed, not disappointed at all.

On the contrary, he wondered if the not yet made, ten-thousand-dollar proposition to her would be enough to convince her to change her venue.

Chandelier was mesmerized as he watches Eldorado ascend the pole and then slide down effortlessly after flipping her body back, with the skill that only a season dancer could execute.

He also took notice to the other patrons, reaction to her, as he noticed that they could not take their eyes off Eldorado as well. To them, she might as well have been the oxygen that they were breathing in that room, including him.

There was so much money that was thrown up on the stage during her performance; it rained down like green confetti.

Chandelier smiled, revealing some of his gold implants. Yeah, he thought, he would have no problem making his ten-thousand-dollar investment back in a month with a star attraction like her in his club.

"She's something else huh?" another patron asks him, that was sitting close by at a table by himself.

"She sure is Pops," Chandelier said, tossing back some of the drink that the server had brought him.

He eyeballed the other patron sizing the old man up before deciding to invite him over to his table for a drink. Not that it looks like he needed another one he noted.

"The name is Chandelier, what's yours?" he said.

The stranger eyeballs him back with equal suspicion, as he reluctantly shakes Chandelier outstretched hand.

"Rufus," he said.

"How fitting," Chandelier stated.

"What are you drinking Mister Rufus?"

"Anything wet," Rufus replied.

"My kind of guy," Chandelier said.

Chandelier waved the server over in the hot waitress uniform that was a Victorian corset, hot shorts, spandex, and black leather knee-high boots.

"Give my friend here a tall glass of ice water," Chandelier requested, with a smirk on his face.

Out of the side of his eye, he could see Rufus, stir in his chair, and shoot him an incredulous glance.

Chandelier looked over at Rufus and laughed. "I am just fucking with you, my friend."

"Make that a double shot of Jack D and coke for my new friend."

Rufus cleared his throat as if he had something stuck in it; Chandelier got the message loud and clear.

"No Coke," said Chandelier.

He then raised his almost empty glass. "And a refill doll on whatever this is?"

"You not from around, here are you?" Rufus asks.

"No, I am not my friend, are you?"

"All my damn life," answered Rufus.

"What do you know about the girl that was just on the stage?" Chandelier asks him.

"Trouble, like you," Rufus said.

"Good observation my old friend," Chandelier said, as he finishes the rest of his drink.

"I take it you haven't heard about the disappearances of some of the customers that used to come here, have you?" Rufus asks cautiously.

"No, why should I give a hot shit Pops?" Chandelier said as his eyes met the servers breast as she sat both drinks down on the table for the men.

"Put it on my tab," he said and tipped her a twenty.

"Maybe you should," said the old man as he took a sip of his new drink, paid for by his new friend.

"Look pops I appreciate the warning, but I don't scare easy, if you know what I mean," Chandelier said firmly.

"I ain't trying to scare you, Mister, all I am saying is just be careful, especially with that one you just ask about," the old man pointed out.

Chandelier swirls the ice cubes around in his glass as he watched the next girl that was upon the stage during her thing, he had to admit that this place seems like it had a better stock of girls than the ones he had at his joint.

When he gets back to Vegas, he definitely had to make some upgrades, he thought to his club, and get rid of some of the fatties.

"Thanks, for the heads-up thirsty, but if it's left up to me, that's the last time you will be setting your eyes on that dime-piece," Chandelier said with a grin on his face and a nod towards the stage.

"I hope so," said Rufus.

"Thanks, for the drink Mister, and have a safe trip back to Vegas," he added.

"What did you just say?" Chandelier said as he turns to face the old man, only to face a now empty chair.

"Creepy old fuck!" Chandelier muttered to himself as he took another sip of his drink. His thoughts went back to *Eldorado*, as he observes the next dancer come on stage and begin wiping the pole down before she begins her performance.

What did the old man mean by the statement? Be careful with that one? He pondered when he had inquired about *Eldorado*. What was so foreboding about her that he had to take precaution? Now his interest in her was even more peaked. As he put in a special request to the floor server to have Eldorado join him once she was finished with her set on the stage.

He now watches her as she made her way over to his table. She had change costumes if you can call g-string panties and a bra with a duster coat that? Just a different color. But it complemented her svelte but slightly curvy figure nevertheless.

Chandelier like what he saw, and more than that he like the idea of unlimited potential in this new creature that exuded sexual tension in the atmosphere, she could be a viable asset he thought.

"Hi, may I join you?" she asks.

"Yes, you may," he responded with a smile, never taking his eyes off this vixen of sensuality.

She sat down on his lap. Her body next to him felt and smell good, as Chandelier size her up.

"What's your name, handsome?"

"Chandelier and yours?"

"Eldorado," she answers.

"You mind if I smoke?" she said.

"Baby, you can do whatever you wanna do? As long as you do it with me," Chandelier said with a grin.

"I plan to," Eldorado said with a smile.

* * *

The provocative music was bumping inside a local Las Vegas strip club called *Puss & Booties*. The dancer on the stage seemed like she was in a world of her own as she gyrated her body in sexual positions that were just as titillating as the music she was dancing too, moves and music that held her captive audience under her spell.

In fact, if one was to evaluate the situation from the outside looking in, they could have come to the simple conclusion, it would not have mattered to her at all if they were not even there. (her captive audience) As long as they left their wallets at the door, and the stage continues to rain dollar bills by some unforeseen force.

The results to her would have been all the same as the song by **Dire Straits,** (Get your) *Money for nothin' in this case tricks for free.*

They were under her spell, and she knew it!

Eyes in the crowd that were full of lust, that hypnotically watch her every move, with erotic thoughts on their minds about just how good she would be in bed? Men with wives, fiancees, girl-friends that were willing to drop their last dollar on their uninhibited fantasies.

On a fantasy that most likely would never come true. A fantasy that had the worst betting odds than any Casino in town, because it was built on like-minded fantasies and lost dreams.

Las Vegas,

The *Rat pack, Elvis, Bugsy Siegel.*

They came, they conquered, and they left.

The dancer who had everyone captivated in the strip club was *Eldorado;* her co-workers called her *Elda* for short.

She was a very attractive girl of Armenian and African heritage in her mid-twenties with sharp features, long jet black wavy hair, and a lean, curvy body that was a product of her employ and strict vegan diet that she adhered to most times.

Sometimes.

It appeared as if she was levitating down the pole as she executed her signature descent down the top of the pole as if she was walking on air. Her shapely legs outstretched and floating in a synchronicity motion with each other making it appeared her feet were touching stairs that were unseen by the human eye.

The all-black costume she wore or the little of it that she was wearing, reminded him of the costumes that Prince, protégé Vanity used to wear.

Her long black see-thru duster coat swayed in the wind when she walked down the stage like a superhero's cape. It soon came off as she set it down in one corner of the stage, revealing her tight dancer's body to her audience even more explicitly.

Eldorado unsnapped her black laced bra, as easily as if she was drinking a glass of water and tossed it in the same corner with her duster coat. As she cupped her small but firm breasts, pinching the nipples as she teasingly met eye contact with one of the club's frequent patron's a man by the name of Larry Forrester.

Larry watch her as she lifted one of her breasts to her mouth and stroke the nipple with her tongue.

He watched captivated, he watched spellbound.

Eldorado was the only dancer he had come here to see, and it was nothing on this earth he wouldn't do for her.

In contrast, Larry was once a family man that had a nice home, a good job, a loving wife, and two kids that he adored.

Now for reasons, unknown to him that he did not know, nor was he able to explain, he was willing to throw it all away to be with Eldorado, sitting in a dark strip club on the other side of town in Las Vegas eagerly anticipating her arrival.

He could not get her voice out of his head, her scent, her face, that body.

Larry had now spent so much money that should have been going to his family on her, and the strip club, he had lost count.

What had innocently enough started as a boys night out from work, with his friends had somehow become a full-time addiction to him that he had no control over.

It was like air and water to Larry. He had to be at this particular strip club; he had to see Eldorado, or else he could not eat, sleep, or function thru the day. His wife Allison had noticed the changes in him, subtle at first before they inevitably started to escalate.

Now Larry Forrester found himself sneaking out of the house at odd hours of the night and morning when his family was sleep to be here at *Puss & Booties* with his favorite stripper Eldorado. He found himself making lame-ass excuses and telling lame-ass lies when his wife questioned him about his whereabouts.

Behavior that in the past had not been characteristic of Larry Forrester.

But the real grim truth was, Mr. Forrester did not know himself these days at all. When he looked in the mirror at himself lately, it was like looking at an empty vessel of the man that he once was. The dark circles around his puffy eyes were the tell-tale signs that he was sleep-deprived, he had lost over thirty pounds in just one month alone and was subsisting off of cigarettes and energy drinks with the occasional upper to keep him afloat and a downer to put him to sleep.

His life was literally off the grid of any normalcy he had known before he cast eyes on the seductress he now watched in a hypnotic-like trance named Eldorado.

He had recently emptied all his bank accounts, investment accounts, joint accounts with his wife, and any future savings that they had set aside for their children's future education, to finance this cancer of an obsession with Eldorado, to provide and placate her with anything that she desired.

Like the Casino's in Las Vegas, she had taken him to the bank and clean him out. He could make deposits but would not be getting any returns on his investments into her in the long run.

As he stared at her in his trance-like state, he reflected on how it all started, how it all began. How she deliciously persuaded him against his better judgment to a private lap dance in one of the V.I.P. rooms in the club.

How Eldorado while mounting his lap and rubbing that beautiful body up against his whispered the words seductively in his ear, "Vous Estes `a moi," (You are mines) in French.

"Je vous possede et Je vous possede," I own you, and I possess you.

He was not literate in French, so how was he suppose to have known? It just sounded good and sexy to him against the beat drop of the provocative music spun by the club's resident deejay.

But he wanted her, and he wanted to possess her as well.

But this was Eldorado's house, and like any Casino, the deck was stacked against him. From the time he walked in until the time he walked out.

"Je vous possede et Je vous possede," she whispered in his ear.

"I own you, and I possess you."

And indeed she did. It was now 4:00 am, and the strip club would soon be closing. Larry knew that Eldorado no longer had any use for him after all his financial resources had run dry.

But he had to have one more lap dance from her, feel the sensation of her beautiful body press-up against his when she whispered the last words that he would ever hear from her again, but this time in English.

"You are mine in life, but even more in death."

This time Larry understood perfectly well, every single word that Eldorado had just spoken to him. What directive that she had just given him, as he slowly walked out of the strip club like a zombie, like the broken man he was. He knew now what he had to do, to make all of this right again.

The parking lot to Puss & Bootie's was now desolate except his car that set like an old relic waiting for him to return to its caverns.

Tears now rolled slowly down Larry's face, as he sobbed to himself, as he looked down at the note that he was leaving his family. If he could turn back the hands of time and do things differently, he would have. But that was not the case, and so here he was *decision time.*

Larry placed the note inside an envelope and gently placed it on the front passenger seat next to him. He then drove to an even more desolate area several blocks from the strip club, parked his car.

Larry looked into his rearview mirror at his glazed over eyes that appeared even more zombiesque. He then reached into his glove compartment and pulled out the new 9mm handgun he had just purchased, put the gun to his temple, (smiled) when he heard Eldorado's voice clear as day say "do it!" and blew his brains out all over the car seats all over the – letter.

Back at the club in the dancer's dressing room, Eldorado set at her vanity, cleaning the make-up off her face, preparing to go home.

When suddenly she grabbed her neck and inhaled, as she felt the life leaving out of ex-client Larry Forrester's body. Her eyes appeared to glow red at that very moment as she then proceeded to relax again.

And although the expression on her face was solemn at best, that was not the case of the reflection that looked back at her from the mirror, eyes luminescent red, smiling, with an evil grin on its face.

The image in the mirror faded into the background, faded into darkness, now Eldorado was looking at herself again, at least the image on the surface that she wanted to project.

The lipstick was the last thing to come off, as she tossed the cotton pad in a trash can underneath her vanity desk.

Men are fools, she thought.

Lustful fools to be toyed with, played with, and then drained of everything that they had in this world, everything that she could get out of them.

Everything.

She liked the arrangement, or you could say the deal that she had struck up with the owner of the strip club, a flamboyant and nefarious character by the name of Marius Chandelier, part-time pimp, all-time hustler.

Money for souls was her proposal to him. She would make him a wealthy man and in return, let's say he would just let her do her thing.

And boy, would he find out she was good at it, doing her thing that is.

Eldorado he would find out wasn't like (his words) any bitch that had just walked off the streets that now wanted to make a living at the strip game and maybe wanted to sell some occasional pussy on the side.

No, Eldorado was the strip game and made the men and women that came to see her fans forever.

Forever, until she owned them, or until she decided to let them go.

Chandelier you see was unaware that he had made a deal with the devil.

Literally, that is.

He was also unaware that he had made a deal with something as ancient as time itself, made a deal with an enchantress, a demon, a succubus.

And part of that deal that Mr. Marius Chandelier had so reluctantly agreed to with her or "it" was? That he with Eldorado's assistance, of course, would make one human sacrifice a month inside the club.

When the dastardly deed was carried out by the two of them, the victim's body afterward would be cut and sliced up by various tools of the "serial killer trade" he kept hidden on the premises.

The flesh of the victims once separated from their bones would then be boiled, fried, or baked depending on what was on Chandelier 's menu that week.

Then unknowingly consumed and cannibalized by the patrons and employees in the club in the form of pastrami sandwiches, hot dogs, chili, pizza garnishments or other imaginative delectables of the flesh sold off a food truck that he ran in the parking lot of his club.

A neckbone in the greens was a neckbone in the greens.

It was a deal with the devil that had made Chandelier a rich man.

The deal was money for souls, souls, for money.

And his had been the first one up for bid.

Eldorado smiled at the thought that she could not have picked a better place Sin City, Las Vegas, where everything is for sale, and everything has a price.

Sheeple she thought, designed to be led to the slaughter.

Eldorado had been human once, but she too like Chandelier had gotten herself in bed with the devil when her spirit was weak. And when she allowed many of his minions to come into her and take over, the dominant of the many took hold and thus was born Eldorado.

Whenever, the house deejay would announce her name before she got on the stage (Eldorado) the whole house would go eerily quiet as all the focus would go to her. She became the club's premier dancer, the main attraction, a star.

Chandelier knew right then that he had himself something special, but how special? He did not know.

The fact that he had pretty much fucked whatever girl he had wanted in the club except her, already made her special in his eyes.

But he did not trust her and for a good reason. Marius Chandelier knew that women like her with the power of persuasion that she had over men and women could be a dangerous thing, because he possessed that same power also, but not to her degree.

That's why he always had the other girls watching Eldorado, watching his back.

Chandelier walked up slowly behind Eldorado in the dressing room and placed his hands on her shoulders. She felt his presence before he had stepped one inch thru the door.

"Goodnight Elda," he said as he massaged her shoulders.

She knew what he wanted.

"I guess," she said in a nonchalant voice, as she applied another shade of lipstick to her lips.

She peeled Chandelier's hands off her shoulders as she stood up to leave with her purse now slung over her shoulder.

"You are one hot number Elda," he said, as he saliciously looked her up and down with a glint in his eye.

His silk Hawaiian print shirt was obstructing her vision.

"Where did you steal that line from an 80's movie?" she said, as she shoves a roll of cash in his hands.

Her boss, Chandelier, looks down at the cash with a greedy grin on his face.

"A good night indeed," he says.

He takes his finger and strokes her left shoulder with it gently.

"How about you and me celebrate," he asks.

"I would, but I might break you," Eldorado says as she removes Chandelier finger from off her arm.

"Ouch, don't be so rough," Chandelier says playfully.

"Anyway, I need you to keep your mind on business and not my pussy understood?" Elda said, firmly with a tone in her voice, Chandelier did not like.

"Trust me, I can do both," Chandelier shot back.

Eldorado smiled at him, to her Chandelier was just a grown insecure little boy that wanted her to make him feel like a man. Unfortunately for him, she was not up for that task.

"I bet you can, but don't forget the arrangement we have, you keep up your end of the bargain I'll keep up mines, understand?"

Chandelier slowly nodded his head yes, in defeat.

"Good, now stop aiming so high and go and fuck one of those stupid tramps out there," she said, Chandelier eyes narrowed.

"You know you're starting to talk to me like you're my boss," he said angrily.

"How else am I suppose to talk to you?" Eldorado snapped back.

"If I wanted you to lick the crack of a hobo's ass, do you think you could resist? Do you!" Eldorado shouted out.

Chandelier stood frozen as he watched her face begin to change and take on a monstrous appearance; her pupils become red pinpoints.

"Do you?" she asked again this time in a deeper, more masculine voice.

Chandelier responded nervously with a stutter, "You wouldn't make me lic.. lic.. lick a hobo's ass would you?"

"Either that or you could be his bitch for the day, that Hawaiian silk shirt would make a nice mini dress Marius," she said bluntly.

"Are you starting to get the picture Marius Chandelier?" Eldorado added her face now back to a human appearance.

"Loud and clear," Chandelier answered nervously.

"Good now stay in your lane," Eldorado said, as she walked out the dressing room.

Chandelier remains silent as he watches her leave; he was right that crazy bitch or whatever that thing was *masquerading* as a human was *extremely dangerous*!

Why had he gone this far he thought, and what was he thinking?

He now begins to realize no amount of money in the world was worth the hell he had created for himself.

There was though a way out of this he reasoned, how could he destroy it soon? Before "it" decided he was no longer of any use and came after him first.

* * *

Eldorado was aware that she had a lot of eyes on her, on and off the dance floor, and that one pair of those eyes belonged to a co-worker and dancer that went by the stage name Misty Grant.

Misty was one of the few girls that she was close to in the club on a personal level and one that Chandelier had requested that she take under her wing and tutelage as a protégé.

And although Misty was a pretty and shapely girl in her own right, Chandelier knew that she lacked the enigmatic qualities that Eldorado possessed, but she would at least make a good spy he thought. But unknown to him Eldorado had already suspected as much but chose to go along with the program as if she was oblivious to this fact.

"Keep your friends close, but your enemies closer," was after all one of her "mottos" that she had made her own. The "little girl" as she termed (Misty) was not only a mortal but a novice to her, so she fed her what she wanted to feed her as far as information.

Information that was impertinent to Eldorado and just enough to keep Marius Chandelier baited and happy.

In reality, the only thing that she would miss about Misty Grant in case she had to dispose of her was she was a good bed warmer and the numerous lustful tryst they had shared. She had to admit she liked the way Misty felt in her mouth, soft, supple, and warm.

But if she had to get rid of the bitch, she thought, Misty like the rest of them, once she had gone thru the "meat grinder" would make a nice pastrami sandwich on rye bread served a la carte.

Eldorado licked her lips wet at the thought, as she set her sight on her next victim in the strip club, a middle-aged man with a prominent bald spot that he unsuccessfully tried to cover up with a combover and some hairspray.

But she could also see that he was dress very nicely and that his polyester pants might contain more than just his excitement at the various dancers, that took turns displaying their assets and wares on the stage and the pole.

The patron set at a table with a small entourage of his own as Eldorado walked over to join him upon his request.

"How it's going tonight handsome?" she asked him as she walked up to his table, zoning in on him and picking him out of the other three men in his group. He looked her up and down as he took her by the hand that she had offered him. "Fine doll, now that you're here," he said.

"Have a seat," he offered.

Eldorado set down on his lap; she could feel the other men at his table watching her and him with envy like grinning hyenas.

"Hot damn! You're gorgeous; what's your name beautiful?" he asked.

"Eldorado," she answered.

"Like the fabled city of gold?" he asked.

"Who says it's a fable," rebutted Eldorado.

Her *mark* laughed, revealing overly white teeth if there was such a thing.

"Is there gold down there?" he asked, as his eyes went down between her legs towards the black g-string that she was wearing.

"Would you like to find out?" she whispered in his ear.

"Oh boy, would I," he replied with a big grin on his face revealing those too white teeth again.

Eldorado massages his arm, causing his sleeve to go up revealing a nice Rolex Cellini gold watch on his wrist.

She smiled as she mentally noted that his one wrist alone was worth at least fifteen thousand dollars. She was right about Mr. Polyester pants he had more than just an erection in his slacks, he had deep pockets, and she for one did not mind burying her hands deep inside of them.

It was time to start digging.

"Would you like a private dance in the V.I.P. room," she asked.

"Show me the way," he said cheerfully, as he picked up his drink off the table.

Several other girls had now joined his friends at their table to the party, so his "associates" were now too distracted by the other skimpily clad vixens around them to worry about what the hell their friend was doing or where the hell he was going.

Eldorado took Mr. Polyester pants by the hand and guided him to the VIP room. That would be the last that they would be seeing their friend for the rest of the night.

The last time they would see him again.

Back in the V.I.P. room in a more intimate setting Eldorado now slid her upper naked body down Mr. Polyester pants exposed chest as she straddles him.

He sat back with his mouth agape, and his eyes glazed over a ghastly white color.

"Je vous possede et Je vous possede," she whispered in his ear.

I own you, and I possess you.

Chandelier fastens the watch onto his wrist. "Nice Rolex," he said out loud, to himself, admiring the timepiece. He then took a handkerchief out of his pocket and wiped a speck of blood off of the glass face of the watch. "Aaaahhh, much better now," he said, holding his wrist up towards the light.

Eldorado observed him from across the room, the strip club was now empty besides the three of them, and the bloody parts of a mutilated body cut up in various pieces like meat from a butcher shop on a large plastic tarp sprawled out on the back kitchen floor.

It is this part of the bargain (the killing and dismemberment) is what Chandelier soon detested the most.

Murder.

To him, Eldorado had now made him an unwitting accomplice to her succession of murders and her insatiable appetite for bloodlust, thus making him into (he wanted to vomit whenever he thought of this) a fucking serial killer.

He took the watch off and put it back in his jacket pocket underneath the plastic apron that he wore.

Eldorado stuffed the polyester pants with the other remnants of clothing from the victim into a small garbage bag, all of this with his bones in another bag would go to dumping sites familiar to only her and Chandelier.

She calmly smoked a cigarette as she surveyed her and Chandelier's handy work.

"Hey, no need to be squeamish he won't bite back I can assure you that," she said sarcastically.

Chandelier wiped the sweat off of his forehead as he contemplated the grisly task ahead of them.

"Put the bones in the bag and the meat in the grinder," Eldorado said.

"I know, place the bones in the bag and the meat in the grinder," Chandelier repeated.

"You don't have to tell me twice," he said angrily, as he tossed a limb into one of the garbage bags, nervously eyeing the gruesome sight of the victim's headless upper torso on the tarp.

"Are you forgetting something?" Eldorado asked as she pointed out to Chandelier a gold and black ring with the initials MC on one of severed hands fingers. "Oh shit, I didn't see that!" Chandelier picked up the severed hand and tugged at the ring to remove it from the finger, but despite his attempts, it would not come off the finger that it was attached too.

Eldorado quickly snatched the hand away from Chandelier, tossed it on the kitchen counter and in the blink of an eye swiftly cut off the finger with a meat cleaver that she held in her other hand.

Eldorado pulled the ring off the bloody finger and tossed it to Chandelier. "See how easy that was," she said with a smirk.

Chandelier caught the ring and went to stuff it in his pocket but in his nervous ridden haste missed the inside of his pocket; the ring went tumbling unnoticed by him or Eldorado to the floor with a ping.

It was hot as hell in the back kitchen, and he just wanted to be done with this task and move on, it would be another month until she or it would demand another sacrifice, which was fine by him.

The rank smell of blood and guts filled his nostrils, as he wiped the sweat from his forehead, leaving a smudge of blood in its place. He could not understand how Eldorado could be so detached? Was never nervous, never broke a sweat or batted an eye while she carried out these heinous murders and dismemberments.

Yes, technically he had never murdered any of the victims, although he had been a willing participant in the latter. Not that it would have mattered much to the police if they had discovered what he and his discompassionate co-part had been up too.

Bang bang bang! The loud knock at the front door startled them both or at least him. "What the fuck now?" he said underneath his breath.

"Diesel see who is at the goddamn front door will ya?" he screamed out at the large doorman and bouncer that was in the front area of the club.

"Sure boss!" he heard his employee scream back at him from the front.

"We need to get this shit bagged up and out of here," Eldorado said.

"Shit!" Chandelier blurted out as he watched wide-eyed as his bouncer came crashing thru the kitchen double doors with a shotgun pressed up to the back of his head, accompanied by three-man, which included the guy with the shotgun to his noggin.

"Sorry boss," he said nervously.

"It's okay Diesel," Chandelier said to him.

Eldorado recognized the three men right away; they were the ones sitting at the table earlier.

"What the fuck is going on in here?" shouted out one of the goons as he looked at the bloody scene.

"It looks like these sick fucks done had themselves a party," said his friend.

"Drop the meat cleaver bitch! And the both of you need to get those hands in the air," the first one that had made the inquiry ordered, he appeared to be the leader out of the three.

Colorado dropped the meat cleaver to the floor, which made a loud clanging noise as it made contact.

"I recognize her; she was the one that came to the table for Mike," said goon number two.

"I think you got me mistaken," Eldorado said firmly.

"Bitch! You calling me a liar?" he rebutted.

"I am saying you're mistaken," she said, holding her ground.

"Who is this on the floor?" the leader demanded to know.

" Trust me he's no one that you should be concerned about," Chandelier said.

The words had almost not fully left his mouth before he got a quick smack across the lips with Goon number one's pistol instantly splitting it and drawing blood.

"Motherfucker, we are not here to play games!" he said.

"We are looking for our friend Mike, he did not go home, and the last place we saw him was here," said the leader.

"We don't know your friend Mister, and if he came with you he should have left with you," Chandelier said, as he wiped the blood off his lip.

"Yeah, that's the only thing you got right asshole," the leader said, as he looked over at his other associate with the shotgun to the bouncers head. A slight nod was all his trigger man needed, as their eyes met.

And just like that, he let loose with the shotgun, Blam!

The bouncer's brains were all over the kitchen floor, the big man's body dropped face forward, with a loud thud to the floor, revealing a now large and gaping hole to the back of his head. A whiff of blueish gunsmoke creeps up out of the wound and into the air.

Chandelier and Eldorado jumped back startled by the brazen execution of the bouncer and doorman.

Chandelier looked on in shock; it was the first time that he had seen Eldorado respond emotionally to anything, maybe she still had some humanity left in her after all he reasoned.

"Now do you think we are serious?" the leader asked them unsympathetically.

Goon two smiled.

"Now unless you two twisted fucks want to join your friend "Dead engine" here on the floor, I advise one of you to start talking and quick."

In all the chaos that had ensued, no one had noticed that Eldorado had discreetly slid the meat cleaver that was in front of her, behind her with her foot when no one was looking.

Goon two eyes went over to the metal table to the severed hand and the chop off fingers of the victim, one of them pointing in Eldorado's direction.

The leader of the group eyes went straight to Eldorado, it was something about this broad he did not like but just couldn't put his finger on it right now.

"Hey man check that out!" Goon two said to his two friends while motioning to the table.

"The finger is saying the bitch did it," he said.

Goon three held the shotgun on Chandelier and Eldorado, ready to drop them like a bad habit, at the least sign of aggression by either one of them. His expressionless face and intense glare said it all "Move, and I'll blow your fucking brains out all over this place!"

"Maybe a message from the grave?" the leader said, staring dryly.

Yes, he knew what it was now, it was something about her eyes that he did not like, they almost seemed to him, that if you stared into them too long, they could hypnotize you put a spell on you real…

"Hey you, pick that up off the floor!" his associate wielding the shotgun ordered Chandelier to do after he spotted what looked like a piece of jewelry.

Chandelier looked down at the spot that the gunman had pointed his weapon and that is when he saw the ring that he thought he had put in his pocket, lying on the floor. A lump suddenly forms in his throat that he is unable to swallow.

"Slowly genius," the leader said with his weapon aimed at Chandelier.

Chandelier reached down slowly as instructed and pick up the black and gold ring off the bloody kitchen floor.

"Toss it to me."

Goon number one (the leader) caught the ring in his free hand and wiped the blood off of it with his fingers, as he held it up for close inspection. It was a familiar piece of jewelry that he had seen before, two spades on each side of it and the initials MC in gold on a black onyx background.

This ring could belong to only one person that he knew of, his boss and friend a mobster by the name of Mike Castellini.

But he wanted to be for sure before he took the next step.

"What did you say your name was bub?"

"I didn't but its Marius Chandelier." Did he call me bub? Marius thought.

"Is this your ring ten-watt?" the leader asked.

"Yes."

"Describe it to me."

"It has my initials MC in gold on a black background Mister; it was a gift from my daughter."

Eldorado watched quietly at everything that was playing out, and every time one of the goons took her eyes off of her, she eased herself closer to the light switch on the wall panel next to her, as she slid the meat cleaver behind her, along her path.

"Is that all?" was his final question.

Chandelier looked back at him with anxiety and a sense of warranted dread; maybe he had a way out of this mess after all.

'Yeah, and it was all of that bitch over there idea," he said, pointing over to Eldorado.

His interrogator smiled as he tossed his friend goon two the ring.

"That's all," said the leader.

Goon two looked at it, smiled, raised his gun to Chandelier's head, and pulled the trigger.

Chandelier brain matter flew out the side of his head before he hit the floor dead.

Click, the lights then went out in the kitchen, leaving them in complete darkness. Bang- bang-bang-bang-bang. A succession of rapid gunshots now let loose as muzzle flash from the three goons guns lit up the darkness in the kitchen.

"Stop shooting you fucking morons, before you kill us all!" shouted out Goon number one.

The gunfire ceased, followed by a scream of pain and agony by one of his associate's Goon number two, as Eldorado surgically implanted a meat cleaver in the middle of his forehead, he fell to the floor cross-eyed, convulsed for a few seconds, and died.

Goon number three was able to find the light switch and flip it back on, but not before Eldorado swiftly came across his throat with a butcher knife severing his trachea. He reactively dropped his shotgun and grabbed his throat to stop the bleeding.

Goon number one watched on in shock as the blood squirted between his friend's fingers as he tried to speak. He put him to rest with a bullet to the head, after firing several shots at Eldorado and missing.

He stuffed his semi-auto pistol in his pocket and picked up Goon number three's shotgun as he proceeds out of the kitchen to the front of the strip club. This psycho bitch had dropped two of his best men he thought, and he was going to make sure she paid with her life.

They had underestimated her (his men) and paid dearly with their lives, he promised himself, as he made his way thru the club searching for her, he would not make that same mistake.

Pumping a slug into the shotgun, he cautiously scans the dimly lit club when dance music suddenly starts playing from the club's speaker system "startling him" causing him to spin around towards the DJ booth.

He lets loose with the shotgun blowing a hole thru one of the clubs walls.

"Folks and all non-believers get ready for the hypnotizing and mesmerizing Eldorado," a voice says over the music.

"What the fuck?" Goon one says to himself, as he now watches Eldorado walk slowly out on the stage in black lingerie and a duster coat to the beat of the music.

Whomever the mysterious voice belongs to is right, she is one of the most stunning women he has ever laid eyes on, why hadn't he recognized that at first sight, he wonders? But this is fucking crazy he thinks, he wants to kill her, wants to make her pay for what she has done to his friends.

Her eyes meet his as he lowers his shotgun, she puts her finger in that lovely pouty mouth of hers, never breaking eye contact with him, as her body sways rhythmically back and forth to the beat of the music. The duster coat comes off, exposing more of her lean voluptuous body, as he imagines being inside of her, taking her lean body in his mouth.

Eldorado slowly removes her bra exposing breast that even Venus De Milo would be envious of, as she slowly gyrates to the music as she wraps her body around the dance pole like a charmed viper emerging from its nest.

She now climbs up the pole maneuvering and flipping her body down with the gymnastic skill of a seasoned veteran, her legs spread wide and body perfectly arch as she descends the metal phallic between her legs.

She dismounts off the pole to the pulsating beat of the music, as her only customer Goon number one, fights the urge not to keep his eyes on her, it's as if she is taking over his thoughts, taking over his mind.

"What the fuck is she?" he says to himself.

The stage and the front of the club suddenly go dark.

Goon one snaps out of it quick enough to catches a glimpse of the shadow of something running quickly up the wall and behind him making guttural noises.

Staring up at the wall, he cannot believe what is looking down at him.

A bat-like a creature with white pinpoints eyes that glow in the dark and the tail of a serpent, extending down from underneath its muscular legs.

It releases itself from the wall and comes down at him, with an ear-piercing shriek, with something shiny and pointy in its hand; Goon one lets loose the pump, blowing a hole thru the demon, as the blast from the shotgun propels the creature back off of him and onto the floor.

It makes those weird guttural sounds as he approaches it, but this time it's different as if it's struggling to breathe.

Goon number one pumps another round unmercifully into the twisted winged abomination struggling to breathe on the club's floor.

Silence.

AFTERMATH ONE:

Vinnie watches from a distance, as flames engulf a seedy strip joint that he just set on fire, called *Puss & Booties* per order of the Boss. He listens to the fire engines now fast approaching in the distance, to no doubt put out his five-alarm masterpiece.

He throws the cigarette and the pastrami sandwich wrapper down to the ground, extinguishing the cigarette bud with his foot. Walks around to the back of his cargo van, looks at the three bodies of his deceased associates and closes the back doors to the van.

From here on out he concludes strip clubs is definitely off his radar, especially the ones in Las Vegas.

Two months later: Somewhere on the east side of Atlanta, GA at a local strip club called "*The Crave.*"

The music is bumping as the Deejay sets the pace for the night and the main attraction that everyone inside the club has been waiting for and anticipating.

He begins his announcement: "We have a very special treat for you tonight folks, this beautiful creature is in a league of her own, put your hands together for the hypnotizing, and mesmerizing

Eldorado."

* * *

It had now been one year since Vinnie's boss, and his crew had been slain at Puss & Booties. Vinnie had attempted to put the whole sordid ordeal behind him the best that he could and had started up his own crew up in Las Vegas. A venture that kept him pretty busy and his mind occupied with their various business interests, of loansharking, shakedowns, truck hijackings, drugs, prostitution, and money laundering that made up his criminal enterprise.

When he had reported what had happened to the other bosses in their organization, they thought that he had gone ape-shit crazy. And he had to do everything within his power to convince them otherwise.

After much back and forth wrangling and meetings on the matter it was determined by the Capo's that the only logical explanation to what had happened to his boss, Mike Castellini, and their crew was that their drinks must have been laced with a hallucinogenic and shit went to hell in a handbasket after that occurred.

The only part that Vinnie could agree with was the latter part of course, but he did not want to rock the boat or compromise his position in the organization, so he decided it was best to go with the flow and their determination.

That is until one of his men a gent by the name of Pauly that he had sent on a business trip down in Atlanta, came back and told him a story he could not believe. About a strip club named "The Crave" and an exotic dancer that work there. Not just any exotic dancer or stripper to use layman terminology.

But one in particular, a dancer who went by the name of "Eldorado." That according to his soldier Pauly had every man in the club so mesmerize and seduced by her mere presence alone he was surprised the owner didn't go around with a collection plate so that they could drop all their wallets and cash in and their children college funds.

Could it be her Vinnie thought? The same demon that he thought he had killed here in his city one year ago, to date. That abomination that he had destroyed all evidence of in that fire he had set at Puss & Booties.

What did she look like this "Eldorado?" Vinnie asks Pauly as he sat across from him in his office, in the back of a bar, his organization ran on the north side of Vegas.

Pauly smiled at his boss "Like a vision from heaven," he said, as he took a sip of Amaretto out of a glass, he was holding in his hand that had been resting on his lap.

"Can you be more specific?" Vinnie ask.

"A pretty African American girl of biracial descent. I was informed she had some Armenian in her, but I prefer if she would've had some of me in her if you get my drift," Pauly said, as he laughs and takes another sip of his Amaretto.

"This is some serious shit Pauly," Vinnie said unamused.

The smile disappears off of Pauly's face because the last thing he wanted to do was piss off his boss Vinnie. He then remembers the pic he had taken with some of the girls in the club, something you normally were not allowed to do, but he was connected, and those rules did not apply to men within his organization.

"You know what boss, I took a few pics with some of those strippers in that club on my Celly, and I am sure she's in one of those pics," Pauly said confidently.

Vinnie face lit up.

"I always said you were smarter than you look Pauly, so where are the pics?" he asked.

Pauly pulled out his cellphone, open up his gallery, and pulled up the pictures he took at Crave and passed his phone over to his boss Vinnie.

Vinnie surfs through the pictures, Crave did have some hot strippers he noted and in the middle of this bevy of beauties was his foot soldier Pauly with a cigar in his mouth grinning like a Cheshire cat. But something also stood out as well, and at first, Vinnie thought it was just a fluke until he went through all five pictures Pauly had taken that night at Crave.

He passed Pauly back his phone because he wanted to confirm this anomaly himself.

"Is it the girl in the black outfit that's behind you?" he asks him.

"Yeah, how did you know?" Pauly answers.

"Look closer Pauly at the pictures."

Vinnie watched as Pauly's finger swept across the face of his phone as he scans through the pictures.

"Shit, that's weird. This broad's face is blurred out in every freaking photo! How can that be?" Pauly said befuddled.

"Maybe she doesn't want to be seen in those photos," Vinnie said.

"I don't understand? What'cha getting at boss."

"What I am getting at Pauly is that bitch ain't no common stripper, and she might be that thing that took out Mike and our crew all in one night."

"*A succubus demon* – boss?"

"I thought you were just pulling my leg with that shit," Pauly said nervously.

"I wish that were the case, Pauly," Vinnie stated somberly, as he then raised from his chair walked out from behind the desk he was sitting at and walked over to a small decorative treasure box that set on a credenza.

Vinnie opens the lid to the decorative box, reached in and pulled out a small satchel and toss it onto Pauly's lap.

Pauly set his drink down on the desk and picked up the bag off his lap, he reached inside nervously and pulled out the contents in the satchel, but as soon as his eyes laid sight on it he threw it on the desk in revulsion and shock!

"Is that what the fuck I think it is?" he said.

"And what in the fuck you think it is Pauly?" Vinnie asks as he made himself a drink from his office bar.

"It looks like a fucking ear, but it's all pointy and shit," Pauly said, staring at the strange-looking ear that still seemed too well preserved in its severed state.

"I cut it off the creature, Pauly and the damn thing has not changed from the day I took it off its ugly head."

"No decomposition, no nothing."

"That is weird as shit!" Pauly said.

"Look closely at it," Vinnie said, handing Pauly a magnifying glass.

Pauly took the magnifying glass and zone in on the gargoyleish ear on the desk.

The thin hairs on the ear appear to move back and forth as if the wind was blowing on them; the ear though severed appeared to react to sound.

Pauly made the sign of the cross across his chest with his hand.

"This ain't right boss," he said.

Vinnie walked over to the desk, picked up the ear and put it back in its satchel back into its box on the credenza.

He turned around to face Pauly.

"I agree, that's why this thing – if it still exists, must be destroyed," he said.

"And how do you suppose we do that? If you already filled it with lead and set it on fire," said Pauly.

Pauly walked over to his wall that held several mounted samurai swords above the credenza. He lifted the middle one off its rack that was slightly different from the other two and held it by its grip, admiring the craftsmanship of the gleaming blade.

"What are we fucking ninja's now?" Pauly said sarcastically.

"I purchase this particular beauty a while back ago, my friend. From an antiquities dealer out in South Dakota."

"South Dakota? Are you kidding me?"

"Yeah, he swears up and down that it was used to slay demons," Vinnie answers.

"What is this guy some kind of fruitcake?"

"No, I don't think so, Pauly," Vinnie said as he walked back over to his desk and set down with the sword still in his hands.

"Then what gives?" An unconvinced Pauly asks.

"Sometimes you know what you know," said Vinnie.

"Anyway, this antique dealer tells me that when you slay a demon with this sword, you must decapitate it and bury its head and body separately on hollow ground."

"And if you don't?" asked Pauly.

Vinnie laid the sword across his desk.

"I think you know the answer to that question," he said.

"I need you to get a coupla' of our guy's together we are taking a trip down to Atlanta Ga, to check out this broad."

"Consider it done boss."

"And Pauly."

"Yeah, boss?"

"Keep this between us; I don't want to get none of the other guy's spook, understand?"

"Yeah, Boss," Pauly said.

Vinnie winks his eye at Pauly.

"Good then this meeting is adjourned until we meet up again tonight and go pay our little friend a surprise visit," he said.

Pauly shook his bosses' hand and then exited his office.

As Pauly left, Vinnie watched him closely, very closely. And he would have one of his other men keep an eye out on him from here out. If what Pauly was saying was true, and the pictures were real. He had come into contact with the demon "Eldorado" and was now a probable liability to him and the organization. He knew what this monster was capable of, (Her power and persuasion over men) After all he had a dead boss and two deceased friends from his old crew as a constant reminder how lethal this creature could be when its back was up against the wall.

If she was using Pauly, he thought, and this was a trick to get him and his men down to Atlanta and massacre them all, she would be in for a big fucking surprise, that's for sure, he concluded.

Vinnie took a sip of the Jack that he had just poured and smile at the fugazi line of bullshit that he had intentionally fed his man Pauly regarding how he plans to take out "Eldorado." Why? Because he could not trust that Pauly had not been compromised, which he suspected, and he hopes a great deal of that bullshit that he had just fed him had sunk into Pauly's brain just in case he felt the need to warn Eldorado of their plans.

He knew the only way to truly destroy this creature was to remove its black heart while it was still beating in her chest while she was still in human form and then make sure it was buried somewhere that it could never be found again by anyone.

And although he had lied about purchasing the Samurai swords from an antique dealer in North Dakota, he had made one viable purchase from the dealer. An ancient dagger that the dealer had informed him had been made, been blessed and design just for the kind of job he had in mind.

Normally he would not believe in such "hokey pokey," but he had seen one of these demons up close and personal and wonder if the antique dealer that seemed quite knowledgeable in the matter, may have as well.

Nevertheless, he had personal business that needed attending to in Atlanta, and if Pauly was wrong about all of this and it was just some dancer using the same name as the demon, he had killed. Then the worst scenario that he could imagine would only have played out in his mind, he thought.

But something inside of Vinnie told him that this would not be the case, something inside of him told him to prepare for the worst.

Vinnie walked over and pushed a hidden button underneath the credenza. One of his pictures on the wall opens up, revealing a concealed safe. Vinnie walked over to the safe and put in the code that opens it revealing cash and other contents.

He removed the ancient dagger in its scabbard from the safe and closed the door, punching in the lock code.

"Eldorado I am coming for you," he said in a low whisper of a voice to himself.

* * *

Vinnie could not believe what he was looking at, but there she was on the stage gyrating to the music from the strip club's dee-jay. The same damn girl that he thought that he had killed a year ago at Puss & Booties. The same damn demon that he thought he had destroyed in the fire.

She moved the same, slow, and sensually to the music as she caresses the pole with her shapely legs and six-inch stilettoes, as she made love to the aluminum phallic extended out of the floor. Vinnie looks around at the audience in the club and notices that the reaction to her was the same to her as the previous club she killed at in Vegas. She held the potential pastrami, and corn beef sandwiches captivated.

But this time would be different Vinnie thought as he sat there at his table with his crew five strong. Men you did not want to cross or meet in a dark alley at night.

"So Boss is that her?" Pauly asks nervously.

"From her titties to her toes," Vinnie said as he puffs on a fat cigar.

"It's hard to believe looking at ..."

Vinnie shot him a sharp look cutting him off in mid-sentence.

"Never mind," Pauly said.

"Don't believe that illusion up there Pauly that bitch is more of a killer than me or you and she ain't nothing to be trifle with – you understand?" Vinnie said.

A lump formed in Pauly's throat as he gulped.

"I understand," he said.

"Now we will wait until this club close and when she leaves for the night that's when we will grab her, got it?" Vinnie said.

"Got it, boss," Pauly answers as the rest of the crew nodded their heads in agreement.

Vinnie watches Eldorado closely as she exited the stage after her performance and mingle into the crowd of lusting men at the strip club. She had hardly batted an eye at him on the stage or looked in his direction while she was performing. He begins to wonder if this might have been a look-alike that had just assumed the dead demon's name or maybe even a twin demon, he had to be for sure though before he made his move.

Vinnie addresses one of his soldiers sitting at the table with him and Pauly.

"Hey Bruno, I need you to get a little background info on our girl up there and get back with me as soon as you find out something Kapish."

"No problem boss," he said.

"Hey boss, why not me?" Pauly said, slightly offended.

"Pauly, you've done enough, but thanks," said Vinnie.

Vinnie watch as Bruno excused himself from the table and made his way over to the bar where Eldorado was at entertaining a patron. He was a large and imposing man but affable in his demeanor and most women Vinnie discovered found him easy on the eyes.

Vinnie now watches as Eldorado turn around as she watches Bruno approaching the bar. The gentleman seated across from her that she was entertaining, seemed to look up at Bruno but did not say anything but uneasily shifted in his barstool as his attention all of a sudden went onto his drink that set on the counter. Smart move on his part, Vinnie thought, because you cannot sip a drink and look cool with a broken jaw.

He watches now as Eldorado took her attention off the square and begin to engage in conversation with his soldier Bruno.

That's right put that Bruno magic on her, Vinnie thought.

He looks across at Pauly at the table who had a slight scowl on his face as he watches his associate in action. Another one of his soldiers a man they nickname "Scotch" notice it and laughed. Pauly gave Scotch a fuck you look. Vinnie's other two soldiers Tony and Joe watched the action quietly from an adjacent table both packing enough artillery underneath their blazers to turn this strip club into a disaster zone.

Bruno walked back over, set back down, and begin to give Vinnie the run-down of his conversation with the stripper.

"Is she, or isn't she?" Vinnie asks bluntly.

"I don't know boss she claims she moved here from Queens, New York, and she's never been to Vegas before," Bruno said.

"Did you ask her if she had a sister that looks like her?" Vinnie said.

"Nah no sister, she said. But a brother back in upstate New York."

Vinnie shook his head in sideways in disbelief.

"Upstate, huh? Did she give you her real name?"

"Boss, you know how that shit goes," Bruno answered, taking a sip of his drink.

"Yeah, I know just how that shit goes," Vinnie said, looking at Pauly with a skeptical gaze.

Vinnie set at the table quietly for a moment going over things in his head before he responded again to his crew.

"I think that bitch is full of shit, we grab her tonight," he said.

Eldorado or whoever she was had only got a few blocks from the club when Vinnie and his crew made their move and quickly.

They strategically block her off with one car at the intersection. As two of his biggest guys quickly approach her vehicle, they smash her windows out unlock the doors and snatch her up out of her car before she can figure out what is happening, they throw her into a nearby van and speeds off to an isolated location.

Vinnie opens the van's back doors and instructed the two men that set with a blindfold, bound, and gagged Eldorado in the back of the van to bring her out.

The chains that bounded her clinked as they helped her outside of the van.

"What do you want?" she asked, feebly with fear in her voice.

Vinnie motions for one of his men to pull the blindfold down from her eyes.

Eldorado blinks as her eyes attempted to focus from being obscured by the dark cloth now pulled down to her chin, how long had they been driving for almost an hour now she thought? Vinnie's face was the first one that came into focus.

"Do you remember me?" he asked.

"No, should I?" she answers.

"Yeah you should," he said solemnly.

Two of his men stood on each side of her, just in case she attempted to escape.

"Well, I don't know what the fuck this is about Mister? And why am I out here?" she said.

Vinnie looks for some recognition in her face of him but could not find any.

Then his hand went across her face splitting her lip, drawing blood.

Eldorado spits out the blood from her mouth, onto the ground.

"Well let me jar your memory little lady one year ago you were the bitch that kill three of my friends and family to me at a strip club in Las Vegas," said Vinnie.

"Ready for the cherry on top Sister, after your little massacre, you changed into a demon bat fucking thing and attempted to kill me!" he said.

"Man, that's crazy, I don't know what you are talking about I swear?"

"You don't huh?" Vinnie said unconvinced.

"No, Mister, you got me all twisted, sorry about your friends, but like I said I am not that person," the girl said.

"Well, you sure do look like her," Vinnie said.

"And you look like an ass hole, are you?" she said defiantly.

His crew laughed.

Vinnie scowled at their reaction bringing the laughter to an instant halt. Then he punched her in the gut, causing her to double over instantly in pain.

"Yes, I am," Vinnie answers.

Vinnie pulled out the dagger and wiped it off against his pants leg, brandishing it in front of Eldorado's face.

"I know who you are Eldorado, and I am going to make sure this time I do it right."

Vinnie had been watching Pauly out of the side of his eye all this time he had been interrogating to Eldorado. And a good thing he had too, because no one seems to notice but him that Pauly was slowly reaching for his gun in his waistband while he was nervously looking at him with hate in his eyes every time, he laid a hand on Eldorado.

Every time …

The dagger quickly left Vinnie's hand as he spun around and hurled it straight into Pauly's chest before he could get his gun out to kill Vinnie.

His other men quickly realize what was happening let loose with a barrage of bullets that ripped through Pauly's face and chest taking him down to the ground.

"Fucking Judas," Vinnie said before he put another bullet in the dead man's cranium.

"Fuck me," Scotch said.

As Vinnie pulled his dagger out of Pauly's chest, he could not help but notice the glazed overlook in Pauly's eyes as if he was under a spell.

"Yeah she had gotten to him too," he said in a whisper of a voice to himself.

"Party times over," Vinnie said, to the sound of laughter coming from Eldorado, as he turns around to face her again staring into her now ghastly white pinpoints for pupils encased in black sockets of the sclera.

"I knew it!" he says to himself.

The transformation had now begun.

"Shut up bitch!" Joe said as he grabbed Eldorado by the back of her neck.

Eldorado broke out of the chains that bound her wrist and with lightning-fast agility grabbed Joe's wrist off her neck and snapped it back so hard his bone popped out of it., tearing through the skin as he screams out in pain.

Tony reacted on the other side of her but not quicker than her scorpion-like tail that went through the back of his neck and out the front of his throat, the tail then receded, and the jagged point of it smash through Joe's eyeball straight into his brain killing him instantly.

The flashbacks came to Vinnie in rapid succession as he witnesses her once again change into that lethal creature that he had encountered one year ago at Puss & Booties in Vegas that had massacred his deceased boss's crew.

He watches helplessly to stop it, as it once again destroys his soldiers one by one ripping them apart as if they were just objects in the way of a bigger kill goal.

Him?

"What the fuck are you?" Bruno said as he let loose with the Uzi on Eldorado who had now fully changed into a gargoyle-like winged monstrosity.

The creature snarled at him, revealing a mouth full of pointed, jagged teeth as it took flight behind a hail of bullets from him and his boss Vinnie.

Some of the bullets struck one of the creature's venous wings as it flapped loudly in the night air cutting through the atmosphere as it provided the creature lift and ascension.

A vile and inhuman screeching noise came from the creature's mouth as It continues to ascend higher in the air, escaping Vinnie and Bruno's gunfire.

"Follow that motherfucker!" Vinnie said as he and Bruno ran towards the van.

"What the fuck is that thing boss?" Bruno ask.

"Something from hell," Vinnie said.

Vinnie grabbed a set of night vision goggles off the van seat and put them against his face looking up at the sky.

With some adjustments, he spotted what appeared to be the creature headed west.

"Go west down this road,' he said.

"You are not getting away this time," Vinnie said, as they sped down the road at almost one-hundred-miles per hour.

"Hand me that fucker now!" Screamed out Vinnie pointing to a high-powered rifle rigged with a night vision scope that set upright between them inside the van.

As Vinnie quickly adjusted the night scope on his rifle, he could now see the creature was less than one-thousand yards out and about 30.48 meters high, (100 feet ca.30m) flying low, maybe he or Bruno had got in a good shot, after all, he thought and injured one of its wings.

Vinnie popped a customized rifle mount out on the side of the door and attached the high-powered rifle to the rack and then sighted back in on the creature as it appeared now as if it was descending.

"A little bit closer!" he said to Bruno.

"Closer," he repeated.

Here goes nothing he thought to himself as he pulled the trigger on the rifle twice. The shots rang out in the night as the high-velocity bullets crack through the night air. Vinnie watch as what appeared to be the creature take a nosedive to the ground.

"I think I hit that sonofabitch!" he said, as he picks up the night vision goggles to get a more precise location on where the creature might have fallen.

"Over there," he said excitedly, as he directed Bruno to turn down a dark, desolate stretch of the road about less than a mile down with overgrown giant reeds on both sides of the road.

"Man, I can't see shit!" Bruno said as he drove the van through the reeds mowing the tall stalks down in his path.

Suddenly they heard a loud thump on the roof of the van.

"What the fuck, was that?" said Bruno as he eyed the roof nervously and tried to keep his eyes on the road at the same time.

Vinnie reached down, pulled out a gun case open it, and took out a Smith & Wesson XVR 460 Magnum.

"Good lord, that cannon's big enough to take down an elephant boss," Bruno said.

Something on top of the roof begins scraping against it as if it were trying to get through.

"I think that sonofabitch is on top of the roof!" Vinnie said.

The van now begin to violently rock back and forth as if whatever it was? Was now attempting to topple the van. Both men inside were thrown back and forth as Bruno attempted to maintain control of the van.

"Goddammit! I can't keep this van stable, get it off us," shouted out Bruno.

A large bat-like wing flapped over the vans front windshield, startling both of them as it blocks Bruno's view.

"Fuck you!" Vinnie said, as he cut loose with the 460 Magnum, the rounds went through the van of the roof like a butcher's blade going through butter – effortlessly. A loud screech of pain could be heard from the creature as the mini- missiles made contact. In retaliation, the creature gave the van another hard jerk, and this time it was successful as the van went toppling over on its side, skidding through the reeds before coming to a dead and crumbling halt.

The creature made its way to the van slowly, injured. And as soon as it was close enough to breach the van muzzle flashes appeared as several shots rang out in the deadness of the night.

Then quietness, then nothing.

AFTERMATH TWO:

"Hey, is anyone alive in there?" the voice brought Vinnie out of his state of unconsciousness, as he slowly came to looking over at his driver Bruno.

"Bruno, are you okay?" Vinnie said as he pushes on a slump over Bruno who had been knocked out cold when his head met the steering wheel.

The voice again, "Hey, is anyone alive in there?"

Bruno slowly started to come to with a visible wound to his forehead.

"Yeah barely," Vinnie answers back out to the stranger.

Vinnie kicked out the rest of the broken front windshield and him and Bruno exited the vehicle through the opening into daylight.

"What the fuck happen here?" said the stranger, who was an old man that just happened to be driving by when he noticed the van turn over on its side on the road.

"Oldtimer I don't think you want to know," said Vinnie as he took out a cigarette, lit it, and took himself a long drag, while surveying the damage.

Bruno, stagger around to the front of the van looking at the oily blood trail left by the creature. The trail ended no less than twenty feet from the van and disappeared from that point.

"Fuck it's gone," he said still dazed.

"I am not surprised," Vinnie said, as he looks out beyond the reeds.

Vinnie took out a roll of cash, peel off some Benjamins and put it in the old man's hands.

"Can we slum a ride back into the nearest town with you old-timer?"

"I think I can manage that?" he said.

"Is the big fella over there going to be okay?" he asks.

"Oh sunshine, you don't have to worry about him," Vinnie said with a grin.

By the way, old-timer what's your name?"

"Rudy from South Dakota," the old man said, scratching his head as he looked at the overturned van.

"That must have been some damn good whiskey," he said.

"The best "Rudy from South Dakota."

"We got some equipment to put in your truck; do you have a problem with discretion?" Vinnie asks.

Rudy looks down at the roll of Franklins still in his hands.

"Nah' I ain't got no problem with that, but I can't do no lifting, oughta I got a bad back."

Vinnie smiled as he flicked the cigarette to the ground stomp it out and then looked up at the morning sky.

"Look like it's going to be a beautiful day," he said

"If you say so Mister," said the old man.

Vinnie looked down at the creature's bloody eyeball staring back at him from the ground.

"Yeah, I say so."

THE LOTTERY

ello, my name is Ronald Avenue. My friends call me "Ronnie" for short. I am an African American male fifty-six years of age, a Detroit resident with a nine to five job that barely gets the bills paid, never married, no children, not even a freaking dog. Just a few expensive saltwater fish in a fifty-gallon tank that I can barely afford to feed and keep.

But fish need a home, too right?

My life sounds pretty boring, huh? I would agree, that's why I have been continuously chasing the dream of hitting it big in the State lottery since I was a teenager, and my mother's boyfriend, Macy, was sending me to a local party store to put his poorly handwritten numbers in on ripped off pieces of paper he kept in his pocket.

Three-digit numbers, four-digit numbers, Super Lotto, Fantasy Five, Mega Dollars, you get the picture.

Back then, if the big jackpot was over 20 million dollars that was a big deal, now it's nothing even to bat an eye at, to get the masses out, you need to have a jackpot over 100 million or more to get the greedy buzzards hovering.

Not me, "my friend," I am a simple man. If I just hit one million dollars, I would be stark raving butt ass naked happy! And at least I could probably get back some of the money I've been losing since I was a young sixteen years of age, maybe younger. Keep on dreaming right? Yeah, I know, they say the lottery is a suckers' game for those who are bad at math with the odds at almost one in one billion now or more of hitting that top jackpot with that magic ball.

And statistically speaking they say the odds are better of getting struck by lightning or killed by a shark. But you know what I say? Fuck them odds. You know, there's another saying also, "If you ain't in it, you can't win it." And that being said, I got about thirty-eight years of my hard-earned money invested in the game, so why quit now?

Did you know that some lottery statistician said that most lottery players quit when they are close to winning the big one? No shit. So, I figured if my ship's coming in, I damn sure do not want to be the one to miss it because I didn't have a ticket to board.

Therefore, for the last thirty-six years plus the two when I was a teen, I've been putting my lottery tickets in every week, like some brainwashed church folks put in their tithes in the collection plate. For their pastor's goal of buying themselves that nice shiny Bentley that God told them in a dream that he or she would be getting, courtesy of their congregation of course.

Pastor: I am telling all of you, my brothers, and sisters that the Lord brought me a vision, last night, that it was his will that my family and I be the owner of a safer and better car that represents our church better.

Congregation: That's right, reverend, that's right, preach on.

Pastor: Yes, yes, yes, and I had a vision that the car was like a chariot used to spread the gospel of his gloriousness, and it had a distinguished-looking letter on its grill.

Congregation: Amen, preach on reverend, what was that letter?

Pastor: That letter was a "B" for blessed, for bountiful, for Bentley.

Congregation member: Oh' that's a nice car reverend, mmm-hmmm.

I am just keeping it real, my friend. It has always been hard for me to sit up and listen to any so-called pastor preach about how prosperous I am going to be when it seems like the only one getting prosperous is them and their bank accounts.

They are driving their Cadillacs and Benz's, while I am driving a finally paid off plain car that is now a finally paid off piece of hooptie one shit wheel from the junkyard.

Their spouses are beautiful, while all the recent dates I have, have been sit-ins and midnight matinees. (You can only date these people at night) Now, I am not saying that I am the catch of the litter either, but truth be told, two ugly people have never produced one pretty person, I don't care what the statistics say. And we both know rich ugly beat poor ugly all day.

Yeah, I could probably tolerate a rich ugly spouse. But a poor ugly spouse? They would have to be like Michael Jackson and just beat it!

You can consider me an asshole, my friend, but I am just keeping it real until my ship comes in.

Yeah, another boring day at work and now I am sitting here in my apartment waiting for a little shit named "Scratchy" to bring my lottery tickets back before I kill the rest of this forty-ounce I got sitting in front of me on the table, and watching the Lion's lose another winnable game.

It's almost time for the evening draw, where is that little shit? He should have been back thirty-minutes ago; I conclude as I check my knock-off Rolex watch on my wrist.

Bzzzzzzt – bzzzzzzt. Hold up; someone is at my door.

"Speaking of the devil, I was just about to go looking for that little prick."

"Who is it?" Ron yelled out as he looks through his peephole.

"Scratchy."

"Where the hell you been Scratch? I thought you got lost."

"Man, my bad, I had to make a run for my grandma too," said the young man who could not have been any older than eighteen with a wild look in his eyes and dirty clothes on, scratching like he got a bad case of lice.

"Man, you need a bath, you still smoking that shit?"

"No, sir. I don't mess with it like that anymore," he responded.

I knew Scratchy was lying to me, but what could I do about it? He was born an addict, thanks to his crack head Momma, and now here he was repeating the same misery that had brought him into this world.

His mom who everybody knew by her nickname "May Day" was a street whore known for turning tricks for ten dollars a pop to support her drug habit.

And his farther a "Vietnam vet" was M.I.A. and I am not talking about war M.I.A. either. Rumor has it he had acquired a nasty addiction to heroin doing a double tour over in Nam and came back with a shitload of problems that he had been fighting back and forth with the government to address.

The kid just compounded his problems with a wife that could not keep her legs close to the neighborhood dope slingers when she hit the bottle and the pipe, so he split. It was the nature of the beast and this kid called "Scratchy" had to feed the beast, its claws and all "digging in his back" unfortunately.

Maybe – just maybe if I hit the big one tonight. I could put Scratch into drug rehab, set up a trust for him and get him off the streets for good. Maybe.

"Are all the tickets there?"

"Yes, sir." He answered back, enthusiastically.

I handed Scratchy ten dollars for his troubles.

"Don't spend this on drugs, on food, understood," I told him firmly.

"Yes, sir," he said again, sniffling.

"Okay then, stop by tomorrow, and get a hot shower and a meal, I also might have some old but fresh clothes you can have."

"Can I ask you a question, Ronnie?"

"Yeah, what?"

"Why do you give a fuck about what happens to me? When no one else does."

"Look, if your stinking ass ain't around to run my lottery tickets for me, who do you think I am going to get to do it this cheap."

"Fuck you, Ronnie," he said laughing.

"Fuck you too, speaking of that, tell your Momma to drop by I got – ten dollars with her name on it."

The kid gave me the finger; I would have given it to me also, maybe I was an asshole after all.

But this was a tough neighborhood, where we lived on the east side of town. Cold and raw. And if your ass couldn't handle, it? You best be making plans to move your marshmallow ass up outta here before it got roasted over a toasty fire.

I sat back down on my sofa and acknowledged there is a god because my forty-ounce was still cold.

"Good evening players, this evening drawing is just minutes away, the jackpot is now one hundred and fifty million dollars. "Good luck," said the lottery host on my television.

* * *

The lottery host was an older white lady, but not too shabby, in a glittery dress. Yeah, I'll tap that ass, I thought as I took another sip of my cold forty.

"The winning balls are... Yeah, I got some balls for you, I thought, my mind still in the gutter. *6, 14, 21, 33, 05, and the magic ball is 17 good luck, and that concludes our evening drawing."*

I set my cold forty down as I went through all twenty of my tickets, those numbers to me seem quite familiar for some reason.

I flicked through my tickets, scanning the numbers. "Nope-nope-nope…"

I have been down this road before, I thought, and the name of that road is Loserville.

Nineteen? I'll be damned! That is when I discovered that little shit forgot to give me all my tickets at the fucking count of nineteen.

Lucky for me though I had written all the numbers down that I had given him on another sheet of paper.

I rechecked my numbers against what I had written on this paper. *6, 14, 21, 33, 05, 17.*

6, 14, 21, 33, 05, 17.

I sat there slack-jawed and eyes wide staring at the paper in an almost catatonic state of mind in total disbelief. I even checked the lottery numbers over several times to make sure they were correct, after rewinding the lottery drawing that I was recording. Was I in reality or dreaming? I could not tell. I did not even hear myself scream at the top of my fucking lungs, but my neighbor across from me must have, because the sound of my doorbell buzzing, snapped me out of my dream-like state of consciousness, back into reality.

Bzzzzzzzt – bzzzzzzt.

"Fucking doorbell again."

"Who is it?"

"Ronnie, open this door it's Brenda."

"What's up Brenda?" I said, trying to conceal my excitement.

"Man, I heard you screaming over here like you done lost your mind, is everything okay?" My noisy neighbor asks.

"Yeah everything is tight, how's the family?" I said, trying to divert the conversation.

But my nosey-ass neighbor Brenda was not letting me off that easy.

"Family is family Ronnie, but you alright, you are screaming like you won the lottery or something over here.

And there it was, I could not believe that she had uttered those words. It was like I was watching her ashy lips move in slow motion when she made that declaration.

"Brenda, you be tripping, I was watching the game," I said.

"What game you are watching, because the one you are talking about just ended thirty minutes ago," she said trying to peep in my apartment as I intentionally blocked and obscured her view with my body.

"I recorded it if you must know, maybe you want to put some lip gloss on those lips and something nice on and come over and join me."

"Ronnie, you know you can't afford this good shit, so stay in your lane," she said.

Despite, her ashy lips Brenda had a semi-cute face and an exceptionally banging body, and when she dressed up, she was the kind of girl that I knew would not give a working slug like me the time of day. Her goodies were strictly reserved for slingers and ballers which was fine by me if that is the way her stinking ass wanted to Rock & Roll, but unknown to her, she was not even on my level, now. Soon I'll be able to buy a hundred like her or more, so how was she going to stand at my doorstep and shoot me down.

"What do you mean? Stay in my lane," I said offended.

"Boy you know what I mean, I see those nightcrawlers that you be dating, creep-creep," she said making fun of me and waving her hands in a clawing motion.

"Fuck you, Brenda, I ain't got time for this dumb shit! So, bounce."

"No, fuck you nigga, and you need to stop screaming like a little bitch over here with a dildo up your ass because you are waking my kids up."

"Kids? Those two lazy grown motherfuckers, ought to be at some jobs," I said.

"Keep talking shit, Ronnie and my son's (job) is going to be to come over here and put his size thirteen up your ass."

"I ain't hard to find Brenda."

And with that, I shut my door in her face. If I weren't one hundred and fifty million dollars richer, I would have invited that lurch ass son of hers over for a two-piece and a biscuit. The nerve of her, threatening me like that? And then it hit me like a ton of bricks! Here my dumbass was standing in my doorway, arguing with a hoochie mama, while a crackhead named "Scratchy" was running around with my one hundred and, fifty-million-dollar lottery ticket in his musty pants pocket.

"Nigga, you need to get a grip," I told myself.

Do you know how much crack a hundred and fifty million dollars can buy? I could get half of Detroit high off of money like that. No, I needed to do one thing now, and one thing only, and that was get my ass out on the streets and locate him and recover my ticket before he loses it or worse.

In my mind, I could now visualize him sitting on a mountain top of crack rock smoking it up at my expense, with a runaway model type giving him a half-and-half job on his nasty little wiener.

He smiles with a mouthful of new bling attached to those new teeth of his, as he mouths the words, "Thanks Ronnie, you poot butt ass sucka."

"I couldn't have done it without you," he says, grinning a hundred and fifty-million-dollar smile, as he comes up off the crack pipe, and blows dollar sign crack vapors magically into the air.

I shake this disturbing vision out of my head, to clear my thoughts.

"Poot butt ass sucka, huh? "Wait until I get a hold of your little raggedy-ass Scratchy, you better have my fucking lottery ticket or else…"

There it was, or else? That thought had never pervaded my mind until now, but what was I really willing to do to him if he did not produce my lottery ticket? Was I capable of hurting him really bad or something worse? Something like murder.

Maybe.

After all, would he not be killing a lifetime dream of mine, in retrospect killing me? If he did not produce the one thing that could change my world around for the better for the rest of my life.

The life of my loved ones and maybe unloved ones if I was in a generous mood.

But you cannot put a monetary value on human life they say.

Bullshit! I say.

My job and maybe yours, do it to us every day at thirteen dollars an hour or less with shitty benefits and an even more shitty retirement plan waiting for me in my shitty old age.

And if that is the case, that being said, I might have enough money left over to buy my depends and some adult Enfamil, to give me the shitty runs to buy more adult diapers for my old shitty ass if I am lucky.

It's like reverse infancy when you get old, and even worse when you are old and fucking broke.

If you are a baby and you shit on yourself in your diaper, the person that cares for you and love you might *say, "It's okay you made a stinky again you little snuggle-wuggle."* But if you are old and trapped in a nursing home that is not known for being senior-friendly, because of its discount rates and questionable staff, hired from an even more questionable temp agency, your stinky becomes: ugly nurse telling you, *"Not again! You nasty old bastard, I just changed your shitty drawers."*

"You old shit stain."

But if you got money.

Pretty nurse: "Ohhhh, Mr. Avenue, you had another accident or boo-boo?"

Me: No, I just shitted on myself.

Pretty nurse: "Don't worry, I gotcha boo."

Me: And I want some head later.

Pretty nurse: Don't worry, I gotcha boo."

Me: "I love it when you dress up in that nurse costume and role-play with me."

Pretty nurse: "I luv your shitty old rich ass too, boo-boo."

Now, do you get my point? Forgive me if I rather the later future than the prior future.

Yeah, both scenarios may be sad in their own way. But, let me tell you the chance of a seventy-year-old broke guy getting some good *enthusiastic head* from a woman half his age because he is in touch with her feelings, I believe is about as high as seeing a leprechaun fucking a unicorn in the ass on St. Patty's Day.

Not enthusiastically, unless she is a broke bitch too, and that is another story for another time.

Damn! Suddenly, I remember. Scratchy is like a one out of one thousand crack heads, that actually owned a cellphone.

A raggedy flip-phone prepaid, but he has one.

Beep-beep-beep-beep-beep-beep-beep.

Ringgggggg-ringggggg.

"Hello," answers a drowsy voice on the other end of the phone.

"Scratch, is that you?"

"Yeah, what's up? Ronnie," he answers back, although I could tell he was zooted.

"Scratch listen very closely, check your pockets to see if you still have any of my lottery tickets left in your pocket," I said, trying not to sound too anxious.

Scratchy snorted before he answers back. "Man, didn't I give you all your goddamn tickets!" he said, annoyed.

I had to bite my tongue on that one because I knew when Scratchy was using dope, his mouth often wrote checks his narrow little ass could not cash.

"Look Scratch, stop giving me shit you little… just check your pockets boy," I caught myself, trying not to lose my cool and reveal anything that would get his little crack mind to thinking.

"Hold on Ronnie," he said, sniffling like he had a cold, a crackhead cold no doubt.

"Ronnie! You're not going to believe this boy!" he said excitedly.

"What?" I said, now so nervous I could almost piss on myself.

"You were right; I still got a ticket in my pocket. My bad bro, I will bring it to you tomorrow," he said.

"Why can't you bring it to me now?" I demanded to know.

"Because bitch, I am getting high right now, that's why!" he said angrily.

"Whoa! Did you just call me a bitch?" I said, as flashes of red and me beating his little punk ass to a pulp played out in my mind.

No answer. Just quietness, on Scratch's end of the phone now.

"What the cat got your tongue, you little crack-nerd-motherfucker!" I screamed into the phone, heated.

"My bad dog, I was getting annoyed by all your damn questions, no offense intended," he said apologetically.

"Well I am offended you little black bastard, and you are lucky if I don't implant my annoying foot in your narrow-ass when I see you."

"Why can't you bring me my shit?" I reiterated.

"Because I am on the other side of town on Chalmers and Rochelle," he answered, now choosing his words more carefully with me since I promised him an ass-whooping.

"What the fuck you doing over there? I didn't know crack-heads travel that far."

"We do and fuck you!" he says.

"What's so important, anyway? It's just one ticket why can't you wait until tomorrow," Scratchy asks.

Goddammit! That's the last thing I needed it now, is an inquisitive crackhead. Scratchy was dumb, but he wasn't that dumb. I now had to diffuse somehow the spark I had ignited in that little doped up brain of his and quickly before he put two and two together and sell my one-hundred and fifty-million-dollar ticket for a nickel or dime bag of crack cocaine.

"You right, Scratch. I can wait until tomorrow, but if you get a chance drop by tonight and drop it off and will throw back a few beers with a coupla sandwiches, aighttt."

"Yeah, that sounds cool, so you not mad at me anymore, Ronnie."

"Naw dog, it's all good." I lied.

"Bet, because I am about to go over to Juanita's and get me a piece," he said.

"Stinky Juanita?"

"Ronnie, why you gotta call her that."

"My bad, stink ass Juanita," I said, correcting myself.

"Yeah, it may be a little smelly, but to me, it's like an aphrodisiac," he admitted.

"That's because you don't wash your ass either," I pointed out.

"She still on Rochelle Street?"

"Yep," he replied.

I hit the end button on my cell phone; that's all I needed to know.

That area in Detroit that Scratchy was hanging out at on the east side of town (Chalmers and Rochelle St.) was notorious for being grimy. Not that my neighborhood was ever going to make the cover of *Better Homes & Gardens* itself.

But there were just some places in Detroit that when you venture off in them, it was no if or buts about if you were in the hood, the only question you needed to ask yourself was: What were you willing to do to survive once you placed yourself in that element, you dig? So, I concluded I might need some back-up just in case things got a little nasty, so I called someone just as grimy as that neighborhood, my crazy cousin "Mookie."

Mookie had just finished doing a ten-year bid up at Kinross, for attempted murder, and assault on a rivalry drug dealer. He had sworn that he had now cleaned up his act and was going down a straight and narrow path. I did not doubt that his path had some zigzags in it. But hey, I was willing to give anybody the benefit of the doubt, until shown otherwise.

Mookie just wasn't one of them. If he were a monster, he would have been a fucking werewolf. The kind of person that walks around in human form, but if you fuck with them and cross 'em, you were guaranteed to see the beast in them emerge, and by then, it would be probably too late to save your ass.

And then, there were times with him the beast would be just there on the surface, sizzling like bacon on a hot skillet. Unpredictable and ready to pop.

"Hey, Mookie,"

"Yeah, who's this?" he said, suspicious.

"Your cousin Ronnie nigga," I answered.

"Cousin Ronnie? Man, I ain't heard from your ass, like forever, I thought you had died," he said.

"Naw, Cuz, I'm still here, alive and kicking," I replied.

I could hear the sound of faint moaning in the background.

"I need you to do me a solid though or you busy? I ask.

The moaning grew louder; it sounded like a woman's voice.

"Hold up, my nigga! I ain't heard from your black-ass in ages, and you dare to call up and ask for favors?" he said.

"Take this baby," he added.

There was that beast I mention, rearing its ugly head.

"Now turn that ass over," he said.

"What?" I said, confused.

Ronnie starts laughing; it was a high-pitch sinister laugh he had.

"Cuz, I wasn't talking to you, I'm getting my sausage wet right now, in some juicy booty," he explains.

"Oh," I knew that" I said.

"Anyway, I was just fucking with you boy, you know you one of my favorite cousins, what's up?" Mookie said, through grunts and moans.

"I need you to make a run with me if you can," I reluctantly said, not so for sure if this was a good idea calling him after all.

"Nigga you know I got your back, let me wash off my pecker, and I'll be by shortly."

"Let me wash it off for you, Mookie," I heard a woman's voice say.

"Then open up your mouth, freak," I heard him reply.

Then I heard what sounded like gargling, but I am sure she was not gargling mouthwash.

"Bet," I said, ending the call.

Now it was just a matter of me waiting on my cousin "Crazy Mookie" to finish his acts of hedonism with one of his probably numerous skanky baby mama's so that I could go and collect my ticket and get as far away from him, and all this madness in Detroit.

I'll give him some bullshit story on the run we were making and treat him to a little weed and a forty on the way there, – he'll never be the word the wiser so to speak.

That was the plan, but as we all know, things don't always go as planned, do they?

"Man, I thought your ass would never show up," I said to Mookie as he finally arrives at my crib, with a shit-eating grin on his face.

"I told you, my nigga, I was breaking me off a piece," he said, laughing.

"Really? But how long does it take to break off three inches?" I ask, teasing him.

"Yeah, but you're talking three inches wide homeboy," he said, high fiving me.

Mookie's elevator did not only go all the way up to the top, but he was a big dude. An easy six-foot two, of muscle and short temper. A powder keg waiting to explode for those who were either brave enough or dumb enough to light the fuse.

Pick your choice.

I happen to be one of the fortunate few, amongst the relatives that Mookie actually liked and did not want to put his foot off into my ass when he saw me.

I guess a few prison visits and me putting something in his account so that he could buy himself some ho ho's and bam bams (treats) out of the commissary when he was on lockdown had earned me that respect.

Don't get me wrong; it was not that I didn't have love for my cousin Mookie. He was just one of those guys – family or friend that you did not want to get to close too or relax around because it was like putting your head slathered in meat sauce in a hungry lion's mouth and saying "Fuck you! I dare you to chomp down."

Chomp! You only have yourself to blame you headless bastard.

Mookie looked around my place with that wild-eyed look on his face like he was about to hold me up and rob the joint.

"Something wrong," I asked.

"Man, I am just thirsty, you got something to drink in this bitch?" he asked.

I walked over to my fridge and got a tall can of beer out and tossed it over to him as he caught it in those big mitts of his.

"Here you go, thirsty. Now we gotta ride!" I said.

"You the boss," Mookie said as he popped the tab back on the can and took a long swig of the beer, belching and then wiping his lips.

"And can you guzzle that tall boy, I don't need the po-po, stopping us on no bullshit," I said.

"No problem, I gotcha Cuz," Mookie said, as he turned the can up and finished off the remaining sixteen ounces before I could bat an eye.

"You got another one of those I can borrow?" he said, wiping his lips again.

"Mookie lets go," I said, losing my patience.

Mookie's shifty eyes danced around in that big noggin of his before he cracked a smile at me.

"Man, I am just fucking with you!" he said.

"Who's driving?" Mookie asked.

"You're big fella," I said, tossing him my keys.

Mookie caught the keys in one hand.

"Damn you are feeling generous today! Letting me grip your baby," Mookie said, with a grin on his face.

"Real generous," I replied, thinking that once this was over and I retrieved my winning lottery ticket and got my affairs in order, I would gift him this piece of a shit car wrapped in a "red bow" since he liked it so much.

I might even leave a gift card in the glove compartment to *Red Lobster* if I am feeling overly generous that day.

Yeah, I know what you're saying, "This guy has a one-hundred and fifty-million-dollar lottery ticket, and that's all he can do for his favorite cousin?"

First, I never said Mookie was my favorite cousin; I don't have any of those kinds of cousins. And second, you know how they say, some people got relatives so scurvy that if they did hit a lottery jackpot, the least and the last thing that they should do is let any of those mofo's know that they are now rich with lottery winnings.

Guess what? I am one of those people, and Mookie is one of those mofos.

No, I am not going to be that guy surrounded by a bunch of relatives, holding an enlarged size card of my lottery ticket with a big cheese-eating grin on my face. Relatives that if my black ass were on fire, they probably wouldn't piss on me to put it out but pour gasoline on me, so I can burn quickly.

Contrary to that, though, I can assure you that they would feel some false sense of entitlement to some of my winnings because we are blood-related, and I ought to share my blessings.

Hey, I got plans to share my blessings, alright! On booze, hookers, and gambling.

And if I am feeling generous, (yeah that's-that word again) maybe, I'll send them a postcard of my many soon to be trips and adventures, with my happy hookers.

Maybe.

Damn, as we cruise the east side of town now through one of many neighborhoods in Detroit that looks like one of our foreign enemies drop a bomb on it. I look at one of the many burnt out and abandoned homes in the Chalmers area that my little friend Scratchy could be held up in piping on that skinny glass dick with those white rocks in it with pieces of brillo pad stuffed inside.

"Man, that crack head could be anywhere Cuz," Mookie said, as he scanned the forsaken landscape with me.

"But he's not. I can smell his stinking ass," I said, as I spotted a small posse of men, hanging out on the corner street.

"Pull up over there," I said.

One of the young men quickly walked up to my car with his hand inside his shirt next to his waistband.

"What up Hoss?" he said, as he looked suspiciously at Mookie and me inside the car.

"What's up player?" I said.

"Y'all the po-po?" he asks.

"Nigga, do we look like the po-po?" Mookie responded.

"Man, I wasn't asking your big fried chicken eating ass I was talking to your partner aighttt," the young man snapped back at my cousin Mookie with his hand still inside his shirt next to what we could only assume was his heater.

"Little nigga, what' cha you just say?" Mookie said pissed.

"Man cool it! We did not come down here for this," I said, quickly trying to de-escalate this situation.

I turn back to our guest.

"No, we are not the fucking po-po, we are looking for a dude that goes by the name Scratchy," I said.

The young man rubbed his chin, never taking his eyes off of Mookie.

"Man, what y'all looking for that crackhead, fo?" he asked.

"Because that crackhead is my cousin," I lied.

"What's the info worth to you?" he asks.

I took out a twenty-dollar bill and held it up.

"Thatta work," he said, as he removes the twenty from my hand.

"He's over in that two-family flat across the street," he said, pointing to another house that looked like all the other houses on the street – fucked up.

"Thanks," I said.

"Hey, big boy! You might want to lay off them fried foods it's probably got your blood pressure elevated," he said to Mookie, laughing.

Mookie just gave him the finger and a look that could cut through ice.

"Play nice," I said to Mookie under my breath.

The young man walked back over to his entourage, showing them the twenty-dollar bill, I had just given him and pointing at our car.

"Man, if that niggle were my celly, I would have put that smart mouth of his to good use," Mookie said.

"I bet you would have," I said, not meaning for it to sound like I was approving whatever Mookie had going on up in that twisted brain of his right now.

"Anyway, what the hell is a niggle?"

Mookie gave me a weird look and laugh.

The sooner I got this over with and dropped him off, the better. I thought.

Plus, it was getting late, and the area we where in was one of the more notorious sides of town. I definitely did not want to end up as an unreserved guest at the Wayne County Coroner's Office tonight with a one-hundred and fifty-million-dollar lottery ticket in my pocket that would be then useless to me at that point.

Because "dead or alive" I was a firm believer in the fact: You cannot buy your way into heaven, but one thing I was certain of "Hell" always had a price "alive or dead."

I could feel the eyes on me, and my cousin's back from across the street as we made our way into the crack house that our informative guest had pointed out to us, where my so-called cousin had set up camp to smoke up his rock in one of the dilapidated palaces on this street.

"Man, I got a bad feeling about this place Ronnie, but if shit hit the ceiling Cuz, know that I have your back," Mookie said, as he showed me the .45 pistol that he had tucked inside the waistband of his pants concealed by his jacket.

I stop in my tracks, grabbing my cousin by the arm.

"Mookie are you crazy, don't you know as a convicted felon, you are looking at twenty to life if you get caught with that thing if something goes wrong," I chastise him.

He brushed my arm aside. "Nigga if something goes wrong, twenty to life is going to be the least of our problems," he said.

What could I say to that? Maybe he was right.

As we made our way into the dilapidated crack house, a conglomerate of refreshing odors of *piss, shit, ass,* and vomit hit our sensory receptors full force.

The house inside was dark and dimly lit running off electricity that was illegally stolen from rigged up lines attached to one of the many utility poles nearby. Drunks and addicts were everywhere in the house lying around and some sleeping in different corners of the house. Garbage of all kind, fast food wrappers, drug paraphernalia littered the floors like it was part of the décor of the house.

Random drug dealers popped in and out of the place to make small deals with the house inhabitants to keep the party going.

But the most overwhelming part was the stench of lost souls in this place. If there was such a thing as hell on earth, then I was convinced that this shithole drug – den had to be one of them.

"Hey Mister, ten-dollars for a blow job," said a young sister to me, that could not have been no older than seventeen.

"Naw, I am good," I said as I stepped over someone's lost child. But I intentionally drop a crumpled up twenty on the floor as a gesture of benevolence as I passed her and watched her scamper to pick it up out the side of my eye. Twenty dollars after all would soon be like two dollars to me or less.

As we made our way into the third room of the house that was just as gloomy as the other rooms in this hellhole, that is when I spotted him, the man I had been looking for all night that had my golden *"Willy Wonka ticket"* in his fucking possession.

My favorite crackhead in the whole goddamn world – Scratchy!

I could tell he was out of it as Mookie and I made our way over to him in another corner of the room. He was hugged up with some scant about his age whom I did know. But I could tell she probably would not be half bad with a delouse and ten-hot showers.

They also, both looked as if they were half-asleep in a crack induced haze.

"Hey Scratch, wake your ass up, its Ronnie!" I said as I shrugged him to get his attention.

He brushed my hand aside, off his shoulder.

"Who?" he said as he wipes the drool off his mouth, barely making eye contact with me.

"Ronnie, fool!" I said again.

Scratchy looked up at Mookie and I and this time his eyes set on my face and though the look in his eyes was vapid, I could see the recognition set slowly in his feeble brain of who I was and what the hell I was there for after all.

"Ronnie? He said.

"Yeah, It's not *Mickey Fucking Mouse!*" I said.

Mookie laughed at my response, as he kept his eyes on Scratchy, his companion and pretty much everything else that was living, breathing, and stinking in that house.

"You here for your ticket?" he said.

"No, I am here to sing you a fucking lullaby!" I said, as I open-handed Scratchy across his face stunning him.

The blow was powerful enough to snap his face to one side, and also let him know I meant business at the same time, and I had no time to be pussyfooting around in this dumpsite.

Scratchy grabbed his face in shock as he jumped up to face me.

"What the fuck you do that for?" he said.

"To snap you back into goddamn reality you little shit stain! Now give me my ticket," I demanded.

Mookie and I watched Scratchy patiently as he reached in his pocket searching for my ticket, then the next pocket. When his hand finally came out of the last pocket on the clothes he was wearing, the only thing I saw was lint in an empty hand, the only thing I saw was my dreams vanish like a puff of smoke.

"Search his pockets!" I ordered Mookie.

Mookie quickly grabbed Scratchy by the collar and threw him up against the wall almost before I can get the last word out of my mouth and begins to go through Scratchy's pockets turning them inside out expeditiously. The only thing he did not do was hang Scratchy's little skinny ass upside down by his ankles.

"Man, this crackhead ain't got shit!" Mookie said, releasing him and throwing him back down to the floor next to his crackhead scant girlfriend.

"That's because you sold it too *Quick* for a rock, remember stupid," the girl said to Scratchy.

"What the fuck you just say?" I said, now astounding.

The crackhead zombie starts swaying her head from side to side before she spoke again, through her crack white ashy lips.

"I said, he sold the rock to homeboy Quick for a rock nigga, what's wrong with your hearing? You deaf?" she shouted out to me.

"Nothing is wrong with his hearing you stinking bitch! You better watch your mouth," Mookie chimed in, on my behalf.

Scratchy sat there watching this whole scene play out wide-eyed between us, but I could tell he did not give a fuck at this point in his crack-induced hazy brain. But once I brought pain into the element he would, and that I was now more than ready to do if I did not retrieve my fucking ticket! My fucking life.

I grabbed Scratchy's ass by his dirty collar and pulled him up off the floor.

"You better hope for your sake, this joker name Quick is still within the vicinity because if not, I am going to make sure that you are never able to smoke another rock in your life unless someone is sticking a crack pipe in your breathing tube," I said.

Mookie snickers.

"What about her?" Mookie asked as he looked down at Scratchy's newfound girlfriend.

Scratchy looked at her disgustingly, "Big mouth, bitch!"

"Watch the way you talk to our homegirl Scratch!" I reprimanded him. I looked at the girl.

"C'mon stinky, we might need your services too," I said.

"What's in it for me?" she asked.

"Living," I glumly replied.

She gave me a one-hundred-yard-vacant stare that told me that what I had offered her she could take it or leave it. The shape she was in, I understood. I forgot I was talking to a crack zombie and that her mere existence was only based on getting high every day, like a zombie's existence, was based on eating non-zombies, preferably other human-beings.

"How about a twenty?" I said.

She smiled, revealing maybe three healthy teeth in her mouth.

"For that amount, I'll suck your balls through your eyeballs," she offered.

"No thanks, I like my eyes and my balls where they're at," I graciously decline.

* * *

The stench of the crack house was starting to make me nauseated, and I welcome the cool night air as we made our way outside of the house.

"There he is!" Scratchy said as he pointed to the big young muscular brother with the yellow-doo-rag on and the yellow and black leather jacket, counting his cash out openly.

From the way the other young cats surrounded him, it was obvious he was the Alpha of the group.

Mookie and I sized them up as we made our way over to them, this would require some special finesse if I were ever going to recover my ticket, especially from these young hoodlums.

Before we were able to get close to him though, two of his boys quickly stepped in front of us, with their guns drawn, blocking our path.

"Relax fellas; we come in peace. Are you Quick?" I asked him. Cutting to the chase.

"Yeah, who wants to know?" he asked, as he pulls a small lollipop out of his pocket in plastic and begins to unravel it.

"I do," I said.

"Who's I do?" he said, never missing a beat as he popped the green-colored sucker in his mouth and began twirling it around.

"Ronnie and this is my cousin Mookie," I replied.

"Mookie you a big nigga," Quick said.

"Big enough," Mookie replied as he sized every one of the young wannabe gangsters up.

I could tell by the look in his eyes he was debating which one of the five of them he was going to take out first and then work his way on down from there.

But hopefully, I could resolve this before the shit hit the fan! I thought.

I grabbed Scratchy by the collar and shuffled him in front of me.

"Tell him what you did Scratch," I said, with as much menace as I could muster up in my voice. Because I wanted him to know that if things didn't go as I planned, his ass was on the line, literally.

"That tick-tick-ticket, I sold you is not mine Quick," he stuttered.

"I know, it's mine-mine-mine," Quick said to the outburst of his posse laughing.

"No, it's his ticket Quick, – Ronnie's," he said.

"You know, that's why your mama should have swallowed you Itchy," said Quick.

"No, it's Scratchy," our crackhead associate said, with more balls than I thought he had.

"Whatever Itchy," said Quick with a grim look on his face.

And in the blink of an eye, Mookie and I found out why they call this guy Quick.

He grabs Scratchy, spun him around in a headlock, and slit his throat with a straight razor from ear-to-ear, in what seemed like one lighting fast move that I am sure took him repetition to perfect. The blood squirted out of Scratchy's throat as his bug-out eyes got even buggier.

Stinky let out a scream in horror only to be put to sleep by a KO punch to the jaw by one of Quick's homies.

Mookie went for his piece but not before a baseball bat to the back of his head wielded by one of Quick's boys put my cousin to sleep and out of commission as he hit the concrete face first and so hard, I wonder if he was dead.

I threw my hands up quickly in surrender, what else could I do? Shit had now hit the fan, quicker than a New York minute.

I still had one thing going for me. I was still standing, I was still breathing, for now.

Quick flip the straight razor close, with a wicked grin on his face.

"Now give me One-hundred-and Fifty-Million-reasons why I should just hand this ticket back over to you my nigga," he said.

My mouth dropped, Quick wasn't as dumb as he looked or was, he?

"Because it's the right thing to do?" I said.

To another outburst of laughter from his posse, right before everything went black and silent for me from a blow to the back of my noggin. Most likely with the same baseball bat that had put my cousin sound to sleep. Not enough to crack my skull, but just enough to send me to La, la, land.

I had foolishly and naively walked myself and my cousin into a death trap, and now I might pay for it dearly with our lives.

But before that happened, my cousin and I would take a five-hour drive to Chicago in the back of separate car trunks for what Quick called an out-of-town disposal run.

And I had yet to even lay eyes on the lottery ticket that may cost us our lives.

I had one-hundred-fifty-million-reasons to live, but unfortunately, Quick had the same amount to kill my dumbass.

My head hurt like shit, and I had a splitting-ass headache as they pulled me out of the back trunk of the car that looked as if they had parked inside a big-ass warehouse of some kind.

I watched as they popped the trunk to an old school black Lincoln Continental with enough trunk space to put a horse inside. To my surprise, that horse happened to be my cousin Mookie as they reached in and got him out of the trunk of that car onto his feet with his hands tied behind his back. Just like they had done mine.

A relief suddenly came over me, to see he was still alive too. I know it sounds selfish, but the first thing that came to my mind is at least I would not die alone. But I am sure Mookie probably did not feel the same way. Not that I could blame him. I had fucked up and fucked up royally.

I could already picture and hear the sound of our executions in my mind, as they forced us down on our knees and put the cold metal of the barrel of a gun to the back of our heads.

The click of the trigger, which activated the firing pin in the gun, would activate a bullet that would actively blow the back of our brains out, spilling what little intellect we still had left on unknown concrete floors. Yeah, three actives in a row, how lucky could we get? I ask myself.

And as this thought entered my mind, it was the first time surprisingly that I realized through this whole ordeal, that a winning lottery ticket should be the least of my concerns right now.

"Where the hell are, we?" I asked.

"Oh, while you fellas were sleeping, we decided to drive down to Chi-town (Chicago) for a little R&R," said Quick.

His crew laughed, at his response like cackling hyenas.

"What part of Chicago?" I asked, not that it mattered.

"Southside, warehouse district. Last stop for you two Mensa geniuses," said Quick, popping another sucker, this time an orange one in his mouth.

I imagine sticking something else in his mouth and making him choke to death, and guess what? It wasn't a sucker.

"Punk ass niggas ain't man enough to take care of y'all business in Detroit huh?" Mookie said as he spits blood out of his mouth onto the floor.

Quick look around at his crew and then back at Mookie.

"I guess not," he replied to their laughter.

It was five of them against the two of us, and if we could stall them for a few more seconds, unbeknownst to them, they had missed a small knife on me, that I had been using discreetly to cut myself free of the ropes they had my hands tied up with behind my back.

"Go ahead and laugh it up, but all of you punk ass niggas would have been my bitches in the joint washing my dirty drawers," Mookie said.

Keep it up Mookie you're not as dumb as I thought. I said in my mind.

"What the fuck you just say nigga?" one of Quick's boys said.

"You heard me niggle!" said Mookie, not backing down.

Now it was either do or die, and the punk kid knew it with his friends snickering at him to see what he was going to do?

He walked over to Mookie and slapped him across the face like a bitch.

Mookie quickly responded in kind with a hard head butt to the kid's nose that not only broke it but sent the scrawny kid out to the floor like a dead cat.

"Motherfucker broke my nose!" he cried out in pain as the blood shot out from his nostrils like snot.

He went to his waistband for his Glock; I guess the fight was all out of him. Can't say it surprised me, this was just how a lot of these dudes was these days, quick to settle their disputes with a pistol, but short on heart when it came to the fisticuffs.

Fucking punk! I wanted a piece of his sweet ass too.

"Stop!" Quick yelled out to him.

"You got what you deserved, he said to his underling, and he will get his," he said confidently with that same shitty grin on his face.

The punk kid stuffs his Glock back into his saggy pants.

Then, Quick did something that I was not expecting. He pulled out the lottery ticket and began reading the numbers off of the little pink piece of paper.

"06, 14, 21, 33, 05, 17, does that sound about right," he said, holding the ticket up to my face.

I could remember those numbers any way you repeated them. Backwards, forwards, sideways, unilateral, I thought because those were my goddamn numbers.

"Sounds about right to me," I said through clenched teeth and a splitting ass headache that would not subside.

Quick, put the ticket back in his pocket.

Mookie looked over at me, giving me the fucking reaper face.

I know Mookie, I thought, I told you the ticket was only worth five-hundred-dollars, what can I say? But I grossly misrepresented its true value. Now that misrepresentation was coming back to bite me. No, Bite us in the ass like Karma.

"Well homeboys, it's been fun, but me and the fella's got some estate planning to do before we go cash in the big one!"

I am just dropping off you bloods for a special friend of mine that has something special in store for the both of you," he said.

"What a three-way with your mama," Mookie said.

I laughed through my headache at that one. Bingo! My rope was cut enough, whereas I could slide right out of it. My eyes went to the closest gun next to me about five or six feet away. Mookie and I made eye contact again; I sent him a Morse code with the blink of my eyes. That was the smartest thing that we had put together before we made our way to the crack house that evening.

If we find ourselves in a life and death situation and it was time to Rock & Roll, we would need a way of signaling each other, to let each other know when it was about to go down.

I just hoped Mookie remembered.

Did I hear a flapping noise? I thought.

"Hey, niggle (little nigga) your nose still hurt?" Mookie said, to the punk that was still nursing his nose.

The punk kid looked up at him; his eyes went wide.

"That's it. I am going to smoke this fat motherfucker!" he said, pulling out his Glock and raising it at Mookie.

But before he could get off a shot, a bullet from Quick's pistol hit him in the chest taking him down.

"I told you, No!" Quick yelled out after taking one of his own men out.

I seized the moment and rushed the punk next to me, tackling him and taking him down to the ground as we started wrestling for his gun.

I could hear the flapping noise getting closer in my struggle as a bullet whizzed past my ear into the floor tearing up concrete next to me.

Then a strange thing happened, the lights went out! Now I had the darkness to my advantage.

I heard Mookie yell! Then the sound of more gunshots cutting through the air.

I got a hold of the gun and fired blindly straight in front of me, something wet splash on my face, then a body fell on me! I pushed it aside. It was pitch-black darkness; I could not see shit! Not two feet ahead of me.

I heard more agonizing screaming! It sounded as if some animal was tearing someone apart limb by limb.

I fired in that direction, something flew past me, above me quickly, hovering. I could only see its shadow, and I knew whatever it was, it was large.

My mind was racing; I could only think of one thing, where the fuck had Quick taken us? Where, something deadlier than all of us was now killing all of us off – one by one.

The last scream sounded, and the building now went silent.

And just like that, the lights came back on.

But when they did, I could not move. Because the area now looked like a fucking slaughterhouse. A bloody fucking slaughterhouse! I stood there, frozen like a child, unable to move a muscle. I was in shock of the carnage laying out before me in the warehouse-like a Serengeti buffet created by wild lions.

My eyes went straight to my cousin who still had his hands around the throat of one of Quick's guys he choked out.

"Stop it, he's dead," I said.

The dude's eyes looked like they were about to pop out of his head, and his lips were an unsavory blue.

Mookie got up on his feet, and that is when I saw that he had been shot in the leg. A look of terror suddenly came across his face at me; now I thought I am going to have to kill him too. But wait a minute, I soon realized he was not looking at me. He was looking past me.

At it?

I turned around, and that is when I saw what I could only describe as a creature straight out of my worst nightmare! I fired off the last shots, but the bullets bounced off the gargoyle-like creature's leathery chest like it had on a Teflon fucking vest.

It then transforms into a man right before our eyes. I almost shitted on myself, as I dropped the gun to the floor.

"What are you?" I ask.

"What am I? That is no concern to you and your cousin Mr. Avenue," it said?

"What I can do for and to the both of you, should be."

My eyes went over to Quick's face that was now staring up at me on the floor. His head was separated from his body, but at least the lollipop was still in his mouth I thought.

"My name is Mr. Piper, but you and your accomplice may call me Jonathan," he said.

Mr. Piper looked over at Mookie who was frozen like me, waiting for it to tell us what to do. Mr. Piper then looked back at me and ordered me to get the lottery ticket out of the headless body's pocket of one Mr. deceased – Quick.

Then, he gave me specific instructions. Specific instructions that he demanded that I follow down to the very last detail.

He would allow me to take the ticket cash it in, but half the winnings would go to him. That is seventy-five million in case I was bad at math. He would set up the arrangements for the deposit and transfer in the future. As for the rest of the money, he did not care what the hell I did with it. Although he did suggest, I might want to show my cousin Mookie some real appreciation for putting his life at risk for my wanton greed.

I concurred without any objections; wisely might I add.

Now here is the bad news: If either one of us were ever to mention this moment or speak of him, he assured us he would kill us both and all our family members for breaching our agreement.

Mr. Piper looked at the clumps of bloody body parts strewn out in various areas on the warehouse floor. My eyes follow his and Mookie's followed mine's.

A lump formed in my throat as I surveyed all the bodies that lie mutilated across the floor in a bloody mass like a machete had been taken to each of them.

I did not doubt that he'll fill his end of the agreement if we did not uphold ours.

Jonathan Piper looks over at the "75" Lincoln Continental, black with white top.

"Now, take that beauty and get the fuck out of my warehouse," he said as politely as he could.

Mookie threw his arm around my shoulder as we made our way to the car.

Just then, his voice cracks the air again, freezing the both of us in our path.

"Excuse me, gentleman, do you two believe in God?"

We both shook our heads up and down nervously.

"Then our agreement should be easy," he said.

And just like that, he was gone, just as quick as he had come.

Mookie looked at me in shock. "What the hell do you think he meant by that?

"Come again, what in the hell are you talking about?" I said angrily.

It was a Faux pas and a slip of the tongue that I could not afford in the future from my cousin Mookie.

Then it dawned on me as I felt the cold metal of the gun in my waistband before the long ride back to Detroit, I might have to decide if both of us were going to make it out of this warehouse alive, out of this nightmare with this secret.

Sorry Mookie.

SOLDIERS OF MISFORTUNE

—⟨⟡⟩—

Vietnam Da Nang, 1968, I was assigned to the 3rd Brigade, 5th Infantry Division, Charlie Company. Over here in this hellhole, I am simply known as "Sarge" or Sgt. Martin. If someone were to ask me if I had anything to say about what was now my second tour into Nam, I would say that it is hot, humid, and sweaty as hell over here despite the monsoons.

The stench of death permeated the barely breathable air, and blood-sucking malaria-carrying mosquitoes are the size of fucking baby birds. Wisely, I came to the grim reckoning earlier in my first tour, that every day that I woke up was one day more or less that brought me closer to death's door maybe with grace, maybe without. It was after all, all around me. Life hanging by a thread in the atmosphere of a place that I thought was lost back in time.

But there was something else here in the air that was just as palatable. And that was a tension of fatality that was just as thick as the humidity that hung over the platoon with every patrol that we went on as we navigated our way through the rice patties, land mines and booby traps that could wipe out most of our men at any given minute.

And those were the good things I had to say, now imagine the bad, Will you? But maybe, I was a glutton for punishment; after all, I was into my second tour. Or perhaps, I was trying to make atonement for my first tour after seeing good men die that I felt was much better men than me, fighting a war that most of our country back home did not even fucking support or give a rats ass about because it was not easily relatable.

But that is another story, so let me get down to the nitty-gritty. Our marching orders had come down from the top. In response to the Tet offensive, sweep these villages right inside of the Son Tinh District, South Vietnam, for Viet Cong and sympathizers.

Destination: Mai Lai.

Captain Mendoza had made it clear during our platoon briefing that when we arrived at these villages, we were to "destroy everything in those villages that was walking, crawling, or growling."

And that is what we did and more. Heinous shit I did not agree with ethically or morally.

In short, it was a fucking massacre of innocents and Staff Sgt. Horatio Duck was right in the fucking middle of it all. He was like a boil on my ass, and I was a thorn in his for sure. He was also into his second tour, and I had discovered for all the wrong reasons.

His hatred for the Viet Cong ran deep, which I could understand after all this was war, and they were the enemy. But his hatred for the people that we were supposed to liberate from their communist oppression ran just as deep unfortunately for people who looked just like them.

You see, Sgt. Duck was a fierce proponent of the "Mere Gook Rule" an unofficial policy in which soldiers would be prosecuted very leniently, if at all, for killing or harming Vietnamese civilians, even if the victims of this unofficial racist policy turned out to have no connection to the Viet Cong or the North Vietnamese Army.

Whereas I was there for atonement, he was there for revenge, and it became obvious to me that all his many demons would not let him rest until he had his fill in blood and death.

As we stepped foot into Mai Lai and begin to conduct our sweep for Viet Cong and sympathizers that was reportedly hiding out amongst the civilians in this village or what we referred to as hamlets. It was obvious to me that most of the villagers were getting ready to go to the market that day to sell their goods.

We immediately began rounding all of them up and clearing them out of their stilt houses, searching for Viet Cong soldiers and sympathizers for interrogation per Capt. Mendoza's orders. And that is when things went Fubar real fast. And for those of y'all who do not know what Fubar means, Its – "fucked up beyond all repair."

The villagers had no idea what was coming, and neither did I, to tell you the truth. Therefore, they were cooperative and did not panic or attempt to flee when we began herding them into one of the hamlet's commons.

Then, all hell subsequently broke loose from there, when I observed fellow team member Corporal Riggs let loose with his M-16 with a bullet straight to the head of one of the elders in the village, blowing his brains out all over the red dirt.

Capt. Beck then yelled out! "Burn this fucking village down to the ground!"

Amongst the screams and cries of the villagers that repeatedly shouted out to deaf ears. "No, VC! No, VC!" as they were led to irrigation ditches and cut down by bullets by our M-16s and even M79 grenade launchers. Have you ever seen what a human head looks like after it's has been fired upon with a grenade launcher? Of course not. I unfortunately have and have two words for you, "fucking unrecognizable." Not resembling anything close to human after being hit by the 40x46mm grenade.

Death spared no villager that day, men, women, and children all needlessly murdered. It was hard to keep the bile from coming up out of my throat as I watched this unnecessary massacre surreally take place before my eyes.

I pretended that my weapon had jammed as I was reluctant to fire a shot on people that I felt were no threat. Nevertheless, that did not stop some of my fellow troopers' bullets from meeting their intended targets.

I will never forget the look in the old woman's eyes as she mouthed the words "I curse you all," before a killer's bullet met her between the eyes.

Like I will never forget the grin on Sgt. Duck's face as he ordered the men to gun down people who we should have been protecting.

"I curse you all!" said the old lady before her death.

The women villagers that did survive were only left alive for the pleasure of some of the men in my platoon who viciously sexually assaulted them, despite their cries and pleads not to and was then killed afterward.

As far as I was concerned, we were no better than the Viet Cong that day. We were worse, animals at our most savage base.

I did not sign up for this kind of shit! This shit is not what we were about, or were we? As I raised the barrel of my M-16 to Sgt. Duck's head and assured him that this time, my weapon would not jam.

It was not until the gunships arrived and a brave enough helicopter pilot, a warrant officer by the name of "John Tanner" from company B that would not back down after flying over Mai Lai and seeing all the dead bodies, did the killing stop.

As warrant officer Tanner and his crew witnessed some of these atrocities being committed, such as Captain Mendoza kicking and shooting an unarmed woman at point-blank range, who he claimed that he thought she had a hand grenade. Tanner landed and told his crew that if any other soldiers from my platoon fired on any more villagers while he was trying to get them to safety, they were to open fire on these soldiers plain and clear.

When the killing had stopped, it was as if the devil himself had set foot in Mai Lai that day.

Hundreds were dead, and the stench of death and an eerie quietness now hung over the burnt-out village.

I could still see the old woman's face now embedded in my mind.

"I curse you all!" she said.

There was someone in the government that attempted to portray Tanner's actions as cowardly when they were nothing short of heroic after the truth came out of what had happened that day in that village.

All I know, with the barrel of my weapon to Sgt. Duck's head, he never fired another fucking shot that day at an innocent.

Like I said earlier, I was a thorn in his ass, and he was a boil on mine.

After the dust had settled the motherfucker tried to have me court-martial, but It ended up backfiring on him and opened up all kinds of investigations that got him an undeserved general discharge.

He got off easy, so I thought.

It was not too long before I began to notice some strange events that began to occur as I came to the end of my second tour in Nam.

Strange events such as all the soldiers in my platoon that had participated in the Massacre in Mai Lai began to die gruesome deaths on the same soil that they had needlessly taken lives. At first, I thought it was just Karma, but no, it was more than just that.

Captain Mendoza, who had given the orders that day that led to the all-out slaughter of the villagers, died in a helicopter crash in Hanoi on a recon mission.

Corporal Riggs, while on a military furlough in Saigon, went to get his pecker wet in one of the numerous whorehouses. But unfortunately for him, one of the prostitutes was *"The Spider,"* a nickname given to a Viet Cong sympathizer who was notoriously known for putting razor blades carefully and strategically inside her vagina, as a welcome gift for horny American soldiers.

By the time he got back to base, his penis, from what I had heard from a Medic, looked like it had been through a meat shredder and split in two. It became so swollen; Riggs became temporarily confined to a wheelchair.

Despite the Military's best medical care and effort, he developed a gangrene infection in his traumatized penis, and they had no other choice but to castrate him as a result of his mutilating injury.

He could not deal with the aftermath of the surgery nor his actions that led up to it that day. And with the same M-16 that he had used to kill Vietnamese in Mai Lai. Corporal Riggs strategically place the barrel underneath his chin before he was scheduled to be ship back to the states on a medical and psych, and made sure they inconveniently found his brains, that is, what was left of them, dripping off the ceiling the next day in his hospital room.

"I curse you all," she said.

* * *

I had now made it back stateside in one piece, It was 1975, and the Vietnam war had finally come to an end. This war had affected me in ways that I cannot even begin to explain. When I hit the tarmac of the LAX in "71", it was no big reception for me or us coming back home, unless you want to include the spit reception that we received.

And after what I had seen, I never questioned why. Vietnam was not a popular war, and to that, I understood the answers to why more so than why not. You had to be there to understand. You had to leave good men and friends that was a better man than you behind that did not make it out of those jungles and off those rice paddies to understand.

As I crossed the street to catch the bus on Fifth and Second, that is when I saw him, and all the memories of Nam came flooding back full force.

None, good. All bad.

Sgt. (Fucking) Horatio Duck!

I do not know if his eyes met mine before mine met his, nor does it matter. All I know is that he still had that same evil motherfucking grin on his face that he had when he was gunning down those poor Vietnamese in Mai Lai.

Had the old lady been wrong? I thought. If there were ever someone who had been deserving of dying of a *death curse,* it would be this treacherous sonofabitch, I thought.

How had God allowed him to live so long, with the type of atrocities he had committed. If there was a God, I thought.

I shook my head in disgust as I lessen the distance between us with every step that I took. He pointed at me as if making a gun motion with his hand snapping his hand and thumb back as a trigger finger.

I blew him a kiss back with a middle finger as its partner.

Sgt. (Fucking) Horatio Duck!

As he hit the curb, he never saw the 12:41 bus coming in front of him and it did not stop at 55mph (ca. 89km/h).

Splat!

His body was like a bug on a windshield as I watched it explodes, and the rest of him go under the bus.

As the bus came to a screeching halt, I watched in shock as the passengers one by one under the supervision of the bus driver who was just as shock and dismayed as I was all started to disembark off the bus.

I stood by looking as the blood from Sgt. Ducks crumpled and disintegrated body begin to pool and run out from underneath the buses' undercarriage.

Suffice to say it looked like his body had been thrown in a meat processor and spit right back out on the hardball in pieces.

The last passenger to get off the bus was a small elderly woman who turned around and looked at me affably, nodded her head, and gave me a wink.

"What the fuck...?" I said under my breath, unable to get the rest of the words out of my mouth as I look on horrified and speechless.

I knew that face from only one place; it was the one that I had seen that very day and many times in my nightmares, that face that had cursed us all in *Mai Lai,* in that small desolate village in Vietnam.

The face that had recognized me for what my platoon members and I were when we set foot in her village that day, soldiers that brought death and destruction.

Soldiers of Misfortune.

ZOMBIE PIMP

Breezy as he was known on the streets of Oakland, California was a well-known pimp and wheeler and dealer in the skin trade game. A pimp that took pride in having some of the best **ass-sets** money could buy working the tough and gritty streets of Oakland.

"If your head ain't in the game your ass better be," was the favorite line he would say to the new girls that he introduces into what he calls "the business."

"But I would prefer both," he would add. Often to the new girl's nervous giggles.

He had a team of twelve girls that he was working bringing in twelve-thousand dollars a day on an average three-hundred-sixty-five thousand on a good month, which came to four million three hundred and eighty thousand dollars and maybe some cents, a year, if the girls got their tricks for their pocket change too, all tax-free.

See, Breezy had figured out what most men did not know; the government had already figured out how to tax pussy, it was called marriage, so he was just subleasing it as a commodity from good Ole' Uncle Sam.

When business was slow, which was seldom, Breezy would loan some of his girls out to the porn industry to make some spank your monkey movies on VHS and Beta tapes.

He was a ruthless millionaire pimp that had to climb his way to the top by turning out young girls on the streets with the finesse and verbal skills of a master manipulator, as well as a verbal virtuoso of telling them just what he thought they wanted to hear as he lured them into his inner circle.

"Wine 'em and dine 'em then trick 'em and pimp'em was one of his mottoes.

His street cred was established, his pimp game un-challenge by up and coming pimps and old heads that had been around in the game for some time.

With all the money that he had coming in, Breezy definitely did not have to be out on the streets, watching his girls while they work. It was a task he usually left up to his right-hand man "Big Jesse" who he appointed as a manager and look-out for the girls while they work.

Big Jesse, was also was responsible for making sure that their asses were up, and their heads were down as they put in their shifts, because as Breezy had told him "No play, no pay." And making sure that those dead presidents came in correct and they weren't skimming any of their earnings off the top and stuffing it up their va-jay-jays to spend on getting high later. Just like every master pimp would, worth his glass heel Stacy's and mink fur coat into Pimpdom hood.

Breezy's bottom bitch was a butterball who he referred to as "Whiplash" that kept the other girls in check when they got catty, and out of order. She also oversaw and ran his whorehouse for his more exclusive clientele, like businessmen, politicians, doctors, judges, and lawyers. Men whose rich wives had come up with them in status but were no longer interested in what their penises look like unless they were attached to the young teenage pool boys, strapping gardener and occasionally the bartender or waiter at their favorite high-end restaurants.

They were old men with lots of money and power that still wanted to feel desired by the pretty young things that were willing to do whatever they ask to separate that almighty dollar from their almighty wallets.

Breezy reflected on a joke that one of his high-end clients had once told him about his wife. "That if he would have known that she would stop giving him blow jobs once she had her first million after one year of marriage, he would have dished that one million out to her one buck at a time."

"Tricks were bitches and bitches are tricks," he thought, with a smirk on his face. As he watches one of his street girls turn a trick in a clients car from a distance inside of his brand-new white on white Caddy, (exterior and interior) with white walls, shiny aluminum rims and an eight-track player in the deck belting **out the smooth sounds of the impeccable Marvin Gaye.**

No, Breezy normally would not be out on the streets playing lookout and babysitter to one of his street whores, but tonight was different.

Different, because he had got the word that a suspected "serial killer" that the police had dubbed "Hands On" was on the loose in Oakland and had already brutally raped and killed several of his competitor's girls.

This sonofabitch he felt needed to be dealt with and dealt with quickly.

Breezy's attention went back to the car of "The John" a brown Riviera that was parked in front of him. Inside that car was one of his girls's a southerner he nicknamed "Dixie" servicing a john with some righteous head game.

Although it was dark, he could see a silhouette of her head bobbing up and down through the Riviera's back window, like a bobblehead.

The guy must have been hung like a horse for her to keep coming up for air like that he first thought. But upon closer observation, Breezy could see that was not what it was at all. He could now see the trick had his hands around Dixie's throat forcing her head down inside his car. He could now see the trick was attempting to kill his street girl as she struggles for her life.

"Motherfucker!" Breezy shouted out to himself, as he took out the gold plated .45 with a pearl handle grip, from his glove compartment and chamber a round into its slide.

Breezy exited his Cadillac quickly, with the .45 hanging alongside his right leg as he made his way over to the John's vehicle. The trick never notices Breezy as he stealthy crept up next to the driver's side of his vehicle with pistol in hand. Maybe because he was too busy choking the last bit of life now left out of Dixie as her eyes bulge out of her head as she struggles to breathe.

Breezy gave the car door handle a tug, but it was lock and would not open. He then rapped on the trick's window loudly with his gun to get his attention and to stop the assault on his working girl.

"Motherfucker open this door!" Breezy shouted out at him.

His aggressive directive caught the man's attention inside the car as he stops strangling Dixie and released his death grip from around her throat. She gagged for fresh air, grabbing her throbbing and aching throat. As he turns around to face Breezy, she pops the door lock on the passenger side and quickly escapes the vehicle almost falling out of it before she gains her footing.

"You sick sonofabitch!" she shouted back at the trick.

"What the fuck?" Breezy said, jumping back startled! As the John's or Trick's hideous face came into view. It had to be the worst case of disfigurement he thought that he had ever seen on someone. With his girl Dixie out the car, Breezy fired several shots into the window of the car, shattering it, and striking the man in his chest multiple times. He could see the trick now slump on his seat after the bullets had torn into his chest. Breezy cautiously approaches the car with his gun still pointed at Dixie's assaulter as he went to open the trick's car door.

The man suddenly sprung up with a growl, through rotten teeth, staring at Breezy through grayish cloudy cataract like pupils.

Breezy fires off another round that struck the trick in his shoulder, but that did not stop "The John" from pushing the door open violently knocking Breezy down in the process as the door flung open striking him.

Dixie let out a scream as she watched what now look like a monster to her, the same monster that she was performing oral sex on earlier exit the car slowly, walking towards Breezy, grunting and growling like an animal.

"Breezy, no. Get up, baby!" she shouted out.

"Get up!"

Dixie rushed the trick in defense of her pimp (Breezy) with a straight razor that she had retrieved from her purse. As she swung the blade, it met the trick's ear and completely sliced it off as if it were a piece of fungus attached to the head of a cabbage.

"How, you like that motherfucker?" she said.

But the ear had come off too easy, she thought, with little resistance.

Almost as if all you would had to do is tug at it and it would have fallen off on its own.

Unfazed by the loss of its rotting ear, the thing only growled inhumanly, before it backhanded Dixie in the face and sent her sprawled out to the sidewalk.

What the hell is this thing? Breezy thought as he reached for his .45 that he had dropped when he was knocked down by the car door. Suddenly he felt the thing's rotten teeth sink into his arm.

"Goddammit!" he screams out in pain, as he punched the thing in its face with his free hand while jerking his bitten arm free out of its rotten mouth.

Boom! It sound like a cannon had went off as Breezy watched the thing's head explode like a melon in front of him, splattering blood matter all over his face and his fine threads.

"What the fuck took you so long?" he said.

"Sorry but my corns on these damn feet had me moving slow," Big Jesse said, wielding the saw-off shotgun that was still smoking at the barrels as he helped his boss to his feet.

"What the fuck was he on PCP? Big Jesse asked.

'How the fuck am I supposed to know? All I know is that mother-fucker almost killed Dixie and tried to bite my fucking arm off like it was a delicious slab of ribs!" Breezy said, retrieving his .45 off the ground as he brushes himself off.

"You okay baby?" he asks Dixie.

"My throat hurt daddy," she said as she wiped dead penis flesh from off her mouth.

Big Jesse looked at her with a smirk on his face.

"That motherfucker look like "*The son of Frankenstein*" why would you want to get in the car with him?" Breezy ask, as he took out a handkerchief and begin to wipe the dead man's cerebral cortex off his face and clothes.

"I am sorry daddy, it was dark," she answers feebly.

"Ain't that much darkness in the world," Breezy retorted.

"And that motherfucker stinks like something dead," Big Jesse added.

Breezy looked down at the deceased man's mushy head at least what was left of it and noticed a name tag badge clip onto his coat.

Apex Labs & Bioresearch – Dwight Kimbo – Lab Tech.

Breezy unclips the name tag and stuffs it in his pocket.

"Do you think this joker is *"Hands On?"* Dixie asks in a Southern drawl.

"Could be?" Breezy answers apprehensively, while massaging his goatee.

"Get anything that can be trace to us cleaned up – Jesse, and meet us back at the pad," Breezy instructed him.

"No problem Boss," Big Jesse said.

"Good, I gotta get "Doc" out and get a rabies shot and this bitch some glasses," Breezy said, pointing to Dixie.

"Sorry Daddy," Dixie interjected.

"Get your ass in the car," Breezy said, as he shoves Dixie in the front seat of his Caddy.

Big Jesse laughed.

"That wasn't meant to be funny," Breezy said with a stern look on his face.

"Sorry Boss," Big Jesse said apologetically.

"By the way, I have another job for you when you finish this one."

"Yeah what's that boss?"

Breezy reached in his coat pocket and took out the name tag badge and toss it to Big Jesse who caught it in his mitts and begins examining it.

"I need you to get the 411 on this biter?"

"Consider it done," replied his crony.

Big Jesse watched as his boss Breezy walked back towards his car before he begins his task of cleaning up all evidence that they were involved in the demise of the clump of shit that now laid headless on the sidewalk.

He takes out a small bottle of cologne opens it up and sprays his fingers, then dabs his nostrils to deaden the scent of the headless body.

As Big Jesse begins the arduous task of cleaning up the scene something to him does not sit right with this dead guy right off the bat as he goes through his pockets for other proofs of identification. One, this cat has only been dead for a few minutes now but smell and looks like Rigor Mortis has already set in and two, could it be that he had already been dead and stinking for some time.

Growing up on the streets of Oakland California, Big Jesse was no stranger to new death or old death but to him this was a weird mixture of both. As he gathers up the shell casings from his bosses gun, he could hear the distinct sound of "Five O" in the air approaching; he hurriedly picks up the remaining evidence. It was time to get the fuck out of dodge he thought as the sound of the sirens grew even closer. And find out who and what they were dealing with before he reported back to his million-dollar pimp boss, and the nostril cologne stop working.

* * *

According to Big Jesse's resources and connections, Mr. Dwight Kimbo was about as L-seven as you could get with a wife and some kids in an affluent neighborhood up in Orange County, and a good job at ***Apex Labs & Bioresearch.*** He had also been reported missing by his wife several days ago but had not yet made the local news, until his body was discovered in Oakland with his head blown off to pieces.

The cops were investigating it so far as a carjacking or robbery went wrong and had not tied the trick in as being the serial killer "*Hands on.*"

Question, was, "What the hell was Mr. Kimbo doing on this side of town strangling prostitutes?" See, Big Jesse had also got another piece of information through his paid informants on the Police payroll. Information that had not been released to the general public yet.

Information such as, "That the serial killer at large had not just killed his victims but had cannibalized them as well."

And if his memory serves him right, this cat did attempt to take a nice chunk of meat out of his boss arm before he spread his brains like jelly all over the sidewalk with his trusty street sweeper.

Two plus two always made four as far as he knew, and he was sure once the dental records came back along with the fingerprints that Mr. Kimbo would be identified as the sicko that was going around "offing" women in Oakland.

Furthermore, this was solid information he could relay to "Breezy" as he entered the spacious confines of his boss's laid out digs, decorated with white art-deco furniture and zebra print rugs laid out across the floors jazzy pimp style.

Breezy was being attended to by an older gentleman that Big Jesse only knew as "Doc" an on-call physician on Breezy's dime and payroll.

"That should do it Mr. Breezy," Doc said, as he secures the wrap around bandage on Breezy's arm.

He hands Breezy two bottles of pills one for pain and one to prevent infection.

"Take these as needed, and make sure you change the dressing," he said.

Breezy opens one of the bottles and pops two of the pain pills in his mouth and downs it with some E & J.

"Thanks, Doc," he said, as he caught the doctor side-eye balling one of his girls, a pretty almond colored curvaceous girl that had just turned twenty-one named Cashmere.

Breezy reached in his pocket and pulled out several hundred dollars and handed it to Doc.

"Does this cover it?"

"More than enough, kind sir," Doc said.

Breezy laughed, what incredible luck he had, he thought. He must have been the only pimp in the hood with a Black British Doctor.

Doc's admiration of Cashmere had not gone unnoticed by him either.

"Do you like her?" Breezy ask him, as he pointed at Cashmere.

"Yes, she's quite lovely indeed," said Doc, wiping the sweat from his forehead with a pocket handkerchief.

"Indeed," said Breezy.

Big Jesse smiled, watching the whole scene unfold from across the room as Dixie made him a drink at the bar.

Breezy waved Cashmere over to him.

"Take care of Doc before he leaves," he said.

"Okay Daddy," she said, as she took the doctor forty years her senior by the hand and began to lead him to one of the nearby bedrooms.

"Cheerio," Doc said with a grin.

"And fruit loops to you too," Breezy said sarcastically.

Big Jesse walked over to where Breezy was sitting and sat down across from her on the beanie chair.

"Give me the low-down Jess, and give it to me real," said Breezy.

"24-7 Boss," said Big Jesse.

"But before I begin, how's that arm?"

"It still hurts like shit, but I'll live," said Breezy.

He handed Breezy a sheet of paper with all the information that he had recently gathered up on Dwight Kimbo. His address, his wife's name, his children, employer, next of kin, etc.

"What are you telling me? This guy's an L-seven that just decided to turn and become an undercover freak and killer at the same time; something is not right here?" Breezy said.

"My thoughts exactly, boss. This cat has no history of violence, domestic or otherwise, that I could find," Big Jesse said, as he took a sip of his drink.

"Weird," Breezy said.

"Unless the sonofabitch is just good at what he was doing," Dixie interjected.

"What was that?" Breezy said.

"I said…"

"I know what you said, bitch! Now speak when spoken to you," he said, cutting her off sharply before she could finish her sentence.

"Sorry Daddy," Dixie said submissively with her eyes downcast.

She knew that she had stepped out of line by speaking out so openly by not asking permission first from her pimp "Breezy" because the name of the game was not only was she his girl, but also his property to do as he please.

And "In this business," property was never equal to that of its owner; hence the word – landlord.

Only one of his girls had the diplomatic immunity to speak out openly and that was his bottom bitch "Whiplash" who just happened to saunter into the room as he put Dixie in her place.

What's up Daddy?" she said, as she greeted Breezy first, then Jessie.

"What's up baby doll?" he said, as she planted a light kiss on his cheek.

Big Jesse watched her admirably; she was all woman he thought from her head, to her titties and toes. A curvaceous ebony butterball that could curl any men's toes and having him screaming like a bitch in the bed while he called out her name, as she put that magic box down on him mercilessly and empty his wallet at the same time. Her multi-tasking skills were second to none.

The purple tight-fitting mini dress she wore, with matching stiletto heels, showed off her ample butt cheeks and big shapely legs.

Big Jesse had gotten the pleasure of sampling her goodies and had been a fan ever since.

Whiplash looked over at Dixie at the bar sipping on a cocktail.

"Bitch, I know you had a hard night, but rent doesn't pay itself," she said.

"Put a scarf around that neck and get your skinny ass back on the block," she ordered.

Breezy grinned from ear to ear. He liked watching his bottom bitch in action, for some reason it gave him a hard-on.

"Damn girl you out cold," Big Jesse said, chuckling.

"Yeah, but the rest of me is all hot & juicy!" she said flirtatiously.

"I know that's right," Breezy said, with a smile, for a minute forgetting his pain.

"Girl sit your fine fat ass down," Breezy said.

Whiplash complied sitting in a plush chair across from Big Jesse.

"Dixie, before you leave, pour Whiplash a glass of that peanut noir," he said.

"You mean Pinot noir?" Dixie said, with attitude.

"Bitch you blind and deaf? That's what I said," Breezy replied agitatedly.

"Relax baby, she's had a hard night; she don't mean no harm," Whiplash said, in her defense.

Dixie hands Whiplash her drink.

"I'll talk to you later," Whiplash said to, Dixie.

Dixie's mouth dropped as she nervously hurried out of the house back onto the streets, because that is the last thing that one of the girls wanted to hear from his bottom bitch Whiplash.

"I'll talk to you later."

"I heard a freak almost choked her out?" Whiplash said as she took a sip of her fresh glass of wine.

Big Jesse's eyes never left her as he sat there quietly.

"Yeah, she might need some retraining; getting lackadaisical in her choice of clientele," Breezy said.

"I didn't know we had choices daddy," Whiplash said.

That comment took Breezy by surprise. As he was about to say something he stopped and looked at Whiplash soaking in the merit of her statement.

"Yeah, you're fucking right!" he said, as they all broke out in laughter.

He was what he was, a demon in fine threads.

"Breaking News!" the tv reporter said on the big television screen right across from them.

"Shhh-shhh, I want to hear this," Breezy said.

"It has just been confirmed, that authorities believe that the victim of what was thought to be a recent carjacking "Dwight Kimbo" a lab-tech at Apex Labs & Bioresearch, might now have been the victim of vigilante justice while he was living a double life as a serial killer the police gave the nickname "Hands On." At this time, they say all their gathered evidence points to him!"

"I be damned, wasn't there a twenty-five-thousand-dollar bounty on his head?" Breezy said.

"I think so," Big Jesse answered.

"Only one problem boss," said Jesse.

"What's that?"

"He's got no head," Big Jesse said, with a smirk.

They all laughed again.

Although Whiplash was sitting across from Breezy, she could not help but notice that his smooth dark complexion, now had an ashen color to it and he looked sick.

"Daddy are you okay, she said?" as she set her wine down on the table and walked over to examine him further.

"I am fine baby, except my arm hurts like a sonofabitch!" Breezy said.

As Whiplash approached Breezy closer, she could now see that his complexion had not only taken on an ashen color, but the veins from his neck were grotesquely pronounced and throbbing. When she felt his forehead, it felt as if he was on fire.

"Something ain't right with you daddy," she said wide-eyed and nervous.

"Jesse, get Doc's old ass off that young snatch and out here right now!" Breezy demanded.

"Right away boss," Big Jesse said.

"Doc put them old English balls back in your pants and get your ass out here!" Big Jesse shouted out.

"Coming mate just give me one moment to zip up," Doc shouted out from behind the closed door.

The old man shuffles out the door looking dishelved as he tucks his shirt inside his pants.

"What seems to be the problem?" he said.

"Breezy he's not doing too well," said Big Jesse.

Doc rushed over to the sofa where Breezy was to examine him; in the short time he was in the bedroom, he was quite surprised at the transformation that Breezy had made from the last time he had examined him and treated his wound.

"Mr. Breezy no disrespect, but you look like bloody hell!" he said.

Doc touched Breezy's neck and forehead and noted he was uncomfortably hot. He then took a glass thermometer from his doctor's bag, removed it from its plastic wrapping, and placed it under Breezy's tongue, look at his wristwatch for a few minutes removed it from his patient's mouth. He was now astounded by what he saw, Mr. Breezy's temperature was one-hundred-and five-degrees.

"Bloody hell! We need to get you into an ice bath now, Mr. Breezy." Doc said.

"Sounds good to me it's fucking hot in here," Breezy said.

"Whiplash and Big Besse," Doc said.

"It's Jesse," Big Jesse corrected him.

"Get every piece of ice you can find and make the coldest bath water for Mr. Breezy," Doc said unperturbed by Jesse's interruption.

"This man is literally on fucking fire, move your asses now," Doc said, tensely.

"I need to lower the core temperature of his body immediately before he goes into shock!" he said.

Big Jesse and Doc both assisted Breezy into the bathroom after Whiplash and Jesse had prepared the ice bath in his jacuzzi bathtub at the request of Breezy's on-call doctor.

"Okay, I think this is the part where Breezy would prefer only one dick in the bathroom," Whiplash said, as she took over for Doc and Big Jesse.

"Roger that mate."

Doc releases Breezy and hands him over to Whiplash as he nodded his head that it was okay, to Big Jesse.

"I am going to just stick around for a while love until he is stabilized if that's alright with you."

"No problem Doc, you can finish getting your little pecker wet for all I care," Breezy said.

Doc shook his head as he exited the bathroom while Big Jesse stood there looking at Breezy with concern.

Breezy raised his head up despite his condition and spoke to their to surprise.

"Scram Jess, I don't need another man admiring what I was blessed with you dig?"

"I dig," said Big Jesse, as he exited also.

Whiplash got all of her pimp's clothes off and got him into the cold bath water.

"Daddy it's going to be okay," was the last words he heard before he passes out and went into a deep coma-like sleep.

* * *

When Breezy opened his eyes, it was as if the whole world had changed while he was asleep, and he was now viewing the world through different lenses.

He was no longer in danger of overheating because his body was now as cold as the blood that now ran through his veins, as he emerges from the bathtub of melted ice cubes.

He reached over and as if by instinct alone, put on the nearby purple Turkish cotton bathrobe that hung on the wall's hook. He tied it's purple belt around his waist tightly as a craving hunger now swept over him as his brain demanded raw nourishment of any kind.

A craving that was the driving force that made him put one foot in front of the other as he slowly walked out of the bathroom, as drool ran slowly down the corner of his mouth.

All he felt was hunger, pain, as he looked through glassed over grayish pupils, as he enters his living room – humans, – food.

"Hey daddy, I see you're awake," said Whiplash. The first one to greet him as she sets her glass down and walks over to him.

She dabbed the drool off his chin with his robe collar as she touched his forehead.

"He's much better now Doc, cool as a cucumber," Whiplash said.

Breezy looked at her through those dead pupils of his with no recognition, grunting.

Hunger – pain – food.

Breezy gently placed his hands on the side of Whiplash's face and then sunk his teeth into her face and begin chewing into it as she let out a deafening scream of terror and shock! while struggling to pull away from his grasp.

Big Jesse and Doc watch in horror.

"What the fuck?" Big Jesse shouted out as he jumped up off the sofa and ran over to assist Whiplash who had been taken down to the floor by Breezy who was now cannibalizing her face.

Doc wet himself and broke for the door.

"Come back Doc!" Big Jesse screamed out to him, while he attempted to wrestle Breezy off of Whiplash.

But Doc was gone and now Big Jesse was on his own.

After much effort and struggling, he finally managed to get Breezy off of Whiplash with half her nose still intact as he threw him off of her, Breezy went crashing into a piece of the furniture nearby.

Whiplash grabbed her face, as blood poured down it.

"Oh, it's on now you skinny bitch motherfucker!" she said, as she then made a beeline for her purse and retrieved a .38 revolver.

Breezy was back on his feet and headed back towards Whiplash.

"Whiplash no!" Big Jesse yelled out.

But it was too late; she pops off three rounds into Breezy's chest sending him crashing through the glass coffee table in the living room.

"Bite that you old raggedy ass pimp!" she said.

"What the fuck just happened?" Big Jesse said as he looks over at what appeared to be his now deceased boss.

Cashmere and several of the other working girls came running out of other rooms in the house into the living room during the commotion.

"What the hell is going on?" Cashmere said, as her eyes went over to her down pimp.

"Bitch, you just killed daddy!" she said, as she ran over to Breezy.

"Cashmere no!" Whiplash screamed out.

"Aaaargh!"

Breezy sprung up and sank his teeth into Cashmere's neck ripping out her throat.

Cashmere flopped to the floor dead! Blood spurting profusely out of her fatal neck wound.

Breezy was now back on his feet, grunting and sneering at everyone in the room. He could smell all of their insides, and he wanted to rip every one of these creatures apart.

Whiplash aimed the .38 revolver center mass towards Breezy's forehead.

Smack! The metal candle holder went across the back of Breezy's head, knocking him out cold.

The candle holder fell to the floor out of Dixie's hand.

Whiplash lowered her gun down still in shock.

"Bitch, this is one time that I might not be mad at you for disobeying a direct order," Whiplash said.

"I didn't it was just a slow night," Dixie said taking out a wad of cash, throwing it on the table.

"What the hell happened too Breezy?" she said.

"I don't know, but he's like some kind of fucking..."

'Zombie" said Bushy, one of Breezy's girls of Caribbean descent, finishing Big Jesse's statement.

"My fucking nose!" Whiplash screamed out holding a towel to her face.

Big Jesse went to the kitchen, came back with a sandwich bag with some ice in it, reached down and picked up part of Whiplash nose off the floor and put it inside the bag.

"Take a couple of the girls with you and get your ass to emergency and they might be able to save your face," He said.

Whiplash snatched the bag out of his hand.

"That's all a bitch need is a pimp that's a zombie, nose eating motherfucker!" she said, looking down at Breezy.

"The rest of you, get some rope or whatever we got so that we can tie him up until we know what the fuck we are dealing with," Big Jesse said.

"The answer might be here," Dixie said, picking up the ID badge off of the bar that had her attacker's name on it and where he worked.

Dwight Kimbo, Apex labs & Bioresearch.

"We need to find out where this joint is and pay them a little visit, but first I need to get some of my soldiers together," said Big Jessie.

Big Jesse looked down at the dead young woman named Cashmere with her throat ripped out lying on the floor.

"Can someone throw a blanket over her Goddamitt!" he shouted out.

Big Jesse walked over and picked up the cordless phone off the table and dialed one of his soldiers an ex-nam veteran.

A man with a deep voice answers on the other end of the phone.

"What's up Big Jesse?" he said.

"I got a situation "Coldpiece" that needs handling, you down?"

"Brother I am ready if you steady," the man shot back.

"Good, round up a some of the crew and some choice hardware, we got a run tonight."

"Sounds like you got some serious "Action Jackson," shit in mind.

"Maybe? I'll fill you in with the details when we all meet up."

"Copacetic," replied Coldpiece.

* * *

Breezy had now been confined to one area of the house where he could be monitored, now secured with rope and chains to a chair that is bolted to the floor. But that did not stop the sound of his whaling and grunting from reverberating off the walls, he could be heard throughout the house.

"Can you shut him the fuck up!" Dixie said, not believing at first those words had come out of her mouth, as she looks up the address to Apex Labs & Bioresearch on a Macintosh home computer. She had never been outspoken before without risking the consequences of being reprimanded by her pimp. But this was different, although technically speaking Breezy, was still her pimp he was nevertheless, now a *Zombie-pimp.*

A pimp who's only desire was to devour human flesh like it was filet mignon.

"Muffle him," Big Jesse ordered the other girls in the room.

"That shit is starting to creep me out too," he said.

Big Jesse said "Who the fuck can that be?" at the sound of the doorbell going off, as he looks at Dixie suspiciously.

He took out a 9mm from his waistband and made his way to the door.

"Who is it?" he said.

A feeble voice answer back.

"It's Doc."

Big Jesse said with a frown as he opened the door and greeted the runaway doctor.

"I be damn, it's the cowardly lion, welcome back," Big Jesse said.

"Mate, please accept my sincerest apology for my hasty retreat," Doc said.

"Sure," Big Jesse said waving Doc into the house.

"By the way Doc, you have something on your nose?" Big Jesse said.

"What?" Doc said checking his nose.

"This!" Big Jesse punched Doc in his face and sent him sprawled out to the floor.

"You sonofabitch what did you do that for?" Doc said as blood gushed out his nostrils.

"If you ask that question again, you might wake up dead," Big Jesse warned him.

"Duly noted," Doc said, fearfully, as he swallowed the lump in his throat, took out a rag and applied it to his bloody nose.

"Get this asshole an ice pack for his face," Big Jesse said to one of Breezy's call girls, a seasoned whore that went by the name of Tasty.

"If you run away again, I'll make sure it's your last time, understood Doc?" Big Jesse said grimly.

That lump came back in Doc's throat as he elevated his head to stop the bleeding, still holding the rag against his nose.

"Loud and clear mate," he said.

Graarghhhhhh!

"What the blimey hell is that godawful noise?" he said.

"Do you really want to know?" said Big Jesse.

Doc nodded his head reluctantly.

Why the hell had he come back, he thought?

"Follow me," said Big Jesse.

Doc gasped and was stunned by the quick transformation and deterioration of his employ's appearance, during the short time that he had left.

"Good lord, he looks like a Zombie…"

"Pimp," Big Jesse said, finishing Doc's sentence.

"I am afraid you took the bloody words right out of my mouth," Doc said wide-eyed.

Tasty finally tied a rag around Breezy's mouth muffling – his inhuman bawling.

"Don't be afraid, he's secure," Big Jesse assured Doc.

Doc cautiously steps forward closer to examine Breezy's condition.

"All I can say is that at the rate, that he appears to be degenerating, we will soon have a walking corpse on our hands," said Doc.

"I see medical school wasn't wasted on you," Big Jesse said with a roll of his eyes.

"No, I graduated in the top ten of my class," Doc replied.

"I didn't mean that as a compliment," Big Jesse said.

Tasty laughed.

"Is this Cat serious?" she asked Jesse.

"I am afraid so," Jesse answers.

"Hey Jesse, I got a hit on that lab it's in Hidden Valley California it's about two hours from here," Dixie said.

"Okay good, hey Doc guess what? We are going for a ride," said Big Jesse.

"You two keep an eye out on the boss and make sure he don't go nowhere," Big Jesse said to the other two girls in the room.

"Dixie and Tasty you are coming with us."

"Whoo-wee, we get to have some fun," Tasty interjected.

"I got a bad feeling about this mate," Doc said.

"Good you'll, be the first one through the door then," Jesse said.

"Are you serious?" Doc replied, almost choking on the lump in his throat.

Big Jesse just gave him a firm look and said nothing.

"Dixie make sure Coldpiece gets that information, and he meets us at that spot in two hours," he said.

"Okay boss," she replied.

Big Jesse smiled at this; she was right. He was boss, at least for now.

He looked back at the dark corner where his boss was sitting, and that is when he could see the glow of Breezy's pupils in the darkness like those of a wild captured animal.

What the fuck was he turning into? Jesse thought as a chill went through his body.

* * *

Apex labs & Bio Research was a fairly well-concealed facility on acres of privately-owned land in Hidden Valley, California. And despite Big Jesse and his crew having an address to the facility it took some geographical navigation to reach this fenced in compound.

But as Big Jesse and his crew pulled up to the gates of the facility, he quickly noticed that the fence that outlines the perimeter was no ordinary fence, but more like the one you would see at San Quentin prison where he had done a five-year bid for armed robbery and assault as a young street thug.

An armed security guard sat inside a guard booth at the gate's entrance and watched them as they pulled up slowly to the gate.

He got out and slowly walked over to their van, peeping inside, with a small flashlight in his hands.

"Evening can I help you?" he said.

"Yeah boss, we got some supplies that we need to drop off," Big Jesse answer back, as he handed the security guard a clipboard with some official looking forms on it that corresponded to the fake magnet sign on the side of the van that said, (*John Trick lab supplies & equipment*).

The security guard looks at his schedule.

"I see the delivery, but I don't see the name of your company," he said.

"There it is on the side of our van boss," Big Jesse said cheerfully.

The security guard shook his head sideways, "That's not what I mean, Mack" he said.

Dixie smiled and wink at the security guard as they made eye contact.

"I know boss, just funning, but we can take this shit back to the warehouse, all the same to me if you want," said Jesse, with an intentional tone in his voice that conveyed to the guard he didn't give a damn one way or the other, he was just a delivery man.

"Naw and get my ass, chewed out, this shit happens all the time," replied the guard.

"How're you doing little lady," he said to Dixie with a smile on his face, taking his focus off of Jesse.

"Fine handsome and you?" she said flirtatiously.

The security guard grinned back as he handed Big Jesse a clipboard and an electronic visitor's pass.

"Sign this Mack," he said, the tone of his voice now less affable.

"How long you been on the job?" he asked Dixie.

"Today is my first day, Wilbert's showing me the ropes" she answer.

"Wilbert is that so?" said the guard as his eyes cut to Big Jesse annoyingly, for a second and back to Dixie.

"Yes sir, Mr. Officer," she said.

"Well, I hope to see you around."

"Me too," Dixie said, with a wink and a wave.

"They're okay, let them through," the guard yelled out at another security guard who steps out of the darkness and hits a button on the gate causing it to slide back and open.

"Wilbert?" Big Jesse said.

"It worked," Dixie said, with a giggle.

"Yes, it did," Jesse agreed, but he had not even seen that other rent-a-cop hiding in the shadows, and he could not help from wondering why they had this place on lockdown like Fort freaking Knox.

But one thing was for sure, in the back of his fake delivery van were enough hired guns to find out the reasons why? As the van slowly drove up to the paved delivery area and loading dock of the lab, under the watchful eye of Apex's security cameras.

Big Jesse and Dixie exited the vehicle and used the temporary electronic card pass given by security to them to access the building. Once in, Big Jesse opened the back doors to the van and begin unloading the lab equipment which consisted of Coldpiece, three of his hired hands, Tasty and Doc.

As Coldpiece and his three goons exited the back of the van, Big Jesse noticed that him and his crew had indeed taken his advice and brought with them some serious firepower.

M16A2's and Heckler & Koch MP5's locked and loaded and ready to rock & roll.

"If you don't mind me asking, Big Jess. What in the hell are we doing outside a Research Facility?" Coldpiece asks.

Big Jessie removed several Polaroid pictures from his pocket and passed them over to Coldpiece.

Coldpiece shined a mini Maglite on the pictures, as he looked them over. "What the fuck, who dug up the corpse?" he said.

"That corpse is Breezy, and that corpse is still alive," Jesse said.

"You jiving me man?" Coldpiece said.

"No jive, our man Breezy is a *zombie-pimp* right now," Jessie stressed.

His other crew looked at the pictures.

"I heard of shit like this, but I thought shit like this only happens in Haiti, man," one of the men in Coldpiece crew said.

"Well consider this the new Haiti because I killed one of those mutherfucking dead things that bit Breezy and infected him," Big Jesse said.

"That's some wild shit!" Coldpiece said.

"And guess where that thing worked at?"

Coldpiece and his crew's eyes went towards the building.

"Exactly!" Big Jesse said as he then pointed at the Research Facility for emphasis.

"So, I need to find out what the hell is going on inside there? And how its related to Breezy and if there is some fucking cure for this shit, dig it?"

"You damn skippy," Coldpiece said.

Doc looked at all the armed men and women around him then his empty hands.

"If it's not too much of a problem mate, can I have something like what they have to protect myself in case shit goes bonkers?"

"No, but you can have this and try not to shoot yourself in the foot," Big Jesse said as he slaps a .38 in Doc's hand.

"By the way, it's only one bullet in the cartridge so, don't waste it if you don't have too," Jesse said to Doc.

"One bullet? But it holds six?" Doc said nervously.

Coldpiece and his crew laughed because they knew that Big Jesse was only screwing with Doc.

"Stay close, I'll protect you honey buns," Tasty said, to Doc, as she patted him on the ass then pumped a round into her Mossberg shotgun.

"Okay everybody, enough talk. Let's find out what the fuck they're hiding up in there," Jessie said.

"Disarm those fucking cameras and let's sweep this compound and see what kind of Frankenstein shit that they got going on up in here," Jesse said giving his final instructions before they proceeded inside.

Dixie shook the can of spray paint up that she would use to blacken out the security camera lens.

Doc gripped the .38 tightly as he made his way with the rest of them towards the building, sticking close to Tasty. He had a bad feeling earlier about this whole plan and unfortunately for him that feeling had not gone away.

He was headed into the "belly of the beast" just like the rest of them and the only question that remained now, was how many of them would get out to talk about it tomorrow.

* * *

Big Jesse and his group now made their way back inside. He ordered Cold-piece and his crew to search one wing of the building while Dixie, Tasty, Doc and he searched the other wing of the facility.

They would all communicate with each other via headphone walk-ie-talkies sets that he had supplied them with for contact.

Big Jesse had no clue what they were looking for inside the lab. But he suspected whatever it was had to be somewhere in this building, as they cautiously made their way inside the loading dock area of the facility.

"Here goes nothing," Jesse said, as he took Dwight Kimbo's employee badge out and stuck it in the card reader next to a door inside the drop-off area, that led to access into the more sensitive area of the facility.

It was a gamble he knew he was taking regarding "If the access badge was still active or not?" lucky for him it was a gamble that paid off as the LED light turned a bright green on the reader, and the door unlocks.

"Baby we're in," he said.

"Let's do this," Coldpiece said, gung-ho, his MP5 at the ready to rock and unload.

As they made their way through the corridor of the facility, Dixie and Tracy hit the camera lenses that follow them from above with a shot of spray paint blinding them from their movements or whoever was watching them.

Big Jesse knew that it was probably only a matter of time before Apex's security discovered that he and his team had breached the facility, and all hell would break loose. That being said, he knew damn well whatever it was that they were looking for, it had to be found quickly before shit hit the fan! Fast and hard.

His crew came upon a door that had the word *"Testing"* on it; this was as good as a place to start as any, he thought as he opens the door to the antiseptic facility. He could hear what he thought was a human voice behind the door.

"What the fuck?" He said as him and his crew's eyes locked on to three corpses dressed in prison uniforms and strapped down on gurneys across from each other.

"Man, this is some deep doo-doo!" Tasty said as she made her way into the lab with the rest of them, her Mossberg at the ready.

"So, this is the alternative to death row," Jesse said as he pointed out the Prison jumpsuits the corpses wore.

"What in the bloody hell is going on here?" Doc said as he looked over at the strapped down corpses and sophisticated lab equipment and charts on display.

"What does it look like?" Jesse said.

"Ggggrrrrrr," growled one of the corpse before it reached out and grabbed Tasty by her jacket and pulled her towards it for consumption.

Tasty scream out! Right before she broke loose and fired off a buckshot into its head sending it slumping back down on the gurney this time dead for sure.

Its other two buddies seemed to spring to life and started grunting, going into a rampage as they tried to break free from their straps.

"These fucking things are alive!" Dixie shouted out as she fired off a round into the chest of one of the creatures, causing it took slump back down on the gurney as well, but it was not dead. Unlike the two others it appeared to be of female orientation.

It snaps back up growling as black mucus oozes out of its rotten mouth.

"You're one ugly bitch!" Dixie said, right before she put a bullet, this time dead center in the middle of its forehead.

"Fucking zombies," Jesse said, as he and the rest of them stood there in the lab room in awe of what they were dealing with inside this obvious lab of horrors.

"Take pictures of this shit," he said to Tasty, who then got a small camera out from around her neck and began snapping pictures of the lab and its contents.

"I would not do that if I were you," a voice said in the distance.

"Who in the hell are you?" Jesse said, to the men in the white lab coat with salt and pepper hair.

"Dr. Dick Dickerson and I am in charge of this research facility," he said arrogantly.

"It would be a dick in charge of this," Tasty replied.

"And who and the hell are you people and why are you trespassing?" he asks.

"My boss got bitten by one of your little playmates, and I need the fucking cure," Jesse said curtly.

Dr. Dickerson adjusted some pens in his lab coat pocket.

"Aaaahhh, my lab tech Dwight Kimbo, that was an unfortunate accident, how he got infected," Dickerson said.

"He was a good man."

"Fuck him and fuck you! I need the cure for this shit!" Jesse said angrily, pointing his assault rifle at the doctor.

"And do not come any fucking closer," he warned.

Doc had been reading a medical journal of notes that Dr. Dickerson had written and been keeping on one of the tables in the lab.

*Notes: That spoke of a zombie virus that was created and would be administered and tested in a mandatory vaccination for population control and to eradicate the undesirables in a society that was not of good gene pools and a burden and dredge on society. All inner cities ridden with crime and other malfeasances would be the first operative targets, and this new virus would be given the name **Z-1 Prionisis** by this research facility once it was perfected and ready for mass distribution.*

Collateral damage was expected, equated, and assessed outside of **Z-1 Prionisis's** *targeted demographics. But it has been determined through research and testing that this new virus benefits to new world order will far outweigh any negative consequences that it may have on a global scale once its activated and epidemic in its highly contagious and genetic form.*

Apex Labs & Bioresearch.

Dr. Dick Dickerson

"This is bloody madness!" Doc, shouted out, with the journal in his hand.

"Sanction Government madness," Dr. Dickerson said with a smile.

"What'cha got there Doc?" Jesse said.

"A lab journal on genocide, on us…" Doc said gravely.

"Goddamn fucking domestic Nazi's!" Tasty said.

"Let's do this motherfucker now," said Dixie.

Big Jesse threw his hand out to an agitated Dixie to not shoot.

"Hold up!"

"Dr. Dick is there a cure?"

"There's always a cure," Dr. Dickerson said grinning.

"Question is…" he paused.

"What?" Jesse asks.

"Can your black ass afford it?" Dickerson said, snickering as he unfastens the last strap on one of the zombie's on the gurneys.

"No!" Jesse yelled out.

But it was too late – as the zombie lunged up off the table and attacked an unaware Dixie going for her throat as she fired rounds helplessly into the air.

The zombie bit into her neck as she attempted to get away from the creature.

Big Jesse and the others watch frozen for a moment in terror.

"Get off her motherfucker!" Big Jesse yelled out, as he let loose with a barrage of bullets that tore into the flesh of the creature, propelling the walking dead abomination off of Dixie as it ate the bullets like a fat kid eating cake.

Doc walked up behind it and put two .38 bullets straight into its head, sending its brain matter out the front of its skull and onto the floor.

More gunshots could be heard throughout the facility as the building alarms went off flashing strobes of red from its overhead sensors.

Just like Big Jesse had predicted it would "shit had hit the fan and hard!"

In all the melee the other creature had unnoticeably been unstrapped by Dr. Dickerson also, as he fled.

The undead came up off the table but did not fair as well as its predecessor, because Tasty quickly raised her Mossberg and obliterated whatever little brains that the she-zombie had left all over the lab floor.

"He's getting away," Tasty said, as she noticed Dr. Dickerson exiting the testing lab with some folders and a briefcase in his hands.

"He won't get far," Jesse assured Tasty, as he caught sight of the doctor quickly going out the door.

Coldpiece came in over the headset walkie-talkie *"BJ we taking fire and we got one down, these muthafuckers are everywhere like cockroaches!"* he said.

"CP hold it down we are en route and b.o.l. on a dick headed your way," Jesse said.

"A what?" Coldpiece responded, not sure he heard Big Jesse correctly.

"White male, 5-10, salt and peppered hair, Dr. Dick Dickerson."

"A dick gotcha," said Coldpiece.

Big Jesse could hear the loud sound of gunfire in the background.

"Let's move, maybe we can catch up with that asshole," he said.

"What about Dixie?" Tasty said.

Big Jesse looked down at Dixie who was moaning and holding her bloody throat.

"Put a bullet in her head to make sure she doesn't come back as one of those things."

Coldpiece was right Big Jesse thought as they made their way into the corridor. The undead... they were everywhere. It was as if Dr. Dickerson had unleashed every test subject in the building to do his dirty work while he got the hell out of dodge.

A horde of the walking dead now surrounded the halls feasting on Apex security guards and whatever else they could sink their cannibalistic teeth into as they walk aimlessly about in an almost vegetative state, sniffing out the air for the smell of fresh meat – human meat.

Now it was up to Big Jesse and his two companions to cut through that hoard if they ever had any serious intentions on making it out of the building alive and catching up with Dickerson.

As the zombies headed in their direction, they all let loose with their artillery and began mowing every walking dead creature that stood in the way of their path and freedom down.

"Shoot for the head, don't waste no damn bullets!" Jesse yelled out.

"Over here," Coldpiece yelled out! As he and another gunman hidden behind a barrier fired into the hoard.

Their bullets ripped through the zombies, flesh, tearing off ears, noses, and fingers. Blowing out eyeballs! But the horde still kept coming as if they were mindless invincible machines of death.

"Help me, help me!" someone screamed out in fear.

Big Jesse turned in the direction of the voice to see who it was coming from in the corridor.

It was Dr. Dick Dickerson coming out of one of the adjoining rooms with a zombie hot on his heels and neck.

"I'll help you," Jesse said, as he nodded at Tasty.

Tasty aimed the Mossberg towards the zombie that had now grab hold of Dr. Dickerson's lab coat and was pulling him in towards him.

Dr. Dickerson smartly came out of the lab coat, leaving the zombie confused.

Tasty took her sights off the zombie and aimed it at Dickerson's leg and pulled the trigger.

The doctor's leg exploded right from underneath him as the buck shot's tore into his calf and sent him collapsing to the floor in pain.

"You fucking black bitch, what have you done?" he shouted out.

"I don't know? Improve race relations," Tasty shouted back at him with a smile on her face.

"That's okay, if I don't make it out, none of us will," Dickerson said as he took out a detonator switch and began laughing.

"Fuck me!" Jesse said.

"You see, I created the zombie virus especially for black bastards like …"

"Shut the fuck up, honkey!" Coldpiece said, as he brought an ax down on Dickerson's arm severing it from the forearm, the detonator rolled out of Dickerson's hand onto the floor as he screamed out in agonizing pain.

The zombie was still standing there behind Dickerson looking perplexed, as it fumbled with his lab coat. Then he looked down at Dickerson.

Food.

Big Jesse walked over and picked up the suitcase and that is when he heard the detonator beeping.

"Let's go; this place is about to blow!" He screamed out to his crew.

As Dr. Dickerson held onto the stub of his arm, he felt something crawling up his backside; it was no mistaking what it was as its rotten jagged teeth ripped into the back of his neck, gnawing into his flesh.

Boom!

The explosion was so loud behind Big Jesse and his crew it shook the very foundation that they were standing on as they barely made it out of the facility alive.

Kaboom!

A second explosion erupted as they now watched the facility from a safe distance erupt into a blazing ball of fire.

Big Jesse opened the suitcase, lifted a foam cover off six golden vials of the antidote nestled in the case with syringes.

"There's always a cure," he said softly to himself.

"Goodbye Dickenstein," Tasty said, as she threw up her middle finger at the burning building they just narrowly escaped.

A silhouette suddenly appeared out of the darkness not too far away walking towards them.

Big Jesse raised his assault weapon at the unidentified target.

"No, he…"

"Wait!" said Tasty interrupting him as she pushed his weapon down.

"Dixie?" she yelled.

Big Jesse looked at Tasty.

"I thought I told you to, never mind," he said.

"It's not as bad as it looks," Dixie said, holding her neck as they helped her into the van.

"I hope for your sake this shit works," Jesse said, raising up a briefcase marked "antidote" that they had taken from the lab.

"If it doesn't put a bullet in my head, right?" Dixie said.

Big Jesse looked at her and Tasty and shook his head sideways.

"You crazy bitches got balls," he said.

"We have to, the streets of Oakland are unforgiven," Tasty said.

"When this shit is over perhaps, I'll talk to Breezy about a career change for you two," Jesse said.

"Yeah, I could use two bad ass bitches on my team to," Coldpiece said.

"From one bad ass bitch to another I'll take that as a compliment' Tasty said.

Coldpiece laughed.

"Can yall shut the fuck up my neck hurts!" Dixie groaned.

"May I?" Doc said.

Big Jesse handed Doc the briefcase.

Doc got the antidote and the syringe out of the briefcase; it was time to see if this zombie in-reverse shit worked.

As they entered the pad, Big Jesse could immediately sense something was wrong as he called out to the two girls that were supposed to be attending to Breezy. The house for one was all in disarray and furniture was all turned over and broken.

"What the fuck happen here?" Tasty said, as they cautiously made their way deeper into the confines of the house.

Big Jesse flipped the light switch on to the kitchen, and that's when all their mouths dropped at the sight of the two women left to watch Breezy lying dead on the spacious kitchen floor with their guts hanging out and chewed on as if a wild animal had viciously mauled them and torn them apart.

Their eyes then went straight to the creature kneeled with its back to them feasting on raw hamburger meat straight out of the refrigerator, with car tree pine air fresheners pinned to its clothes.

"Breezy?" Jesse said.

Breezy turn around with a growl. It was too late for his boss, Jesse could see it in his clouded over dead greyish eyes as he gorged into the raw hamburger meat, as saliva and pieces of meat dripped off his decayed chin.

He had gone full "***Zombie – Pimp***" and there was no coming back.

Tasty raised her Mossberg shotgun and aimed it at Breezy's wretched head.

In the background, a reporters voice could be heard on a nearby television.

"We have breaking news that renowned virologist Dr. Dick Dickerson has perished in an unfortunate lab fire caused by a possible gas leak at the Apex Labs and Bioresearch facility, in Hidden Valley California. We will keep all our viewers informed as further updates come in on this unfortunate tragedy. In other news today, the brutal serial killer known as "Hands On..."

THE WEIGHT ON MY SHOULDERS

I sit here in the dark haunted, unable to sleep because I can feel its claws digging into my shoulder, the weight of this entity on my back.

I smell a sulfuric musty odor, permeating my nostrils as it whispers its demands like an unwelcome muse with cold breath in my ears. As my compulsion from killing gets weaker and weaker by the day, the entity becomes stronger and stronger as I fill its insatiable bloodlust for murder and mayhem.

All the days now that I sit in this apartment after I come home from a night out hunting and putting work in at the direction of this putrid thing sitting on my shoulders staring down at me with its vapid black eyes. I feel that I am now subjected to a life of surrealism by proxy and I am just a viewer now and puppet participant tuning in for the next nightmarish episode of its making.

I was not born a killer, nor was my inspiration ever to be a killer. I only play the hand that I was dealt with in this life and the cards that were spreaded out on my table. And when I saw the card that stared up at me from that table, a grinning reaper with a scepter in its hand, I knew what my true calling was – good or bad.

The thing about me is, I could be your next-door neighbor, your co-worker, your best friend or worst, your lover. And you would never know in a million years what I was truly capable of until it was too late for you, too late for me, too late to stop this compulsion that venomously traveled through my veins, through my soul like heroin travels through a needle to the mind of a junkie.

But this thing sitting on my back and my shoulders knew exactly what kind of heinous acts of murder and debauchery I was capable of because this thing was with me during every act when I slashed, stabbed, mutilated, and violated every one of my victims in the worst ways possible.

I know this sounds like a confession, but it is not. It is more like an awakening for me from a constant state of denial of what kind of monster I have truly become and my disgust for anything or anyone that I decided due to lack of self-control. Or perhaps, some sadist compulsion propelled by the power of this thing on my shoulders to erase any life that I came into contact with when I was haunting and prowling the streets of Oakland, California looking for my next target, my next victim, my next rush.

I saw a weird thing the other night when I was out cruising for my next target. Something that made me do a double take. I had stopped at a traffic light in East Oakland, and another car had pulled up beside me a– brown Riviera.

I cannot say what compelled me to look over at the next driver, but I did. Only to find the other driver already staring at me between gritted teeth with a ravenous look on his face. I could see clearly in his eyes. Just like myself, he had lost his way also, had lost his soul.

I could see that just like myself, he was a creature of the night as he stared at me malevolently through bloodshot eyes. Unfazed, I stared back, and when the light turned green, he continued on his way and me on mine.

I had business to attend to after all, while the night was still fresh and young, and all I wanted to know was if one of my favorite girls I had laid eyes on a few nights ago was out here working these gritty streets tonight. She looks like she needed someone to save her and remove her from this life of sin. Fortunately for her, I and this monster on my back were more than happy to oblige.

I would be afforded some relief from this merciless entity once the deed was done and I left my calling card.

Those are the times that "it" would remove itself from my shoulders and back and sit across from me in the darkness of my apartment leering at me salaciously. Knowing damn well that it knew all my deepest secrets and my innermost thoughts, and it was absolutely nothing in this world I could do about it, other than erase myself out of existence or submit to its control of my mind, body, and soul.

I guess I cowardly chose the latter, so therefore now I must deal with the consequences of those choices.

My first and last mistake, I assure you.

I watch the life leave my last victim's eyes as I held her life in my hands. But it was something different this time about the last victim that I had chosen. I had stepped out of Oakland, this time. Stepped out of my comfort zone.

I had drifted off into a more affluent area and had abducted and killed someone who had come from a wealthy background that the authorities would now actually give a shit about and not write off as a statistic of their environment because of poverty, lifestyle, etc.

Now with the assistance of her family who was prominent members of their community, I had a half-million-dollar bounty on my ass, and a bounty hunting team way out of fucking Montana called the Bone-squad looking for my ass on the streets of Oakland, California.

The only real break I had caught was when this virus epidemic had hit our city that was making people go bat shit crazy! Almost like bath salts and they were now fucking eating each other's faces off and making me look tame by all appearances.

But fortunately for me, it was the break I needed to relocate and set up shop elsewhere, maybe head east. This thing that was on me like a backpack on a hiker's back agreed. I had no problem anyway leaving my little shit job and equally shit apartment, and the only thing that I would truly miss was my girlfriend Lillian, who I had been kicking it with for two-years now.

Maybe I will send for her once I get settled into wherever I end up setting up shop for a while.

There was still a little bit of daylight left as I now hit the road eager to put as much distance between me and the city of Oakland, California as possible. The entity on my back had not been taunting me today, and it felt like it had dismounted itself from me and went on fucking vacation.

Hooray! I guess you can say I felt fucking fantastic as I hit the freeway eastbound towards my freedom.

Ding-ding-ding-ding.

Shit! My gas light came on, less than a quarter tank of gas is sure not going to get me where I wanted to go, so I pulled off at the next exit where I saw a fuel sign.

I could smell the rain in the air as I made my way into the gas mart to pay for my gas. I like the rain, it always made everything smell extra special to me and also it was good for washing away evidence.

Maybe I'll take a break I thought, when I get where I am going, lay off a few years before I start back up if this thing on my back allowed me to attempt to live some semblance of a normal life.

I paid for my gas at the counter with the cute young cashier, as I imagined my hands around her throat, as she stared into my eyes, stared into the abyss.

"Thank you, sir," she said, bringing me out of that visual back to reality.

"Thank you," I said, making sure to touch the top of her hand as she handed me back my change.

She made me want to get a hotel nearby and come back and pay her a visit so that we could get to know each other better. Lucky for her, I was in a hurry and had no time for such extracurricular activities.

"Howdy stranger," said a tall and pretty woman in a black Stetson and western attire entering the gas mart.

"Howdy to you too," I said with a wide grin on my face as I held the door open for her as she walked inside, the smell of her sweet perfume hit my nostrils.

"Oh, you're quite the gentleman," she said.

"Hands on," I replied.

Her jeweled skull and crossbones belt buckle also caught my eye. I have to say, "I had never seen a pair of jeans fit a woman's ass so perfectly," I thought as she passed me by. I have to say; it is at this point all thoughts of the cashier became obsolete in my mind.

I think this stranger must have known I was still looking because she turned around and smiled at me tilting her black Stetson as she walked over to the cooler.

And that is when I noticed also, she had a smile like one of those girls on a fucking television commercial all white and pearly.

But as I stated, I had business elsewhere and the thing on my back whispered in my ear with cold breath I no longer had the luxury to linger around and watch the show.

I filled up my truck and just as I was getting ready to leave the gas stop, I observed Ms. Cowgirl exiting the gas mart, I tried to be discreet as I watched her walk over to a black Econoline van with tinted windows where this muscle head was putting gas into its tank.

"The pretty ones always go for the losers," I thought as I got into my truck and began pulling out the gas station lot.

Trying to be inconspicuous as (it) told me not to linger.

But I made it my business to pull over close to the van to get one more look at her before I exited the lot.

When I looked up in my rear-view mirror, I caught a reflection of her staring at my truck as I exited the lot. It must have been a trick of the light because her eyes almost seemed to be illuminating amber in the reflection.

The first drops of rain began to fall, hitting my windshield lightly, like I said, today is going to be the first day of a new start for me in my life, or at the very least, I hope so. Oh, by the way, it appears that the van from the gas station is following me.

Oh goody, I have a surprise for them.

Your friend sincerely,

Hands On.

MIDNIGHT RAIN

—⚜—

The torrential rainfall had now been coming down for several days as a posse of five bounty hunters with two prisoners rode their horses through the tumultuous weather to get to the town of Red Rock, New Mexico.

They had a bounty to collect of one-thousand dollars a head on the two alleged cattle rustlers and murdering thieves the Chantling brothers, Rickie, and Monroe from El Paso Texas.

The five men in the posse made up of Charley, a rancher and farmer from Arizona, Sanders, a thief himself turned bounty hunter, Peck from Nebraska - a former miner, and Tito, and their leader Eli Boone both ex-soldiers in the Civil War (on the same side of course) and farmers themselves.

All men from different backgrounds but with one thing in common for sure: they were all hardened cowboys and quick and handy with their pistols and had somehow come together to pursue one common interest – bounties.

This posse had been riding their horses for days now with no sign of rest when they stumbled onto a small and desolate town outside of Amarillo Texas that was not on the map a town named Solemn Creek.

Eli looked at the town's welcome sign through a pair of small binoculars he kept in his saddle bag.

"Let's get these horses dry, fed, rested, and some grub in our bellies, and we can start up tomorrow," Eli ordered.

"Sounds like a plan to me. I am tired of riding wet balls in a saddle," replied Sanders, as he pulled back on the reins of his horse to settle him.

"Solemn Creek, what in the wurl kind of name is that for a town?" asked Charley as he spit some of the tobacco he was chewing on the ground. "Yeah, it ain't that inspirational is it?" Tito stated frowning.

One of the Chantling brothers started laughing that was riding rope saddle and shotgun under the watchful eye of Eli's men.

"What's so damn funny?" Charley asked, eyes narrowing.

"I be damned, I ain't never heard a nigger be so ambidextrous with the white man's language, have you, Ricky?" Monroe said grinning.

"Can't say I have," answer Rickie with a tobacco stain and missing teeth grin.

"You do know what that word ambidextrous mean don't you boy?" Monroe, said, taunting Tito.

Tito rode his horse over to Monroe and put his shotgun underneath the rustler's chin and unsheathed his blade from his scabbard strap around his leg and stuck it in Monroe's gut.

"Blow your cracker brains out while gutting you at the same time boy?"

Fear formed in Monroe's eyes as he looked into Tito's and seen that this was a man highly capable of doing just what he said he would do and no doubt with little or no remorse.

Monroe broke into a crooked smile.

"Why's I believe you got it, no need for unnecessary violence," he answer back - conceding.

"Well you keep flapping those cracker gums boy, and I am gone blow out your cracker brains, do you understand?" Tito asked.

"Compren'da amigo," Monroe said, still smiling.

"You kill my brother, you're going to have to kill me too boy," Rickie chimed in.

Tito turns around and looks at Rickie.

"Well that was the plan - boy," Tito said bluntly.

The rest of the posse laughed, but Rickie Chantling did not find it all that amusing.

"Fucking bushwhackers," he said, with disdain.

"You two are lucky you are two-thousand dollars' worth of dumbness," said Eli to the Chantling brothers.

"Well our Mammy always said we were blessed," answer Monroe, looking over at Tito for a reaction, he got none just a cold dead stare back from him.

"You ain't gone to be such a smart ass when your neck's at the other end of a rope boy," Peck pointed out.

"You know I'll cross that road when I get to it Mister," said Monroe.

"Oh, you're getting to it fast," Eli assured him.

"Boys let's pay Ole' Solemn a visit shall we," Eli said, as they all set mounted on their horses on a ridge staring at the mysterious town below them in the valley.

"Sounds good, like I said, I need to get my sack dry," Sanders grumbled.

"Will you please stop yakking about those wet balls, Sanders," Charley protested.

"Yeah as soon as they get dry," Sanders replied.

Peck chuckled at his compadres antics.

"Hey, you two clowns cut the horse shit and keep your eyes wide-open we still don't know jack rabbit shit about this town we are riding into and why it's not on the map," said Eli wiping the rain out of his eyes.

The two of them nodded apologetically at Eli out of respect.

"Okay let's go," Eli commanded.

Eli and Tito took the lead as they all rode down to the town of Solemn Creek against the sound of the pouring rain and crackling thunder. Their horses' hooves beat the muddy dirt, sloshing through the treacherous terrain, down to a town that was mysteriously not on their map down to a town that was so far at least to them - unknown.

As they rode their horses through the dirt road into Solemn Creek, they could not help but notice how eerily quiet it was on the dirt streets of the town even the Saloon seemed empty which they all knew was uncommon for any town large or small on the weekend.

After all, that was the place where most locals raised hell on a Saturday and were in church on a Sunday to repent for their rousing rebel ways.

"I don't like this Eli, this town is so quiet it might as well be dead," Tito said observantly.

"You might be right about that Tito, but do you smell that stench in the air?" Eli said, with a scowl on his face.

"Like a hot pot of chitlin's," Tito replied back.

"Goddamn what they paved this street with horse shit?" said Sanders holding and pinching his nose.

A young man suddenly appeared out of the darkness of teenage years from one of the structures on the dirt street; he was dressed in old worn out clothes with a floppy hat on his head.

"Hey Mister, can I help y'all?" he yelled out to the strangers on horseback as he looked at them with one hand over his eyes to block the rain coming down.

"Yeah, we need to get bunkered down for the night and get these horses fed and out of this weather," said Eli.

"Okay," answers the young man as he continued staring up at them.

A few minutes pass by, and he had said nothing else, he continued staring up at them strangely.

"What's wrong with that boy, is he short a tater or two?" Charley asked.

"Maybe," Sanders replied, as he eyeballed the young man suspiciously.

Eli finally broke the uncomfortable silence between them and the boy.

"So, boy are you going to stand up there and get drenched staring, or are you going to direct us to where we can get a hot meal and a bunk for tonight," he said.

"Sir if I was you…"

"Aiden get those horses in a stable and send them gentlemen over here!" interrupted and commanded a voice in the distance.

"Peck give 'em a hand," ordered Eli.

Eli and his men dismounted from their horses and took what was important to them out of their saddle bags before they made their way over to the voice with prisoners in tow behind them, that had instructed the boy to stable their horses.

The voice had come from the silhouette that Eli had made out standing in front of the doorway of the Saloon and the closer he got, he saw that the silhouette was a pretty young woman in a white dress maybe in her twenties at the most.

"Greetings, y'all the law," she asked, looking at the two men with them bound with rope around their wrists.

"Good evening to you ma'am I guess you could say that. These two fine fellas got a date with the hangman's noose in Red Rock, New Mexico, and we gonna make sure they get there promptly."

"Is that a fact," she asked.

"Yep, that's a fact," Eli answered.

"And who do I have the pleasure of conversing with?" Eli inquired.

"My name's Charity and that boy out there is Aiden that took your horses in, but he's a little touch if you get my drift," she said.

"I told you that boy was on the short coach," Charley said, to Sanders.

"Well, thank you for your hospitality Charity. I will gladly be willing to make your acquaintance and introduce you to the rest of my posse once we get out of this unforgiven weather."

"What about those two," Charity asked, looking over at the Chantling brothers who were eyeballing her intensely with grins on their wet faces.

"Ms. Charity, can you inform your sheriff that we might need use of his jail for tonight?"

"The sheriff's not here, he's out of town," she said.

"What about your deputy?"

"Him too."

"You telling us you ain't got no law in this one-stable horseshit town?" Monroe asked, wringing the rain water out of his scraggily beard.

"We do now," Charity said looking at Eli and his men.

Monroe and his brother started laughing.

"No dandelion, what'cha got yourself here is a bunch of blue bellies and a nigger!" he said.

Tito quickly went across Monroe's jaw with the butt of his rifle knocking out the last rotting teeth he probably had in his mouth. The blow also sent Monroe straight to the ground as he grabbed his jaw in pain spitting up blood and teeth chips.

His brother Rickie lunged towards Tito in his defense only to be knocked out cold by the butt of a rifle to the back of his head by Charley.

"Fucking nigger broke my jaw!" Monroe bawled as Eli's men help him to his feet.

"You better shut that white trashy mouth of yours son, before you be making the hangman's noose early," Eli warned again.

"That ain't nothing but vigilante justice; you heard him dandelion."

"I'll have Aiden show you where the jail's at so these boys can get a good night's sleep," Charity said.

"Thanks Dandelion, that's mighty white of you," Monroe said sarcastically.

"Get that turd up off the ground," Eli ordered, pointing at Rickie who was slowly starting to recover.

"Goddamitt how am I supposed to eat now?" asked Monroe holding his jaw.

"Suck it up through your ass now, it ain't no differ," Tito said.

Charley, Sander's and Peck all chuckled.

"Aiden show these men where the jailhouse is and come right back and get something hot in your stomach," Charity said.

"Yes ma'am," responded Aiden.

Eli and Tito followed Charity into the Saloon while Sanders and Charlie on Eli's orders escorted the reluctant Chantling brothers to the town's jailhouse for their evening quarters.

* * *

In the darkness of the night hidden in the shadows, two adolescent children, a girl, and a boy no more than ten years of age watched the arrival of the new strangers in their town with the intensity and focus of a wolf watching a rabbit through eyes the color of midnight.

It had been a long time since the both of them had been fed and they could smell the warm blood pumping through the veins of the strangers as their mouths watered in delight and their little bellies grumbled for the divine meal soon to come.

"If y'all need a bed and a bath, it's a hotel two buildings over, Mr. Buckley and his wife Mildred run that operation."

"Much obliged, thank you ma'am " said Eli.

"Can I get you gentleman something to drink?" Charity asked as she walked behind the bar.

"Yeah, two whiskeys," Eli said, taking in his surroundings.

"Where's everybody at?" Tito asks as he looked around at the empty Saloon except for their presence.

"I guess the bad weather got's everybody hunkered down for the night," she answer as she poured the two men two shots of whiskey.

"Is that so?" said Tito as he looked around the empty bar suspiciously.

"Yep, that's so Mister?"

"Tito," he corrected, looking at her with equal suspicion.

"Tito," repeated Charity.

The two men threw back the shots of whiskey and Charity refilled their empty glasses as soon as they hit the bar counter.

"How old are you, Charity?" Eli asked.

"Old enough to breed Mr. Eli," she said.

"And how old that might be?"

"Nineteen, in fact, it seems like I've been nineteen for a long time now," she reflected, as she threw back a shot of whiskey, she poured for herself.

"Oh," Eli said quietly to himself because he thought she was much older.

"It's too damn quiet around here," Tito whispered to Eli.

"How do we get some food around here?" Eli inquired.

"It ain't much, but I can whip y'all up some beans and pork with some yellow bread," Charity proposed.

"Ms. Charity, our bellies would be most thankful," Eli said.

"What them two men do that you have in your custody?" she asks.

"Oh, those two fine upstanding citizens, they ain't nothing but cattle thieves and cold-blooded murderers," Eli answer back.

"And I take it there is a bounty on their heads?"

"Dead or alive," Eli replied.

"Girl, you always so nosy?" Tito said.

"No, just curious," Charity said, smiling.

"The same damn thing," Tito replied.

"He sure is a friendly son of a gun," Charity said as she looked over at Tito.

"Overly," said Eli with a grin.

"What in the hell's taking Peck so long?" Tito asked.

"Speak of the devil," Eli said as Peck came walking through the saloon doors drench and soaking wet.

"Goddamitt, is this monsoon ever going to let up?" he said, as he walked over towards the bar and took off his cowboy hat, beating it against his leg to get some of the rain out of it, and then plop it back on his head.

"I'll take one of those if you don't mind," he said to Charity pointing at the whiskey in the shot glasses as he set some coins down on the bar to pay for his drink.

"Coming up," said Charity as she took up the coins.

Peck looked around at all the empty chairs and tables in the saloon.

"Where the hell is everybody, church?" he asked, curious.

"Looks like it," Tito answer, shaking his head sideways.

"Man, that's one strange boy, hardly had two words to say to me when we were putting up the horses," Peck whispered to Eli and Tito.

"How so?" said Eli.

"I don't know, it was like he wanted to say something but just couldn't muster up enough nerve to do so," Peck said.

As Charity set Peck's whiskey down, all of the three men went dead quite.

"I'll round up some grub for you and your men," Charity said.

"Much obliged," Eli responded.

"Well for starters I asked him where his Pa was? And he said he don't know," Peck said.

"Is that so," said Eli as he listened intently.

"I then asked, well where's you and your sister's Ma?"

"He said that ain't my sister, Mister, and I ain't got no (Ma) no more," Peck said, nodding in the direction of were Charity had exited.

"That sounds like more than Two-words to me," said Tito.

"Point taken asshole," Peck said as he tossed back his whiskey.

"What I am saying is, I almost had to dig a corpse's grave to get any-thing outta the boy," Peck said.

"Is that right," replied Eli as he swirled a toothpick in his mouth.

"You damn right Eli, something's not right about this place," Peck stressed.

"I was saying the same damn thing myself," said Tito.

Eli could feel it in the air also, something that did not sit quite well with him about this town, the minute they rode into it, but the truth was he felt this way for the sake of caution about every town they rode into, but this time something was different as if the danger was more imminent.

"We'll rotate sleep shifts, keep your eyes and ears open, we leave at sunrise gentlemen," he said.

"Sounds good to me," agreed Peck.

Tito nodded okay, but in his head, he thought the sooner, the damn better.

"Hot grub coming up, make y'all self-comfortable at any table," yelled out Charity as she carried plates of food.

"Make sure y'all get some food down at the jailer for Charley, Sanders and those two assholes and fill them 'em in on what's going on," instructed Eli.

"No problem, boss," said Peck.

"What the hell," said Eli as he drew his shotgun quickly and his men drew their weapons just as swiftly as something shot passed them at lighting fast speed like a blur and ran into one of the corridors of the saloon, followed by childlike giggling and laughter.

"What in the hell was that noise?" Eli asked startle.

"Yeah, don't mind them, in this town the children tend to sleep during the day and play at night," said Charity as she set the food down on the table.

"Well that don't make no rabbit ass sense, children ought to be in bed at this time of night, not running around playing Hide & Seek in a goddamn saloon," said Tito.

"I agree with you Mr. Tito, but that's just the way it is, here in Solemn Creek,"

"Well, them two little goblins can play Jack & Jill for all I care I am about to dig into these beans and pork," said Peck.

Tito went over to the area in the saloon that he had seen them run through.

"Where in the hell did, they go? They are not here," he asked confused.

"No telling," Charity answered back nonchalantly.

Tito and Peck looked at each other and read the suspicion on each other's faces as they looked back at Charity and then Peck stuffing his face with beans, pork, and yellow bread.

"Are you two cowpokes gonna let your food get cold?" she said.

"Food?" Eli said, as if he had forgotten it was there on the table or maybe he was just now awestruck by Charity's alabaster complexion that he had not noticed before, as she was quite pretty.

He noted the last time he had seen a complexion like hers was on an embalmed corpse. "Did the Lord's sun not shine it's grace on this place," he wondered as he continued to stare at her ghastly pallor?

"No, much obliged for the food," he said snapping out of his trance-like state.

"No worries, I am sure you and your men will square up with us before sunset," she said smiling.

"We will," said Eli as he went over to the table to join Peck in some fine dining on beans, pork, and yellow cornbread.

"You boys go ahead and eat; I'll have Aiden take some food over to your men at the jailhouse."

"Thank you, Ms. Charity, you're too kind," said Eli.

The three of them at the table watched as discreetly as they could as the boy Aiden entered the saloon and he and Charity conversed, but they could not make out what they were saying to each other because their voices were barely above a whisper.

Charity took off the apron from around her dress and hung it up on a post behind the bar.

"I am retiring for the night, gentlemen, if you don't mind, but before I do so, I will inform the Buckley's that y'all will be checking in shortly for some rooms," Charity said.

"Please do," said Eli, tipping his cowboy hat in gratitude.

Charity looked around the bar and she could sense all the men's eyes at the table follow her as she did so.

"Eli, you and your men are welcome to drink what you want, I am sure you will square up with us before sunset," she said again.

"So, I've been told," Eli said with a wink.

Charity cracks a half smile at Eli's response, and then she and Aiden exited the Saloon with covered food in hand.

"I don't trust that bitch," said Tito.

"Me neither," agreed Eli.

"I second that motion, but those beans were sure tasty," Peck said as he swiped the small piece of yellow bread in the last bean juice he had on his plate and plopped it in his mouth.

"You two check out that so-called hotel next door while I go down to the jailhouse and check on Charley and Sanders," Eli said.

"Do you want me to go with you Eli?" asked Tito.

"No, I'll be alright."

"I'll meet you two back at the hotel next door in about twenty minutes."

"And if not?" said Tito.

"Then you know what to do," said Eli as he racked his Winchester.

Tito nodded his head and felt the ivory handle of his pistol.

Hehehehehe – the faint sound of children's laughter could be heard again by the men, but for some reason unexplained, it now made the hairs stand up on their arms like a porcupine's quills on its back.

"You damn brats show yourself!" yelled out Peck.

All of them look around the saloon again three hundred and sixty degrees, searching for the children and the direction their voices came from inside.

"I think I know where they are hiding," Eli whispered as he pointed across the room at a wall.

Eli walked over to one end of the saloon to what he noticed was a closet door that blended in with the wall. Tito and Peck followed behind him.

"You smell that?" Tito said, referring to the awful stench behind the door.

Eli nodded his head yes, as he begins to slowly open the faux wall closet door, they could hear the buzzing of flies, as the glow of the flame from one of the saloon table's oil lamps held by Eli, illuminated the mummified remains of a male corpse stuffed inside the closet.

"Well I'll be damned," Eli blurted out.

"Yep, looks like we found our bartender," Tito said, as he swatted away corpse flies buzzing in front of his face.

"I bet you that prissy bitch knew this poor soul was in here all along," said Peck.

"I don't know, but I am damn sure going to find out," Eli said, as his eyes went to the empty plates on the table, Tito and Peck's eyes followed.

The men then simultaneously stuck their fingers in their throats and began to hurl up all the food that they just consumed onto the saloon's floor, chewed, and digested beans, pork and yellow cornbread that looked and smelled nothing like it did before going into their bellies.

"I knew those beans and pork taste funny, but first, I thought it was just white folks cooking," stated Tito, wiping his mouth off with his sleeve.

"Charley and Sanders, we need to get over to that jail now!" Eli said urgently, remembering Charity and Aiden were delivering them meals over at the jail.

"Poisonous bitch is going to Hang High if something has happened to Charley and Sanders," Peck said angrily.

"Stop your yapping, let's go!" Eli order.

As Eli and his men rushed out of the saloon, the closet door closed shut, by an unseen force, followed by the echo of children's laughter.

* * *

"How y'all going to lock us up in this cell with no sheriff around," asked Monroe, as he stood up looking from behind the bars of the jail cell, he shared with his younger brother Rickie.

"We put the key in and turned the lock," answer Charley as he set at the sheriff's desk reading an old newspaper after finishing his dinner.

Sanders let out a hearty laugh at Charley's response as he sat at an adjacent desk across from the town's sheriff desk that gave him a peripheral view of Monroe and Rickie's temporary living quarters.

"Jackass," said Monroe displease with the answer.

His brother Rickie was stretched out on his back on the wooden jail bench with his arms folded behind his head like he did not have a care in the world.

"Monroe, you might as well be talking to a rock then versing with those two Rhodes Scholars out there," he added.

"I think you might be right little brother," Monroe said, rubbing his sore jaw.

"Them two out there dumber than a pork rind egg sandwich without the crunch," he said.

He then directed his attention back to the two bounty hunters that were guarding him and his brother.

"So, how in the hell are we supposed to protect ourselves if something goes wrong locked up in this cell?" Monroe asked.

"Don't worry we won't let anything happen to you two cow turds, but a good ole' hanging - dandelion," responded Charley, chuckling.

"I graciously decline y'all's protection and prefer you let us out and give us some pistols to defend ourselves, Mr. Charley," Monroe replied.

"Boy, you're denser than a mole hole," said Sanders as he struck a wooden match on the desk and lit his cigarillo.

Ricky chuckled at Sanders' remark about his brother.

A loud pounding on the jail's main door which was locked by two-four by door bolts, interrupted the men's conversation, and brought it to a halt.

"Who is it?" Charley yelled out.

He waited for a minute with all eyes on the door but received no answer back.

"Are you hard of hearing, I said who is it? Goddamitt!" he yelled out angrily the second time.

"Aren't you going to go answer it Ole' Charley boy," Rickie said who had got up off the bench and was now standing beside his brother inside the cell, poking his oily face between the bars.

Charley cut Rickie a mean look before he got up from the desk with his Winchester rifle in hand and made his way over towards the door.

Bam-bam-bam-bam!

"I said hold on, Goddamitt!"

Sanders stood up from his desk with his two six-shooters pointed dead center at the door with his cigarillo smoking, hanging from his mouth.

Charley unbolted the door and slowly opened it with his foot at the bottom of it just in case it was an ambush, he peered out between the crack of the door seeing no one until he looked down at the two cherub faces of the little boy and girl staring up at him, both soaking wet from the rain.

"What in the wurl?" he said.

What'cha two little angels doing out at this time of night?"

The little boy and girl said nothing but only stared at Charley with blank expressions on their alabaster faces.

"What, the cat got y'all tongue? You two come on in from out of that cold downpour," he said.

With that invitation, the two children that could have been fraternal twins stepped inside the jail and out of the rain.

"Looks like big ole bad Charley was scared of two sawed-off gunslingers that come to bust us out little brother," Monroe said laughing.

"Looks like," his brother Rickie echo him.

"Shut the fuck up you two dipshits!" Charley said.

Sanders holstered his pistols and set back down at the desk; he took a fresh cigarillo out of a small canister carried in his pocket and put it in his mouth. He struck another wooden match on the desk, but this time as he did so, his hand grazed across a sharp loose nail instantly lacerating the side of his hand as he screamed out in pain.

"Goddamitt!" he shrieked in pain.

"You gonna need a Tetanus shot for that boy!" Monroe said grinning.

"Yeah, I hope your hand doesn't rot and fall off," Rickie chimed in with a grin.

Charley ignored the brothers taunting as the blood flowed from the open wound of his hand, the children's eyes unknown to all of them were fixated on that blood that now flowed freely like sweet nectar to them from a honeycomb.

And just as Charley brought his hand to his mouth to suck the blood out of it, the boy leaped from across the room like a wild animal and grabbed Charley's hand and bit down into it like a little beast penetrating flesh and bone.

"You little shit!" Charley screamed out as a backhand from him to the boy's jaw sent the child sprawled out to the floor.

"No need for that, we got some left-over beans and pork if yaws children are hungry," said Sanders as he picked the plate of his leftovers off the desk and showed it to the boy's sister?

She was over to Sanders as quickly as her brother had attacked his partner Charley, but what the little girl did next shocked Sanders when she slapped the plate of food out of his hand, sending it and its contents scattered to the floor.

"You little pissant that was plain rude I ought to take you over my knee and…" Sanders, suddenly froze, as he watched the innocent features to the little girl's face change into that of something else.

Something evil.

Sanders reached to unholster his pistols but was not as quick as the little creature that lunged at him and was now on his neck with its fangs deeply embedded in his jugular. And although it was small, it was unnaturally powerful as it took Sanders down to the floor as it ripped the rest of his throat apart as Charley and the Chantling brothers watched in shock and horror!

"What are you waiting for, shoot that sonofabitch!" Monroe yelled out.

Charley aimed his rifle at the back of the creatures head, but just as he pulled the trigger, the boy jumped on his back and sank his teeth into the side of Charley's neck causing his rifle to go up and turn as he got a shot off.

The boy creature, claws dug into Charley's eyeballs as he fought to get the little hellion off his back. He now felt himself fading as the creature drained the life force (his blood) out of his body.

"Fuck you! You little bastard," Charley said, as he put his rifle in his mouth and pulled the trigger blowing his brains and the boy creature's eyeball out at the same time.

The creature fell off his back writhing and snarling in pain, as Charley fell to the floor dead.

Monroe laid dead in the cell with a smoldering hole in the middle of his forehead after being accidentally shot by the first bullet that was discharged from Charley's rifle, as his younger brother Rickie wept over his body.

"That sounds like gunshots!" Eli said as he and his other men rushed over to an old building with a sheriff's sign mounted below its eaves.

Eli and his men, with their weapons drawn, entered the jailhouse cautiously once they made their way to the entrance.

"Charley, Sanders!" Eli shouted out as they entered into a scene of carnage.

"Holy Mother Mary what happened here?" Peck said.

"Looks like a slaughter," Tito replied.

"I only heard two shots though," Eli said, as he inspected the dead bodies of one of his men.

Tito kneeled over Sanders examining his dead body.

"Eli, I don't know what to make of this?" he said, confused.

"What do you mean?" Eli asked as he walked over to Tito.

"Who would rip out a man's throat," Tito responded.

"Get me the fuck outta here before they come back!" Rickie screamed out from inside the cell in fear as he shook the bars violently.

"Who's they, Rickie?" Eli said, walking over to the cell.

"The children, they did this" Rickie said as his eyes slowly went up to the ceiling, Eli's and the others followed.

"How in the tarnation did you two get up there?" Peck said.

The two children scrambled to another corner of the cathedral ceiling, defying the laws of gravity, hissing, as their pupils illuminated in the dark like the creatures of the night that they had become.

"What in the fuck?" Peck said jumping back startled.

"I don't think those things are children," Tito said softly.

"Kill 'em!" Eli screams out.

As they all let loose with a blaze of gunfire, the creatures dodged the bullets with supernatural speed as they ran upside down on the ceiling. The boy and girl creature then went in for the attack as they dropped down from the ceiling towards Eli and his men with the same lighting fast agility that they had taken out Charley and Sanders with, unfazed and not slowed down by the bullets ripping through their unholy flesh.

Tito threw his rifle to the floor, smashed one of the desk chairs and broke off its wooden leg, he took out his pistol and shot a piece of the wood off the end giving it a sharper edge. The boy creature, when it landed turn in his direction, snarled, display animal-like canines and went in for the attack! Tito impaled the creature with the chair leg through its chest as it screamed out in agony before bursting into flames and disintegrating to ashes, leaving only a skull behind, right before all of their eyes.

"What in the hell?" Eli said, shocked.

The girl creature snarled and jumped through the glass window shattering it, as a hail of lead followed her escaping the fate of her brother.

Eli turns to Tito.

"How the hell did you know?" Eli asked.

"My grandmother use to tell me stories of the Tikoloshe that fed on the blood of children in her village," he said.

"Tikoloshe?"

"Yes, here in America I believe y'all call them vampires," Tito said.

"I told you those little murdering bastards was monsters!" Rickie bellowed.

"That piece of turd doesn't look like he got killed by no vampire," Peck said, looking through the bars at Rickie's dead brother, with the bullet hole in his head, and now pale as a ghost.

"He didn't, Sanders accidentally shot him in the head while that little demon bitch was ripping out his windpipe," Rickie explained, distraught.

"Is that so?" Eli said.

"You damn Skippy, now are you clueless bastards going to let me out this cell or what?"

"Let this weasel dick out," Eli said, as he tossed the jail key at one of his men.

"Bullets don't seem to affect these things much, so we gonna need some more of these stakes Eli in case we run into her kinfolk," Tito said.

"You heard the man break off some more of these chairs, broomsticks, anything that we can make into stakes to defend ourselves!" Eli ordered.

Eli's men began smashing up the chairs and removing the chair legs carving the end of the legs with sharp bowie knives into a point.

As they were finishing up, the sound of their horses in distress accompanied by an inhuman shrilling noise like they never heard before stopped them in their tracks.

"They know that we know," Tito said.

"The horses!" Eli said.

"Can I get a gun?" Rickie asked nervously.

"Boy have you been listening?" Peck said.

"Well if I shoot out their eyeballs, they can't see to bite me," Rickie answer.

"Yeah, but they sure can smell your dumbass!" Tito said as he handed Rickie off a wooden stake.

"Well I never said I had all the answers," Rickie said.

"We need to get our horses and get the hell outta this town," said Eli.

"That's the smartest thing I heard all night," agreed Rickie.

"And what about my brother Monroe," he asked.

"He won't mind, he's dead," Eli answered.

"That's not what I meant," said Rickie flatly.

"You sure we can't leave him behind boss," Peck said, referring to Rickie.

"No, he still worth something even if he's just a lowlife lying piece of cattle thieving murdering piece of horseshit," Eli said.

"Can you be more descriptive," Rickie asked him.

As the men slowly entered the stable, they now saw what all the fuss was as they all froze in disbelief at the site of Charity, Aiden, and the little girl all feasting on their horses. Only three of the horses were still alive.

"Fucking bloodsuckers!" Peck shouted out! As he started firing in their direction, all three of them scatter and ran for cover in the shadows of the stable.

"Get the rest of these horses out and burn this sonofabitch down to the ground!" Eli said.

"That's a slow burn with this rain," Tito pointed out.

"Well, I am not sticking around to find out, are you?" Eli said.

The horses neighed and buckled as the men gathered them up and escorted them out to safety.

Peck threw the lit lantern on the floor of the barn as it slowly caught fire to some hay and begin to burn.

"We need something stronger to get this fire going," Tito said.

"It will burn, let's go," said Eli.

Outside, Eli and his men saddled and mounted the last three horses as they prepared to leave Solemn Creek.

Rickie rode piggyback on Peck's horse.

Eli looked over at the saloon as he gathered the reins up to his steed in his hands.

"That's where all our problems started gentlemen," he said.

"Well let's burn that sonofabitch down too," Peck said.

"Let me have the honors, in my brother's memory," Rickie insisted, as he unmounted Peck's horse.

Eli tossed Rickie a box of wooden matches which he caught.

"Don't be long," he said.

The three of them watched on horseback as Rickie entered the saloon.

Less than a minute had passed when they all seen the first flames erupt inside the Saloon through its stained windows.

"Good job shit stain," Peck said.

The saloon doors opened, but it was not Rickie that walked out, it was Charity and what Charity was carrying in one hand made Eli and his men's jaws go slack, Rickie's decapitated head!

Charity tossed Rickie's head to the ground as she confronted Eli and his men.

"Mr. Eli, y'all wasn't going to leave without squaring up, first, was you?" she asked.

"Under the circumstances - yes," Eli responded.

Charity laughed. "Well I am sorry if we have not been as hospitable as you expected."

"Overly," said Eli, as he looked up at the roof of the saloon and seen the little girl sitting there staring down on him and his men with cold dark eyes.

Charity looked up at her and waved at the girl. It waves back.

"Oh, don't mind little Tessie, she can't wait to rip y'all throats out for what you did to her brother."

"I see you are raising her right," Eli said.

Charity laughed again.

"I try."

"Of course, it's hard with so many other children and mouths to feed,"

"Somehow I am sure you manage," Eli said, spitting his chew to the ground.

"I do," she said.

Eli and his men slowly turned around and see that they are flanked by at least ten other children in the rear of them. All dark silhouettes of various sizes and ages waiting silently in the dark, waiting silently for the command from their Countess, Countess Charity.

"I see," said Eli.

"Good, so shall we square up now Mr. Eli?"

"Much obliged," Eli said, holding his shotgun in one hand and the stake in the other.

Charity smiled, and this time Eli did indeed notice her perfect row of vampiric teeth illuminating in the darkness, on her pretty ghastly face, an illusory mask in place of grim finality through the unrelenting haze of the midnight rain.

THEY CALL IT IZZY

THE BEGINNING

The large cockroach scurries along the floor of the dark room of the abandoned house in search of food and water amongst all the trash and other litter scattered about on its decrepit floors. Old and used drug paraphernalia brought in by addicts using the house as a drug den also decorates the interior of its numerous rooms floors.

The musty stench of decay and decadence hangs in the air of the abandoned house that was once inhabited by several generations of families, busy with the noise of births, birthdays, and even deaths. But that was the past this is now, soon the relic-like home in the not so good neighborhood, which people like to coin as the "Other side of town," will eventually be condemned by the City of New Orleans and razed like similar and other homes within the vicinity.

The cockroach now nibbles on an old piece of dried up pizza crust as its antennae flicker back and forth feeling and smelling out its environment, as another nocturnal creature now appears out of one of the numerous holes in the room's baseboards. It stands up on its hind legs sniffs the stale air with its pink nose and pinpoints the tasty little treat that the roach has discovered. The rat now runs along the floorboard in the direction of the cockroach for a two-in-one meal. The roach senses that it's in danger and dashes off quickly with a tiny piece of the pizza crust still in its mouth. The rat follows suit as it watches the roach run into one of the holes in the wall. The hole is small, but the rat pushes its head thru first now attempting to squeeze the rest of its body thru the wall hole, when something bites its nose, it lets out a squeak!

Another bite, squeak, then another, squeak! Something crawls into its mouth, large wet and slimy, the rats incisor-like teeth crush it spewing out its pus-like insides into its mouth, but then another one comes, trapping the first one in the rat's throat before its able to digest it completely, proceeded by another parasitic invader and so on and so on.

The rat now has a horde of carnivorous invaders inside of its mouth and throat all fighting for space, cutting off its air supply as it struggles to breathe. The rodent's hairless tail does one last death wiggle before the rest of its body is snatched inside of the hole by its new-found friends.

The large bait roach from its colony finishes up the last of the pizza crust and joins in for a more furry and tastier meal.

INTRODUCTION

Two junkies now enter the abandoned home to shoot up their dope then afterward sleep off their high. They walk over to a corner of the house, sit down and begin taking their drugs out. The male takes a clear plastic bag filled with what looks like white crystals out of his jacket as his female companion looks eagerly on.

It is cold inside of the abandoned house, but that is of little concern to them right now as she rubs her hands together in anticipation of her hit on the glass dope pipe. She watches as her boyfriend takes a long drag on the pipe, inhaling the vapors of the crystal meth inside. "Stop fucking around and let me hit that glass dick baby," she said. Her companion looks at her wild-eyed as he hands her over the pipe. "I wish you stop saying that kind of shit it makes me feel weird," he said.

She lit up the meth from the base of the pipe and took a long drag herself, inhaling the vapors, and laughed. "You sure it's not all this good dope going to your brain making you paranoid babycakes?"

The both of them looked as if they had not slept or bathe for days.

The boyfriend scratched the open meth sores on the side of his face and his neck with his fingers.

"All I am saying "is" that if that (glass pipe) is a dick that would make me a "Homo" and I don't appreciate that shit," he said annoyed, as he snatches the drug paraphernalia out her hands. His companion eyes rolled back in her head as she laughs because she knew how to push his buttons.

"Calm down baby, it's not my fault you got skills," she said, as she proceeded to imitate performing fellatio with her mouth and hand while making slurping sounds.

"Fuck you," he said as he sucks on the glass meth pipe.

She smiled and looked at him, coyly. "After I hit that glass dick homophobe."

"You are one twisted fuck baby," he said with a grin on his face.

"Yeah, but you like it and this stinky stink," she said, as she rubs her groin and then begins to remove her clothes.

In the distance of the house, something watches them, in a corner, patiently, its eyes glowing ambiently in the darkness, waiting its turn to bring the two of them back into a whole new, different kind of reality, a grim one.

After they have their way with each other, it will have its way with them. And not in the nicest manner. Because visible on the wall above them as they engage in a drug-infused passion of intimacy are the words written in dried blood "Beware of Izzy," A warning they should have taken more seriously.

CHAPTER ONE

Sam felt as if she would never stop falling, but when she finally did. The dark lake water felt like she had fallen thru concrete before plummeting straight into its cold abyss.

The temperature in her body immediately started to drop once she hit the cold water that couldn't have been any warmer than thirty-six degrees. Sam knock-out by the fall begins to descend to the bottom of the lake inadvertently taking in gulps of lake water, she begins the process of drowning, when suddenly her eyes pop open into the hazy darkness. Instinct now kicks in as she held her breath and began swimming to the top of the lake. That's when she hears another splash, in the water and a growl.

The creature was still in pursuit of her and now swimming in her direction, its amber eyes eerily glowing luminescent in the dark. Sam had reached the top of the lake now but was still disorientated; from the fall.

As Sam struggles to get her balance and composure back, she suddenly heard someone calling out her name in the darkness of the night. All she had to do now Sam thought, was follow the direction of that person's voice, back to safety.

The earthy taste of the lake water filled her mouth and nostrils as she swam faster back towards the shoreline. Sam was almost there when suddenly something grabbed her ankle from behind and began pulling her back deeper into the lake, deeper into the darkness.

Sam screamed out in shock as she attempted to wiggle free of its vice-like grip, as its claws dug into the flesh of her ankles. She kicked one more time, and her foot made contact with its eye causing it to release her ankle. Sam took off swimming again and made it back to the shoreline. As she emerges out of the lake wet and cold, she could now see familiar faces although they were blurred waiting for her in the distance, it was her mom Gina, Sheriff Alvarez, and Cody Smith. "Sam watch out!" her mom shouted out. But it was too late as the big creature reached the shoreline behind her grabbing her by the collar. Sam turned around to face the creature and was met by the amber eyes of a killer by the eyes of a werewolf. Her scream was, just a gulp in her throat, which never came out not even when she woke up.

Sam wiped the cold sweat from her face as she looked over at the alarm clock on her nightstand that illuminated in red digital numbers, it was 4:00 "am." In the morning.

The sleeping pills that she had taken last night was not working, and she would have to ask her doctor for something stronger she concluded. Sam looked over beside her and noticed her boyfriend Brandon was still sound asleep. She rubbed her fingers thru his thick brown hair, staring at him in the dark. Brandon was always a sound sleeper she had noted, but of course, he did not have to deal with the visions and nightmares that had plagued her ever since she had left Harper Creek four years ago and taken a job in Chicago either. Sam could not help but harbor a jealous sense of envy of him in that respect, although she knew it was not his fault.

Sam quietly got out of the bed and made her way into the kitchen area of the spacious and comfy loft that she rented on the north side of Chicago in Lincoln Square.

She walked over to her kitchen counter and removed one of the small teacups that dangled off the rack mounted above the counter. Sam placed a small chamomile teabag that she had retrieved from a tea jar on the counter inside the cup, poured a small amount of water from a bottle into the cup and placed it inside her microwave. The microwave made a beeping sound as Sam pressed the buttons on its keypad to heat up the cup of tea.

The skyline of the Chicago river reflected thru her glass living room doors that gave access to an upper patio providing her with a spectacular view. Sam may have been a long way from home and the mountains of South Dakota, but in a way, she could not explain how she felt not oddly at all at home in Illinois.

The microwave beeped alerting Sam that her tea was now ready as she sat at the island bar in her kitchen in front of her laptop going over a news story that she was writing for her paper "The Night Turner Tribune." Sam felt something soft brush up against her leg as she got off the bar stool to get her tea. "Meow." It was a long-haired tabby she named Hi-Cee because of its orange coat. A rescue cat that she had adopted from the local shelter. She picked up Hi-Cee off the floor, cuddling the cat in her arms as she rubbed its fur.

"What's wrong boy? Are you in the mood for morning brunch," she said.

"Meow," answer Hi-Cee as it looked up at her with big green eyes that reminded her of bright green emeralds.

"Okay, boy I'll see what mommy can scrounge you up," Sam said, as she sat the cat down.

Hi-Cee bolted towards the glass patio doors as soon as its paws touch the loft's shiny wood floors.

Sam shook her head sideways as she watched her cat now scratching on the glass doors whining to get out. "Just like most men, you can't make up your mind what you want huh boy?" Sam said as she walked over to her patio doors to let Hi-Cee out for some fresh morning air.

The cat shot through the patio doors as Sam opened them and jumped up on one of the patio chairs. Sam took a sip of the hot tea that she had retrieved from the microwave that contrasted with the cool wind coming off the Chicago lakefront. A lone figure of someone standing across the street in front of her loft caught Sam eye. She gave a friendly wave to the stranger who's dark silhouette she could barely make out because of the morning mist still in the air, and the fact it was still dawn.

The stranger did not respond but just stood there staring in Sam's direction. Sam was sure whoever that person was, could see her, and she now began to feel creeped out about their presence.

"Are you okay?" he asks, slightly startling her from behind. It was Brandon. Sam turned to face him and gave him a peck on the lips.

"Good Morning babe, I am fine. But maybe we should ask our friend across the street," Sam said.

"What are you talking about babe, there's no one there," Brandon said.

Sam quickly turned back around, Brandon was right there wasn't anyone across the street. Somehow her gazer had disappeared quietly into the streets of Lincoln Park, as quickly as they had appeared.

"I swear someone was there," Sam said confused.

"Hey, it could have been just a drunk or some kid playing a prank," Brandon said, trying to offer Sam some reasonable explanation.

"I guess so," Sam said still surveying the streets for her ominous gawker.

Brandon could still see that Sam was still slightly disturbed by the incident as he rubbed the side of her arm.

"Hey look, Sam, if you want me to go down and take a look around outside, I can do that babe," he offered.

Sam thought about his proposal for a moment, what was she doing to herself, to them? She thought. "Nah, that's okay babe, whoever it was is probably long gone by now, and it might be what you said it was," Sam's mouth stated, but her brain was telling her better. Anyway, she thought it was best now to change the subject.

"Hey, babe you want some tea?" Sam ask.

"Sure," Brandon said as he stared at Sam wondering how someone could still be so damn beautiful so early in the morning.

Brandon watched Sam as she walked over to the kitchen in his shirt to make him some tea, he loved how his shirt seemed to hug her ass, the creases in the shirt moving symmetrically with every stride her long legs took towards the kitchen. How did he get so damn lucky he wonders? As, he watched Sam make his tea.

"Cream and sugar?"

"Just sugar," Brandon responded.

But if anyone were to ask Sam she would have said; she was the lucky one. When the two first met thru mutual friends, Sam had to admit to herself it was not exactly "love" at first sight for either one of them, but they knew it was something there between them, a spark that could maybe become a flame or an explosion. His first impression of Sam was that she was tough and driven and spoke her mind. And boy, was he right on the money about the third assumption.

He was impressed that she had come down to a tough city like Chicago to pursue her career in journalism if you could survive on the streets of Chicago his attitude was you could survive anywhere. He should know, being that he was a war veteran of Desert Storm and now a two-year rookie officer on the Chicago Police Department who was up against a different kind of war that now infested the streets of the City most people still knew affably as "Shy-town."

But Brandon Crust was different because every decision he had made during his adult life was by choice, not a necessity. At least in the aspect that most people make decisions in their lives. Because, unlike most cops on "the job" he had been born into a life of privilege, in Chicago's Old Town where one- million dollar homes were about as common as caviar were as an appetizer and cocaine was as Chanel.

His father Jonathan Crust was a well-known bigwig and shot caller in the world of finance in Chicago. A Banker by trade he had founded his own company Crust Holdings LLC. Which had its stake in real estate, restaurants, entertainment and anything else that the Senior Crust thought could generate him a buck or two? There had even been some rumors of mafia ties associated with some of his more lucrative business dealings.

Brandon Crust meanwhile had observed his father's wheeling and dealing from afar, and although he had been his son in name and birthright, he had not been the prodigy son that his father expected and had not displayed his father's interest or his passion for chasing dead presidents stamp on mint green paper.

If one were to ask, he would say, Brandon was more like his mother, Brandon's mom Sarah, which he felt was an inherent weakness, which his son possessed.

That the boy that was now a man gave a damn too much about trying to make sure that the underdogs and those members of society that did not have the wealth and privilege he had came from did not get screwed. Yes, it was a noble way of looking at the world, his father agreed, just not a realistic view of how things were in the concrete jungle he had to survive in. On the other hand, Senior Crust viewed the world thru a different set of binoculars; whereas in this world it was survival of the fittest to him plain and simple.

As they both sat at the island bar sipping on tea, Brandon gazes into Sam's eyes.

"Having those nightmares again I take it?" he asks concerned.

"Damn he's perceptive," Sam thought before she answered.

"Yeah, they come, and they go," Sam replied, trying not to sound to concern herself about the matter because the last thing she wanted was Brandon to worry about her while he was out there on some of the dangerous streets of Chicago trying to do his job as a police officer.

She wanted him to stay sharp and focus.

"Sam, can I ask you a question?" Brandon asks as he takes another sip of his tea.

"Sure," Sam said.

"Everyone knows, that the Night turner Tribune is responsible for some pretty (I hope no offense taken) outrageous stories, and I was wondering as talented as you are why you are not with a more…" Brandon thought it was best for him to stop there.

"Reputable paper," Sam interjected, finishing his thought.

"The only thing I can tell you babe, is because of that factor alone is why I wake up every day ready to take on this world because, in this crazy job of mine, I never know what to expect," Sam said.

"I can relate to that," Brandon said with a smile.

Sam was now between Brandon's legs as she held his face in her hands and gently kissed him on the lips.

"Don't worry about me so much babe, I am a tough bitch!" she said.

"So I've heard," Brandon acknowledge.

Sam put her hands between Brandon's legs and begin to massage his crotch.

"That means I won't break," she leaned forward and whispered in his ear softly.

Brandon loved the way Sam smelled in the early morning hours when they made love to each other even more he loved how her flower budded and tasted in his mouth.

"I'll go easy on you," Sam said, as she looked into Brandon's eyes.

"Promise?" he said.

"Nope," Sam answered back with a smile as she took Brandon by the hand and led him into the bedroom.

Avery Denton, the Night Turner Tribune's Editor & Chief was on the phone engaged in a heated conversation with someone on the other end when Sam, knocked on his office door to enter. He saw her thru the glass pane in his door that had his name and title on it and waved her inside of his office.

"All I am asking of you is that you make sure that when my reporter gets down there, you keep her in the loop, agreed? Good, I'll keep in touch." Denton hung up the phone.

"Jerk." He muttered, and then he looked up at Sam as if he had almost forgotten that she was standing there.

"Good Morning Chief, should I come back at another time?" Sam said with an awkward look on her face.

"No, not at all." Her boss said as he pressed his vest down with his hands. "Please have a seat, Sam, I think I have a helluva assignment for you," he said.

Sam looked at him confused.

"But Chief I am already working on the Langelli case."

"Maria Langelli the exorcism case, I know Sam, but we are going to have to put that on hold for now," Denton stressed, much to the disappointment of Sam. He knew that she had been working long and hard on the Langelli case, but it seemed like these days demonic possession cases were a dime a dozen. What Denton felt was that his paper needed something fresher to bring up its readership numbers and this next story might be the magna cum laude to do just that.

" You know you're one of my best reporters Sam, that's why I am asking you to put the Langelli case on hold because we have bigger fish to fry," he said confidently.

"How big?" Sam asked her curiosity now peeked. "Magna Cum Laude big," Denton said with a poker face. "Okay, chief I am all ears where's the action?" Sam said.

"New Orleans, I need you to fly out tonight."

"Louisiana, what am I looking into down there?"

"I have information thru a reliable source Sam, that there's been a string of strange homicides down there in New Orleans, and rumor has it that some of the locals believe the murders were not committed by anything or anyone human but something not of this world," Denton said.

"Such as?" Sam asked.

"Brace yourself, for this one. A demon."

"Interesting Chief, and does this demon have a name?" Sam asked.

Denton leaned back in his chair with his hands folded in his lap, studying Sam's face. "Funny that you asked Sam, but it might," he said.

"Well, what is it?"

"Well, according to our sources at each crime scene they found 'Beware of Izzy' scrawled on the wall in blood," Denton answered.

"How very Manson," Sam said.

"I know," he agreed.

She had absorbed everything her boss had just told her; but she knew that she could be chasing a demon of the two-legged kind, just as well as one of the supernatural.

"One more thing, Sam."

"What's that Chief?"

"Be careful."

Sam winked her eye at her boss.

"Always," she said as she exited his office.

"That's what I am worried about," he said to himself shaking his head as he watches Samantha leave out of his office.

CHAPTER TWO

Sam's flight from Chicago O' Hare to Louis Armstrong New Orleans International Airport had finally arrived two and a half hours on its schedule. Sam now made her way briskly thru the busy hub of the airport after collecting her luggage from the baggage claim the only thing she wanted now after her two-and-a-half-hour flight in was a hot shower and a soft bed in a comfortable hotel room.

As Sam now rolled her luggage behind her, she visually scanned the airport lobby area for a liaison by the name of Tracy Leaumont that her newspaper agency had arranged to meet her there at the airport and provide any assistance that she needed during her time in New Orleans.

Sam looked thru the crowd of airport pedestrians at the signs with the names printed on them held up by chauffeurs and strangers, until her eyes came to one that said, *Sam* on it. Sam waved over to the stranger that held the small sign in his hands with her name printed on it catching his attention, as their eyes locked on each other, he smiled back at her as he headed over to assist her with her luggage and introduce himself to Sam.

"Welcome to New Orleans, Ms. Jackson. I am Tracy Leaumont," he said.

"Nice to meet you, Tracy, you may call me Sam by the way," she said, shaking as his hand.

Her liaison was not what Sam was expecting; he was a very attractive young man around her age, tall, dark and handsome with a winning smile. And although Brandon was no slouch, she doubted if he would approve of a liaison to her that looks like he had just stepped off the cover of a men's Vogue magazine. She wondered if Denton was unintentionally setting her up.

"May I?" Tracy asked as he looked at one of her luggage's on wheels.

"Thanks, be my guest, " Sam said, a gentleman she thought to herself.

Tracy took hold of one of Sam's luggage by the handle. "This way to the garage," he pointed.

"You lead I'll follow," Sam said grateful for his help.

"I know you must be very tired after your flight in, what hotel are you staying in?"

"The Daupont Orleans Hotel," Sam answered.

"Oh, I know that one, it's a very nice hotel in the French Quarter."

"Do tell," Sam said, as they now loaded her luggage in the trunk of Tracy's car.

"Do tell," Tracy repeated with a smile and a wink, as he opened Sam's car door for her.

Sam was thankful that the drive from the airport to the hotel took less than thirty-five minutes as she graciously took in the sights, sounds, and smells, of New Orleans. It wasn't long before they had arrived in the French quarter section of the city, the Creole cottages and Historical mansions pop out at Sam, giving her the feeling that she had stepped back into a time machine and was viewing another era of history in Louisiana's past good and bad.

As they pulled up in front of the Daupont Orleans Hotel Guest Parking, Sam took in the sight of the hotel.

She noticed It was a quaint and elegant French colonial-styled building painted in a yellow pastel. Similar to the other beautiful French or Spanish colonial buildings that adjoined it and decorated the quarter.

"Here we are," Tracy said as he exited the vehicle to help Sam unload her luggage.

"Thanks, for the ride Tracy," Sam said as she gathers up her luggage out of the trunk of his car.

"Would you like to grab a couple of drinks after you check in?" Tracy asked with a smile, as he closed the trunk of his car down.

"I am really, tired Tracy, so I am going to have to take a rain check tonight, but how about brunch tomorrow, and we can start fresh."

"Sounds good, I'll see you in the morning," Tracy said.

Sam followed his eyes towards her luggage, she did not want to appear rude, but she was butt ass tired and ready to hit the sack.

"I'll take it from here, thanks."

"Goodnight," Tracy said, before he smiled, and waved goodbye.

"Thanks again, same to you," Sam said.

Tracy stopped at his car door before he got in and watched as Sam headed into the hotel lobby, he had to admit to himself she wasn't what he was expecting. Denton never told him that the reporter he was sending was young, beautiful and "well" Sam.

Sam noted that the inside of the Daupont Orleans Hotel was no disappointment either. It was well lit and furnished with a touch of "Creole class" one could say.

She walked up to the registration desk in the lobby that was being manned by one Daupont employee to check in.

"Good evening, how may I help you?" the employee said as Sam caught her attention.

"Good evening, I have reservations here," she said as she handed the receptionist her driver license and corporate card.

Sam watched as the receptionist took her documents and pulled her reservations up on the computer in front of her.

"Ah' here you are Ms. Jackson," she said in a cheerful voice, as she handed Sam back over her documents.

"Welcome to New Orleans."

"Thank you," Sam said.

"Here you go."

The receptionist handed Sam two access key cards for her room.

"Enjoy your stay with us, Ms. Jackson," said that cheerful voice again.

"I'll try," Sam said with a smile, that hid the fact that her tired body was in desperate need of a hot bath and a soft bed.

Her brain, now told her it was time for her to make a bee-line to her hotel room and fall out on her bed before the very-polite receptionist decided to exchange more pleasantries to make her feel right at home.

Sam inserted one of the key cards into the door's card lock, a clicking sound emitted from the hotel door card lock letting her know the door was now unlocked.

She turned the door's handle and entered the nicely decorated hotel room with her luggage in tow, Sam walked over to the hotel bed and dropped one of her bags on onto it. She watched the bag sink into the bed with envy.

Sam then unzipped the bag and took out her laptop, and it's accessories and set all of it up on a nearby desk table in the room. Just as she was finishing up, she suddenly heard a knock on her hotel door. Who could it be she thought? "Room service," said the voice on the other side of the door. "Just a minute," Sam said as she made her way to the door.

Sam looked thru the peephole on the door, thru the hole she could see room service dressed neatly in a similar uniform to the front desk receptionist. Sam unlocked and opened the door. She did not recall ordering anything? She thought.

"Good evening Ms. Jackson, I have a bottle of Pinot noir for you," room service said pleasantly with a smile. Sam looked at the bottle of wine inside the ice bucket on a small silver cart next to a wine glass, and a plate of appetizers. "Good evening, "wow" it looks delicious, but I believe there's been a mistake," she said.

The employee smiled and looked at her room number on the wall as if he knew something that she did not.

" You are Samantha Jackson?" He asked.

"Yes," Sam answered back. The employee looked at his notepad. "Right person, and it has already been taking care of Ms. Jackson," he said.

"May I?" he added.

"Sure," said Sam as she allowed him to enter with the cart.

"Thank you," Sam said as she handed him a tip. The employee nodded his head in appreciation.

"Thank you, Ms. Jackson, and have a very good night."

"Same to you," Sam responded.

"By the way Ms. Jackson, I hope you don't find this inappropriate to ask?" he said with hesitation in his voice.

"Go ahead," Sam said anticipating the question.

"You wouldn't be Samantha Jackson, the writer, at The Night Turner Tribune?" he said nervously.

"Yes, guilty as charged," Sam said with a smile she manages to put on her face to put him at ease.

"Wow, I read all your stuff, Ms. Jackson, you're like a legend in the world of paranormal," he said excitedly. Sam rolled her eyes.

"I don't think I am that old or seasoned, but I am flattered by the compliment, nevertheless, so thanks."

"You're welcome, keep up the good work Ms. Jackson, the world need's to know what's out there."

Sam closed the door behind him. I don't know if the world is ready for that she thought, as she walked over to the wine cart and lifted up the little card attached to the bottle of Pinot noir. *"Welcome to New Orleans, enjoy! Tracy Leaumont.*

The card attached to the bottle of red wine fell out of Sam's hand, as she stared off into the distance of the room.

The room begins to take another shape of its own as if she was looking thru a Kaleidoscope of revolving colors, spinning around in her brain. A room that is now metamorphosing into a thing of another dimension.

All the light in the room now starts to fade away as Sam finds herself falling thru the darkness, frozen in space and time as she stares into an abyss of nothingness. The room now starts to allow light to get thru, to penetrate the darkness.

The smell of candles, hang in the damp air, accompanied by the smell of decay and rot. As more light shines through, Sam's vision becomes clearer, less obscure. She can now see that she is no longer in the fancy room of the Daupont hotel, she is in somebody's basement.

The chains and shackles attached to the basement walls catch Sam's eyes, as she heads slowly over to them. For some odd reason, she cannot explain, she feels a strange familiarity with those shackles of bondage.

The closer she gets to them she can now see that they are dripping with blood, fresh blood. Sam stops. What was that? She can now hear someone or something else entering the basement walking down its creaking steps, creak, creak, creak. It is getting closer and closer to her.

Sam's mind is now racing because she wants to run, but there is no place to run too. She wants to hide, but there is no place to hide but underneath the concrete floor permanently.

The thing has now descended the basement stairs; she can see that it is massive in its size and weight. It stares at her silently and malevolently waiting for her to make a move, any move. Its whole being is covered in shadowy darkness.

A cold chill runs thru Sam's body "Who are you?" Silence. "What do you want?" No answer, as the creature takes a step closer to her in the barely breathable confines of the basement. Sam takes a step back in synchronicity with the creature's step forward. Her eyes go to the glistening dagger in its left hand.

"Who are you dammit?" Sam screams out one more time, as her eyes now go to the various weapons mounted on the basement's wall above a Baphomet statue. If she can reach one of those weapons she reasons, maybe she will have a chance to make it past the behemoth and out of this dirty hell-hole.

"You are Sam," the creature said, a creature that was more beast than man. Its stringy hair from its head hung in front of its face-obscuring Sam from visually making out anything "fathomably human" behind its greasy, and dirty tresses.

"Yes asshole, I am Sam, and who in the fuck are you?" Sam shouted out defiantly.

"I have many names; some people call me The Butcher, The Highway Strangler, The Creeper, I like *The Slayer* personally," the creature said in a diabolical tone. Sam eyes quickly shot back over at the wall of mounted weapons; one of the weapons was an ancient ax its wooden handle wrapped in twine.

"You should not have come back here Sam; you should have stayed away," the creature said as it advanced closer towards Sam.

"Fuck you!" Sam shouted out as she lunged herself towards the wall, grabbing the ax off its hooks. No sooner than when she righted herself back on her feet the creature is almost upon her with the blade in its hand. Sam swings the ax with all of the strength left in her body.

As the sharp-edged blade of the ax makes contact with the creature's neck, it slices thru cartilage and bone. The creature lets out a bloody scream and stumbles back. Its neck is now barely attached to its shoulders. It fights to maintain its balance as it wobbles from side to side.

"Slayer my ass," Sam said. The creature than charges at Sam wobbly neck and all, as she swiftly dealt the last fatal blow to its neck, decapitating its head from its body.

Sam watched as the head with the greasy, stringy hair roll onto the floor, separated from its body. It's soulless black eye's now staring up at her.

It was a twisted face with those black pupils that was almost barely human to her, but she recognized that face despite its inhumanness. That face belongs to a man named Elwood Holmes.

The face smiles at her and winks one of its souless eyes. "What the fuck?" Sam said, as she reactively jumps back and comes down on the head with the ax splitting it in half.

That is when she notices a beeping noise. Sam looks up and sees the red led lights pulsating in sync with the beeps all around her. That is when it hits her, the fucking place is rigged and is about to blow-up. A hand suddenly reaches out and grab her by the ankle. It's the headless body of Elwood Holmes. "Nooooo!" Sam screams out while looking down at the body as she struggles to break free.

She begins hacking at the headless body's wrist with the ax until its hand that has her ankle is no longer attached to its arm. "Fuck you, Elwood," Sam said defiantly again as she breaks free, kicking the hand across the floor. The beeping stops. Sam looks up at the ceiling in the basement. "Noooooo!" she screams out again, but it's too late.

The explosion, disintegrates her body and the one on the floor, next to her, tossing her into nothingness again, into darkness.

* * *

Beep-beep-tap. Sam hit the silence button on the chirping alarm clock on her nightstand, as she woke up from the nightmare that she had just had.

She rubbed the sleep out of her eyes as she looked over at the half glass of red wine on the metal cart. She did not remember pouring it, and she damn sure didn't remember having any of it last night. But she must have? She thought. Because there it set on the cart half-full reminding her of last night and of course, she reasoned the bottle did not pour itself into the wine glass.

Sam looked over at the desk clock again; it said 6:00 am. "Time to rise and shine," she said to herself, as she pulled the blanket away and from off of her, exiting the bed, and making her way to the bathroom that was just a few steps away. She had promised Tracy that she would meet him for a light breakfast this morning to go over the details of the homicides that had happened in the lower ninth ward of New Orleans. One of the areas that were hit hard by Hurricane Katrina.

The lower ninth ward was still struggling to get back on its feet despite being slated by the government for funding and redevelopment.

A neighborhood that was predominately inhabited by African Americans that was now starting to see an influx of white millennials along with the new development that most of the residents viewed as gentrification to inevitably push them out. The question no one appeared to be asking is where they would go? Or could it be simply that those with vested interest and money did not care about people that were there long ago, before the levees ever broke and were now considered disenfranchised and disconnected by the struggles of poverty, to whatever faith those with the power, money, and vision had in store for them?

The New, New Orleans some were calling it. To Izzy, it was all the same. Her favorite colors used to be pink and blue; she used to love to laugh and play. No more of that. Now all she sees is red and darkness, and it makes her angry, very angry.

The small café that Tracy had chosen for him and Sam to have breakfast in the French Quarter was bristling with activity from a mixture of locals and tourist. The sound of dishes clanging and people talking filled the air, as they both sat across from each other at a small bistro table dining on a breakfast of Bananas Foster Belgian Waffles and a side order of Praline bacon, that Sam could not help with every bite fine sinfully delicious.

Sam, could feel Tracy's eye's on her as she bit into her bacon. She wonders what he is thinking of all of this, what he is thinking of her? "Thank you for the gift last night, the wine was a delicious nightcap," Sam said, appreciatively.

"You're welcome Sam; I am glad that you enjoyed the Pinot, it was my way of saying no hard feelings for rejecting my offer to have a drink with me last night," Tracy said. Sam raised an eyebrow at this comment and was about to say something when Tracy cut her off. "Just kidding," he said with a smile that Sam noticed lit up his distractingly handsome face even more. "I hope not," Sam replied with a smile to match his.

Sam now watched as Tracy's expression on his face suddenly went from gleefulness to confusion. "Just kidding," she said with a smile. Tracy shook his finger at Sam while laughing. "You almost had me."

"That will teach you not to let your guards down," Sam said.

"With you?" Tracy asked. "With everything," Sam answer, as she took a sip of her coffee.

Tracy looked at the woman that sat before him even more curiously now, just as he had thought there was more to her than meets the eye.

"I hate to mix pleasure with business, but what can you tell me about the recent deaths in the ninth ward Tracy?" Sam asked.

Tracy shifted uncomfortably in his seat now; Sam could detect a change of tone in his voice a tone of uneasiness.

"What can I say, Sam? Other than I know that these recent deaths are homicides, and they're some of the most brutal and strangest homicide scenes I have seen yet. And trust me I have seen some strange shit happen down here."

"But don't take my word for it, see it for yourself," he said, as he handed Sam a manilla envelope out of the messenger bag that hung on his chair beside him.

Tracy watched Sam's face as she pulled the photos out of the manilla envelope studying each one carefully.

He was quite surprised at how she seems to look at them with an expression on her face that did not convey any sense of what she was feeling. He knew what the photo's portrayed and how shocking and disturbing they could appear to anyone that viewed them. But unknown to him, Sam was not just anyone. She had seen far gruesome things in her life and profession. And thus, she had learned to develop an emotional disconnect when necessary, to make a clearer assessment of the cases she was reporting and writing about. One of the photos showed a possible suicide or homicide victim pick your choice, hanging from the rafters of an old house. The other photo was of a male impaled by a beam thru the chest. The horrid look on his face told Sam he never saw his death coming.

The question then to Sam was who and what was behind these deaths? The third photo though was the one she found the most disturbing and was of a young girl that couldn't have been any older than ten or twelve, and it was obvious by the photo evil and unspeakable things had been done to the child. Sam could also tell by the photo, that it appeared that the killer had staged the girl's body and crime scene to fit their twisted fantasy. Sam also noticed that the one thing that all these victims appeared to have in common was, the deplorable conditions that they had died in – abandoned homes, she presumed in the lower ninth ward.

She stuffed the photos back into the envelope and handed it back to Tracy. "The child, how is she related to the two other victims?" Sam asked. Tracy leaned back in his chair rubbing his chin. "She's not, she was the first," he answered solemnly.

"Any leads on who her killer might be and do you think theirs a connection?"

"I don't know? The police are just as stumped as they are about the other two homicides," Tracy said.

"Not good for the community with a monster like that still walking around out there looking for its next victim," Sam said.

"You think?" Tracy said. Sam ignored the reply.

"The two adult victims what's the story on them?" Sam wanted to know.

Tracy now held both of his hands together in a triangle formation. "I don't know if you can classify those two as victims with the history they had between them, or was it more like karma's time to collect," Tracy rebuttal.

"What do you mean?" Sam said.

"This," Tracy said, as he handed Sam a few pages of paper with their arrest record and history printed on it.

Tracy was right; Sam thought as she viewed their rap sheet, these two had been far from upstanding citizens of their community. Burglary, Narcotics, Child Abuse, and a conviction each of Criminal Sexual Conduct first degree against a minor under sixteen years of age.

These two fuck up's Sam could see were just like that man she heard about in Brunsdale Fargo, that slather barbecue sauce on his pecker for a joke and dangle it over a hungry pit bulls mouth. Bad shit was bound to happen eventually when stupidity met faith.

The legal system Sam knew was, unfortunately, a revolving door that allowed freaks like this to slip thru the cracks way too often. Tracy was right; the chickens had come home to roost.

"I think I'll pass on the dessert," Sam said as she handed Tracy back the police file.

"I figured you would," Tracy said as he took the file from Sam and placed it back in his messenger bag.

Sam looked around the Café and noticed the breakfast crowd was starting to wind down as customers were beginning to leave. "May I ask, how did you obtain this information?" Sam said curiously.

"Let's just say it's good to know the right people in this town, and when you look out for them, they don't mind looking out for you," Tracy said with a grin on his face. "I see and are you one of those right people?"

"I could be," Tracy answered with a glint in his eyes. "Are you ready to see another side of New Orleans?" "I thought you'd never ask?" Sam said. Sam then raised her hand to get the attention of their waiter. "Check, please," she requested. The waiter nodded his head in acknowledgment. After, only a few seconds had passed by he returned with the check. Sam quickly took the bill from the waiter went over it just as quickly and paid it and the tip.

"Wine's on you; breakfast is on me," she said To Tracy.

"Thanks, big spender," Tracy said. "All on the company's dime," Sam replied with a wink as both of them then rose from the table gather up their bags and exited the Café into the bright sunlight and cool morning air filled with the sounds and smells of the French Quarter.

The drive down to the lower ninth ward took longer than Sam had expected due to the morning traffic congestion but eventually her and her liaison Tracy arrived in a neighborhood that she could see had probably long suffered economic despair before Hurricane Katrina had unleashed its wrath and devastation on the area.

Sam could not help but feel a tinge of guilt as she viewed the dilapidated homes and overgrown lots that her occupational and educational status afforded her the luxury of a higher standard of living. But there was another thing that she knew in her heart as well, that guilt is not what this neighborhood and the residents needed. They needed action and support from their local government agencies and representatives to make a true comeback to stability and recovery. Sam could only imagine with a sigh as she looked on that the red tape of bureaucracy here was probably as long as the Industrial Canal, a shipping channel that cut off the lower ninth ward from the rest of New Orleans. Tracy pulled the car in front of one of the many abandoned-looking homes in a neighborhood, that had an almost war zone look to it.

As they both exited the vehicle, Sam looked around the neighborhood for a sign of life; there was none. "Is this where the last homicides happen?" Sam asked Tracy as she adjusted her Nikon camera that hung by a strap around her neck. "It is and a lot more I am sure," Tracy said looking in the direction of the old house.

A cool breeze swept by, blowing debris in the direction of their feet, as they now made their way towards the abandoned house that they could now see had no trespass and condemned signs taped on the front of its boarded-up windows. A stream of yellow crime scene tape hung out the crack of the dilapidated door fluttering whenever a cool breeze blew by.

"Nice digs," Tracy said sarcastically. Sam looked at him, "You think?" The both of them was now standing on the front porch of the two-story home. The front door opened up with a creak and little resistance as Tracy tugged at it. "Watch your step, Sam," he said as they both entered the house. Despite being morning and daylight outside it was very dark inside of the house with only shimmers of light seeping thru the cracks and crevices of its walls and boarded up windows. "It stinks in here," Tracy said.

"Death usually does," Sam retorted. Tracy reaches into his messenger bag and pulls out the yellow manilla envelope. He then opens it up and pulls out some of the homicide photos of the recently deceased couple that had the misfortune of attempting to use this place to get high and slap monkeys (sex). Sam aims a small led pen flashlight on the photos then back on the cracked, dirty walls of the room.

She has now verified the room they're standing in matches one of the photos that Tracy is holding in his hand.

"Wow look at this," Sam said as the lumens from the penlight illuminated the words sprawled out on the wall in front of them.

"Beware of Izzy!"

"Is that blood or paint?" Tracy said as he stared at the warning written in letters that appeared to be oozing down the wall. Tracy walked up to the wall closer. "Wait a minute is that fresh blood?" he said, upon closer inspection of the wall. The warning to him seemed to pulsate with a life of its own.

Click, click, flash. Sam took a picture of the wall and the warning. Tracy reached out to touch the warning, to see if the letters were blood, fresh blood. Bang, Clanggg! "What the fuck?" Tracy blurted out. The noise stopping him in his tracks.

"Don't!" Sam screamed out.

"Are you two kids having fun?" a voice said coming out of nowhere. Two men in suits and ties stood in the corridor behind them. It was no mistaking what they were – cops. "I guess you two don't know what the words no trespass mean?" said the older of the two that had initially addressed them.

"We do, Detective Devereaux, but we weren't expecting you so soon, short line at the donut shop?" Tracy said.

Sam felt a sense of relief come over her, that Tracy knew these two.

"Fuck you," the detective responded. A smirk came over the younger cop's face. "Tracy I didn't know she was your type," he said. Tracy winked at him. "She's not; I like my men with some oink in them." "And may I ask who do we have the pleasure of meeting in such palatial surroundings?" The older cop said, turning his attention to Sam.

"Oh hi, I am Samantha Jackson, from the Night Turner Tribune." "Another reporter huh?" said the younger cop.

"Glad to meet you too sunshine," Sam replied.

The older cop laughed. "Yeah, we got a report of suspicious activity out here, are you two aware that this was a recent crime scene?" Devereaux ask. "No, we just came in here to smoke a little crack," Tracy answered.

"Well you pick the right place," Devereaux said.

The younger detective shook his head sideways in disapproval. Tracy ignored him. He turned his attention to Sam. "Where are you from Ms. Jackson?" "Chicago, sunshine." Devereaux chuckled. His partner Canty, unfortunately, did not share his same sense of humor.

"Detective Canty," he said flatly, rolling his eyes in his head to express his annoyance. "Gotcha," Sam said, hoping that her conciliatory acknowledgment might loosen the proverbial stick stuck up in Canty's ass.

Sam, curiously looked back over at the strange writing on the wall in what appeared to be an ominous warning to trespassers.

"Anyone knows who Izzy is and why we should beware?" she asked.

Detective Devereaux turned in the direction to face the wall and studied the cryptic message scrawled on its surface. "Oh, that? Izzy was the nickname of the little girl that was murder here." "Isabella?" Tracy said.

"Yes, Mulder," Canty said sarcastically, referencing the fictional character of the X-files. "But why would someone write her nickname up on this wall as a warning?" Sam inquired.

"Because not only are the locals poor in this community Sam, they are also very superstitious, and they believe the spirit of that little girl is still haunting this place," Devereaux said. "For what?" Sam asked. "Lady, are you always this persistent?" Canty interjected. "If I was a man, would you ask me like that?" Sam said, with a glance that told Detective Canty he did not want to go there. Lucky for him, he didn't.

Devereaux shook his head sideways and chuckled again.

"I like her Tracy; she's a tough cookie," Devereaux said. "You meant tough bitch," Sam said. "If I may respectfully oblige," Devereaux said with a smile. Canty looked on with that smirk on his face. "Now the answer to your question Ms. Jackson, why do the residents around here think that poor little-deceased girl is haunting this shitty place?"

"That might be a question that you best ask them."

"Now if you don't have any more questions for my partner and me I think we can find some real police work to attend to."

"Like a beignet with your name on it," Tracy said, condescendingly.

"Don't let the door hit you in your sweet ass on the way out," Canty said.

"I am not worried as long as you're watching it, big boy," Tracy said, with a wink. Detective Canty raised both of his middle fingers to Tracy on his way out.

Tracy threw up the call me sign to Canty with a grin on his face as he watches both men leave.

"Did I miss something?" Sam asked. "Not much, Devereaux is just trying to do enough to make his pension, his partner Canty has got repressed sexual feelings for me and doesn't know how to deal with them."

"Wow, I wasn't expecting all of that," Sam said. "Hey, Ms. Nosy you asked, I answered," Tracy pointed out. "Fair enough, and since Detective Devereaux was intentionally being evasive and would not answer my question, I guess that leaves us little choice but to ask around the neighborhood about why the spirit of this little girl is haunting this house?." Tracy was now taken aback by what Sam had just proposed. He had to ask himself, was she crazier than he thought she was? Or just willing to take more risk than he was at this time.

"That's a real noble idea Sam, but you did you happen to see the surrounding neighborhood when we were driving up?"

"It's not exactly the Taj Mahal," Tracy pointed out.

"Get out! And don't return!" a booming voice commands them, startling them both. Sam and Tracy turn in the direction of the house that they thought they heard the ominous warning, they see no one.

"Hey is there anyone else in here?" Sam shouted out.

Silence, dead silence.

"Man that was some Scooby Doo shit," Sam said.

Tracy turns towards Sam; his face says it all, now might be a good time to leave.

As Sam and Tracy, both exits the dilapidated house, the sunshine is almost blinding to them as they step out into the daylight. The smell of cool fresh air permeates their nostrils.

A familiar booming voice from a disheveled looking stranger greets them again. *"Get out! And don't return,"* he warns them again.

"You are not a ghost after all," Tracy says, with a sense of relief to the stranger.

"No more of a ghost than you two are," he answers back, in a gruff voice.

As they approach the stranger closer, Sam greets him politely. "Hello, my name is Sam, and this is Tracy, we are doing a story on the murders that occurred here in this house." Sam extends her hand to shake his; he does not acknowledge it, leaving it drifting in the air untouched, as he looks them both over suspiciously.

"I don't give a tater's ass if your names are Puss n' booties you don't need to be snooping around these parts," he barked out firmly.

"Furthermore her family needs to mourn that child in peace," he added, scratching his stubble chin.

"And we couldn't agree with you more, but if our report on what happened to that innocent little girl, moves one person to come forward and give some evidence, that might be crucial to catching a child killer Mister..." Sam paused, hoping that the eccentric figure before them would take the bait. "Rufus," he said. There it was, she now had a name to go with their antagonist. She gladly then finished her question to him.

"Rufus, don't you think it would be worth it?"

Their new hobo-like friend scratched his stubble chin again, looking downward at the ground as he contemplated what Sam had just told him. Tracy watched him closely with guarded eyes.

"Maybe you're right; maybe you're wrong," he answers back.

It wasn't the answer that Sam was looking for, but at least in its apparent ambiguousness, it was a start. Sam and Tracy watched as Rufus removed a bottle of something with a clear liquid in it and took a long swig of it. To their surprise, he offers them some of its contents. They politely decline.

"Mr. Rufus, did you know that little girl?" Tracy asked.

Rufus wiped his lips off with the back of his hand and placed his bottle back into his tattered coat pocket. "Yeah, everyone did, sweet little girl, but not anymore," he said.

Sam could now smell the scent of alcohol coming from his breath.

"What do you mean by not anymore?" Sam asked.

Rufus looked nervously at Tracy back to Sam. "Word has it that she has come back from the dead for revenge, but the only thing is, what came back is not her, it's something else," he said. *What is it?* Sam pressed on. Rufus' eyes begin to widen even more as if he had been struck by a bolt of lighting. He then begins to tremble, as if something had now taken hold of him.

"What is it?" Sam shouted out. The sound of her voice seemed to snap him out of his catatonic spell.

"Izzy!" he shouted back with as much vigor as he did in his earlier forewarning to them. "Isabella," Sam said softly. "No Izzy, not the same," Rufus said.

"look I've said too much already, I gots to go, and I advise y'all to do the same and never come back," he warned.

Sam reached into her jacket pocket and pulled out a twenty dollar bill and offered it to Rufus. He looked at it discriminately. "What is that? I can't spend that in hell," he said, offensively.

His eyes went back to the twenty dollar bill Sam still held out to him.

"But on second thought, *Jojo's Beer and Wine* will accept it," he said, snatching the twenty dollar bill rudely from Sam's hand.

Tracy watched on with that guarded look still in his eyes. "Thank you for the information, Mr. Rufus," Sam said, as they watched him begin to leave.

Rufus stopped in his tracks and turned around slowly at them. "Don't thank me; only three outcomes can come from this," he shouted back at them.

"And what's that?" Tracy shouted back.

"You catch the killer or meet the devil," Rufus said, as he began to walk away again.

"Wait, what's the third outcome?" Sam shouted out.

Rufus stopped again and looked back at them both, but this time Sam could see it was something different in his face, his eyes.

"Both," he said.

Tracy turns to Sam to address her, she can tell by the look on his face he saw the same thing that she did on Rufus.

"Maybe he's the killer?" Tracy said.

"Maybe," Sam repeated back.

"Welcome to the neighborhood," Tracy said, with a grin on his face.

"Do you still feel a need to talk with the neighbors Sam?"

"Only if they are engaging as our Mr. Rufus," Sam shot back. Tracy shook his head sideways. "I knew you were trouble the minute I laid eyes on you."

"I bet you did," Sam said smiling.

Tracy did not want to ask this question, but he had to. "Sam is it me or did his face appear to change?"

"No, I saw it to Tracy," Sam said. "You said that like its no big deal?" Tracy said.

"Trust me it's not when you've seen the things I have."

They were now back over to their car. "Can you be any humbler?" Tracy asked. Sam looked over at Tracy, who was now leaning against the car with his hand on the roof and a worried look on his face.

"No," she said.

"Sam we are definitely going to have to talk about some things when we get back to the hotel." "I look forward to it," Sam said with a wink.

"I bet you do," Tracy replied.

Sam laughed.

As Sam now sat in the car as they cruise slowly thru the neighborhood, she now wonders if Tracy should have done his research better on her newspaper, "*The Night Turner Tribune.*" It was after all "*The Night Turner Tribune.*" A nationally syndicated paper that wasn't necessarily known for its feel-good stories and diet ads.

And this particular reporter from there didn't chase stories she chased monsters, real and imagine and whatever else went bump in the night.

Yeah, she would have that talk with him, and it would be his decision from there if he wanted to follow her into the unknown into the abyss. Because the fact was once, they went down the rabbit hole; she couldn't guarantee his safety or her own. Because, she never knew what was waiting at the bottom of that hole for her, but Sam did know one thing, *faith* in this game was like gold in *King Solomon's mine* if you didn't have it you'd wish you did especially in times of peril.

Faith.

When you reach the bottom of the abyss you look back up and discovered, you now got no rope to climb back out of the darkness, but somehow you will find a way out.

Faith.

It turns out you did not need that rope, after all, to climb out of that abyss.

Sam knew what that was like, the descent into unknown and forbidden territory working in the area of paranormal investigation and reporting for her newspaper agency, *The Night Turner Tribune.*

The car was starting to feel stuffy to Sam, so she let the window down for some fresh air. The cool morning breeze blew in her face and threw her hair. She now noticed that there were more people out in the neighborhood, outside of their homes.

She wonders if Rufus had tipped some of them off about the two nosey reporters snooping around their neighborhood asking questions. Sam could feel some of their eyes on their vehicle as they drove past their homes. "It looks like the locals have got word about their new guest," Tracy said.

"Yeah, it looks that way," Sam replied.

Tracy looks in his rearview mirror to make sure they are not being tailed.

"What do you think about what the old man said, about the child coming back for revenge as a…" Tracy paused, unable to get the word out of his mouth.

"Demon?" Sam said.

"I guess," Tracy responded sheepishly.

"I've heard stranger things, but the only real demon to me is the one that murdered that child and is still out there roaming free," Sam affirmed.

" Speaking of that, do you know if Detective Devereaux has any solid leads on any suspects?"

"Good question, I don't know, but I got ways of finding out," Tracy said confidently. "Did I ever tell you I like the way you think," Sam said with a smile.

"All the time," Tracy said.

Sam looked back out the open window as the houses pass them by, it was good people in this neighborhood, she was sure of it, that did not deserve what had been cast upon them. Isabella's family did not deserve this, no family did. She silently swore to herself that she would do everything within her power to make sure that the person that was responsible for this heinous crime would eventually be brought to justice before she left New Orleans. The killer was out there somewhere, she knew it, still lurking and waiting for his next opportunity to strike again.

If she could bring him back out from whatever rock he slithered back under, like any dangerous viper, he could be cut off at the head.

"Tracy, you wouldn't happen to know the address of Isabella's parents would you?"

"In fact I do."

"I would like to pay them a visit I need to know who Isabella was?" Sam said.

"Do you think that's a good idea?" Tracy asked skeptically.

"No, I think it's a great idea," Sam said assuredly.

Tracy glanced over at Sam in the passenger seat. What was she up to now? He thought as he punched in Isabella's parents address into his car's navigation system.

His glance did not go unnoticed by Sam, and she knew somehow instinctively what he was thinking.

Yeah, she would have to have that talk with him, before they went down the rabbit hole, maybe, perhaps, together.

Isabella's favorite colors were pink and blue, this Sam could see from her bedroom that had been left untouched and undisturbed from the day she had gone missing in the neighborhood, it was decorated nicely with colorful wallpaper. Isabella's favorite stuffed toys a teddy bear and a plush cat set on her bed, staring blankly into the unknown.

A few posters of her favorite boy – pop bands, adorned the non-wall paper sections of her wall.

If one were to imagine what a twelve-year-old girl's room was to look like in their mind, it would probably be this, Sam thought.

Pictures of her and family members set on various shelves in her room.

Isabella was only twelve years old at the time but looked younger than her age. She dotted on and looked up to her older brother Ben Jr. according to her parents Ben and Sharon. They were indeed good people as Sam had expected.

Just your typical working-class family that was trying to raise their children the best way that they knew how.

They had all survived *Hurricane Katrina*, and somehow they would all survive this, with the help of the Lord, the father Ben so eloquently stated to her. It did not take long for Sam to see after talking with both parents, that they held strong religious convictions and those beliefs and their faith, is still what held this family together. But there was another thing that she could not ignore as well, and that was the pain in both of their eyes as they spoke about their deceased daughter Isabella.

The only thing that Sam could assure them of is that she would do everything in her power as a reporter, to make sure that her daughter's story gets told to the public.

And although Sam could not promise them anything, in the way of finding their daughter's murderer, after all, she was not a cop.

She knew Isabella's story once published, could be a tool or the catalyst that leads to the arrest and hopefully prosecution of Isabella's killer.

Sam would make sure she would keep Isabella's story out there in the public's eye, as she silently vowed after speaking with the parents, that she would not let Isabella's death be in vain.

They thank her and Tracy for their kindness and bid them a safe trip back to the hotel.

No, Sam was not a cop.

And unknown to the killer that made her more dangerous to him, than had she been one.

CHAPTER THREE

The drive back to the Daupont Orleans Hotel was mostly silent, both of them deeply lost in thoughts on the morning events, expected and non-expected. It had been a rough day for both of them and what better way to unwind Sam thought than some good drinks and dinner in the Hotel's lounge. "How about you meet me back here at six o'clock for some dinner Tracy?"

"Sounds good Sam." "Also, don't forget to check into those leads for me," Sam reminded him. "I will give one of my contacts a call over at the Sex Crimes Unit and see what they got," Tracy assured Sam.

"Thanks a million, Tracy," Sam said.

Tracy could see there was something else on Sam's mind. Also, she just appeared hesitant to say what it was which he found unusual for someone that always he felt spoke their mind.

"Is there something else?" he asked.

"Come to think of it, there is, and forgive me if this second request sounds a little bizarre, but I assure you its necessary," Sam said between grinding teeth.

"What?" Tracy responded curiously.

"Do you know any good psychics?" Sam said. "What?" Tracy repeated himself. "Do you know a good psychic?" Sam said, the request flowing out of her mouth easier the second time around.

Tracy shook his head sideways in disbelief, this person he had just met over a day ago, was truly almost unbelievable, he would have to be more discreet in who he offers his liaison services to next time, he thought.

"Darling I don't have one on speed dial, but I can look into that for you," Tracy said, with a hint of condescension in his voice.

"It pays to know people," Sam said, with a smile as she exited the car. "Where have I heard that one before," Tracy said, with a roll of his eyes.

Sam laughed.

"Is there anything else you like Sam, like a *Scooby Doo Van* to go with that psychic?" Tracy asked. Sam looked at Tracy's small compact sized car.

"Well now that you asked, this little ass car is kind of crampy, a van would be roomier darling."

"Bitch," Tracy said under his breath.

"Likewise," Sam said as she gave him a smile and a wink.

"Three o'clock," she said. Tracy laughed, he had to admit to himself, he liked her. He only wished he knew where she was going with this ghoul hunting shit, as he pulled out of the hotel's parking lot.

He shifted in the rental car seat to get more comfortable; she was right a van would be nicer. Tracy decided he'll check into that later. After that is, he finds her a psychic. Which shouldn't be that hard to do, he reckons in a city entrenched in what some would consider unorthodox practices of religion, like New Orleans voodoo. But to other people that lived here, it was a part of everyday life, like a good bowl of Creole Gumbo, what you put in it, more than often determine what you got out of it in flavor and taste.

Tracy now wondered if he had gotten himself into something that was above his pay-grade. He had important questions that nagged at his subconscious, like who was Samantha Jackson? And what was she doing here? He would have to do some digging and some soul-searching at the same time, he thought.

Nevertheless, though, he could not deny the fact that there was a child-killer still on the loose, and if he could be instrumental in catching the sonofabitch, he was all hands on deck.

Because maybe that was a risk he might have to take, to make the streets of New Orleans safer, from this particular type of monster.

But first he had a psychic to look up, what the hell did Sam have up her sleeve? He thought as he pulled into the driveway of his house.

Psychics? What next UFOs' he thought, hold up, I better not put that out there in the universe, he thought to himself.

"Things were already weird enough, and it'll be just my luck if things got weirder," he mumbled to himself as he exited his car.

As he made his way to his front door, he just so happen to glance up at the sky just for reassurances nervously.

"Hey babe, how's it going down there in New Orleans?" the cheerful voice said on the other end of the phone. "Great baby," Sam said to Brandon. It was good to hear his voice. "I miss you," he said sweetly. "I miss you too," she reciprocated.

"How's the weather down there?" "Cool, but lovely," Sam said. "I wish I were there Sam." "Awww, me too," Sam cooed, empathetically. "Do you have any idea when you'll be back?" "Hopefully by next week baby, but you know how these assignments go," Sam said.

"Yeah, I know, that's what I get for dating a big-time investigative reporter," Brandon quip.

"Reporter, yes, big-time I don't know about that?" Sam said, with a laugh.

"That's what I love about you Sam you're so humble about your awesomeness," Brandon said.

"Hey if you're trying to talk your way up to some phone sex, it's not happening today," Sam said, with a smile on her face.

Brandon laughed. "Guilty as charged," he said. "Okay baby I just got dispatch for a run, I'll give you a call later on tonight," Brandon said with a sudden urgency in his voice. "Okay, baby be safe." "I will."

Sam, could hear the dispatcher voice on Brandon's patrol car radio in the background giving out the information on his run, for some reason this always made her feel slightly uncomfortable.

'I love you," she said. "I love you too," Brandon reciprocated. "Awww ain't that sweetttt." Sam heard another familiar male voice in the background say. "Who's that Ty? Tell him I said Hi," Sam said with a laugh. "Sam said Hi Jerk," Brandon said to his patrol and squad car partner, Tyrone Johnson. "Hi, Sam," she heard Ty shout out to her in the background. "Okay, babe I gotta go."

"Okay, baby, be safe," Sam repeated herself. "You too," Brandon said.

Sam ended the call on her cell phone; she had always made it a point, especially since Brandon, had started his job with the Chicago Police Department as a police officer, to tell him that she loved him, even if they had a disagreement or lover's quarrel earlier.

She knew how dangerous his job was and if something was ever to happen to him out on the tough streets of Chicago, she could not fathom him remembering, that the last time that they spoke with each other, it was of anger and not love.

Sam knew this was a selfish and unrealistic expectation of herself and him, but it was better than the latter, and that's all that matter to her right now. All she could do is hope that her request to him (To be safe) did not go unheeded and that he would return home safely. In retrospect though, she was sure he felt the same way about her.

"Enough of being a worry wart," Sam thought, as she sat the cell phone down on top of her hotel dresser. She knew worrying did no one any good, not even the worrier; it was she felt, a reaction that in fact produce inactive solutions if not viewed from a logical perspective of the dynamics of the issue, personal or non-personal.

Bottom line was Brandon could handle himself and so could she. And right now she knew she had more pressing matters at hand like a six 'o clock dinner date with her liaison Tracy Leaumont. Sam poured what was left over of the *Pinot noir* in a wine glass, and headed off to her hotel's bathroom for a hot shower and to get ready for what she was sure was going to be anything but an unremarkable evening, rest assured she would not be disappointed.

It had not been easy for Tracy to locate a reputable psychic that one of his contacts could vouch for but finally, after numerous attempts, he had come by one that a longtime friend and associate had sworn by, a psychic that went by the name of Madame Ashante Delacroix.

After contacting her and after much negotiation and assuring her that he would make it worth her time she had agreed to meet with him and Sam tomorrow at the crime scene, to discuss the case of the most recent homicides in the lower ninth ward. When he questioned her about why she had proposed to meet them there, instead of at another location, she went into a spill about that she had to be there on-site where the murders had taken place to get the best results thru her clairvoyant abilities. It sounded weird enough to be believable, so he reluctantly accepted her terms.

The truth of the matter was though, that old dilapidated house gave him a bad vibe one that he felt even a good hot shower couldn't wash off. But he could not deny either that he was curious to see if this Madame Ashante was the real deal. Tracy looked at his wristwatch; he was fifteen minutes early as he pulled into valet parking at the Daupont Orleans Hotel.

The tattered blueish gray cat made its way stealthily down the street of a row of abandon homes in the eighth ward. It went about its business unnoticed like the dilapidated homes that set on this street.

The cat was cold and thirsty from its journey and had not eaten or drink anything in a week. The cool water puddle from the rain that had recently fallen was a welcome watery banquet as it lapped up gulps of it with its tongue. Its five senses of feline perception were on full alert as its bright green eyes took in its new surroundings. It massaged the side of its body up against a broken mailbox post purring in delight.

But that only brought her temporary satisfaction; her mind told her that she was close to him, she was home. The tattered cat jotted off into one of the abandon homes to find her something delectable to eat to sustain herself for the task she came all this way to complete. She was looking for a particular rat to catch, one that had evaded her in the past. She could smell his stench nearby, sense his presence, he was crafty and good at going undetected, but so was she.

Oh, he wasn't the kind of rat you could lure with a piece of cheese, he had other things in mind, other things on his agenda.

Oh, but again, so did she and that's how she would catch him, that's how she would ensnare him. And when she finally had him in her claws, his beady little black eyes will look again into her bright green ones and realize playtime's over – endgame.

The smell of decomposing fish wrapped up in a newspaper caught a whiff of her nostrils; She walked over there slowly to it and cautiously to inspect her find.

Did someone know she would be here, did someone know she would come?

Meowww.

She begins to feast, on the pungent fish. Her belly will be full tonight.

And then she will find a corner or some hidden place in the abandoned house and cuddle up and sleep until night comes.

The cat stopped eating and raised her head again sniffing the air, her pupils widening, the hairs raised on her back.

The smell of the rat nearby was almost as pungent as the fish she was eating.

Maybe he was miles away, she thought, maybe he was close? Not that it matters she reasoned, the outcome would be the same.

Meowww, – death.

CHAPTER FOUR

He was an unassuming individual, someone that you would pass by on the street and never notice. And frankly, he liked it that way. A man of measurable girth, with greasy hair and a five o clock shadow of stubble on his face, he had eyes that appeared to look straight thru you when he was talking to you.

His name was Moby, and he was a janitor by trade at the local High School nearby in the ninth ward, he was married and had a sixteen-year-old stepdaughter of his own that he despised with a passion because the wife dotted on the little brat like she was the second coming or something he thought. To him, all she was he thought was a selfish little bitch that got way more than she deserved from her mother and him.

Things had been fine he thought between her mother and him until she came back onto the scene to live with them at fourteen years of age because she wasn't getting along with her biological dad.

Moby now felt that his marital bliss had suddenly turned into three years of living hell. In a way, he felt envy and empathy for her biological father being able to tolerate her so long and envy for finally being rid of the brat.

(Secrets).

Moby had them big and small. Secrets that he kept hidden from her and his wife. Big ones like he had served time in one of California's State Prison, for Rape and Assault with Attempt to Commit Murder. He had copped a plea and got twenty but only did ten and got paroled out early on good behavior if there was such a thing for a man like him.

He had moved around a lot after getting paroled from prison but found obtaining a job and keeping one as a registered sex offender was a very hard thing to do, once his employer discovered what he had served time for in the joint. Even harder was finding a community that he could live in that would not ostracize him and ban together to throw his ass out once they discovered who he was.

Meanwhile, he was still fighting his urges, his desires to repeat the behavior that had gotten him that ten years of lockdown in the first place.

Until one day he just said to himself, "Fuck em' all." The probation officer, the registering, the world.

He moved away from it all, and never looked back. He got himself a new identity, and most of all a new start when he touched down in New Orleans. He tried to keep his urges at bay, but the monster inside of him would not allow it.

Moby felt he had been screwed over, for the most part, all his life by the women in his life, especially his birth mom who he thought was his sister up until the age of twenty-five. His grandparents had raised him under the pretense that they were his parent's until; he had discovered the lie.

Moby believed he could have been anything in life if not for the bad breaks due to other people's misconceptions about him. Instead, here he was reduced to the lowly status of a custodial janitor in a public high school cleaning out the Urinals and Shit Stalls of thankless, and ungrateful acne prone pus-popping teenagers who to him was much like his unappreciative stepdaughter.

If he were not married to her mom, he would have – wait he thought.

Was this not the same kind of thinking that had gotten him into trouble before? What his prison psychiatrist had warned him of in his sessions.

His mind wandered back to the little girl; he did not mean to kill her; he had lost control given in to the monster inside of him, he thought.

He was a sick man, but his twisted thoughts and desires would not allow him to admit that he was. But somewhere in the deep recesses of his mind, Moby knew one day he would have to answer to someone, something, for the things that he has done.

What he didn't know was that day was coming sooner than he had anticipated.

Meowww.

A grayish blue cat observed him with bright green eyes from the distance of an open doorway as he put the janitorial supplies up he had been using in a nearby supply closet.

A strange feeling came over Moby as he quickly turned around to see what was behind him.

He watched as the cat quickly darted off out of the open doorway.

"Stupid cat," he mumbled.

The school bell ringed, and the students begin exiting their classes, exiting the school building for the day.

Moby watched them keenly as they left.

Know – nothing's, he thought, as he went back to putting up the janitorial supplies before he also left for the day.

The cat reappeared in the doorway and watched him quietly; one could say almost sizing him up, biding its time.

The sweet smell of revenge hung in the air, and unfortunately for Moby, the little creature that was now stalking him was the only one that could smell its intoxicating fragrance.

The cat noted that the man that now stood before her again had not changed that much at all after its death. He was still as disgusting as ever, a vile pig in human form that took whatever he wanted even the innocence of lambs.

She also knew now in her infinite wisdom that there was no rehabilitating these types that had crossed the point of no return.

What had he told her thru his foul smelling breath that reaped of stale cigarettes? As his massive body weight down on her, almost crushing her small frame. "She was not the first and won't be the last."

Moby was what he was behind the mask that he wore.

A monster.

Isabella knew that. But Izzy knew it better!

CHAPTER FIVE

The Daupont lounge inside of the hotel was just as cozy and quaint as the hotel itself. As Tracy spotted Sam sitting at one of its many dining room tables, he made his way over to join her, while graciously declining the assistance of the host at the front entrance who greeted him.

"Good evening," Tracy said as he joins Sam in the dining area where she was sitting. "Evening," Sam replied with a smile. A young waiter soon approached their table and offered them drinks and a menu.

"Two glasses of water and a bottle of Lambrusco," Sam requested. "Coming up," the waiter said politely.

Their waiter soon returns shortly with glasses of waters and a bottle of red wine; he pours the wine into two additional empty wine glasses he has brought along with the water. Sam and Tracy thanks him, and he agrees to return shortly to take their dinner order.

Sam takes a sip of the water first as she looks across at Tracy dressed in a casual blue blazer with a crisp white shirt. "I must say you are looking mighty dapper tonight."

"Thanks, you're looking pretty good yourself Sam, that white dress becomes you," Tracy responds.

"Thanks, it's just something I pulled out of my suitcase," Sam said trying to be modest. Tracy smiled at her reply.

Sam could almost feel the heat of Tracy's eye's go over her again, and despite his male – model looks, she had to admit it made her slightly uncomfortable or was it she wondered due to the latter.

"You should pull it out more often," Tracy said with that glint in his eye.

Now that took Sam off guard, was Tracy hitting on her? She now wondered, or just testing the waters.

"I think we need a toast," Sam proposed, as she lifted up her glass of red wine. "Too what?" Tracy asked.

"To friendship," Sam stated.

"There" she had strategically placed Tracy in the friend zone, she thought, as their wine glasses clanged together.

"Friends huh?" Tracy said, eyeing Sam suspiciously. "I hope so," Sam rebuttal.

"Friends like girlfriends?" Tracy asked.

"No, friends like friends," Sam said, now wondering if her objective had backfired.

"You mean like professional friends?" Tracy persisted.

"I mean like I don't need this shit you're giving me right now Tracy," Sam shouted out angrily. Drawing unwanted attention and eyes from other patrons toward their table.

Sam noticed that Tracy looked slightly shocked by her reaction, maybe she had gone a little overboard she thought.

All of a sudden to Sam's dismay Tracy started laughing. "What the hell is so funny?" Sam said still pissed.

"The look on your face Sam, I was just fucking with you," he said.

"You was just what?" Sam said, not amused.

"Look you're cute and all, but you're not my type darling," he said.

"The feeling is mutual you pompous asshole," Sam said, as she took another sip of her wine.

Wait she thought, why was she hurt by his admission, wasn't she the one that just put him in the friend zone? And wait, did he "just" refer to her as darling? She was such a presumptuous fool she thought.

She could not help but laugh at herself, Tracy was right she wasn't his type.

"I hope this means that our, dinner date didn't go to hell in a handbasket because of my uncanny sense of humor?" Tracy said, almost apologetic.

Sam smiled, "Your uncanny sense of humor, now that I can toast to," she said.

Tracy smiled and raised his glass." A mental note, I do not unnecessarily get on this bitch wrong side" Tracy thought to himself.

"By the way what is your type?" Sam asked Tracy not willing to let him off the hook so easily.

Sam looked back over at the host that greeted him at the door; Sam followed his eyes.

"I think the host is kinda' cute wouldn't you agree?" he said.

"Nope not my type either," Sam said.

"Bitch!" Tracy said and laughed.

"The feelings mutual," Sam said, raising her glass in the air.

The waiter came back over to the table, and the both of them ordered a light entrée off the menu for dinner with a house salad.

"Now that we have established your sexual preference which was none of my damn business in the first place, can we get down to the business at hand?"

Tracy could do nothing but smile from within at that remark, that was one of the things that he liked about Sam, unlike some people that were just pretentious assholes that would think one thing while their mouth was saying another, he did not get this impression from his new friend.

If she thought about it, you could guarantee that she would more than often say it, good or bad.

"Fair enough, where do you want me to start?" Tracy asked as he played thru the salad in the bowl that was now in front of him.

"Wherever you want?" Sam said.

Tracy smiled, for whatever reason, the atmosphere now felt more relaxed between him and the reporter.

"Well I did contact my contacts over at Sex Crimes and Homicide, but they did not have anyone that they had narrowed down as a prime suspect in the murder of that little girl."

"That's too bad," Sam said disappointed.

"Yes, it is," Tracy agreed.

"Now for the good news, or not. I was able to secure you that psychic you asked for Sam."

"I like the way you put that, who is it?"

"Madame Ashante Delacroix ." Oooh – I like her already," Sam said.

"I figure you would," Tracy concurred.

"So when do I meet this Madame Ashante?" Sam asked.

"Hopefully tomorrow, she has agreed to meet us at the house in the lower ninth ward," Tracy said reluctantly.

"I think I know why Tracy, there is so much negative energy in that house; you can cut it with a knife."

"I think an ax would be more like it," Tracy proposed.

"Thank you," Sam said, as the waiter now set her and Tracy 's entrees on the table. The smell of good hot food now feels both of their nostrils.

Sam had detected that sense of reservation in Tracy's voice about going back to the house to the crime scene. And although he had said he would be going, she did not feel it would be fair to him if she did not address that matter. See to her it all boil down again to rather are not Tracy was on his "own admission" willing to follow her voluntarily down that rabbit hole.

"Tracy you know, I appreciate all your assistance with this case, but I must let you know that it may get very dangerous from here, and if you don't want to continue this investigation with me I understand."

Tracy took in every word that Sam had just said, as he rubbed the sides of his chin with his hand. Here was his chance he thought to bow out or bow in on an investigation that he had acknowledged was above his pay – grade.

He was a lot of things, he thought, but one of them for sure was not a coward.

"Why would I do that you selfish bitch and let you have all the fun?" he said sarcastically.

"Yeah, why would you?" Sam said with a smile and a wink.

CHAPTER SIX

Moby knew he had no business going back to that location again, where he had allowed the monster inside of him make bad things happen again. But something was calling him back, something he could not resist.

That something now kept him awake constantly at night. A desire that was haunting him in what little shut-eye he was able to obtain when he did finally drift off to sleep. It wasn't like he had ever been a man of conscious or empathy towards other people feelings. No! A conscious always played second fiddle or maybe even third to Moby's sociopath and narcissistic twisted desires.

Desire, yes that is what he was feeling, overwhelming in its essence in its depravity to draw him back to the place where he had left little Isabella's lifeless body, lying on the floor in that old dilapidated house in the lower ninth ward. If he did not know any better himself, he would have thought it was the dead girl's spirit itself drawing him back into the tentacles of that place that he vowed never to return to again. But then he knew better than that, didn't he? She had not been his first victim and the way Moby felt right now if he couldn't control that monster inside of him that always wanted to get out, than she surely would not be his last.

And although Moby had bull-shitted and finagled the prison parole board into granting him an early release on the pretense that he was the new-and-improved 3.0 Moby, rehabilitated, he knew all along that he never had any plan or intentions of meeting those obligations now or ever. In fact, if he had been honest with the State of California's parole board and told them the truth.

The truth that all he ever thought about while being locked up was getting out and getting his head back into the game, as he looked over and studied page after page of young women on the illegal contraband (Teen magazines) inside his cell that he was not supposed to have due to his conviction. They would have thrown away his jail key and politely told him to go fuck himself.

He had vowed never to return because Moby knew men like him weren't the most popular amongst other inmates. In fact, Men like him in prison that preyed on the innocent that preyed on children in the real world. (The outside) was like shit scum on a inmates boot.

That is when the killing started after he had made that vow, which he would never return too prison again. He also made another one that he would never leave another witness alive again. Dark promises to himself that he had made good on so far.

No more time for contemplation, who was Moby kidding he thought? The Monster inside of him demanded to be fed. He would return to the lower ninth ward today and use the same cloak of invisibility that had shielded him from detection the last time.

A vehicle that he stored away and only drove on what he called special occasions, a car that Moby had outfitted with all the bells and whistles to look very similar to an unmarked patrol car.

When he drove that car, he was no longer Moby, the janitor. He assumed a new identity, Investigator Mike Fox, just another cop passing thru a neighborhood to the untrained eye, except he wasn't a cop, he was an impersonator and at worst a killer.

Moby raised the garage door up as he looked over his fake police car a black 1989 Ford Crown Victoria Police Interceptor. The Car at one time had been part of New Orleans Police Department's Fleet, but had been decommissioned, and stripped of its police insignia and equipment and sold at a public auction.

That's where Moby step in and restore it back to almost its original status, including a brand-new police scanner so that he could monitor and track police calls.

What better way he thought to slap the cops in their faces and say I am smarter than you "assholes," was to drive around in a vehicle like theirs while he was out committing his atrocities.

Moby smile as he entered the Crown Victoria and put the key in the ignition. He gave the ignition switch a turn and the car rumble to life. He hit the gas pedal, and the car gave an even more throaty rumble from its 4.6-liter Modular V8 engine.

The car with its fake officialiaty, made him feel like he was powerful and indestructible.

"What the hell, one last time," Moby said to himself as he pulled out of his driveway, headed to the other side of town, back to the lower ninth ward.

"Unaware" that's exactly what it would be, one last trip.

CHAPTER SEVEN

Moby had made it a point despite his fake cover, to return to his crime scene very early in the morning before dawn, to avoid drawing any unwanted attention to himself. He was not sure if the police still had the house under surveillance or not, so he parked his fake police car on the opposite side of the street further down from the house to get a feel for his surroundings first. Moby opened up his glove compartment to his car and pulled out the small pair of binoculars he kept inside of it.

He flips them open and puts them to his eyes, adjusting the optics on them so that he can zoom in and get a better look at the house and its surrounding arca. No cops, he thinks, as he shuts the collapsible binoculars and stuffs them back into his glove compartment.

That feeling comes over him again as he sits there in his car staring off in the direction of the house. Bam! Something hits his window on the driver side jarring him out of his trance-like focus. Bam! Again. A closed fist slams up against his tinted window.

"Goddammit!" Moby says as he hits his window switch, slowly letting it down but not all the way. A pair of wild eyes stares back at him thru the crack of the window. "What the fuck is your problem buddy?" Moby asks in the most official police voice that he can muster up.

"Have y'all caught that girls' killer yet?" the eyes answer back.

Moby can smell the strong odor of alcohol coming from his new inquisitive friend thru the window.

"Not, yet we are working on it," in his official police voice.

"Well work harder!" his new friend shouts back at him thru stale breath and red eyes.

Moby lowers his window some more to get a better look at the stranger. The man looks to him like a hobo living off the streets.

Moby watches him as he takes a bottle out of his coat pocket and turns it up to his lips taking big gulps of whatever the elixir is in his glass container.

"Its kind of early in the day for that wouldn't you agree?" Moby said.

"No, I would not!" the stranger answer back defiantly, wiping his mouth off with his sleeve.

"It's never too early in the day for refreshments," he added.

The stranger's eyes suddenly widen as he gets a better look inside the car, a better look at Moby.

"Don't I know you?" he asks Moby, trying to place his face thru a mental fog.

"I don't think so," Moby said affirmatively.

His new friend was now starting to annoy him, and he knew that could be detrimental to them both. Moby reason it would take him two seconds maybe three to cut the bum's throat. He could envision the blood pouring out of the strangers gaping wound onto the seat of his car. He smiled at the thought.

Stick to the plan his voice told him in his head.

One,

Two,

The vagrant stared at him some more. "I guess not," he said.

Moby slid the switchblade knife back between the front seat of his car.

"You guessed right," Moby replied with a solemn look on his face, almost one of disappointment.

Rufus grumbled something incoherently and walked away from the fake police car, away from Moby in the opposite direction of the house.

Moby watched him closely thru slitted pig eyes that almost didn't appear human.

When Rufus had disappeared and was no longer within his eyesight, Moby turned his attention back over to the house; and that is when he spotted her, a young girl that bore a striking resemblance to the one that he had murdered. She now stood no more than twenty-five yards away from the house staring in his direction.

"What the fuck?" Moby muttered underneath his breath, as his brain still tried to register what he was seeing. Was it an apparition, was she even real? He thought. The young girl gesture with her hand for him to follow her as she turned around and began walking towards the direction of the house. Moby watched her too thru those same slitted pig eyes of his as he exited his fake police car.

He looked around to see if anyone was following her if the hobo was still around. The street was eerily quiet. It appeared to him that no one else was around. What the hell was a young girl like her doing out at this time of the hour? He thought. Was this a set-up? Is this why he had been compelled to come back to this location? He reached back into his car and pulled out the switchblade knife wedged between his car seat and stuffed it inside his jacket pocket. He then walked around to the back of his car, popped the trunk, reached in and pulled out a black bag that he had aptly named his kill kit. Moby looked back around and shut the trunk to his fake police car. He did not yet have any of the answers to the questions that he needed, but one thing for sure, he did have the audacity no matter how foolish to go and seek those answers out.

And that's just what Izzy had banked on.

Moby caught another glimpse of the girl entering the dilapidated house.

It had appeared that she had turned around and looked back at him again, but he wasn't for sure. "You wanna play games you little bitch, will play," he murmured with a sinister tone in his voice.

Moby then made his way as fast as his fat frame could carry him across the street with the kill bag in hand to the house the girl had just entered.

Someone watched him quietly and undetected from a distance.

CHAPTER EIGHT

Tracy watched as Sam exited the Daupoint Hotel with a camera around her neck and two cups in her hand. "Nice Scooby Van," she said as Tracy open the door for her, and she entered the vehicle. "I thought you'd like the new wheels," Tracy said confidently. "I do," Sam reciprocated. "How did you sleep last night?" Sam ask Tracy.

"Not much," he said. "And you?"

"Like a baby," Sam said with a smile. "It figures," he said, shaking his head. "Awwww, don't be a sourpuss," Sam said as she leaned over and pinched Tracy's cheek. "Look I brought you coffee," she said pointing to the two cups that she had placed in the front cup holder.

Tracy picked up one of the cups of coffee and took a sip. " Mmmm that's delicious that's not just coffee that's a *vanilla mocha latte*, honey you're redeemed."

"Thanks, and for the record, I did not sleep much either," Sam confessed.

"I knew that," Tracy said with a smirk on his face, as he took another sip of his coffee.

"This Madame Ashante Delacroix, why didn't she just ride with us Trace?" Sam asked, out curiosity.

"I offered, she declined," Tracy said.

"Why?"

"Something about not wanting her energy broken," Tracy answered.

"Bitch," Sam said. "That's the same thing I thought," Tracy stated.

"Why does that not surprise me, Tracy."

They both laughed.

It felt good to Sam that she and Tracy could share this brief period of levity together, helped relieved some of the stress she was sure they both felt working a case like this, that was so intense and demanding.

"Hopefully," she thought this Madame Ashante would offer them some insight into the investigation, if not just a glimmer of information, that might be instrumental in apprehending this animal that was still at large.

Sam need not worry about that though. She and Tracy would get their money's worth and then some. Because Madame Ashante Delacroix wasn't a poser, she was the real deal which they would soon find out.

Sam looked across at Tracy; he appeared tense.

They were now only twenty minutes away from the lower ninth ward, twenty minutes away from the house.

CHAPTER NINE

Moby cautiously entered the house; he had not planned on returning so soon to these killing grounds, he thought. But he had unfinished business, and today he would not leave until that business was finish.

The girl had entered this house; this he was for sure, it was now his job to find her, and once he found her he would make her regret that she called him back here to play. Memories of what he had done here and the innocent blood he had shed flooded his senses, as the familiar stench of the house flooded his nostrils. His eyes darted back and forth across the inside of the house, trying to adjust to its dusty darkness.

Hcchcehee – comes the sound of a young girl giggling out of nowhere, stopping Moby in his tracks, raising the hairs on his arms.

A shadow of something quickly shoots pass him, causing him to spin around with the switchblade in his hand. He quickly ejects the blade, but is too slow and does not see what runs pass him.

Heeheehee, more giggling. His senses are on full alert now, as his eyes scan the room. Moby feels something tap him on the back of the neck. He turns around and swiftly stabs the naked air, nothing is there. Whatever it was is now gone. "What the fuck is going on?" He says in a whisper of a voice to himself.

"Man you are losing it, keep your shit together," he assures himself.

His eyes catch the writing on the wall; he walks over to it to get a closer look. And although the wall is bleeding the words in crimson red, bleeding the words in blood, he can still make out what it said. ***"Beware of Izzy."***

Moby reaches out and touches the words on the wall. "Shit!" he screams out as he quickly draws his hand back in searing pain, but it's too late, his fingers now have first degree burns and quickly starts to blister.

Touching the foreboding words of blood on the wall is like touching acid.

"I am going to enjoy this you fucking little bitch!" he screams out.

"Hehehehe, you can't catch me," she says as she darts up the stairs.

Moby catches a glimpse of a figure in a pink dress running up the stairway; he runs after her. "I got you now you little… aaargh!" Moby screams out in pain as a nine-inch nail protruding thru one of the steps goes thru his shoe into his foot penetrating soft flesh. He loses his balance and doubles back, his fat frame falling down the rest of the stairway to the bottom of the landing, his bag still in his hand.

Hehehehe, the laughter taunting him. "I think you broke my fucking back you little bastard," he says writhing in pain as he attempts to recover from the fall. He throws the kill bag down on the floor away from him. He then watches in awe as the bag moves slowly across the floor away from him as if guided by some unforeseen force, it then picks up momentum and is dragged across the floor by the same unforeseen force into one of the numerous rooms in the house, as it disappears from his line of sight.

"How did you do that he?" He stammers.

"It doesn't matter, I still have this," he says brandishing his switchblade knife, waving it in the air.

"And I am coming for you," he says attempting to hide the fear that is now starting to set in on his mind. His attention goes back down to his foot.

He makes a quick mental assessment of his injuries, burned hand, his whole body aches, from the fall, now a nail implanted in his foot, it wasn't supposed to be this hard he thinks, for God sakes, she is only a twelve-year-old girl or is she?

"All I need to do is get this fucking nail out my foot, and your ass is mine," he warns as he reaches down thru clenched teeth and begins pulling the hot nail out of his foot tearing the flesh off his stubby fingers in the process.

"Fuckkkk!" he screams out as the nail finally comes out.

He tosses the bloody nail to the floor.

"Hehehehe, come and get me," he hears a little girl voice say, which sounds like its coming from one of the upstairs room.

But something in his mind starts to tell him this is no little girl; maybe he should leave he thinks, as he gets back on his feet. Sweat now rolls down his fleshy face; his slitted pig eyes are even narrower as he tries to focus on his surroundings. Maybe he should try a different approach he reasons.

"Do you want to play with Izzy?" he hears the little girl voice say.

Moby looks up the stairs; he hesitates at first to move in that direction, what if it's a trap? He thinks. Fuck it! She's just a little girl he reasons, what the hell is wrong with him? "Get a grip!" he tells himself.

Moby proceeds now more cautiously up the stairway, watching his every step, listening for every sound.

When he reaches the top landing safely, he lets out a sigh of relief. "Now back to business," he tells himself.

This little *Home alone bitch* is not going to get the best of him, he reasons.

There are two more rooms on the upper floor.

Contestant, door number one, or door number two?

An imaginary game show host asks him in his mind.

The game show host smiles showing unnaturally white teeth, but his eyes are what stand out the most they have no color in them both are completely bloodshot red.

Contestant, door number one or door number two?

Roby attempts to shake the image from his head. "Fuck You!" he says out loud to no one in particular.

That is when he catches something out the side of his eye running pass him from one of the rooms, he spins around and grabs a handful of her hair from the back of her head.

"I gotcha now you little bitch!" he says gleefully, as he turns the little girl around to face him.

His face goes blank as his jaw drops in horror! Because what he is now staring at could hardly be misconstrued as a human-less alone a little girl. It's skull-like face stares back at him thru hollow eye sockets, it then slowly smiles at him revealing a double row of rotten razor-like teeth in its mouth.

Razor-like teeth that before he knows it clamps down on his hand. "Goddammit!" he screams out as he releases the thing's hair.

Once released, it quickly wastes no time and maneuvers to his side in a blink of an eye, it grabs the switchblade knife out his hand and plunges the knife up into his scrotum. Moby eyes go wide as an intense sense of excruciating pain hits his brain, pain that locks his throat into a silent scream.

Blood instantly starts gushing out of his testicles running down his pants leg. The knife protrudes downward like a phallus between his legs.

"Hehehehe, do you want to play some more with Izzy, Moby?" it asks him in its little girl voice.

Moby is now trembling with fear the same fear that he instilled in his helpless victims.

"Do youuuu!" it shouts at him in a more masculine voice.

"What the fuck are you?" Moby asks as he crouches over in pain, backing away from the thing towards the stairs. He feels himself now starting to get dizzy; he knows he is losing too much blood, and it is just a matter of time before he goes into shock.

"Isabella," says the thing that is no longer the hideous creature that was standing before him, it is the little girl that he has murdered.

Moby begins to sob and begins pleading for his life. "I didn't mean to kill you, child. I am not a bad man."

Isabella leans her head inquisitively to the side. "You are not"?

"No, I am not. Sometimes, I can't help myself, and the *monster* inside of me makes me do bad things," Moby said, coughing up blood.

Isabella stood there, now silent.

The knife to Moby felt as if it was tearing his insides up, it had to come out. He blocks out the pain and reaches between his legs and pulls the knife out with one jerk! He almost passes out.

"I have a present for you," he says with a grin, as he holds the knife towards Isabella.

"I have one for you too," she says calmly.

"What?"

Her face changes back into the skull mask.

"Death," she answers.

"Fuck you!" Moby says defiantly, as he begins making his way towards Isabella, wielding his knife in one hand.

Meowww, a black cat lunges at Moby out of nowhere and is on his face with its claws in his eyes before he takes another step towards Isabella.

Moby let out a shriek of pain as he fights with the little black beast that was now on his face, clawing and tearing!

"Get the fuck off me!" he yells as he backs up blindly to the upper edge of the stairway.

He manages to rip the cat off his face but loses his balance and falls back down the flight of stairs, one of his legs snaps on impact before he finally lands at the bottom of the stairs on the floor.

Moby lays there for a moment before he finally comes too.

Meowww, the cat watches him unhurt at the top of the stairway.

One of his legs is now a bent and broken mess, as he attempts to crawl towards the front door towards freedom.

"Help me! He shouts out. Please help meee!"

Hehehehe.

"Don't you want to play?"

CHAPTER TEN

Tracy pulled the van up behind an orange compact sized Volkswagen with a soft black top, parked in front of the condemned house. "That must be her," Sam presumed. "Must be," Tracy echoed, as they both proceeded to exit the van. The sound of the van doors closing broke the silence in the morning air.

Madame Ashante exited her vehicle, upon seeing Sam and Tracy pull up behind her. She was an attractive woman of medium build, with a honey brown complexion and braided hair, wearing a colorful dashiki dress with various protective amulets and beads that hung around her neck.

"Good Morning Madame Ashante," Sam said as she greeted her. "Good Morning you must be Samantha?" Ashante said as she shook Sam's hand.

"And you must be the gentleman I spoke with on the phone?" Ashante said as she turns in Tracy's direction. "That's correct, Tracy Beaumont in the flesh," he said with a smile, as he shook her hand.

"Glad to make both of your acquaintances, how can I be of help?"

"As I discussed with you on the phone Madame Ashante this is the house where that little girl was murdered. If you can come inside and get a feel of the place, any information you can provide us with now or later would be greatly appreciated," Tracy said.

Ashante looked over at the house.

"I don't know why for the life of me they leave places like this still standing?" she said with a sense of disgust.

"It's not only a blight on the neighborhood. It's a blight on the soul," she added.

"I could not agree with you more," Tracy said.

"Just standing here in front of this house, I can feel the negative energy surging thru it," Ashante observed.

"Well let's see what secrets she has" Ashante proposed.

"Sounds good to me," Sam interjected.

The three of them proceeded towards the front porch.

"I would not go in there if I was you!" A voice commanded, stopping them in their tracks.

All three of them turned around to face the voice it was old man Rufus.

"Rufus we don't have any time for your nonsense today," Tracy said.

"Nonsense you say? You have no idea what you are dealing with Mr. Beaumont!"

Madame Ashante instantly felt a psychic connection with Rufus as her eyes rolled back in her head only revealing the whites of them she starts convulsing, as she stretches out her hands towards him.

"Madame Ashante are you okay?" Tracy asks concerned.

Sam quickly intervene. "Don't touch her Tracy! She's okay; she is in a trance right now," Sam said as she pushed Tracy aside.

"Look," Sam said as she pointed to Rufus.

Tracy looked on in amazement, Rufus eyes too were a ghastly white also, and without color, and he was shaking uncontrollably as well while still standing on his feet.

Madame Ashante Delacroix could see it all as the visions of what had happened flooded her head. The sadistic killer is assaulting the young girl, leaving her on the floor to die. Leaving her in the filthy confines of the decrepit and condemned house to die alone.

Wait! She wasn't alone when she died. Madame Ashante could see now that someone had come along right before Isabella took her last breaths here on earth and performed a ritual on her to come back and seek out her murderer before her soul was at rest.

That someone, was a Shaman, and that someone, was no one other than Rufus.

Madame Ashante snapped out of her trance, and her eyes returned to normal at the same time Rufus appeared to simultaneously snap out of whatever held him in a hypnotic state as well.

"What did you do to her? she asked him firmly.

Sam and Tracy looked on in confusion.

"I did not... not kill her!" he stammered.

"I only gave her the ability to return from beyond to make things right," Rufus insisted.

"To make things right," he repeated softly this time.

"Revenge," Madame Ashante said.

"What's going on?" Sam asked.

"Rufus, here is a Shaman, he came upon the girl after the killer had left and performed a ritual on her to bring back a spirit that would seek out revenge for the girl's death," Ashante said.

"That is some heavy shit," Tracy said, wide-eyed.

He looked over at Rufus who had his head down. "Next time can you just dial 911."

A scream interrupted them coming from the house.

"Help me!" A voice shouted out in agony.

The door to the house this time seemed like it took forever to breach, as Tracy rammed his shoulder into it several times before it finally burst open.

The three of them entered the house slowly, only to see the shocking sight of the bloody figure, "Moby" crawling towards them while pleading for there help.

"My God," Tracy whispers.

"God has nothing to do with this," Ashante says.

The whole room suddenly feels as if it's vibrating as the three of them watch as a fault line begins to form in the ceiling, as it begins to crack, they all try to keep their balance as the house shakes and rumbles as if seized by an earthquake.

The heavy metal chandelier swings from the ceiling above and begins to loosen from its foundation as plaster falls from the ceiling like rain.

"Helpppp!" Moby screams out again.

Tracy attempts to make his way towards Moby when Sam tackles him to the floor. A split-second before the heavy metal chandelier disengages itself from the ceiling and plummets down on Moby's head splitting it like a bloody melon, as it burst open, spilling his brains out all over the floor with the rest of the garbage.

The house stops shaking and is now eerily silent.

"Fuck!" Tracy blurts out as he looks on in disbelief at the unknown man underneath the chandelier.

"Who is he?" Tracy asks.

Sam slowly walks over to the black bag that's open on the floor she looks inside of it and sees duct tape, rope, and various tools of torture.

"I suspect the killer," she says solemnly.

Hehehehe, giggling in the distance of the house. "Did you hear that?" Sam says.

"Yes, I heard it, and I don't like it," Tracy responded.

The three of them followed the voice of the little girl to an apparition of her dressed in a pink and blue dress standing at the top of the stairway.

Madame Ashante walked slowly over to the stairway.

"Izzy."

"Yes," she answered.

"It's okay Isabella, don't be afraid, go to the light," Ashante said.

"The light."

'Yes, go home," Ashante insisted.

"The light is beautiful," Izzy said.

"Yes, it is," Ashante agreed, as a tear flow down her cheek.

They all watched silently as the apparition of the little girl that was Isabella Dupri slowly faded away into the light that now shines brightly thru the boarded-up windows.

"Police!" announces the personnel now entering the house.

EPILOGUE

Police and Fire personnel are now on the scene as well as curious neighbors that have gathered around on the sidewalks to see what all the fuss is about in their neighborhood.

"We found what we believe to be the suspect's fake police car parked not too far down from here," Detective Devereaux said.

"And when the Forensics and DNA results come back, I am sure it'll verify that the piece of shit lying on the floor in there is the man we've been looking for," his partner Canty injected.

"Keep me informed," Sam said.

"Will do," Devereaux said. He looked over at Tracy and back at Sam.

"If you two ever consider joining the force let me know," he said with a smile.

"If that's your way of saying thank you, detective, you're welcome," Tracy said.

"Thank you," Devereaux said.

"Meowww," the cat rubbed up against Devereaux's leg.

"I think you've made a friend," Sam said.

"I'll be damn," Devereaux said as he looked down at the cat that now jotted off.

"What?" Sam asked curiously.

Detective Devereaux rubbed his chin stubble in almost disbelief of what he just saw.

"You know that cat had almost the same color eyes that Isabella did."

"Green," Sam said.

And with that said, they all turned around and watched the cat stop and look back at them as if it knew something that they didn't. It yawned and turned the corner and disappeared down the street on its next mission somewhere, maybe nowhere? Deep within the city of New Orleans.

BLIND DATE

—❦—

A tall and handsome gentleman by the name of Jonathan Piper looks at a pic of the blind date on his cell phone that he has arranged to meet at a night spot and tavern in downtown Chicago, called Logan's.

He scrolls thru the list of other potential suitors on the dating and hook-up app on his phone, different faces of women, with different profiles.

"The twenty-first century does have its perks," he says to himself with a sly grin on his face, as he enters Logan's leaving the cold chill of the December wind behind him on the slushy streets of Chicago.

Jonathan flashes that one-hundred-watt smile of his, as he spots his date sitting at one of the corner tables by herself. A smile that he had mastered to turn on and off at will, to disarm the most cautious of women.

As a successful businessman and investor, not only did Jonathan Piper look the part but was the part you see, and had no problem displaying his wealth and appreciation for the finer things in life.

Such as the pretty young thing he duly noted to himself, as he entered the bar that sat by herself in the corner of the tavern.

He walked over to the table and kindly introduce himself to his blind date. "Hi, I am Jonathan Piper you must be…" "Laura yes," she said nervously interrupted him.

"Sorry," Laura said apologetically, after recognizing that she had cut Jonathan off in mid-sentence.

"No, it's quite alright may I have a seat, Laura."

"Please do," she said," nodding towards the empty chair. Jonathan took off his dark trench coat and draped it over one of the three empty chairs at the table.

Laura could now see that Jonathan was an impeccable dresser, his European dark gray suit with an open white collar shirt fitted his athletic build like, he was a Greek god. She was also sure that anyone looking from afar with the least sense of a fashion acumen, could tell his taste was tailor made and not tailor rack.

She now wonders if he was way above her social and economic status for her to even consider dating a man of this caliber. Wait what was she saying? Was she now not guilty of doing what she would not want anyone else to do to her, judging a book by its cover, she thought?

At the very least with more forethought, she reasoned, she could at least give him the benefit of the doubt, before classifying him as a rich snob fraternizing below his pay grade.

"Wow, you are indeed a very lovely woman Laura," Jonathan said to her with a smile.

" Thank you and so are you," she said.

"What?" he laughed.

"Oh I am sorry, I meant a very handsome man," she said now even more embarrassed than she was before.

If she kept making a faux pas like this, she thought all night; it was no way that she was going to make a connection with Mr. Right.

"No worries, I knew what you meant," he said, with that one-hundred-watt smile, which did not go unnoticed by Laura.

"I hope that I didn't embarrass you by my compliment? he said.

"And why would you say that?" Laura asked curiously.

"Because it has been my experience, that most people seldom resemble their internet profile, you exceed it."

"Thanks again Jonathan, but I feel there is something that I must share with you before this date proceeds on," Laura said.

"Can it please wait for now Laura, I have something as well, I would like to share with you, but I would like our evening together, for now, to be spent on getting to know the inner person and not just what's on the outside okay?" Jonathan politely requested.

"Fair enough, but I still have something to tell you, if not now, later," Laura said, reluctantly agreeing to his terms for now.

The server came over and inquired if they wanted anything to drink.

"I'll take a Gin & Tonic thank you," Laura said.

"And a Bloody Mary for me with extra salt please," Jonathan added.

"I'll get those drinks to you guy's right away," the server said with a smile.

"Thank you," Jonathan said.

"A Bloody Mary that's an interesting choice, you wouldn't be fighting off a hangover would you?" Laura asked.

"I am indeed, from work."

"I see, and what type of work do you do?"

"I am an investor and a software developer for medical applications," Jonathan answered.

"Wow, how exciting! Is there anything that isn't top secret that you are presently working on regarding medical applications that you can tell me about?" Laura asked curiously.

"One Gin & Tonic and one Bloody Mary," interrupted the server as she set the drinks down in front of them.

"Thanks," they both said.

Laura took a sip of her Gin & Tonic out of the cocktail glass while still waiting for the answer to her earlier question.

Her date Jonathan not to be upstaged followed suit with his drink.

"Aaaahhh, extra salt just the way I like it," he said with a look of satisfaction on his face, as he pops one of the olives in his mouth that was impaled on a long cocktail skewer pick inside his drink.

He could feel Laura eyes watching him curiously as he took a sip of his drink.

"Oh' in regard to your question Laura I am presently working on a software application that may be used in the future to preserve the lifespan of donor blood."

"How impressive," Laura said.

"And what is the current lifespan of stored blood outside of the body?"

"Forty-two days at the most," Jonathan answered.

"And what are you shooting for?"

"Now that my dear is top secret," Jonathan said with a grin on his face.

"By the way did we forget something?" he asked Laura.

Laura looks on puzzled at first and then it came to her that Jonathan was referring to her second faux pax for tonight.

She raised her glass in the air. "What are we toasting to?" she said.

"Whatever you want," Jonathan said.

"Whatever we want?" Laura repeated flirtatiously back to her handsome date.

"To life, love, and blood!" she said cheerfully.

"I can drink to that," Jonathan said tossing back some more of his Bloody Mary.

He patted his mouth afterward with his table napkin leaving a light stain of red on the napkin that he set back down on the table.

Laura like the way his lips curved, she wondered how they would feel on the nipples of her breast?

"I think your profile said you were in the Insurance business, am I correct Laura?"

"Yes, but obviously it does not compare to what you are doing."

"I am sure your job is just as important, just in a different aspect," he assured Laura, flashing that hundred watt smile.

"What kind of Insurance do you sell?" he asked.

"What kind do you need Home, Auto, Boat, Life?" she said, trying not to sound too much like a damn television commercial.

"The kind that will assure me that if I ever get sick, I'll get the key to your heart," he said.

Laura looked into his eyes for a moment and smiled before bursting out in laughter.

"What?" Jonathan asked, smiling at Laura's reaction.

"That was so fucking corny but hot at the same time," she said, still laughing.

"Thanks, I try my worst, I guess?" Jonathan said laughing.

He liked the way Laura's mouth formed when she laughed, how those high cheekbones in her face set when she showed expressions of happiness.

But most of all he liked the way she smelled, which made him wonder about how she would taste in his mouth when it was time for her to willingly give herself over to him when she would allow him to give himself to her uninhibited.

Would she be excited, nervous, passionate? Or all of the above when she gave him the key to her lotus flower he thought.

Laura leaned across the table and gave him a gentle peck on the lips. "I like you, Jonathan Piper," she said softly, trying to read his reaction to what she had just done.

"I like you too Laura," he said, as he leaned back in for a kiss that this time lasted much longer than the one she gave him.

He was right; she did taste good.

Wait she thought, what has she done? Laura had not planned on it to go this far. She had to tell him the truth before this date went any further.

She had to let him know about herself no matter how painful the process might be. She had to let him know now! And not later.

"Look, Jonathan, its something I need to share with you before we go any further with this tonight," Laura said.

"You don't have to tell me anything, I already know," he said.

"You already know?" Laura asked stunned.

But how could he? She thought. Had she been that obvious, or was he one of those guys that had a fetish for women like her?

Jonathan took her by the hand.

"Look, Laura, I don't care about the person you were in the past, I care about the person you are now, do you understand?" he said.

Laura looked into Jonathan's eyes and saw something about them that she wondered why she had not noticed it before? That despite his handsome face, they were strange eyes.

Strange eyes, that almost seem to have a hypnotic glow to them. But eyes that seem to have an understanding of the universe, an understanding of who and what Laura was about in the past and the present, and maybe even in the future.

"I understand," she said softly, touching his face almost in a hypnotic state of mind.

Jonathan took her hand and gently kiss the palm of it, his lips felt soft, Laura thought, against her skin.

"Are you enjoying yourself, Laura?" Jonathan wanted to know.

"I think I would enjoy myself better if the ambiance were a little more private," Laura answered with a mischievous twinkle in her eye.

"I see, how private?" Jonathan inquired.

"Private," whispered Laura in his ear.

"I think I can arrange that," Jonathan said with a look of satisfaction on his face. He then removes his cell phone from his coat, calls his chauffeur and orders him to meet them outside in the front of Logan's.

Shortly after Jonathan makes his phone call, a large gentleman of Indian descent dressed in a chauffeur's uniform appears at the front entrance of Logan's.

The chauffeur waves in Jonathan's direction, Jonathan to Laura appears to know the hulking figure; He sees the somewhat distress look in Laura's eyes.

"Don't worry about him he's just a big teddy bear," he assures her.

They both make their way towards the front door held open by his driver.

As they both exit the bar the cold wind off the Chicago river makes Laura snuggle into her coat even more.

Now Laura begins to worry that maybe she has made a bad decision leaving with a guy she barely knows. As Laura looks up her mouth drops open.

A black gleaming Rolls Royce Phantom is parked in front of them, waiting like a chariot for them to enter inside its cavern.

"Is that your car?" Laura asks a bit overwhelm.

"Yes, one of them," Jonathan replied as if it's no big deal with his one hundred watt smile.

"Impressive," she says.

"Yeah, a little bit," Jonathan says with a grin.

"Thank you, Iman," he says to his chauffeur standing by the cars massive suicide doors (backward hinged) as he and Laura enter a car that she knows probably cost more than her Chicago lakefront condo.

As Laura sits down in the cars luxurious seat, she discovers that the car's opulence does not stop at the exterior.

Iman pushes a button on the doors hinges and the massive vaulted doors automatically close shut on the beast.

How rich is this guy? Laura begins to wonder as she gazes above at the multitude of sparkling fiber-optic stars on the headliner of the car.

* * *

The mammoth size automobile powered by a 6.75-liter V12 engine rolls down the city streets of Chicago effortlessly towards the Southside of Chicago to a warehouse owned by Jonathan Piper on Belden St.

As they arrive at their location, Laura is now a little more at ease with the situation, courtesy of the expensive Champagne from the car's fold-out bar "no doubt" she concludes.

But the creepy surroundings that Jonathan's driver has now pulled into, with the mortgage note on wheels has not evaded her sixth sense.

"Why are we here?" she asks Jonathan.

"This is my home Laura," Jonathan states in a voice as if she should have already known.

"What were you expecting a mansion?" he jokes trying to put her at ease.

Laura looks out of the tinted windows at the massive warehouse, she heard about stories like "this" how women against their better judgment allowed themselves to be taken to desolate locations by their blind dates only never to be seen from anyone, ever, again.

She did not want to be one of those women.

"I don't know what I was expecting?" she said after a long pause.

"Laura, I can have my driver take you home if you wish?" Jonathan said, with a look on his face that told her he was fine with whatever decision she made.

A voice in Laura's head suddenly intervene, it was her voice "Why are you hesitating to be adventurous Laura, is he not the man of your dreams?"

"How are you going to live life if you never take chances?"

A second voice intervenes in her head overtaking the first, but this time it was not her's, it belongs to her late Mother's who had passed away recently due to illness.

"Be careful Laura, not everyone will take the time to understand; I love you."

Her mother's voice fades from her head, replaced by the sound of Jonathan's voice.

"Laura are you okay?"

"Yes, why are we still sitting here in this car?" she asks smiling and trying to regain the confidence that she had before they left the bar.

Jonathan leans in and kisses Laura softly on her lips. "Yes, why are we?" he says with a grin.

His chauffeur Iman turns around and looks at his boss.

Jonathan winks his eye at him letting him know it's okay to continue inside the warehouse that he calls his home.

The chauffeur hits a button in the car which activates one of the numerous wide warehouse metal garage doors, that begin to raise up allowing them entry to the warehouse. The buzzing of the door rumbling back on its rails and wheels fill the night air on Belden St.

The Rolls Royce Phantom creeps slowly into the warehouse.

Laura and Jonathan exit the vehicle, and he bids his large chauffeur Iman farewell, giving him the rest of the night off.

Laura watches intently as the mortgage on wheels exit the low lit warehouse and the rolling metal garage door closes.

"You live in a warehouse?" she says to Jonathan befuddle, as she pulls her coat in from the cold draft that comes from the expansive area of the almost empty warehouse, that looks to be at least two football fields long or more to her.

"Yes I do, I know some people may find it strange, but trust me its more to this place then meets the eye," he assures her with a sense of unapologetic confidence or is it swagger, that she found alluring and disarming.

" Well I guess on the bright side you will never run out of closet space," Laura she said feeling now a little apprehensive.

"No, its plenty of space to throw shit out where ever you want around here," Jonathan said with a grin on his face.

A comment that Laura could not help but find slightly disturbing given the circumstances.

"Would you like me to show you around?"

"Please do," answer Laura, trying to hide her nervousness from her new acquaintance while putting her bravest face on to contradict the "willy nillies" in her stomach.

"Please come this way," Jonathan requested politely, as he took Laura by the hand. Laura noticed a small golf cart parked over in one of the corners of the warehouse.

"Are we going to be using that?" she asked, pointing over to the golf cart.

"Not yet, unless you plan on escaping?" he said sarcastically.

Laura smiled slightly at Jonathan's remark, but in her head, the thought of being held a prisoner in this warehouse or any warehouse for that matter did not sit well with her at all.

In fact, she had made a mental note of three possible exits out of the place in case things went south.

The two of them walked over to a large double black vault door with a multitude of gold decorative inserts inside its frame, and a gargoyle head mounted in the middle of its center.

Laura watched in amazement as Jonathan place his thumb on a Biometric access control reader mounted on the side of the door.

The scanner makes a buzzing noise as it lights up in a neon blue and then unlocks the door.

"Impressive," she says underneath her breath as her eyes go back to the gargoyle head in the center of the door.

Laura's eyes go wide again, as the two doors electronically open by themselves revealing a spacious and nicely decorated upscale loft with a fireplace and wet bar.

"You were right it is more to this place than meets the eye," she says.

Jonathan assists Laura with removing her coat and hangs it up on one of the coat hooks mounted on his wall.

Laura walks over to the fireplace to warm herself rubbing her hands together.

Jonathan watches her closely.

"Can I fix you a drink, Laura?"

"Thanks," she responds, as she begins to warm up.

"Gin and Tonic."

"Of course," she says as she makes her way over to the wet bar.

The life-size samurai statue in one corner of the room in full combat armor with sword catches Laura's eye.

"That's a nice piece of Japanese art you have there."

"Oh' that old thing, I've had it for ages I purchase it from a antiquities' dealer some time ago in Louisiana, a gentleman with a very unusual name."

Jonathan passes Laura, the Gin &Tonic he has made for her across the bar.

"Oh' now I remember, I believe his name was "*Solo Chase*," he said.

"That is unusual," Laura agreed.

"How's your drink?"

"Delicious," Laura said, as she sucks on the piece of lime that garnished her drink.

Her Mother's voice enters Laura's head again " Be careful Laura; not everyone will take the time to understand, I love you."

"I have something I think I should tell you before we go any further with this Jonathan."

"No more talking," Jonathan says as he comes from around the bar, takes Laura in his strong arms and passionately kisses her in the mouth. She reciprocates his action, as her tongue searches the inside of his warm mouth.

Jonathan pushes the bar chairs aside and turns Laura around with her back now facing him. She takes off her panties, sliding them off down her legs.

Jonathan unzips his pants and raises her dress up as he moistens his fingers with his saliva. Laura feels the titillating wetness from his fingers on her as she arches her ass in the air ready to receive him, ready to take all of him inside of her.

Laura is tighter then he imagines she would be, as he attempts to enter inside of her, but something does not feel quite right. Despite this his canine teeth begin to become elongated as he sinks them into the side of Laura's neck, blood begin to form, she feels their sharpness, the pain.

"No, Stop!" she screams out.

Jonathan ignores her and continues despite her objection!

Laura manages to grab a decanter bottle off of the bar filled with whiskey and smashes it across Jonathan's head.

The blow stuns him, knocking him to the ground.

"What's wrong with you? I said stop you fucking asshole!" she shouts out to him infuriated.

She watches as he grabs the top of his head, the dark blood gushing out from his wound all over his white shirt as he attempts to get back his composure.

"What were you trying to do, rape me?" Laura asks, still holding the empty decanter now with his blood on it in one hand.

Jonathan now begins to laugh, and it is the most sinister thing that Laura has ever heard before in her life, a laugh that now lets her know she has made the wrong decision to go with this stranger.

Jonathan looks up smiling at her with blood on his face, with a maniacal expression on her face she did not recognize.

"Oh no" I want to kill you! He said calmly, as he flashed that one hundred watt smile of his, that one hundred watt smile now filled with vampire-like teeth.

The glass decanter came across his head again, this time exploding into glass splinters knocking him back down as he attempted to get up.

Just then Laura heard a buzzing noise in the room, and look over just in time to notice that the double black vaulted doors in the room were closing!

She quickly grabbed her coat off of the nearby hanger and dashed towards the doors barely squeezing her way thru it's narrowing opening before they finally close shut on her with a loud bang.

"Crazy muthafucker," Laura said underneath her breath, as she attempts to get some of her composure back.

Laura looks back up at the gargoyle head staring at her on the door. If it could have spoken she was sure it would have said to her "What did you expect was going to happen behind black and gold doors with a gargoyle head mounted on it?"

"Fuck you!" Laura said as she gave it the middle finger.

Suddenly a beep came from the door as the Biometric access control reader lit up in its neon blue.

Laura froze in terror as she watched the door begin to creak open slowly.

"Snap out of it Laura!" her deceased mother's voice demanded.

Between the gap in the door, Laura could now see Jonathan staring at her with a fanged grin on a monstrous alabaster face with red pupils, that hone in on her like laser dots. Gone was the handsome mask that this creature of the night had worn earlier at the tavern.

Laura watched in a state of immobilization, as her body froze up on her.

She attempts to move but is unable to move a muscle in her catatonic state of fear.

"Snap out of it Laura, run now!" her mother's voice screamed.

The creature would be free soon as the door gap continues to widen.

"You must move now Laura, move!" her mother's voice beckoned.

Laura closes her eyes and begins to concentrate on breaking herself free from her state of immobility.

Laura suddenly feels the bottom of her feet becoming unglued from the floor, and with a tug and a little effort she breaks free and makes a dash for one of the exits that she had seen earlier.

A cold breeze blew over her neck as she ran for her life towards one of the warehouse exits and instinctively she knew Jonathan was not far behind.

Not far behind her, shit! She thought as she froze in her tracks.

Laura could now see that he had somehow manifested himself in front of her, and was headed in her direction.

Laura quickly ducked behind some wooden shipping crates that were stacked about eight feet high. She noticed a crowbar on the floor next to the crates, and that is when she got the idea that if she could slide the crowbar underneath one of them, she could shift it enough to create an avalanche effect.

The problem was she knew the success of this idea all rest upon the weight of the crates, and if could she shift it.

The vampiric creature who used to be Jonathan walked slowly and methodically towards the direction of Laura, sniffing the air for its prey, like a wild animal, it could smell her scent, smell her blood.

Laura jams the crowbar underneath the wooden crate and begins to pull up on it with all the strength she could summon up in her body.

At first, the crate barely bulges, but to her amazement, she feels it shifts a little forward then a little more until the top crate rocks back and forth towards Laura as if it's going to fall.

"Shit!" she blurts out as she jumps out the way, alerting the creature now of her whereabouts. The creature reacts to the sound of her voice, moving towards her direction, but it's too late for it to move out the way as the wooden crates come tumbling down on top of its head on top of its body.

Laura lies on the concrete floor with her hands over her head waiting for the crates to pummel her, but they never do, she hears them crash to the floor, but she is unaware of where they have fallen.

Then she hears a moan, but it is not her voice.

She gets up off the ground and walks towards the wooden crates, some smashed, and some still intact on top of the creature's body, who has now transformed back into Jonathan.

Laura terrifyingly looks on at the grisly site of bloody human remains and bones strewn all over the place on the warehouse floor from out of the busted wooden crates.

She then notices movement from underneath the crates as they begin to shift.

"He's still alive," she says to herself as she watches the crates begin to move, the next thing that happens completely takes Laura off guard as she watches in almost disbelief as one of the intact crates resting on top of Jonathan is propelled straight in the air and explodes, spewing carnage all over the warehouse floor.

"Shit!" she says to herself as she takes off running again towards a red door twenty-five yards down that had stood out to her also when she had entered the building with her romantic date turned killer.

"Fuck no!" she blurts out as she gets to the door and notices that it has a Biometric access reader installed on the wall next to it.

Then she gets an idea that might gain her entry, she quickly takes out a piece of paper and a lighter from her jacket and jams the paper underneath the door, setting it on fire! As the burning paper begin to produce smoke, Laura can now feel the presence of Jonathan closing in on her.

"Please, please, come on," she says to herself as she watches the paper that's almost burned out now when (Systems override) pops up in a neon red on the scanner.

The door makes a buzzing noise and then a resounding click, as Laura bursts thru the door quickly closing it behind her, she notices two security bolts on the door and engages them back into their locking position.

Laura turns around with the crowbar still in her hand, ready to bolt again, but comes to a dead freeze when her eyes begin to take in what is inside of the room with the red door.

With widened eyes and mouth agape, she looks on speechless at what looks like people, hundreds of them in rows, all ghastly pale and ghostly white lying on gurneys hook up to life support machines and intravenous lines that lead to large reservoir tubes filled with human -

Blood?

"Sonofabitch," Laura says to herself.

"So this is what you had in store for me."

Banggg! Banggg! Laura startled jumps away from the red door as something hits it so hard that it puts an indent in its structure.

Bang! The door concaves in; Laura looks on in fear knowing its just a matter of time before whatever it is behind it breaches the door.

"Fuck you asshole!" she says as she begins smashing the oversized tank like tubes, spilling their storage of human blood onto the floor.

An inhuman-like growl now comes from behind the door.

Bangggg! The door becomes unhinged and crashes to the floor, as Jonathan steps thru the opening with one thing on his mind, he's going to rip apart and devour this human being named Laura one piece at a time.

"Noooo! What have you done?" he screams out a Laura as he sees all of his hard labor and works spilled out on the floor.

His mind and sensory perception are off the charts with the smell of blood in the air, fresh blood, wasted blood.

And now he is going to make sure she wished she never spilled a single drop.

"No need to hide Laura, I can smell your fear, your human stench, it's just a matter of time before I find you before I consume you," he says as he walks past the gurney of bodies, some splashed with the off cast of blood from the destroyed reservoirs.

Jonathan sniffs the air again, "Just a matter of time my little evasive friend before I find you, (he repeats) before I consume you."

"Consume this motherfucker!" Laura says as she springs up off one of the gurneys covered in blood and drives the crowbar deep into Jonathan's chest.

He stares into her eyes with those penetrating red pupils that now starts to fade as he grabs hold of the crowbar trying to pull the hot metal out of his chest.

Laura counteracts by driving the metal bar in deeper until she hears the crunch of bone and cartilage.

Jonathan collapses to the ground, and begin to cough up blood.

"Cock tease," he says with a wicked smile on his face.

"I've heard that before," Laura says unfazed.

"What a fucking mess you've made human," he says as he struggles to breathe, his pupils now turning a ghastly gray color.

"Can I ask you a question?"

"Yeah sure," Laura responds.

"How in the hell did you manage to topple those wooden crates like that?"

"I did what I had to do, I guess."

"There's been something that I've been trying to tell you all night Jonathan," Laura said.

"And what's that?"

"I identify as a woman, but I was born a man biologically."

"And why should that matter to me now human?"

"Because every relationship should begin and end with honesty," Laura said, a tear rolling down her bloody cheek.

"Laura."

"What?"

"I have a confession of my own."

"And what is that?"

"I am a vampire."

"I know."

CAMP FIREFLY

—⚜—

Entomophobia (also known as insectophobia) is a specific phobia characterized by an excessive fear of one or more classes of insect and classified as a phobia by the DSM-5

Source: **Wikipedia**

Petoskey Michigan, Camp Firefly, 1987.

A warm, humid breeze blows over Wallon lake as millions of stars illuminate its nighttime sky. The sound of insects and nocturnal little creatures big and small also fill the air as they search and forage for food in the burrows and crevices of its dense woods.

It is a typical night like all other nights at this soon to be open summer camp and getaway for children and young adults on summer break.

A typical night with one exception.

The blueish green meteoroid that cracks thru the night's atmosphere at more than *eight thousand miles an hour* the size of a Chevrolet Pacer plummeting towards the earth's surface, only miles away from the campsite.

The meteoroid now becomes a meteorite as it hits the ground with a loud explosion, decimating every living creature within a one-mile radius of its landing, creating a large burning crater in the ground.

The large anomaly now begins to sink into the cavity, as it turns the ground into mush underneath its weight. Blueish-green rays of light now shoot off the hissing rock like strobe lights illuminating the Petoskey woods sky miles away.

A group of men suddenly appear out of the woods in head to toe contamination suits with radioactive devices, as they slowly approach the alien rock.

"Get this cleanup gentleman as if it was never here," orders the O.I.C. of the group.

"Sir shouldn't this whole area be quarantine off, and this area be declared a biohazard zone until we find out what we are dealing with here?" one of his men ask.

The commander looks down on the ground and kicks a dead rabbit out of the way.

"Our orders as I stated is to get this shit cleanup and ally hoop out of here like we were never here before," he barked.

"Any more questions?" he asked annoyed.

"Sir with all due respect that doesn't sound like proper protocol?" The same team member said.

The commander unholsters his forty-five semi-automatic pistol and fires one round close range into the head of his oppositional team member; the bullet penetrates his subordinates face mask, shattering it in blood before he drops dead to the ground.

The other team members look on in shock.

He shines a flashlight on the ground, bends down and picks up his shell casing.

"Is that protocol enough for you," he says bluntly.

The commander looks over his remaining crew.

"Any more damn questions?"

"No sir," responds his second in command.

* * *

Southfield Michigan, home to Jordan B. Cunningham, 1987

It was the biggest one that Jordan had seen yet slithering on the basement wall with what looks like a million tiny little legs all moving in a creepy cadence with each other. Oh! how he hated going down to the basement to retrieve anything that his mom "Deanna" may request at any given moment, all the wrong moments as far as he was concerned when he was at home.

Because Jordan forebodingly knew he was most likely at any given moment bound to run into any one of the many creepy crawlers that inhabited the dark and sometimes damp sanctuary of his family's basement. Spiders, Millipedes and Water Bugs that look like overgrown cockroaches.

And to him, the millipedes were the worst of the worst!

He stood there now in an almost catatonic state staring at the hideous creature with what looks like to him a thousand legs attached to its wormy body.

Aaaaaaahhh! Deanna his mother was the first one to hear the scream coming from the basement as she stood in the kitchen drying off dishes. Startled by the scream the plate she was drying slips out of her hand and goes crashing to her kitchen floor exploding in pieces.

Their little Pomsky dog, "Boo" reacted as well and started going nuts, spinning in circles and yapping at the top of his lungs.

"Shit!" what now? I swear that child is going to be the death of me," she said as she grabbed a can of bug spray out of the kitchen cabinet and prepared to head down to the basement.

Her older son Michael Jr. came running down the stairs from his bedroom to see what all the commotion was.

"What's wrong with butterfly now?" he asks his mom as he bit into the sandwich in his hand.

"Boy, did I not ask you to stop calling your brother by that name?" his mother reprimanded him.

"Sweep this broken plate off the floor before Boo, or someone cut their foot, while I go and see what got your brother so riled up."

"Probably an itsy bitsy spider," Michael said, making fun of his brother.

His mom shook her head sideways and proceeded down the basement stairs followed by their pomsky, Boo.

"Peanut I don't hear no broom," his mom yelled back upstairs.

"Mom I am getting to it, and pleaseeee stop calling me by my baby name," Michael whined.

"Jordan are you okay?" she shouted out! as she hurried down the basement stairs to the aid of her youngest son.

She quickly spotted Jordan standing in front of the basement wall in a frozen position. Her eyes went to the wall to see what had Jordan's undivided attention.

It was a large millipede or what she likes to call a legger that was making its way down the wall to less conspicuous quarters.

A large puff of spray hit the bug stopping it dead in its track; it slowly loosens its suction cup-like grip on the wall as it begins to curl up before it drops off the wall to its poisonous death on the floor.

"Jordan snap out of it, what's wrong with you?" Deanna said as she grabbed her eleven-year-old son by the arm.

He slowly begins to come out of his catatonic state. He was not even aware that a scream had left his mouth at this point.

"Big, big, bug," he stuttered.

"Jordan its just a harmless millipede and a dead one at that," his mom said, pointing at the now curled up millipede that did not seem so big after all.

"Dead?" Jordan said.

"Yes dead," his mom reassured him.

"Good, punk bug!" Jordan said.

"Yep, punk bug," his mom repeated, now wondering if she had made the right decision to send Jordan to Camp Firefly, despite his therapist assuring her that it was just this kind of activity that would assist Jordan in his development and coping with his insectophobia.

"Did you get what I asked you for down here?"

"My backpack and rain gear Mom?" he said.

"Yes," she replied.

Jordan held up his gear reluctantly.

"But I don't want to go, Mom," he said.

"Look Jordan we've already discussed this, and besides some fresh air and outdoor recreational activities is just what the doctor ordered."

"Well that doctor doesn't know shit!" he blurted out.

"Boy I am going to make you wash your mouth out with soap, now get up there and get ready to go, before we are late for camp," his mom said, tapping him on the butt.

Jordan took off running up the basement stairs to the sanctuary; he was more than glad to get out of the basement of creepy crawlers hidden in the dark just waiting to jump on him.

"Butterfly Bobby" is going to camp, butterfly don't let the bedbugs bite," his older brother Michael shouted out! as he watched his little brother bolt out of the basement door.

"Shut up peanut!" Jordan shouted back.

"What? I am going to get you, you little shit!" Michael said as he dropped the broom, to pursue his brother.

"Ouch!" he blurted out! Jolted from the sting of a hand across the back of his neck. "Boy didn't I tell you to clean this mess up?" his mom said, now standing right beside him.

"He called me peanut," Michael protested.

"You've called him worst, now clean up this mess so that we can drop your little brother off at camp."

"Aw, Mom do I have to go, I promise to meet my boys at the park today."

'Your boys can wait," his mom said not persuaded.

"Jordan let's go!" she yelled upstairs to him.

"Mom I am coming," he shouted back downstairs unenthusiastically.

Deanna watched as her son Jordan appear at the upstairs landing, of the stairwell, dragging his backpack slowly behind him.

"Jordan we are going to be late," she reiterated to him as she grabs him by the arm.

He slung the backpack strap around his other arm, sitting the backpack onto his back and small shoulders into an upright position.

"Let's go slug," his big brother Michael said with a grin on his face as he attempts to ruffle Jordan's hair only to get his hand slap away quickly by his younger brother.

"Cut it out you two, I don't need this horse shit right now!" their Mom said, as they all got into the station wagon.

"That's right it'll be plenty of it when you get to Camp Firefly, Jordan," Michael teased.

"It will probably smell better than your halitosis breath," Jordan said.

"Jordan that's not nice do you know that's a condition that thousands of people suffer from?" his mom interjected.

"I do now," Jordan answer.

"Hey Michael you are not alone," he added.

His brother turned around smirked and gave Jordan the finger.

Jordan looked back at his big brother with a smile of victory on his face as he continued playing a game of Donkey Kong on his Nintendo Game & Watch.

As Deanna headed north on Telegraph road, she was now only fifteen minutes away from the drop off point – Southfield Recreation Center where all the young adults and children that had signed up for the summer camp program would soon board a bus that would transport them up to Camp Firefly in Petoskey Michigan.

The recreational center parking lot was already full of the bustling activity of cars, children and their parents as Jordan 's mom pulled into the parking lot searching for a place to park.

Jordan was silently hoping that his mom did not find a parking space, that way she would not be able to go into the recreational center and send him off to his final demise.

Shit! No such luck, he thought, as he watched her pull into an empty parking space between two cars.

"I have to sign your brother off, I'll be right back," Deanna said to Michael, as she unbuckles her seat belt.

Michel turns around in his seat to face Jordan "I am going to miss you, you little nerd," he said.

"Me too big nerd," Jordan said.

He tossed his brother the Nintendo Game & Watch. "Beat this score," he said.

"No shit!" Michael said as he looked down at the high score on the handheld video game.

The truth was, he liked his little brother, hell no, he loved him. He just had a funny way of showing it by teasing and goading him all the time. Michael watched thru the rearview mirror as his mom open the trunk to the station wagon and gather up all of his brothers camp gear.

The sound of the trunk closing reverberated thru the morning air.

Michael rolled down his car window, "Have fun at summer camp butterfly," he shouted out to his brother.

Jordan turned around and gave him two middle fingers.

Michael snickered, as his eyes went over to a MILF dropping her children off at the recreational center as well.

* * *

"Butterfly," Jordan hated being called that, almost as much as he hated how he had earned that nickname.

His phobia with insects started according to his mom when he was just four years old when a butterfly landed on his forehead; she just happens to understandably so, leave out one important aspect of the event that his brother Michael was more than happy to fill in.

The embarrassing fact that he had peed all over himself while crying like a little girl, according to his sadist brother who swore that was the second funniest thing that he had ever seen in his fifteen years of smelly socks and dookey drawers on earth.

The fact that his older brother Michael also had not missed a window of opportunity to tease and goad him about that up to this day. Hence, the nickname Butterfly Bobby was born. Jordan remembers getting so mad at the teasing from his brother that one day he told his brother that his breath smell like old pootenanny.

When his mother found out what he had said, she asked him what he thought an old pootenanny was. His only answer was, "I came by Grandma's panties on the bathroom floor, and that's the best description I can give." He recalls in his memory how his mom couldn't stop laughing, but at the time he did not know why? Jordan smiles at this reflection, as he looks out the bus window at the passing landscape flying by as the bus makes it way up north.

Another passenger, a young man around his age, had fallen asleep with his Walkmans headphones on with his head resting on Jordan's shoulder. Jordan lifted the young man's head off his shoulder getting the sticky curl activator from his co-passengers Jheri-curl on the palm of his hand.

"Yuck," Jordan said as he wiped the sticky substance on the back of the seat in front of him.

"My bag," the young man said to Jordan as he begins to wake up, yawning, and outstretching his arms, almost hitting Jordan in the face.

Jordan pushed his arm down from out of the front of his face.

"Sorry bro, I was sleepy as fuckkkk, what's your name"? he asked as he put his headphones down over his neck.

Jordan looked at him apprehensively before responding. "Jordan," he answered.

"Jordan, I like that. My friends call me Juice," he said, offering Jordan a handshake.

Jordan shook a hand that was just as sticky as his hair.

"Show you right, " Juice responded, snapping his fingers.

Jordan looked at the other kid's glistening curls with specks of what looks like white lotion in his hair. He talked funny, and his hair was way too wet. Yeah, juice fitted him he guessed, but other than that he seemed cool.

"Nice to meet you juice," Jordan said.

"Don't say that until you get to know me," Juice said.

"Oh," Jordan said as he looked away nervously.

"I am just fucking with you homeboy," Juice said as he brushed up against Jordan's shoulder.

"Loosen up."

Jordan watched outside the window as the bus finally pulled into the Campgrounds, he had to admit the surroundings seemed nice as well as the buildings.

"Okay Campers we are here," the bus driver announce as the bus came to a squealing halt.

"Everyone, please make sure you get your bags and property from the overhead compartments, and luggage, when you get off the bus, and I hope you all enjoy your stay at Camp Firefly."

"I will if there are some fly girls around," Juice said with a grin, as he elbows Jordan.

Jordan had to wait until Juice got his stuff out of the overhead compartment and the bus aisle cleared before he was able to start making his way off the bus.

He noticed the Camp Counselors and assistants starting to divide the children up by age groups as they exited the bus.

"All children 5-8 report over here, to the red group, 9-13 the yellow group and anyone older than thirteen the green group," announce the "young brunette" camp assistant Bethenny Jones on the bullhorn.

"Welcome everyone to your seven-day adventure here at Camp Firefly, if there is anything you need, please let any assistant, counselor or advocate know, and we will do our best to accommodate you," she said with a smile.

"Sounds good to me," Juice leans into Jordan and whispered.

"With that being said campers, please give a warm welcome to our Camp Director Jamie Flowers."

The crowd of kids and teens led by the counselors begin applauding and chanting the Director's first name.

"Jamie, Jamie, Jamie."

"Man she must look like a porn star with a name like that," Juice said to Jordan.

A middle-aged man, balding, with round glasses, banana shorts and striped tube socks walked up to a podium with a microphone positioned in front of the camp attendees.

"There is your porn star," Jordan said, barely able to hold in his laughter.

Juice look on slightly embarrassed.

The Camp Director fidgeted with his mic for a second as he looks upon his waiting audience.

"All I have to say is welcomeee to Camp Fireflyyyy!" he said, met by a raucous applaud.

Mr. Flowers then waited until his audience had calmed down.

"Now hit it!" he said, as a song from Kool and the Gang kicked in on the loudspeakers on each side of him. "Celebrate good times come on," the lyrics blared from the speakers.

"Man my momma think that's the shit!" Juice said as he begins dancing to the song.

"Man you're crazy, and I am tired," Jordan said, picking up his duffle bag off the nicely manicured grass.

"Homeboy don't be an L'seven the party's just started at Camp Fire-flyyy," Juice said, mocking the director.

"Whatever," Jordan said annoyed.

"Group yellow," please allow me to show you to your accommodations and get you guys all settled in," Bethenny said.

"She can settle me in anytime if you know what I mean?" Juice said, to Jordan winking his eye.

"Her or Flowers?" Jordan said.

"Man, don't play me for no fool," Juice said curtly.

"My bag," Jordan apologize.

"I do sweet & juicy, not sweet and low," Juice said, patting one side of his curls while lugging his bags.

"Word up," Jordan said.

Jordan looked back at Juice confused.

"Juice what's sweet & low?" he asked.

Juice laughed.

"Man you're an L seven," Juice replied.

"No, I am not!" Jordan shot back defensively.

The Camp assistant turned around to address both boys.

"Campers, please pay attention to my instructions while I am escorting you to your Cabin," she said.

"Yes Ms. Jones," Juice said.

Juice batted his eyes and broke into a discreet campy impersonation of the Camp assistant. "Campers, please pay attention to my instructions while I am escorting you to your cabin," he said softly.

Jordan laughed, but this time he elbows Juice.

When they arrived at their assigned cabin, number two, Jordan noticed it was fairly spacious inside with eight beds, four across on each side of the room, with footlockers next to them.

"I got dibs on this bed," Juice said as he went over and sat his stuff down on one of the beds.

"Okay guy's I know it's been a long bus ride in, and I am sure, everyone is starving, so get settle in, put your things away, and I'll come back to escort you over to Cedar Hall for dinner at 4:00 pm," Bethenny said.

"Kumbaya," shouted out one of the campers, a chubby kid that was big for his age, causing everyone in the group to burst out in laughter.

"Kumbaya," repeated Bethenny with a smile.

"4:00 pm troopers," she reminded everyone again, before exiting the cabin.

"Troopers? How old do she think we are five?" Juice said quietly to Jordan, his new-found friend.

When she was out of sight, he walked over to Ben, and high five him.

" Kumbaya homeboy that shit was funny, what's your name?"

"Barry."

"Man you built like "the fridge," Juice said observantly.

"I guess," the big kid said shrugging as if he was slightly uncomfortable with his size.

"Barry I am Juice, and this is my homeboy Jordan across from me."

"Word," Barry said sizing them both up.

Jordan nodded his head in acknowledgment and began taking personal items out of his bags and placing them in his footlocker next to his bed.

"Man, look at him Barry, this dude doesn't waste any time," Juice said grinning.

Jordan looked back up at Juice slightly annoyed.

"Well I guess I might as well start unpacking my shit to homey," he said.

Juice begins to unpack his bag as well when something he pulls out catches Jordan's eye.

"Man, what the hell are those?" he asks Juice.

"What these?" Juice says as he holds up his leopard printed underwear.

"Yeah those," Jordan confirmed.

"The latest in men's underwear bee," he answered.

"Those look like my Grandma panties," Jordan said.

Barry smiled and snickered.

"If they do, I would love to meet your Grandma," Juice said.

"Sure, and you can give her back her panties," Jordan retorted.

Barry burst out laughing. "Good one bee."

"Clam it, fat boy!" Juice said as he gave Barry a dirty look.

And although Barry was much larger that tone and look on Juice's face told him that Juice was no one to underestimate.

"I am not fat, just big-boned," Barry said in his own defense.

Still, despite his reservations, he shot back Juice a mean glare, which wasn't lost on Juice.

Juice knew he could probably take Jordan, but the big one Barry would be a whole different story, and he didn't come to summer camp to get his ass whoop on the first day here, so to save face, he felt it was best to keep his cool.

"It's all good ass wipes, y'all momma still buying y'all draws," Juice said, and gave them both the finger.

"And my momma buys my little sister draws like that too," Barry said.

Jordan burst out laughing; It appeared that the big kid had a sense of humor, maybe he wasn't so bad after all he thought.

"Ha, ha, ha, two freaking comedians," Juice said as he threw the underwear in his footlocker angrily.

Jordan suddenly started to feel bad about them teasing Juice; he knew how it was to be teased, to be bullied.

"Juice it's all good we are just messing with you bro," he said extending his hand in friendship.

Juice looked at Jordan's hand and then waited a few seconds before he shook it.

Barry walked over, and Juice did the same.

From here on out or at least for seven days he knew these two would be his cool camp brothers, now where in the hell he thought, did he put his soft n sheen no drip curl activator.

It was now day three at Camp Firefly, days filled with various activities for the camp goers like hiking, campfires, and horseback riding.

And for the more adventurous, kayaking, zip lining, and rock climbing, preceded of course, by more campfires.

Day three in the Camp's Nature Center Entomologist and guest speaker Peter Doogen held the attention span of young and older campers in a classroom, as he gave a vivid show and tell lecture on the various species of insects that inhabited Camp Firefly and planet earth.

All of the attendees seem impressed and interested, in what Dr. Doogen had to say. All of them except Jordan, (that is) who was starting to feel ill. He could feel Juice's eye's on him, how in the hell he thought had he allowed this nitwit to talk him into attending this event, attending his phobia?

He had tried everything possible to talk himself out of attending this thing without drawing suspicion to himself to no avail.

But he knew he could not allow his two new friends to know that he was scared of bugs either, what would they think of him he wonders if they found out?

The last thing he wanted was them to think was he was a puss, a scary cat or uncool to be around.

"Jordan are you okay?" Juice asks.

"Yeah it must be something I ate for breakfast," Jordan said looking noticeably queasy.

"You don't look too good dude," Barry said, sitting at a desk across from Jordan.

How did he let these two talk him into this? Jordan thought again.

Juice: "Hey man wouldn't it be cool to see one of the largest cockroaches on earth?"

Jordan: "No."

Barry: "how large?"

Juice: "I heard at least 3.1 inches (ca. 8cm)."

Barry: cool.

Jordan: "Sounds disgusting."

Barry: "I heard Dr. Doolittle got some mad insects."

Juice: "You in or what homey?"

Barry: "Hey Jordan's not faded by any bugs, right "J"?"

Jordan: "Of course not."

Juice: "Then let's bounce and see some weird ass bugs campers."

It all now came back to Jordan, that's how he had ended up here sitting in a classroom full of the creepy crawling, and slimy monsters that he had feared all his life.

He watched intently as Peter Doogen made his way down the aisle of the classroom, showing off the various insects or bugs that he had discussed earlier to a captive audience of his fellow campers.

Jordan watched as Doogen was now only a few feet away from him with a small aquarium in his hand.

"Man that's one big ass roach!" his friend Juice said.

And that's all Jordan would remember right before he passed out.

"Jordan, Jordan, are you okay?" he heard a voice say as he was slowly coming to, but the faces that were looking at him was still a blur as he attempted to focus.

The camp nurse stood over him staring down into his face.

"Yeah I am okay," he said, his head hurt slightly, and his neck was slightly stiff but other than that he felt okay.

He sat upright in the bed and looked around; he was in the Camp's infirmary.

"Man we thought you were a ghost," Juice said.

"Naw I am straight," Jordan said trying to put on a tough front on for his two friends.

"Man your eyes roll back into your head before you pass out; I thought you were turning into a zombie dude," Barry said, as he then proceeded to give Jordan a brief demonstration by shaking and rolling his eyes back in his head.

"Man you illin bee," Juice said.

"Okay boys give your friend some time to rest, and he will join you later," the nurse said as she hands Jordan a glass of water.

"All your vitals check out Jordan, and we contacted your Mom to see if you had a history of seizures or passing out?" the pretty nurse said.

Jordan shook his head back no, as he passes her back the water.

"A camp counselor will be in here to talk to you shortly," she said.

Jordan looked at the nurse nervously as he already pictured in his mind what the Camp Counselor was going to say, "Why were you in a room full of bugs when you have Insectophobia? This summer program is a step by step process, not jumping out of a plane without a parachute process Mr. Cunningham."

But there were fucking bugs everywhere, and he knew it, especially outside.

After a phone call to his mom to confirm that he was okay and that he had decided to stay for the remaining four days, Jordan exited the infirmary at least with the fact that the staff had not divulged the real reason to his compadres why he had fainted in class.

He knew now that he just had to figure out a better way to cope with his problem, after all, he knew in reality that he was bigger than the things that he feared the most.

"Fuck Butterfly Bobby," he whispers under his breath to himself, as he picked up a rock off the ground and hurled it at a nearby tree.

The daylight suddenly begins to darken as a raindrop hit his face, Jordan wiped the raindrop off his cheek, which was soon follow by more raindrops and the crackling sound of thunder.

"Shit!" he blurted out.

A voice suddenly came over the camp's loudspeakers mounted on its buildings. "*All campers this a weather alert for your safety, please return to your assigned cabins, all campers please return to your assigned cabins or facilities until further notice!*"

"*All campers this is a weather alert for your safety, please...*"

Jordan took off running to his cabin *# 2* underneath what had now become a torrential downpour of rain and thunder.

When he finally made to the cabin, he was soaking wet.

As he entered the cabin, he noticed that some of his fellow lodgers were watching the show ALF on a television mounted above on a bracket.

The Alien puppet's voice resonated throughout the room.

"Hey man you look like a wet possum," a familiar voice said, laughing.

"Thanks," Jordan said as he went over to his area of the room and began removing his wet clothes before changing into some dry ones.

"Looks like it's going to be "pizza night," Barry said, looking out at the downpour of rain beating against the cabin roof.

"Pizza sweetttt!" one of the other young campers in the room shouted out that happen to hear within earshot what Barry had said about tonight's dinner.

"Nerd heaven," Juice said, as he looked over at the other camper.

"Proudly, but at least my pillow cases stay dry juice head," the other camper countered.

"What was that nerd?" Juice said angrily.

"Man chill," Jordan said.

"I know why you like pizza it reminds you of your face," Juice said.

The kid looked up from his bunk and gave Juice the finger.

"Man if I was back in the hood I'll beat the stink off that boy," Juice said feeling disrespected.

"I did not know Farmington Hills was the hood?" Barry said.

"It's not," Jordan answer, giving Juice a "are you for real look" seeing right thru his bullshit as he slips on a dry camp firefly t-shirt.

"Whatever," Juice said.

"How are you feeling bee?" Barry ask.

"Well I could have spent more time with that nurse," Jordan said.

"Word, that nurse was bodacious," Juice said grinning.

"A Brickhouse," Barry concurred.

"Hey, guy's turn that shit down!" Juice scream at the other campers watching the television.

"Who watches TV anyway during summer camp but nerds," he added.

"Hey guy's pizza delivery," Bethenny said as she came thru the door carrying several large box pizzas covered in a bag, another camp assistant accompanied her with a rolling cooler filled with water, soft drinks, and a bag filled with paper plates and eating utensils.

The campers joined her over at a picnic table that was one of two in the middle of the floor of the cabin.

Another camp assistant entered the cabin shortly afterward with more food (Salad) in a rolling container.

"Hey Bethenny," Juice said leering at the attractive camp counselor that was at least four years his senior.

"Hi Franklin," she said.

"Franklin?" Jordan and Barry both blurted out at the same time, bursting in laughter.

"Laugh on clowns," Juice said.

"She is just coy, but once she have some of the juice, she ain't going to want to have milk," he boasted, rubbing his chin.

"Boy, you couldn't tap that if you had a million dollars in your pocket," Barry said discreetly.

"I don't need a million dollars because unlike you I got game scrubs," Juice said.

Bethenny looked over towards them and smiled, Juice wink at her and smile back patting his hair.

"Franklin do you have something in your eye?" she asked.

"No ma'am," he answers embarrassed.

Jordan and Barry burst out laughing again.

"Assholes," Juice said underneath his breath.

Juice felt a set of eyes on him; it was the kid with the braces on his teeth that he had insulted earlier, smiling at him while he ate his pizza.

He gave the kid back the evilest stare he could muster up, but it did not deter the kid from staring.

"Creepy fucker," he said to himself as he got a plate of pizza.

The rain and thunder did not let up until much later that night after all the campers had retired for tonight.

The cabin smelled like ass and feet to Jordan, and all he could hear was snoring throughout the cabin as he tosses and turns to get to sleep, in his bed.

And that's when he heard an unfamiliar sound, like something moving, now slithering on the wooden cabin floor. He sheepishly looked above his covers but did not see anything.

Shoo, shu, shu, shu shu, shu, was the sound. "Hey Juice are you awake?" he said quietly to his neighbor. But all he could hear from his buddy Juice was loud snoring, and the occasional crunching of the plastic cap Juice wore on his head to keep his Jheri-curls moisturize.

Shoo, shu, shu, shu, shu, shu.

"Hey is anyone there?" he asks softly, still afraid to look above his footboard.

Shoo, shu, shu, shu, shu, shu.

Silence.

Whatever it was sound like something with many legs all moving in synchronicity with each other, and Jordan only knew one thing that sounds like that! He finally psychs up enough nerve to sit up in his bed and look above the bed footboard while still clinging to his sheets.

He could hear the rain starting back again accompanied by the crackling of lighting then thunder.

A bluish color light flashed in the few cabin windows when the sound of thunder erupted again.

Jordan slowly eases up in his bed, gripping his sheets and blankets so tight his palms hurt.

His mouth fell open, but a scream never came out of it, as he watches the gigantic millipede quickly slither its way towards Juice's bed.

The twelve-foot long giant insect slithers his way up onto his friend's bed and grabs Juice by his head as his plastic shower cap falls off and begins dragging Juice's body out of his bed, across the wooden floor, out of the cabin.

"Juice, juice, juice…" Jordan wants to cry out his friend's name, but nothing comes out of his mouth, nothing.

Jordan watches as Juice's feet with tube socks on them is the last part of his body to disappear out of the cabin door.

The sound of thunder cracks the night air again sending cold chills thru Jordan's body causing him to shiver as he looks on in a trance-like state.

His gaze never leaves the cabin door that's open letting the rain in, letting whatever's outside. The first thing he sees is the reciprocating antennae of the large insect coming thru the door.

As the insectoid slowly enters he can vaguely make out what it is. It is not until it gets closer that he sees that is an abnormally large cockroach, almost the size of a man quickly skittering across the wooden floor towards his scent. Jordan goes underneath his sheets as he feels the mutation pass him by, he catches the sound of its wings fluttering on its oily back as if it's about to take flight.

Silence.

Then the screams of one of his fellow campers, brings him back to his nightmare, followed by the sounds of the ripping and tearing of flesh by those scissor-like jaws of the monster in his cabin.

The sound of something metal drops on the floor next to his bed.

Jordan peeks out with one eye above his sheet and retrieves the small flashlight that he sleeps with from underneath his pillow. He shines the flashlight on the floor next to his bed only to see it's a pair of metal dental braces with gums and blood on them on the floor.

A musty smell permeates Jordan's nostrils.

Clickety, clickety, click…

Clickety, clickety..

Click.

An audible scream erupts from Jordan's mouth as his flashlight illuminates the large Blattodea (cockroach) crawling up on his bed for another meal.

His flashlight falls to the floor and goes dim.

Barry awakes out of his sleep to what sounds to him like the buzzing of a loud fire alarm.

He gets up out of his bed, stepping into something slimy and wet on the floor.

Must be leftover pizza he thinks, as he lumbers over to the wall and flips the light switch on to the inside of the cabin.

When the light comes on, he immediately freezes in a state of horror and shock as he now watches all the various species of giant bugs wrecking havoc on his fellow campers in a blood-splattered frenzy of insectoid mayhem.

Bizzzzz… bizzzzz… bizzzzzz.

Barry looks around in the air confused, but unfortunately, he does not see the raptor sized mosquito behind him honing in on its target "him."

Barry instantly feels a sharp stab of pain in his neck, as the mosquito's proboscis penetrates his flesh like an oversize razor-sharp needle ripping thru tendons and muscle.

The boy struggles but only for a moment as the insect drives its needle-like nose in deeper, its abnormal weight and size bringing Barry to his knees as he feels the blood being sucked from his body.

The raptor sized mosquito removes his needle-like proboscis from the back of Barry's neck, as Barry struggles to get up, and quickly plunges it into the back of the boy's head paralyzing his prey to the floor like a thumbtack on a paper memo, as it returns to feeding amongst the carnage.

Jordan is jolted from his sleep by the nightmare as he springs into a sitting position in his bed. He is hyperventilating and struggles to catch his breath as he looks around the cabin to see if his fellow campers are still alive, and not torn apart by the monstrous insects in his dream.

He can see that most of them are still sound to sleep, and none of them was dissected and torn apart by monstrous insects like in his dream.

Jordan slowly begins to breath normal again as his heartbeat slows down. He looks over at the bed next to him, where Juice is sleeping, but all he sees is a shower cap on the pillow of Juices bed.

"Juice?" he shouts out loud as he gets out of his bed, to look for his friend.

"Barry wake up, Juice is missing!" he says, shaking his other friend awake.

"No, he's not he went to the bathhouse," Barry says groggily, holding his pillow tight.

Jordan looks over at Juice's bed again, and sure enough, his shower slippers are missing.

"The bathhouse?" Jordan said, as if still not convinced.

"Yeah, what are you his mother?" Barry said, annoyed because Jordan had awakened him and all he wanted to do was get back to sleep.

"I know we homeboys but damn you two don't see enough of each other?" Juice said, coming thru the door in his bathrobe while drying off his wet hair with the towel he held in his hands.

"I saw your plastic cap on the bed, and I thought..." Jordan said stopping in mid-sentence.

"You thought what homey?" Juice said still grinning.

"Nevermind," Jordan said.

"He thought something had happened to you?" Barry groaned, with the pillow still over his head.

"Nope, Juice is still Juice," their friend said patting his body down.

"Yo homeboys do you guys wanna go get some breakfast or not?" Juice asks.

"Sure," Jordan said.

"Barry gets your lazy ass up, and let's go homie," Juice said tugging on Barry's pillow.

"Fuck you," Barry said.

"That's cool it's not like your fat ass can't afford to miss a meal or a hundred," Juice stated.

" Jordan is that pancakes and bacon I smell?" Juice said sniffing the air.

"Smell like it," Jordan agreed.

"I smell'em too, hold up guy's I am getting up now," Barry said.

Juice laughed.

"You dudes know what today is?" Jordan said excitedly.

"No," Jordan said as he tied his gym shoes.

"Man you gotta be joking? Today is the day we get to see flamethrowers in action.

"Oh yeah, the flamethrower event," Barry said as he put on his camp t-shirt.

"How exciting a pyromaniac's wet dream," Jordan said not impressed.

"A pyro what? Homie you trippin we gotta go," Juice said.

"By the way "J" what is a Pyromaniac?"

Jordan looked at Juice was he serious, he thought, then he remembers it was Juice.

Barry shook his head sideways grinning.

"I'll explain it to you later dude on the way to breakfast," he answered.

"Seriously man, you don't know what a Pyro is? You need to get yourself a dictionary bee," Barry teased.

"I don't have to your mama will teach me when your daddy's not home," Juice joked.

Barry gave juice the middle finger.

The flamethrower event was not only designed to teach the young campers about fire safety but also the hazard of playing and being careless with fire when out camping and at home, and of course a short lecture on the history of flamethrowers and their various uses.

Despite all this, the flamethrowers were still no doubt the main attraction of the event and any one of the kids would have loved to have what look like a badass *Super Soaker* that shot flames fifty-feet or more instead of water in their possession.

The local fireman from the Petoskey Fire Department was there also with an engine on hand just in case things with awry.

"Man that's fresh," Juice said as he looks on at the instructors shooting streams of flames in the air, one stream appears to go at least seventy-five feet or more.

"Can we get one volunteer up here?" said one of the Instructors that had a flamethrower with two cylinder tanks already attached to it, unlike the other ones carried by two more instructors that required you to carry a backpack of three-cylinder tanks.

All the campers raised their hands, amongst shouts of "Me, me, me!"

"You young man step right on up," the instructor said as he pointed to Jordan.

Jordan looked back at the instructor wearing what he thought was a ghostbuster jumpsuit rip off stunned by the invitation to participate.

"Me," the word barely came out of his mouth, as he pointed back at himself.

"Yes, you son step on up," insisted the instructor.

Juice and Barry patted Jordan on the back in support.

"Go ahead Jordan show them how it's done son," Juice shouted out.

Jordan steps out amongst his friends into the lion's den.

"Okay camper this is a smaller version of the flamethrower which has two cylinders one cylinder holds compressed gas, the other cylinder flammable liquid call petrol," the Instructor said, pointing at the cylinders as he describes them.

"What is your name son?"

"Jordan."

"Did you just understand what I just said?"

"One cylinder holds compressed air the other fuel," Jordan answered.

"Excellent smarty-pants, now stand behind me, I am going to demonstrate how you fire off this thing, no pun intended, and then I am going to give you a shot at it okay."

"Excellent," Jordan said, causing the other campers to laugh.

"Now it's your turn Jordan," the Instructor said as he handed Jordan off the flamethrower and positioned it in his hands.

"You see that hornet's nest on that tree Jordan?"

"No."

"That's because the tree and the nest are imaginary Jordan," the instructor said, to laughing by their audience which made Jordan even more nervous.

"Okay," Jordan said timidly.

"Now at the count to five you are going to let loose on that annoying hornet's nest that's been plaguing your family's backyard, okay?"

"Okay."

"One, two, three, four, five."

Jordan tilted the flamethrower at an angle and decompressed the trigger on it shooting out a fifty-foot flame into the air at his imaginary hornet's nest in his imaginary tree to a round of applause to those in attendance.

"Good job Jordan, and another round of applause for this brave young man folks," the Instructor said.

"And please remember folks don't try this at home, drunk or stupid."

The campers all laughed again.

"We will have one more volunteer..." before the Instructor could finish his sentence the crack of thunder filled the air, and then it starts raining.

'Okay guy's I guess we are going to have to wrap it up, thanks for your participation and enjoy the rest of your summer camp," the Instructor said to the sounds of disappointment.

The rain hits harder now, as everybody starts scattering and running for shelter and cover.

"Get these throwers on the truck guy's so that we can get the hell out of this rain," says the Instructor that gave Jordan a personal lesson.

"Hey are you guy's staying for dinner?" Camp Director Jamie Flowers ask the boss of the crew.

"You bet Mr. Flowers we wouldn't miss that spaghetti and fish sticks for the world," he shouted back thru the rain, giving him a thumbs up.

"See you at Cedar Hall boys," Flowers said as he took off running towards the camp's dining facility.

"I think that dude's got a thing for flamethrowers," says one of his instructors.

"And yellow shorts," adds the boss, as they all laugh.

"Shit! What the fuck was that?" says one of the other instructors as he slaps at a mosquito on his arm that has just bitten him.

"Lets' get the fuck out of this rain, these mosquitoes out here are vicious as fuck!" he said.

The instructor looks at the size of the bite and the amount of blood running down one of his instructor's arm.

"Dude that looks more like a snake bite to me you sure it was a mosquito?" he asks.

"Yeah I smash the little bugger right here," he says showing the palm of his hand.

"What the fuck?" his boss says as he looks at the palm of his guy's hand completely covered in blood and bug parts.

"That must have been one big ass mosquito."

The instructor looks at his hand, "Boss I think I am starting to feel sick," he says as he grabs his throat and begins wheezing before he passes out and collapses to the ground.

"What the hells wrong with him?" said one of the other workers.

"Hey dickheads don't just stand there he's sick, get him the fuck inside and out of the rain," ordered the boss.

Something flies in front of his face as he swats it with his baseball cap, knocking it to the ground, it lands with a splash in one of the rain puddles.

He walks over to look at it.

It's a mosquito the size of a Side-blotched Lizard 2.5 inches (6.35cm) long, wings crumpled, lying in the puddle dying.

"Holy shit what the monkey splunk is that thing," he says pointing at the puddle with the strange but large crumple insect.

The supervisor of the flamethrower crew ordered one of his men to put the dying crumpled insect inside of a large empty jar, just in case the medical staff on hand at the camp wanted to know what kind of insect had bitten one of his instructors. It turns out to be a good afterthought on the supervisor's part that inevitably saves his co-workers life.

The camp's doctor had informed the supervisor that the man and co-worker that he referred to by the nickname "Reefer" had gone into an anaphylactic shock after being bitten by the mosquito and that he had administered him an epinephrine injection to counteract his allergic reaction to the bite.

He would be fine now and just needed some rest he also informed him.

"Shit doc it looks like me, and my boys are staying for tonight huh?"

"That would be wise so that we can monitor "Reefer's" I mean Mr. Smith's recovery until he's back on his feet."

"Man that's one big ass mosquito Dr. Ward," the flamethrowers' supervisor said looking at the large bluish color insect that was now dead inside the jar sitting on the lab counter.

"Yes quite unusual for its size, the camp's resident doctor agreed.

"That's a fucking understatement!" a voice said that seem to come out of nowhere but soon enter the room, it was Peter Doogen, the Entomologist who had overheard their conversation, accompanied by Mr. yellow shorts himself, Camp Director Jamie Flowers.

"Dr. Doogen," how are you? Dr. Ward said dryly.

"Chipper Dr. Lard," he answered.

"Ward," Dr. Ward corrected.

"Yes, yes, Ward," Doogen said patting Dr. Ward on the arm.

He had long got the impression that Dr. Ward did not consider him a real doctor, and therefore he had no problem, showing Ward equal contempt for his lack of respect for his academic credentials.

Now was Dr. Doogen's time to shine, and he had no problem doing so either. He walked over to the jar with the dead mosquito inside and picked it up, raising the jar above his head as he turns it around in his hands inspecting the culprit that had almost cost a man his life.

"You are a big one aren't you fella?" he said.

"Too big actually," he said to everyone in the room as he sat the jar back down on the counter.

"What we have here is a super skeeter," he said.

"That sounds like a porno movie I've seen," the flamethrowers boss said with a grin.

"A different kind of skeeter I am sure," Doogen said eyebrow raised.

"No, the super skeeter is a "summer floodwater mosquito" usually a half-inch long, this baby is twice its size," Doogen pointed out.

"In fact, it is strangely compatible in size with the largest mosquito in the world which is the Toxorhynchites speciosus endemic to coastal regions of Australia."

"Pete, are you saying we got ourselves some kind of mutant mosquito?" Jamie said.

"Yes, and God knows what else out there?" Doogen said.

The flamethrower instructor looks at them baffled.

"Hey man this stuff is way too heavy for me, you guys don't mind if I grab myself some dinner before those greedy little bastards eat it all up do you?" he said.

"Those greedy little bastards are called campers," Jamie said.

"That's what I meant Mr. Flowers."

"Bon appetit."

The three of them watch the head flamethrower instructor leave the room, and when he was out of earshot, Jamie let loose.

" Shame, shame, shame, all beef, and no brains, I hope that idiot doesn't burn down his house one day," Jamie said tapping his finger on his cheek.

Doogen thought his comment was funny and laughed; Ward remained unfazed. He looks at the mosquito in the jar again; it was something about it that he did not notice before and that was it seems to have a weird blueish glow to it that almost illuminated the jar.

"Doogen, do you think we need to quarantine the children and staff until we find out what's going on?" Jamie wanted to know.

"Jamie that might be the best thing to do at least until I find out what the hell is going on here," Doogen said.

"I am going to take this mosquito and run some tests on it and get back with you," he said picking up the jar.

He looked over at Dr. Ward who had this weird expression on his face and then realizes it wasn't just the academic discourtesy that made the man repulsive to him; it was something else unsettling about him that he just couldn't put his finger on at this time.

"Are you okay, Dr. Ward?" he asked catching him off guard.

"Yes, I was just concern about the children's summer camp being interrupted by what may just be a pebble in the water," he said.

"A pebble that may turn out to be a boulder, if we are not careful Dr. Ward," Doogen countered.

"Yes, excuse the crude metaphor, but shit does roll downhill sometimes eh' Dr. Doogen," he replied with that underlying cynicism that made Peter want to plant a foot in his ass.

"And sometimes up Dr. Ward and sometimes up," Doogen rebuttal.

"I'll contact you Jamie with the lab results."

"Thank you, Peter, and have a safe drive back to Ann Arbor," Jamie said, shaking Doogen's hand.

"I wish you the same Dr. Doogen, and I'll be looking forward to those test results as well," Ward said.

Peter nodded his head at Dr. Ward as he departed, he had a long drive back to Ann Arbor, and it was getting dark.

When the room was empty, and Dr. Ward was sure that no one else was present he nervously made the phone call that he knew he was obligated to make.

He patiently listens to the ringing on the other side, before the other party finally picked up their line.

"Major Stone," a deep, gruff voice answer.

"Major Stone this is Dr. Ward, sir we might have a problem."

"Red Flag," the major said flatly.

"Red Flag," Dr. Ward repeated.

"ETA. Two hours before *Operation Clean Sweep*," Major Stone said.

Jordan had no idea what was up with the weather only that it reminded him of the weather in his nightmare, rainy and stormy with flashes of blue light as he laid in his bed now awake, amongst the rest of his peers who were dead asleep in the cabin.

Jordan raised up and looked over at Juice who was snoring with his mouth open, reminding him of an old lady with that shower cap on his head to keep the moisture in his curls. Jordan shook his head sideways as he laid back down.

He looked over at one of the cabin windows and watched the flashes of blue light illuminate thru every time the sound of thunder erupted in the darkness of the room. A feeling of dread suddenly crept over him, what if the nightmare that he had recently was a warning and a sign of the things to come, he thought.

Jordan raised up and look over at his other friend Barry, he was fast asleep also, counting sheep Jordan thought.

That's it he thought, his mom always said if you have trouble sleeping count sheep. Jordan closes his eyes and begins counting in his mind "1, 2, 3, 4, 5, 6, 7, 8," his eyes flew open at eight. Okay, that didn't help he thought. He found that option more annoying than relaxing.

Jordan took the small flashlight he kept from underneath his pillow, leaned down over his bed and pulled out one of the bed drawers, and reached in and pulled out a Black Beat magazine and begin scanning thru the pages while shining the flashlight on the pages.

He found an interesting story on Grandmaster Flash and the Furious Five and begin reading the article, his eyes soon begin to get heavy midway thru the story, and the flashlight rolled from his hand onto the bed as he finally fell to sleep.

A loud crashing noise and the sound of screams and emergency horns whaling jolted Jordan out of his sleep as he sprung up in his bed eyes wide. And when he was able to focus his eyes, he realizes he was not the only one awake; all his fellow campers were sitting up in their beds too, all seven of them staring ahead, scared in the dark.

How long had he been asleep? He thought, an hour. His flashlight was still on as he picks it up off the bed.

"What the hell is going on out there Armageddon?" Juice said as he got out of the bed.

Screams from outside erupt again, causing most of the children to jump out of there skin as they slowly walk towards the cabin windows and the door.

Ringgggg, ringgggg, ringgggg, "Can someone get the phone," Juice said.

Jordan rushed over to the wall phone and picked it up, "Hello," he said feebly into the phone.

"Do not turn on the lights and barricade the doors we are under attack!" scream a distressed voice from the other end of the phone.

Jordan stood in terror by the sound of the voice and how he was able to get his next words out of his mouth was beyond his understanding, but he did.

"From what?" he asks.

They are coming! Oh! no, they are here, oh, aaaaaahhhhhhhh! Dead silence.

Jordan drops the receiver, "Do not turn on the lights, and we need to barricade these doors, he said we are under attack!" Jordan barked out orders as his brain immediately went into fight mode.

"What the hell are you talking about bro, and who's he? Juice said.

"Man I am going out there to see what the hell is going?" Juice said standing by the door.

"Juice no!" Jordan screams out.

But it was too late; it happens so quick that no one was for sure what had happened or at least wanted to admit to what they thought they saw. But one thing was for sure something large, black, and worm-like snatched Juice up quickly by the head, in its mandibles as soon as he opened that door and dragged him swiftly off into the night kicking and screaming for his young life.

"Juiceeee!" Barry scream.

"Close that fucking door! " Jordan shouted out.

The other campers rushed to the door to close it and begin barricading the door from inside. The only thing that was a reminder that Juice had been standing only seconds ago in that doorway was his oily shower cap on the floor.

"Hey, Jordan check this shit out!" Barry said as he and a few of the other campers stood crammed up by the window trying to get a view of the mayhem outside.

Jordan made his way over to the window, pushing a few of the other campers out-of-the-way so that he could get a better view. And what he was now looking at was even worse than his nightmare, it was as if the gates of hell had opened themselves.

Giant mutant insects where flying everywhere, crashing into things and attacking people joined by other monstrosities of giant bugs of various species, that was ripping the camp and its people apart.

In the middle of this spectacle of mayhem and madness, Jordan noticed the crew of flamethrowers was barely holding their own, as they incinerated any flying or crawling anomaly that was stupid enough to get within one-hundred feet or less of their handheld cremators.

The sound of glass shattering across the room and screams whirls Jordan and Barry around.

"Shit!" Barry shouts out as he sees a giant mosquito on top of one his fellow campers about to drive its sword-like proboscis thru the other kid's skull.

The other kids quickly grab their gym shoes and begin beating the giant mosquito on top of the boy to a bloody pulp, as it makes a loud buzzing noise thrashing back and forward.

Barry screams and comes down on the mutant insects head with a bedpost; its head explodes into a pulp splattering its brain matter all over its combatants.

"Yuk!" says one of the combatants, as it splashes on his face and glasses.

Barry kicks the headless mosquito off his fellow camper, who is in shock but unfortunately unhurt and helps him off the floor.

Jordan looks on in horror and then looks down at the bloody gym shoe in his trembling hand and smiles. He did not freeze this time he thinks; he realizes he has fought back at something much bigger than he has ever seen in his life and this time he was not scared.

"Man, why don't you have any bug juice on your shoe?" Barry asks a camper holding red and white gym shoes that still looks new and unscathed.

"Man these are those new Michael Jordan's are you crazy!" the kid answers.

"Dude seriously?" Barry said,

"Hey guys we need to barricade these windows up and quickly," Jordan said taking charge.

"Let's get these mattresses and dressers up against the windows," he ordered.

Barry walked over to the wall phone and hung it up back on its hook, as soon as he did it begin ringing.

"Hello," he answered.

"Who's this?" the voice ask on the other end.

"Barry."

"How old are you Barry?"

"Eleven."

"Listen, Barry, this is the Camp Director, is there anyone older that's in charge right now with you guys?" he asks with a sense of urgency in his voice.

"Jordan when is your birthday?" he shouted across the room.

"June 26, 1976," Jordan shouted back.

"Yes two months older than me," he said.

"Jordan, Mr. Flowers wants to speak with you?"

Jordan walked over and took the phone out of Barry's hand while his fellow campers look nervously on.

"Yes," he said.

"Son, what's your name?"

"Jordan."

"Jordan how many of you are in the cabin and is everyone safe?"

"It was eight of us, but one of my friends got dragged out of the cabin by a giant worm," Jordan said distressed.

"What? Sorry to hear that Jordan, but we are going to have to evacuate this area and quick, or we all are going to be screwed, do you understand what I am saying to you Son?"

"Yes," Jordan said.

"We are going to bring a bus around in two minutes make sure you get everybody on that bus, do you understand Jordan?"

"Yes, two minutes," Jordan repeated, assuring him that he knew the directive he had just given him.

"Listen, everyone, grab your stuff and take the barriers down from the doors we are leaving by bus in two minutes," Jordan shouted out.

Something large from outside slam up against the cabin rattling it from inside, causing the campers inside to brace themselves.

Jordan tried to listen out for that familiar squeal of the bus amongst all the noise and mayhem.

"It's here!" Barry shouted out as he looked out the windows.

"Let's go!' Jordan shouted out to the other campers.

But unknown to the campers bigger problems was headed their way at one hundred and eighty-one miles per hour, four *Apache Helicopters* equipped with 30 mm guns and hellfire missiles were en route to obliterating everything within that sector and a two-mile radius of the summer camp.

Their ETA was forty minutes and counting.

"Ward you are an asshole," Flowers said.

"You knew all along, but you did not warn us you fuck!"

"Cry me a river, won't you? All you need to know is we need to get on that bus and get the hell out of here Flowers!" Dr. Ward stammered as he took a swipe at something large that had flown by his face.

"Fuck you, Ward! Not before you help me get those kids and the staff on those buses you asshole," Flowers asserted.

Lead by Jordan the other children started filtering out the cabin and headed towards the bus.

"Hurry up you little shits! Can't you see we are under… Dr. Ward never finishes his sentence because a giant flying palmetto bug scoops him up by the shoulders and flies off with him screaming and dangling in the air.

Flowers look on in shock before a smile comes across his face.

"Have a safe fight you asshole," he says, before turning his attention back to the children.

The flamethrowers are still holding their own with the attacking bugs, but Flowers knows it won't be too long before they run out of fuel and then what? He thinks.

Camp assistant Bethenny covered in bug juice and blood runs up to assist Flowers with loading the children on the bus.

Aaaaaaahhhh! The scream of death turns their attention to one of the flamethrowers that are now being overpowered and covered by Palmetto Bugs bigger than humans.

Jordan is the last one to board the bus when he hears the faint sound of his name being called out amongst the chaos.

"Jordannnn, Jordannnn…"

"Jordan what are you waiting for son? Get on the bus," Flower's said with a sense of urgency in his voice.

"Jordannnn, Jordannnn…" the voice called out to him again which now sound more like moaning to him that couldn't have been by his estimates no more than fifty meters away.

"You don't hear that; I think it's Juice! I'll be right back," Jordan said as he runs over to the dead flamethrower that is being devoured by the mutant palmetto bugs, picks up the flamethrower gun, the one that he is familiar with and takes off in a mad dash towards the direction from which he thinks he heard the voice calling out his name.

"You got five minutes son then we are leaving!" Flowers shout out behind him.

He looks at Bethenny standing next to him on the bus. "Who is Juice?"

"That would be Franklin sir," she answers.

"Oh," he replies.

"Who the hell is Franklin?" he asks.

"Juice where are you?" Jordan shouts out as he searches in the dark for his friend.

"Jordannnn over here, help me!" He hears the voice call out closer now near him.

Jordan sees something that looks like it's all tightly wrapped up in a spider web-like mummy cocoon to him, so he walks over to investigate it.

The mummy coughs, its mouth breaks thru the web, then the words come out startling Jordan.

"Jordan help me."

"Juice!" Jordan blurts out excited and begins ripping thru the webby cocoon, slowly revealing his friend underneath.

He then hears something coming up behind him and fast. Jordan spins around with the flamethrower with his finger on the trigger.

"Jordan No!" shouts his friend Barry.

" What in the hell, Barry? I almost burn the stink off of you!" Jordan said.

"Bro, I thought you'll need this flashlight," Barry said grinning, holding a flashlight in his hand.

He looks down at the ground at the partially unwrapped cocoon.

"Is that Juice?" he asks.

"Yeah give me a hand."

Barry sees it first out of the side of his eye as he helps unwrap his friend, something large with lots of legs moving towards them at lightning speed, a giant spider!

"Jordan watch out!" he shouts.

Jordan spins around again with the flamethrower and presses the trigger, but nothing comes out but the hissing of gas.

"Fuck!" he says to himself.

The giant arachnid is almost upon them and closing in quickly.

"Come on, come on," Jordan said as he shakes the flamethrower.

He can now see the spiders mandibles and multiple black eyes staring down at him like he is dinner.

"Eat this!"

Jordan presses the trigger one more time, and this time a flame of fire shoots out from the nozzle of the thrower engulfing the monstrous arachnid in flames, as it lets out an ear-piercing shrilling sound. Jordan and Barry watch as the creature begins to burn, turns and retreats into the darkness from which it came on its spindly legs engulf in a halo of flames.

"That's right run spider bitch!" Barry yells out.

Juice slowly begins to come out of his cocoon state of inanimation. Jordan and Barry lift him off the ground back onto his feet.

"Homeboys am I ever glad to see y'all ugly faces," he said with a smile.

"Likewise Juice, we got to go now," Jordan said.

Juice with the assistance of Jordan and Smith holding him up made a limping run towards the bus.

They could see the yellow school buses were beginning to drive off, leaving all three of them behind.

"No, no, stop, stop!" They all yell at the buses as they ran behind them, trying to catch up.

A shrilling noise came from behind them, and Jordan turn around just in time to see the spider now smoldering in smoke charging towards them.

"Look out!" Barry said as he tackles Jordan and Juice to the ground pushing them out of the way of the bus going back in reverse towards the spider.

Splatttt! The bus collides with the spider, disintegrating it! As the rest of its carcass gets flatten underneath the bus undercarriage and tires.

The bus comes to a screeching halt as the doors fly open.

" You guy needs a ride?" A smiling Bethenny said.

ETA. Twenty-five minutes and counting.

The bus pulled off, tires squealing leaving dust behind, Camp Firefly behind. And when the buses were two miles outside of Camp Firefly's perimeter hellfire missiles, and 30 mm rounds lit up Camp Firefly and every monstrous size creepy crawler and flying abomination like the Fourth of July.

EPILOGUE

Six years later, the official report was that an explosion had occurred at a nearby chemical plant and that the smoke fumes from it traveling miles in the air had caused possible mass hallucinations at Camp Firefly and may have also been responsible for the arsonist acts carried out at the camp.

There is a saying that if you keep repeating a lie over and over again to the masses, even lies eventually begins to sound like the truth.

Jordan and his brother Michael had grown closer as the years past, and the teasing had stopped as soon as Jordan had come back from Camp Firefly six years ago. Jordan was unaware, but Michael had sensed something immediately had changed about his little brother.

Present day: 1993 Saginaw Michigan

Brothers, Jordan and Michael accompanied by their girlfriends, and a few friends sat around the campfire they had set up, drinking beers and laughing when Michael feels something crawling up his back.

He jumps up from where he is seated. "Shit! There's something on me," he says as he begins shaking the back of his t-shirt.

His group of friends think its funny and begin laughing.

Jordan walks over and reaches under his brother t-shirt and grabs hold of a healthy size wood spider and pulls it off his brothers back.

"Bro, get that thing away from me, that joker is a monster," Michael said rattled.

Jordan then remembers how his big brother Michael used to tease him and call him "Butterfly Bobby" when he was younger. How times have changed since then, he thinks.

" Nahhh, bro, I've seen bigger," Jordan states with confidence, as he tosses the bushy spider back into the woods.

* * *

Samantha Jackson, the investigative reporter for The Night Turner Tribune, was at her desk putting the finishing touches on a story that she had been working on before she had left for New Orleans, on the demonic possession and exorcism of Maria Langelli in Lisle, Illinois.

Sam looked up to see her bosses secretary approaching her desk.

"Hey Sam, Avery wants to see you in his office," she said.

"Let me finish this up; I'll be there in a sec," Sam inform her.

Sam knocked on Mr. Denton's office door, and as usual, he was on the phone again about something but this time to her surprise he looks pleasantly happy.

"He looks up and sees her thru the door glass pane with his name and title written on it; *Avery Denton Editor in Chief* and waves her in.

"Hey chief I heard you wanted to see me," Sam said.

"Hi Sam, yes I did, please have a seat," he said gesturing towards the chair in front of his desk.

Sam knew anytime Denton told her to have a seat something must be up. Her question was, what was it this time? She thought.

"By the way Sam, good work on the New Orleans, case."

"Thanks, boss," she said.

'What do you know about Detroit?"

"It's close to Chicago," she said with a smirk.

'I got a case I think you might be interested in that happen at a summer camp up in Petoskey Michigan a while back ago," he said, handing her off the file.

Sam took the file from Denton, open its manilla folder and made a quick scan over a few of the pages.

Giant roaches and mosquitoes the size of pelicans, sound like my kind of story," Sam said sarcastically.

"I know, but something happen down there Sam, and I feel the public is not being told the truth.

"Who's my contact person Chief?" Sam ask.

"Let me see here Sam," Denton said as he ruffled thru some papers on his desk.

"Oh here we go," he said as he picked up a business card off his desk and handed it to her.

Sam look at the card in her hand.

Major Richard E. Stone, United States Army.

THE COUSIN

God knows I should have listened; I should have paid attention. All the red flags were popping up, like a pan of Jiffy pop popcorn on a hot ass stove. But I just chose to ignore them, ignore the haters, as I like to call them. The jealous family members, the naysayers, my wife.

You see my friend, for you to understand this story, you have to understand my point of view, how I was not thinking about what other people no matter how close to me, was trying to tell me about the cousin I grew up with, the cousin I thought I knew, but in truth was never known.

We all make mistakes, that's why when my cousin Alyson Webb who had just got parole from doing a two-year bid up at Folsom State Prison in California, had asked if she could stay with us for a little while until she could find a job and a place of her own.

Aaaahhh, you say? How sweet of me you say. Please save the sentiment for someone else that better deserves it more, my friend.

"Because I believe it was my mother that first introduce me to the phrase, "The road to hell is paved with good intentions."

I had without hesitation and against my better judgment said yes to her so that she could have some place to stay, someplace to lay her head not around strangers but with family.

After all isn't prison supposed to be a place of rehabilitation? That was a debate I had with my wife, Hallie constantly.

"Give her a chance," I said to myself.

"To prove herself?," I proposed strongly.

"It's not what you think," trying to believe the voice in my head.

Someone once said it's not easy to sleep with one eye open when you have someone in your house that is capable of any and everything.

Guess what? That, someone, was absolutely on point and unapologetically correct.

But if insomnia had been the least of my worries my friend, I tell you I would not be writing this story.

We all make mistakes, my name is Dustin Farmer, and my mistake was not listening to my wife, my family members, and my friends. No, let me reword this, *my big ass mistake* was the day I allowed my cousin Alyson Webb back into my life.

But don't listen to me my friend read on and judge for yourself that is why I title this cautionary tale – "The Cousin."

HOW IT ALL BEGIN

Where do I begin my story? That's easy; it would start on the day I pick my cousin up at the Folsom Correctional Facility Prisoner visiting center, the day she was parole from custody, with the clothes on her back and the shoes on her feet literally.

My wife and my young son Josh accompanied me reluctantly might I add, to pick her up from the visiting center of the Correctional Facility.

I was informed earlier by the prison officials if I did not arrive there in a timely fashion, that Alyson would be taken in a prison van and drop off at the nearest Greyhound Bus Station or Amtrak Train Station and given fare to get back home courtesy of the California Department of Corrections (CDCR).

Bottom line once she was released, she was no longer their problem until she fucks up again, so I made it my business to get my ass there early so, she would not have to enjoy the comforts of their escort to her return back to what they call in prison "the world."

Alyson who I should mention is my first cousin on my Farther's brother side. I have to say by all appearances she seemed to be one of those that did prison and did not let prison do her if you get my drift. She had all her worldly possessions in what look like a laundry bag and a beaming smile on her face when she greeted us outside.

Not too long after exchanging nice falsities about how good all of us look and awkward hugs, we all loaded up in the family van and proceeded back home to Scottsdale Arizona. A long drive back home that with a few interchanges of pleasantries between us adults it was mostly a trip back home filled with silence.

That is until my eleven-year-old inquisitive son Josh, ask his Aunt Alyson, the embarrassing question " Aunt Alyson was you a "stud" in prison or a "femme?" he asked.

"Bilingual," she replied laughing and much to our amazement. Needless to say, the ride got much quieter on the way back, while my son googled up the definition of bilingual and had this strange grin on his face that I could see thru the rearview mirror.

Was my Josh just curious, dumb, or both?, or maybe as I stated earlier just inquisitive.

Maybe I should have been more inquisitive, or maybe the apple doesn't fall too far from the tree, excuse the metaphor.

But enough of the self-introspective, I know you're wondering what the hell did Alyson do that cost her three years of her life in prison.

I call it blind love but the court and state call it embezzlement and stealing any sum of money over one thousand precious dollars from your employer especially if you are on probation can get you that amount of time and then some.

In her case, it was over fifty thousand dollars from a real estate company she worked for right underneath her Boss nose while she was fucking him behind his wife's back, and feeding her boyfriend's cocaine habit at the same time.

We all make mistakes as I said. And my cousin had done her time even got an associate's degree while in prison and had discovered Christ from what she told me in her numerous letters.

I had pointed out all her accomplishments to my wife Hallie and even put her on an ideological pedestal as an example of when prison reform actually works for the betterment of a convicted felony's life.

I ignored all the past rumors and innuendos mostly thru family members that my cousin Alyson was unnaturally attracted to me and could be a very manipulative and controlling person.

The thought that her displays of affection were nothing more than familial never cross my mind until she crossed the line.

Family members I rationalize are just jealous of our relationship because now Alyson is trying to get back on her feet, and I am the one supporting her in her effort.

"You are my favorite cousin," Alyson would constantly tell me.

At that time I had no idea what she meant. But I would soon find out.

We had even addressed those salacious family rumors.

"Nonsense," she said.

"What's up with those kissy face emojies your cousin is texting you? Don't you think that's inappropriate?" My wife Hallie asked me, long before Alyson got incarcerated.

"I know it seems strange baby, but I don't think she means anything about that," I said.

"And xoxoxo," my wife asked.

"Don't that mean I love you?" I said.

What was I waiting for you ask? A fucking piano to fall on my head from out of the sky like in the cartoons.

A lesson learned, a lesson lived they say.

Hey, but Alyson was here and goddammit we were going to make the best of it until she moves on to other arrangements that her parole officer according to her was making for her transition back into our world.

"I don't want to impose," she said.

"Not at all Alyson you are family," I assured her with a smile.

I showed Alyson her new room that was slightly off to the left not far from her nephew, Josh. It was a full bathroom in the middle of the two rooms that separated them apart from each other.

"Wow it's been a long time since I've slept on a real mattress, I am going to sleep like a baby," she said, kissing me lightly on my cheek.

"Good to have you home Alyson," I said.

She looked at me and smiled and went into her room.

But I could not help wonder what her life must have been like for Alyson while she was incarcerated.

Three years spent in one of the toughest prisons in California I thought, as I made my way back to the comforts of my bedroom.

Little did I know Alyson did not have to get ready for Folsom prison before she went in. Folsom prison had to get ready for Alyson Webb.

Red Flag number one.

Josh stood up at the crack doorway of the hallway bathroom with his mouth hanging open as he watched his Aunt Alyson standing naked in front of the bathroom sink brushing her teeth.

But what had his attention was the tattoo on her back of the whining snake that appears to slither down her backside with its head going down to her buttocks, its serpent tongue flickering right out between the crease of her cheeks.

"Josh?" I shouted out as I came out of my bedroom and seen him standing in the hall.

Josh just looked at me and pointed at the bathroom door.

I walked over and was just as stun as my son, it was obvious that Alyson had been working out and had the goods to prove it. I did not think it was appropriate; it was now on full display in front of my young son.

"Alyson the door," I said getting her attention.

"Oh I am sorry it must have come open," she said looking at our surprise faces as she closes the door.

I shook my head sideways not sure what to make out of what I just saw.

"Son go use the guest bathroom downstairs will ya," I told him.

"Oh' that's right we do have one downstairs," Josh said slightly embarrassed, but with a hint of sarcasm that I found annoying giving the circumstances.

"Yeah, I don't think it moved overnight," I assured him.

When Hallie got a hold of what had happened, she hit the roof. I have to admit the possibility that Alyson had left the door cracked open intentionally because she wanted us to see her in her birthday suit did not sit well with me either.

But just for peace of mind and to quiet my wife concerns, I check the hinges on the upstairs hall bathroom door, and to my surprise, they did seem a little stiff to me, so I applied a little WD-40 lubricant to both hinges, and the door appeared to shut more easily.

That revelation offered my wife Hallie some relief, but only to a certain degree, might I add.

It was still an awkward breakfast the three of us had that morning together, and I could see the wheels of curiosity turning in my son's head before he opened his mouth to take another bite of his bacon.

"So Aunt Alyson how long have you had that snake tattoo?" he asked.

"Josh do you think that's ..." his mother interrupted before Alyson interjected.

"No it's quite okay, I got it while I was in prison," Alyson answer.

"Wow, It's badass," my son said, obviously impressed.

"Josh watch the language," my wife corrected him.

"Thanks, Josh," Alyson said as her eyes went over to me.

I could not tell if she was trying to read my face to see if I felt the same way as my son? So, therefore, I maintain a poker face as if I had no stake in the game.

I look at my watch, saved by the bell I thought. "Josh eat up, or you are going to miss your bus for school," I said.

"Any big plans today Cuz?" I said. More than happy to take the conversation in another direction.

"Just the usual ex-convict stuff, make contact with my parole officer and start looking for some work," she said.

"Sounds like a plan," I said, trying to sound as optimistic as possible.

"Do you need any extra cash?" I ask.

"Thanks, but I am good, go fix some teeth Doc," she said.

"Oh' by the way I apologize for this morning guys, I did not know the bathroom door was open," Alyson said with what sounded like to me genuine remorse in her voice.

"Don't worry about it Cuz, the only problem is Josh might want to get himself a snake tattoo," I said as my son had left the table by now and was headed off to school.

Hallie gave me that look as she took another sip of her coffee.

"Enjoy your day at work baby, I'll talk to you later," my wife said, as she kissed me on my cheek.

"Thanks,' I said relieved in a selfish way that I had a valid reason (work) for not having to be around my cousin after that uncomfortable exposition of herself this morning, intentional or unintentional.

And it definitely did not help that I still had that image of her embarassedly in my head.

Maybe some time alone with Alyson I thought, would be good for Hallie to maybe bond with her or get to know her better, after all, she was her cousin n law, and she would be staying with us until she made her transition into her "own" place.

The day went fairly well at my dentist office except for the numerous calls and interruptions from Alyson to see how my day was going. I rack it up to being that she was very grateful that we were letting her stay with us and that's how she was expressing or showing her gratitude.

I thought I was overreacting to her numerous calls until my fellow resident dentist and friend Allen, asked me jokingly if I was cheating on Hallie, because of all the phone interruptions.

And I tried to put it nicely to Alyson as possible, that I was busy at the office with my patients and if it wasn't important to please leave a message at the desk with one of my receptionist.

I also wonder though if she was busy with my wife who had the day off from work that day. How in the hell did she have time to call me this much at work? Heck' my wife Hallie didn't even call me this often unless it was something of the utmost importance.

Maybe, I was overreacting, not taking into account Alyson had just gotten out of prison, and her behavior was probably nothing more than anxiety and stress from just getting released. Maybe I should give her a few days to whine down I concluded.

It was a long day, and I was looking forward to getting home. I look at my incoming phone calls on my cars interactive display screen, good there were no more phone calls from my cousin.

The scent of roast beef and potatoes and baked jalapeno cornbread instantly hit my nose as I entered my house.

"Wow, something smells good," I said as I made my way upstairs to shower before dinner.

"Hi there cousin," Alyson said to me as she descended the stairs in a white top that was so tight you could almost see her nipples and some daisy duke shorts that looked like they were painted on her ass.

"Hey Alyson," I said with what must have been a bewildered look on my face as I made my way upstairs.

Was this the same cousin looking like she was going to a white trash rodeo that said she had discovered Christ?

Hallie greeted me and was not far behind me as I made my way up into our room.

"What the hell is she wearing?" my wife lit into me.

"How the hell am I suppose to know, she's been with you all day," I said back to Hallie, I was tired and just wanted to take a shower and sink my teeth into some of that roast beef and potatoes.

"Look I took her to the mall, but I did not know she was going to buy them hoe clothes," Hallie said.

"Shhhhh, she might hear you," I said.

"I don't care if she does, that bitch is going to have to find another house to walk around half butt ass naked," my wife said frustrated.

"If I can cover my ass up and this is my house you don't think I am going to tolerate Ms. loosey-goosey out there do you?" My wife protested, her arms folded with the most serious look on her face that I had not seen in a very long time.

"Hallie calm down, I'll talk to her," I assured my wife.

"You better we got an eleven-year-old son, and Ms. Nasty is not going to be walking around here like this, is the red light district," my pissed off wife said.

"Shhhh, I got this," I said trying to calm my wife down.

As I watched my wife storm out of our bedroom, I had to agree that she was right. It wasn't like Alyson was a teenager we were talking about dressing so provocative; this was a woman that was forty-one years old six years my senior.

High school was over a long time ago.

I made my way down to dinner after taking a nice hot shower and to my surprise guess what? Alyson had changed into a more conservative knee-length flower print dress, had she heard our argument upstairs I wonder? Or did she realize the clothes she had on was just a little to scuzzy for my wife taste, excuse me our taste? I wonder what had motivated her from dressing like a teenage boy's wet dream? To like she was hosting a Tupperware party now. I took a seat at the dining room table.

"Nice dress Alyson," I said.

"Thanks, I was feeling a little uptight about what I had on," she said.

"Excuse me?" I said detecting a possible underlying message in her remark.

'Nevermind Dustin, just because you got it doesn't mean you have to flaunt it right Hallie?" She said.

"That depends on whom you are flaunting it to," my wife answer as she dispenses us all healthy portions of roast beef and potatoes on our plates.

"Amen," Alyson said winking at me, catching me off guard.

"Flaunting what?" my son Josh asks.

"Nevermind," I said to him.

"Let me give you a hand with dinner Hallie," my cousin offers, as she got up from the table and brought over a bowl of biscuits.

'That would be great," Hallie said.

Alyson to all of our surprise said a nice prayer before dinner, and we all ate.

Hallie seemed more relaxed at dinner. Afterward, I help her clean and put up the dishes while Alyson gave Josh a hand with his homework outside on the patio terrace, which gave Hallie and me the opportunity to talk in private finally.

"I guess whatever you told her must have worked," she said looking at me.

"Told her what? I thought you talk to her," I said.

"No I did not," Hallie said handing me off one of the dishes she rinsed off which I then put in the dishwasher.

"You think she heard us?" I said.

"Maybe," Hallie replied.

"What other reason would account for her sudden change in fashion," she said.

"Do you think we owe her an apology?" I said.

"Of course not. We don't want Alyson to think it's okay for her to parade herself around our house half-naked unless you're comfortable with that Dustin?"

"Of course not," I said to my wife.

"Maybe you want me to put on some skanky booty shorts?" Hallie said.

"I would like that very much Mrs. Farmer," I teased her giving my wife a smooch on the lips.

"Old pervert," my wife said slapping me with the dish towel.

I laughed and went in for another kiss and some tickles.

"Let's make some margarita's tonight," Hallie proposed.

"Sounds good to me," I said.

That night after we all had retired to bed, I had the strangest dream that Alyson and I were walking together with her ex-boyfriend Markus when suddenly she fell to the ground and begin to have a seizure.

Markus stood there watching in silence almost detach as I attempted to offer aid to my cousin.

As I placed my hands on her shoulder screaming for help, she suddenly came to and grabbed me by the testicles, her eyes rolled back in her head, and I could only see the whites of her sclera as she begins licking my neck with her wet tongue, a snakes tongue.

I called out her name and screamed at her to let go of my balls, but it was almost like she had a death grip on them as she started crushing them.

"Alyson stop!" And then I woke up. I check my balls, and yes they appeared to be still intact – thank God. I looked over at my wife Hallie, and she was still fast asleep. What the hell did that dream mean, I thought as I got out of the bed to go to the bathroom to get a glass of water, although I required something stiffer to put me back to sleep after that dream from hell.

After I had used the bathroom, I heard a noise downstairs like the television was on. I looked over at the clock on our nightstand; it was 2:00 am. In the morning. Who the hell could be up at this time in the morning, I thought as I made my way slowly down the stairs to the living room. I could see the reflection of the light from the television bouncing off the walls as I got closer to the living room, and I could also hear the sounds of someone having sex in the living room on the television.

I stood there in awe as I watch her in disbelief, as Alyson sat on my sofa with her legs spread apart masturbating to hardcore porn on my television screen.

The male stud on the screen pounded the female porn star from behind into oblivion as she yelled out profanity-lace request to her male counterpart.

My eyes went back to my cousin, softly moaning as she pleasures herself, unaware of my presence in the room or was she?

Red Flag number two, she would have to go and soon I concluded.

I was too embarrassed and ashamed to tell my wife Hallie what I had borne witness to that night in our living room on our sofa. After all, how could I ever Justily bringing a person like my cousin Alyson that had so blatantly disrespected our home and taken my kindness for weakness back into our lives with her bullshit? I couldn't.

It was obvious to me that Alyson was sick and needed some mental health treatment. Contrary to that Hallie and I had an eleven – year- old son, and I could not in good conscience allow this kind of sickness around our little boy.

Alyson apologized for her behavior all the way to the halfway house for her obscene conduct and appeared to show genuine displays of remorse and embarrassment for her actions at my family's home.

On the flip side of that coin, I felt genuine relief when I drop her ass off at her new digs and an even bigger one knowing that I and my family lives could return to some sense of normalcy again.

Alyson name only came up again when my wife she got the cable bill and reviewed the bill and saw that a hardcore porn movie call *The Rough Riders* had been purchased.

I explain to her that I had caught Alyson watching that movie, but I never told her what I had seen, and my wife suprisingly never asked either.

Six years had now passed by with no word or contact from my cousin Alyson when one day I got a call at work from her asking if I was okay with meeting her at a nearby restaurant for lunch.

Alyson explained to me that she had been wrestling with all kind of demons when she had got out of prison and was sincerely sorry for the way that she had shown her gratitude when we had open our home to her six years ago.

She only wanted our forgiveness and for us to see that she had not been a lost cause after all.

After speaking with my wife Hallie about it, I agreed to meet Alyson on a pleasant sunny day at one of the local cafes nearby my office.

To my surprise, I hardly recognize the person that walked up to me that day that was my cousin Alyson. She was very conservative and professionally dressed and gave me a friendly hug before we sat down at our table at the small café.

I instantly notice the wedding ring on her finger and congratulated her on her marriage.

Did I feel slighted that I had not been invited to the wedding? Under the past circumstances, not in the least.

" JT is a handsome man Dustin. I cannot wait for you to meet him," she said.

Alyson explained to me how she had gone back to school and had obtained her master's degree in religious education and that she and JT had now started a small ministry in the San Diego area, but it was still growing.

She seemed sincere in the change that she had made and I it appeared that some great metamorphosis had taken place in her life. Was it divinity from God or some other force? I was not qualified to answer that question.

But I was happy for her and told her I was proud of her accomplishments, over corn beef sandwiches and potato chips.

It had been after all six years since the last time I had seen my cousin Alyson Webb.

Alyson gave me her business card with a long name of her organization on it the "*Ministries of the Enlighten ones*" right before we said our goodbyes to each other.

We parted ways after wishing each other the best of luck in the café that day.

I thought that would be the last time I would see Alyson for a while; I was wrong.

"Hey, baby how was your day?" I said to my wife Hallie as I enter the house.

"Perfect," she said kissing me on the lips.

"By the way thanks for the beautiful bouquet you sent me," she said.

"What flowers?" I said clueless.

"These honey," she said pointing to the ones on the dining room table in the vase.

They were beautiful, and they look expensive, but I hated to burst her bubble they did not come from me.

Hallie walked over to the bouquet just as befuddled as I was and picked up the gift card that I assumed she never read implanted inside the vase.

"From Alyson and JT best wishes to the Farmers," she said.

"Who's JT?" she asked.

"Her husband," I said.

"Alyson?" my wife responded surprise.

"Yes," I said almost unable to maintain my composure.

"Freaky Alyson?" Hallie ask again as if she heard me wrong the first time.

"Yes babe and freaky Alyson is now a minister," I said with a straight face that was starting to crack from holding in laughter.

"A minister to whom? A bunch of rough riders," my wife said.

I burst out laughing at my wife response no longer able to hold it in, as I walked over and grabbed two cold beers out of the fridge.

I open both of them and handed my wife one.

"She said she turned her life around, went back to school and got her master's degree in theology," I said.

"Do tell."

"Yep, and married the man of her dreams and now they've started a ministry somewhere down in San Diego."

"I'll be damn," my wife said, taking a sip of her cold beer.

"I guess that saying is true," Hallie said.

"What's that?" I answered.

"The Lord works in mysterious ways," she said.

"I guess he does," I agreed, taking a sip of my cold beer. But in the back of my mind, I could not forget the devil does also, my friend, the devil does also. Several weeks had passed my friend before I heard from my cousin Alyson again when she called and invited my family and me down to a service at her church in San Diego. I wanted to decline graciously, but something inside of me wanted to give her the benefit of the doubt that she had changed her life around.

She deserved one more chance at redemption. Not that it was mine to give that is. I did not want to be one of those people that believe people could not change for the better if they honestly tried.

Furthermore, I had felt slightly guilty that church or a religious service had not been a part of my family's busy lives in a while. That being said, I had to practically twist Josh's arm to go with us that evening, to weird Auntie Alyson's church service.

He was right the service was weird, it was about ten people altogether that attended that service, and the three of us made up that ten in a small little building in San Diego. But I got the impression that Alyson was doing something that she loved, and at least I had made an effort to show up and give my support.

JT her husband for the most part was a polite and unusual quite man who I got the impression played whatever role Alyson required of him in their lives, her dominance over him in their relationship was obvious by the way she talked to him which made all of us all slightly uncomfortable over dinner, to say the least.

I remember her complimenting "JT" when we had lunch together weeks ago, but now I saw none of that display of affection over the course of our meal. The man appeared to be afraid of voicing his opinion about anything we discussed that evening, and if he did have something to say, Alyson would cut him off like a Ginsu knife in her quest to control the narrative of the conversation.

I begin to wonder if Alyson had changed. She and my wife never interacted much that evening except a few cordial exchanges of pleasantries between them. And every time Josh looked at her I was wondering was he still thinking about the snake tattoo whining down her back to her buttocks? In short, we were all glad when the evening ended, and we said our goodbyes and I doubted very much if we would be seeing my cousin Alyson anytime soon.

Damn, would I be wrong.

A few days later Alyson and her husband JT popped up at our house uninvited, explaining that they were just in the neighborhood and wanted to drop by and say hello, not wanting to be rude Hallie and I invited them in and entertained our company while trying to hide our displeasure for their surprise visit.

Alyson was her domineering self, and JT sat their quietly like the cat got his tongue literally, hanging on to every word silently that came out of Alyson's mouth like a trapeze artist.

But if he did attempt to speak Alyson would cut him a look that would instantly send him into a quiet mode where he would pout like a small child.

It was a spectacle to behold that made me and Hallie completely uncomfortable.

By the time they had left Alyson had gone thru two whole bottles of our most expensive wine and gave us the impression that she would have started working on a third bottle if we allowed it.

Her tolerance and consumption were impressive, and she seemed to have no sense of timing when it was appropriate to leave our home that evening.

Hallie and I both had to work that following morning and had to start displaying signs of exhaustion before Alyson, and her husband finally departed.

By then the both of us were mentally exhausted and physically drained, and I know this sounds rude, but we promise each other if those two ever showed up like that again uninvited, regardless if we were at home or not, we would not answer the door.

The phone calls started back up again at work from Alyson, and despite my declarations to her that I was busy, she seemed to show no regard for my personal time, and space and her phone calls and text messages increased in their capacity.

My wife Hallie started to get mysterious calls at the house, but when she would answer the phone, whoever was calling would say nothing and then hang up.

Hallie, my wife, offered to speak with her about these unnerving disruptions in our life but I told her to give it some time maybe Alyson will go away if I ignore her because I did not want to rock the boat.

That was the wrong answer my friend because unknown to me at that time, the more you ignore some people, the more they become preoccupied and obsess with you.

Guess what? Alyson was one of those people.

They also say with stalkers, rejection builds obsession, which I should have taken heed of my friend because a wrecking ball was coming my way.

And it was up to me to get the hell out of its path.

Red Flag number three.

Alyson's daily and consistent disruptions in my family lives had now become more than just mere annoyances to now outright harassment. The final straw that had broken the camel's back excuse the cliché was when she called me at work and started drilling me in regard to why I had not returned her calls.

Believe it or not, she even dared to ask me when we planned on visiting her cult-like church again? I had a one-word answer for that, *never.*

But what mess me up in the head was when she told me that even though we were cousins, she had been given a vision by God that we belonged together and that anyone that stood in the way of that would have hell to pay.

I could not believe that she had just threatened the ones I loved and me, besides disrespecting my marriage to Hallie.

I informed Alyson as calmly as I could, despite the not so subtle threat I had just received from my cousin, that she was confused and what she was saying to me was wrong on so many levels.

I suggested to her that I thought she needed psychiatric help and that she and JT might want to get themselves into some marriage counseling. But her next words to me was just as stunning as her first and took me completely by surprise and off guard.

"You did not think that I needed help that night Dustin when I was on your sofa, and you were watching me, enjoying the show you fucking little freak," she said.

"What's wrong Dustin? Cats got your tongue," she taunted me.

"Do Hallie know what kind of pervert she has for a husband?" she continues on, obviously enjoying her onslaught of insults towards my character and reputation as a father and a husband.

"No, but she knows what kind of crazy bitch that I have for a cousin!" I shouted into the phone now mad as hell.

"Fuck you!" She said and hung up the phone.

The feelings that she had just expressed in the end was amicable, to say the least, and I now speculated whether or not I should take out a restraining order on a cousin that was unstable. And once again, I decided against my better judgment my friend, to take a more diplomatic approach after discussing my options with Hallie.

I decided to give her husband JT a call, under the assumption that maybe he was not aware of what was going on, and maybe we could work something out and get his wife the help she needed. Instead, I ran into a brick wall.

JT told me he had heard from his wife earlier in their relationship, about me. "That I was the cousin that had amorous feelings for his wife, and I was the one stalking her and better back off." And if I persisted with my lies and allegations that I would be hearing from their attorney soon for my slanderous and unfounded accusations against the stellar reputation that his wife had now earned for herself in their community.

It took all I had to keep the bile from coming up from my stomach and out of my mouth listening to this horse shit.

He then had the audacity to tell me. "That the only reason that Alyson had invited my family and me to their church, was because she believed every soul needs saving including "ours."

The nerve of that arrogant bastard I thought. Could he not see that Alyson was using him? Just like she had used everybody else that had the misfortune of crossing her path.

I did not know if the man was an enabler, a victim or a fool? Or all three. But it was obvious that Alyson was the one calling the shots in their relationship, and maybe he was just a co-conspirator to her madness.

I told JT "He was wrong on all accounts and that he had the real story all twisted, from the lies that his wife had fed him, to the lies that he was now feeding me." The phone went dead silent, proceeded by a dial tone, as I marveled at how well our conversation went.

That goes to show you that you can't rationalize with a grown ass man when he's pussy whip, titty fed and hypnotize, not necessarily in that order, may I add.

If he were sitting in my dentist chair, I'd pull out wisdom teeth that he didn't have without local anesthesia.

A week had now gone by without any contact made by my cousin Alyson, and it was a welcoming relief to myself and my family, and we were all able to rest a little more better.

Maybe her husband JT had taken my advice after all I thought and went and got his wife some help, and check himself into counseling while he was at it.

All of my family and me had retired for the night, and we all felt we could sleep more comfortably with the new alarm system that we had recently installed because of Alyson's threats and stalking behavior. Like I said we all thought. It was 2:00 am when something woke me up out of my sleep, and I went downstairs to investigate.

2:00 am again, it sounded like someone had left the television on, as I made my way down the stairs slowly towards the living room.

That is when I heard what sounded like the sounds of someone having sex again in my living room, but like the first time, it was coming from the television. Once again, I stared mortified at the television screen of the same male porno actor pounding the same female porno actress from behind as she yelled the same profanity-laced sexual demands out to him.

Déjà vu.

"Hallie call the police!" I yelled upstairs to my wife.

"What?" I heard my wife yell back downstairs with the sound of fear in her voice.

"Call the police!" I yelled back upstairs again.

I noticed that the upper deck patio light was on and the sliding door appeared to be slightly open as I made my way to it.

I took one of the hanging cooking pots off of the overhead rack for a weapon as I made my way slowly towards the door. And that is when I saw her my cousin Alyson Webb sitting on my patio deck in what look like her nightgown drinking a beer from a six-pack at my fucking table, on my fucking patio deck.

"Excuse the language my friend, but suffice to say I was mad as hell."

"Hey Cuz what's up?" she said in a cheerful voice like I was happy to see her and I had invited her ass over, two nots in a row. I was not happy to see her and I had not invited her over.

"What the hell do you think you are doing Alyson? You need to leave and now!" I said furiously.

"What does it look like I am doing? I am having a cold beer, that was a long fucking climb up Cuz, and I am thirsty and sweaty," she said non-chalantly.

"You are trespassing Alyson, and I can also have you arrested for breaking into my house, do you understand?" I said pointing at my patio slide door.

"Not even mentioning you are also in violation of the PPO that we have against you," I added.

Alyson laughed at me before she answered back like it was all a big joke.

"Fuck your screen door and Fuck your PPO, Dustin," she said.

"I am going to school you real quick cousin; there are only three kinds of people that put out PPO's where I come from," she said, as she took a swig of her beer.

"And what kind of people are those Alyson," I said, falling into her trap.

"Punks, Pussies, and Old women, cousin," she answers, then laughing so hard she spit out some of her beer.

"You get it PPO," she said.

"Yeah clever, now leave," I said bluntly.

She blatantly ignores me; I see that this is not going to be easy.

"You like the movie I put on? Its' our favorite," she said with a mischievous grin on her face.

I look into Alyson's eye's, and I can now see for the first time, something's not quite right, up there in her head.

"What's going on Dad?" I heard a voice say from behind me.

I turn around it was Josh.

"Go back to bed son its okay," I said.

And that's all it took was that split-second when I took my eye off of Alyson I heard my son scream.

"Dad look out!" in fear.

Right before I felt the seven-inch butcher knife plunge into my shoulder blade cutting thru my flesh that my cousin Alyson had been concealing all along.

Her ferocious attack and assault with the knife drove me back against the kitchen wall, out of the patio doorway. I instantly reached up and grabbed her hand with the knife as I attempted to wrestle it away from her after she had withdrawn the blade from out of my shoulder and went in for another attack. Alyson twisted the knife towards my hand cutting it, and I instantly drew my slice hand back in pain, realizing any closer, and she would have severed my thumb.

Blood was gushing out of my wounds, and I could tell I was losing a lot of it in my struggle as I start to feel faint.

"Aunt Alyson no! Josh screamed out again.

Alyson turned to look at my son.

I took a wild swing at her, and to my surprise, the pot made contact with her head, the blow stun her! Knocking her off balance and a few feet off of me, but she was able to recover quickly and came charging at me again full speed, screaming like a lunatic with the knife held high above her head.

I braced myself for another attack, but I was getting weaker by the minute from blood loss, as my eyes shot straight to the shiny blade in her hand with my blood and flesh already dripping on it and about to get some more.

As she went in for the attack, someone hit Alyson hard from the waist down tackling her as they both went crashing thru the patio screen door. At first, I thought it was my son Josh, but no, my wife Hallie had come out of nowhere and quickly rush her catching her by surprise, and now had Alyson pin down on the patio deck wrestling for the knife wrestling for her life.

Alyson was able to get my wife off her with an elbow to her jaw, that sent Hallie toppling over.

My son Josh instinctively rushed over to protect his mom and was quickly met by a foot to his chest by Alyson that sent him flying back through the busted patio doors onto the kitchen floor. He had underestimated Alyson her three years in Folsom had not been wasted; she was not only deadly but quick. Not far behind, I gain my composure and stumble over, feeling lightheaded but I had to defend my family, and I wasn't stopping until I was dead.

I almost got my wish.

Alyson's knife came within an inch of my throat's jugular vein before I was able to react and evade her attack.

By this time my wife had recovered, taking advantage of Alyson's focus on me, Hallie quickly went in for the attack with a Tyson-like punch to Alyson's jaw that sent her over the deck's balcony and sprawled out on our back lawn KO cold.

"Crazy fucking bitch!"

Don't fuck with my family," Hallie said, spitting down at her below.

That day I could have never been prouder of my wife, Hallie.

"Police!" yelled a voice in the distant. "Of course," I said, and then I faded out.

Alyson was now facing the possibility of going back to prison after she had been admitted to the hospital for psychiatric evaluation while in custody and under the watchful eye of the Maricopa County Sheriff's Office.

The apologies could not have come quick enough from her husband JT who swore up and down that he had no idea of the seriousness of how deep his wife's mental illness ran, and she had been deceiving him and hiding it from him all the time.

I wanted to tell him that "If a sandwich, smell and taste like a shit sandwich, then guess what?" But I chose to be a little more diplomatic and told him no hard feelings, and I wish him the best of luck, God knows he would be needing it and then some.

As our wounds healed and the days passed turning into weeks, the police and courts told us that they would be contacting us for Alyson's court dates. That was good enough for me, being that I was trying to put this whole sordid affair of events behind us, and move on.

Hallie, Josh and I decided no better way to really put this behind us, was to hold a football viewing party at our home for some family members and friends.

It was a nice turn out that day at our home as we all sat around eating football food and watching the Arizona Cardinals play the Chicago Bears.

Arizona and Chicago were in their fourth quarter possibly going into overtime.

"Hey Hallie, you guys got any more of those pretzels and cheese dip?" our friend Tyrone ask.

"You finish with that second bowl already," Hallie said joking with Tyrone.

"What the hell is that noise?" my sister n law Katy asks.

"Turn the TV down," I said.

We could all hear it now; it sounded like something fast and loud approaching the side of the house.

"Get out of the living room now!" I scream to everyone, only seconds before an ambulance came crashing thru the wall of my front living room, demolishing everything in its path.

"What the fuck!" Tyrone said dropping his fresh bowl of pretzels and dip.

Scottsdale police were right behind the ambulance sirens blaring.

It appeared that someone at the hospital had forgotten to give us a call and warn us that Alyson Webb had overpowered a police officer, escaped custody and was now en route to crash our football party and kill us all.

No thanks to them no one was seriously injured that day, and everyone got out of the living room just in the nick of time to have our asses still attached to our bodies.

Alyson exited the banged-up ambulance in her hospital robe, looked directly at me wild-eyed, smiled and shouted the words "Heyyyy Cuz!" Right before Scottsdale police lit her world up with 100,000 volts from their Tasers.

Tyrone looked over at me.

"Man I know you told me you had a crazy ass cousin, but damn that bitch is off the chain for show."

By the way, just for the record, the Arizona Cardinals won that day.

Two years had now passed by since our last contact, but I will never forget the cousin that terrorize my family and our home.

Bringgg, bringgg, bringggggg.

Please excuse me while I get the phone.

Operator: *"Arizona State Hospital, will you accept a call from Alyson Webb."*

Click, dial tone.

THE END

Or is it?

BONUS EXCERPT

IN SHEEP'S CLOTHING

Lee J. Minter

PROLOGUE

The residents of "Harper Creek" a small midwestern town in South Dakota, were out in abundance today at their community park. They were enjoying an Indian summer of unseasonably, warmer weather than the usual, before the cooler weather, set in this time of year. The smell of the charcoal from the barbecue pits and marinated meat sizzling on grills, permeated the warm summer air, along with the resonance of people conversing, children playing and laughter throughout the park.

The music coming from radios and other electronic devices competed with the chirping and squawking of birdsong from the park's winged residents, perched high up in the lush green trees. In fact, the atmosphere and scenery at Harper Creek park were so idyllic; it could have been in a Norman Rockwell painting.

People sat in lounge chairs, enjoying a soda or two and hot dogs, while the children were playing and frolicking at the park's playground.

A young mother pushed her baby in the stroller down the park's cobblestone walkway. Numerous joggers were running along the park's trails; even the bike enthusiast was out today enjoying the warmer weather as well. By all accounts, it appeared this community would have made the perfect picture for a Norman Rockwell painting indeed. But that was not to be the case. Why? Because simply said, today was not that day. See, one essential element had been missing from this descriptive and picturesque day.

That element was the watchful amber eyes, of a pack of six muscular creatures, hidden in the shadows of a more wooded area, across from all this activity.

The iris of their eyes, glowed amongst the darkness of the tree line, like yellow fireflies. A growl of hunger, emitted from the belly of the Alpha male, the largest of the pack, as they watched every movement from their human audience, soon he thought patiently, soon…

CHAPTER ONE

As the young mother pushed her baby in the stroller down the park's cobblestone walkway, joggers quickly sprinted past her, on the other side of the trail, designated for runners. In addition to them, a group of cyclists on their high-performance bikes was pedaling like they were in the Tour de' France, in a convoy formation. The sound of gears shifting, and wheels spinning, could be heard as the cyclists paced themselves, to conserve that last bit of energy, for their final agreed-upon destination, Harper Creek's Café.

One of the joggers was a young female, very fit and toned, dressed in a pink half zip running shirt, black spandex pants, with pink accents and matching running shoes. She is doing her third 1.5-mile lap when she notices something unusual, almost a blur out the corner of her eye.

A blur that is moving extremely fast and headed in her direction and the other runner's pathway. Strange as it seems the other runners seem to be oblivious to what is now taking place before the jogger's eyes and what her mind is trying to comprehend. Is that a pack of wild dogs? She is thinking to herself in a public park? The other joggers continue to run as if they are oblivious to what is going on around them.

The aware jogger then realizes that this is no illusion as her eyes continue to follow the pack of beast headed in their direction. She sees that there is a pack of six, all large, some different colors, huge creatures with fierce yellow eyes that appear to illuminate even in the daylight. It's like everything that is now taking place is happening in slow motion.

The jogger's eyes go towards the young mother pushing her baby, then back to the pack. For "God's sake" she thinks, they're now headed in her direction. She can now see more clearly that these are not just a pack of stray dogs, these are predators, wolves, and the pack is closing in upon the mother and baby quickly with every stride and stroke it takes.

The jogger's mind is racing, confused. She knows she barely has a lead run on the stealthy killers, but to stand by and do nothing is not an option either she concludes. The jogger takes off in a full sprint, hands pumping in front of her for better traction. She passes all the other runners easily in her path. Her only focus now is the safety of the mother and baby. With heart racing, she can almost feel the wolf's heated breath upon her back, and she is now suddenly aware, she is running for her life as well. The jogger yells through panted breath at the mother to run, to getaway! Why isn't she listening? It's as if everything that is happening now is in slow motion again.

The jogger takes it up a notch, now screaming at the top of her lungs warning the others.

"Get the hell out, run now!"

It now appears as if she has awakened the surrounded dead, and they have all come back to life.

Other visitors to the park appear to snap out of whatever trance-like state they were in, including the mother with the baby in the stroller.

All festivities have ceased, the barbecuing, frolicking, and conversing.

The park goer's eyes now go to where the jogger's eyes are focused, over to the pack of hungry beast headed in their direction. It's like coming out of a fog for them, the awareness of the threat of the impending danger, but unfortunately for them, it is an awareness that has come entirely and much too late.

In the blink of an eye, all hell and chaos break out! People in the park are now running and screaming as they scramble for their lives, some of them knocking each other over as they try to get out of the way of the ferocious beasts in their path. Their screams of panic and terror reverberate throughout the park.

A huge gray wolf leaps in the air at one of the fleeing park goer's, grabbing the man by the throat bringing him down in a blur. The wolf viciously rips into the man's throat severing the jugular vein, blood squirts out profusely from the wound.

The muscular beast then proceeds to tear into flesh and bone as easy as a machete cutting a twig. Another victim is almost in her car when suddenly a dark shadow engulfs her airborne from above and before she can reason the shadow is upon her being. A pungent smell of wild stench and bristled fur descends upon her back, taking her quickly down to the ground, as canine incisors viciously sink into her neck ripping her throat out! But not before a silent scream comes from the lips of the victim as darkness overcomes her senses.

The unholy beast, despite the damage already done to his victim, continues to rip out chunks of her tendon and flesh. Snarling and growling in a mind of primal rage as it conducts a symphony of mass destruction upon its prey.

The jogger quickly runs across the grassy field headed in the direction of the baby and her mother. She is now closer to them, so close, she can almost touch them. The mother of the child in the stroller now appears cognizant of what the jogger has been trying to warn her of all along as she now attempts to flee.

The mother's eyes are wide and her mouth agape as she turns in the direction that the jogger is pointing in. But it is too late as the large black wolf with the piercing yellow eyes leaps on her and grabs her by the throat, taking her down for the kill, as the creature tears into cartilage and flesh. The baby stroller rolls away, aimlessly upon the mother's release and begins to topple over. The jogger not thinking only reacting knows this is her only chance.

"Noooo!" she screams out.

The jogger leaps with hands out towards the falling child, thud! She catches the baby in her arms. The jogger now on her feet with the baby quickly scans the park and notices the car keys right next to the lifeless body on the ground. Its killer has now stealthily moved away from the body in search of other prey. The jogger takes off in a dash towards the car, tightly holding the covered baby in her arms.

Sweat is profusely running down her face; her heart is pounding as if it is about to explode out of her chest! Nausea, dizziness, confusion tries to step in and overcome her senses, her body. Must make it to the car she thinks, must make it! The jogger quickly puts the baby in the passenger seat with no time to strap in. She turns the ignition with the keys she has picked up off the ground next to the dead driver's body. The car lets out a weak throaty grumble as it hesitates to start.

"Fucking come on," The jogger shouts out loud to herself.

She gives the key a second turn. The car hesitates, again, and then suddenly rumbles to life.

The jogger hits the gas pedal hard, tires screeching as the car peels out of the parking lot, leaving a cloud of dust and exhaust fumes behind.

She nervously checks her rearview mirror to see if one of those things, "Monsters" is in pursuit. The rearview mirror reflects only one scene, though. And that is the scene of carnage and mayhem behind her. Suddenly she remembers the child; as she then proceeds to pull the blanket from off the baby's face to make sure no harm has come to the infant. The jogger goes pale.

"What the fuck?" she says in disbelief as her mind starts to go foggy.

A bone-chilling reactionary scream of terror comes from her as the baby's amber eyes meet hers encased in sockets with unusually dark long lashes. Pointy little razor teeth glisten from a hairy face that is more Wolfen than human. The jogger blacks out and veer off the road, and the car heads straight into a huge tree. There is a loud "explosion" as metal and fiberglass violently crumple upon an immovable object. Everything starts to go dim as the jogger slips into unconsciousness, but not before she feels the baby like creature crawl upon her chest and sinks its pointy little teeth into the flesh and bone of her neck.

A scream brings Samantha Jackson, out of the nightmare into a sitting position in her bed. Her eyes are wide open; she is not in the park, not in the car, but the comfort of her home. Just for reassurances, Samantha touches her throat to feel the wetness of blood. There is none. Just a dream she thinks to herself, just a silly dream. As her eyes try to adjust and focus on the darkness of her dimly lit bedroom, she hears a howl that erupts in the distance of the night. It is a shrilling howl that makes the hairs on Samantha's arms stand up and a cold chill run down her spine. Suddenly her thoughts are interrupted by a knock on her bedroom door and a familiar voice asking if she is okay? It is her mom, Gina.

Thank you for purchasing this novel , if you enjoyed this novel and found some benefit in reading this, we would like to hear from you and hope that you can post a review of this novel on Amazon. Your feedback and support will help this author to greatly improve his writing craft for future projects and make this book even better.

~ Thanks, from TCP.

ACKNOWLEDGMENTS

My editors Mark Strange and Ray Rodriguez Jr. for your invaluable experience and attention to detail.

Rebecacovers @ Fiverr

My inspirations, the true Masters of Horror and Suspense of film and literature that inspired me to write, Rod Serling, Stephen King, Dean Koontz, John Carpenter, Wes Craven, Rob Zombie, and to all of those I left out but not behind.

And last but not least the fantastic fans of this genre that keeps it alive and exciting.

Lee J. Minter
October 2020

Also by this author are these novels online
and in select bookstores.

LEE J. MINTER
IN SHEEP'S CLOTHING

LEE J. MINTER
THE NIGHT TURNER TRIBUNE
Five Tales Of Terror
SAMANTHA JACKSON

LEE J. MINTER
THEY CALL IT IZZY
A NIGHT TURNER TRIBUNE NOVELLA

LEE J. MINTER
THE NIGHT TURNER TRIBUNE
Five Tales Of Horror + 1
SPELLBOUND

LEE J. MINTER
Zombie pimp
A NIGHT TURNER TRIBUNE NOVELLA

LEE J. MINTER
THE SPELL
A NIGHT TURNER TRIBUNE NOVELLA
Follow me on Twitter @LJMHorror4u
Follow me on Instagram @ mintboogie
Visit me @ my web page at LJMHorrorTales4u.com

ABOUT THE AUTHOR

LEE J. MINTER is back again this time with an anthology of twelve horror and suspense stories to scare the living daylights out of you. Make a hole and make it wide for the new master and self-proclaimed rock star of horror aka mintboogie. Horror will never be the same, stay tuned.

www.ingramcontent.com/pod-product-compliance
Lightning Source LLC
Chambersburg PA
CBHW021443240626
47153CB00001B/277